They Met Robin Hood
&
Robin Hood to the Rescue!

They Met Robin Hood

&

Robin Hood to the Rescue!

By

AGNES BLUNDELL

(*Author of "The Net," etc.*)

Illustrated by Frank Rogers

ST. AIDAN PRESS, LLC

Morning View, Kentucky

They Met Robin Hood & Robin Hood to the Rescue!

They Met Robin Hood. First published in 1936 by Hollis and Carter Limited, London. Reprinted from 1944 edition.

Robin Hood to the Rescue! First published in 1939 by Burns Oates & Washbourne Ltd., London. Reprinted from first edition.

ISBN-13: 978-1-962503-13-6
ISBN-10: 1-962503-13-5

For more information, contact:
www.staidanpress.com
staidanpress@gmail.com

We have made no intentional change from the original text except to correct mistakes in spelling and punctuation.

They Met Robin Hood

"THEY WENT BACK TO THE WOODS, KINDLED A FIRE, CLEANED
THE FISH AND ROASTED THEM ON TWIGS OVER THE HOT
EMBERS."

See page 106

Contents

They Met Robin Hood

OSMUND LAY on his back in bed, indulging in daydreams. He had no clock or watch by which to tell the time, but he could guess it pretty accurately by the light. When he first opened his eyes and sat up, broad awake to greet this most important day, the sun had not yet reached the projecting branch of the great pine tree which he could see from the window. So Osmund judged that it was not yet quite five o'clock and he stretched out a sunburnt hand and turned over the hourglass which stood on a rough stool beside him. His brothers, Eadgar and Stephen, were still asleep so there was no one to talk to, and Mother had bidden him not to dress until she called him—he had a long day before him and must rest as long as possible, she said.

At first the daydream was all glorious. Osmund saw himself speeding along under the trees, greeting anyone he might meet with knightly courtesy. Here he made a digression to wish he were a Knight: a real Knight like Father, with beautiful golden spurs and a full suit of chain armour, galloping on a noble steed over the burning desert in pursuit of wicked Saracens. When he returned to England, Sir Aelfric would doubtless avenge the base oppression of his neighbour, Fulk de Brent, and would regain his own manor and Castle at Southwell. Osmund sighed and returned to the prospect of the day's adventure.

He was to be entrusted with the important mission of doing service to the overlord for their holding. His mother, the Lady Etheldreda, had taken refuge at Welbeck Abbey when driven from her husband's manor at Southwell, and she held her present tenancy from the Abbot, on the usual conditions. Leagues of forest land intervened however, between her present dwelling and the Abbey. The kind monk had indeed given over this distant grange for her use in order that she might be hidden from her enemy in the leafy recesses of the wood.

Osmund muttered over the words which he must pronounce kneeling bare-headed at the Abbot's feet, his hands between those of his patron.

"Hear, my lord! I become liege man of yours for life and limb and earthly regard and I will keep faith and loyalty to you for life and death, God help me."

He must be sure to remember to lay aside his little dagger before swearing fealty. It was so solemn—Osmund wondered how the great lords and barons could repeat these words to the King and then revolt against him. Even his own sons had fought bitterly against the late King Henry! Eadgar said that all the troubles which had fallen of late upon England, were a scourge sent by God in punishment of the false oaths which men swore with so little scruple, and Osmund quickly said a prayer that he might be true to his oath. Circumstances might arise which would make it very difficult, for it was well known that many men in the first positions in the Kingdom were little better than their Norman pirate forebears and preyed shamelessly on the lesser folk. Many a poor man, aye, and even boy! had been imprisoned and cruelly beaten to make him reveal where his lord's jewels and treasures were hidden. The Abbey had its treasures and there were people in the country wicked enough to attack a holy Abbot! However, it was no use worrying about such a thing beforehand. Osmund felt confident that God would give him the grace to die for his loyalty to the good Father Abbot if it were necessary. The thought was rather a gloomy one and he soon began to have misgivings lest he should not accomplish his mission as gloriously as he had pictured to himself. He wished he could ride on a beautiful white charger, with his long sword hanging on his left side, like the hero, Bernard de Balliol, whose exploits he greatly admired. Of course, Eadgar should really have done service as he was the eldest, but Eadgar was so moony and absent-minded that he lost his way in the wood as soon as he was out of sight of the house. Strange that such a clever, book-learned person should be so stupid about everyday things! Eadgar never knew the time, nor which way the wind was, nor when the field should be sown! No doubt he was very wise and always had a quotation from Holy Writ on the tip of his tongue, and he could tell splendid stories too, about saints, and knights and battles. All the same, Hild, though she was a girl and a year younger than Osmund, was more companionable. Eadgar always wanted to read or talk—he never listened to anybody else and spent hours making syllogisms which the others found very dull.

Presently Osmund heard Hild's voice out in the garden— she was up and dressed already, and he longed to join her, and jumped up instantly when Mother presently knocked on the partition wall which separated the loft rooms in which they all slept. Down below was the "solar" or living room, which in this humble dwelling replaced the Castle hall, and which was reached by a short flight of stone steps from the yard. The kitchen was next it and down on the ground floor slept the woodman and his wife and the hinds. These last got no wages except a "luck-penny" to spend at the two great yearly fairs.

Osmund had left all his clothes ready overnight. Since they had been fugitives from their own Manor the family had felt the pinch of poverty. Osmund wore a plain tunic like the peasants, only that he had a shirt under it. His legs were clothed in cloth "chausses," which were something between loose stockings and tight trousers, and for his feet there were his old leather shoes, very much patched, which pulled up over the ankles. His mother had made him some beautiful new ones of purple velvet, cut from a gown of her own, to put on when he reached the Abbey.

Old Goody Alice was always in terror that the boys would break their legs as they came down the ladder-stairs, Eadgar blundering along with a book in his hand, and Osmund descending in two wild bounds. Even Stephen declined to hold on by the rope hand-rail any longer! This morning Osmund only paused to wash hastily at the basin set in a little angle of the wall with a jug of cold water beside it. It was the duty of the person who emptied the jug to fill it up again at the spring, but Osmund decided that as the next user would be Stephen it would not be necessary to show so much consideration for a younger brother. So he tipped the basin into the projecting spout which carried it outside the house wall, flung the towel on the floor, and leaped down the steps into the garden.

Hild was tethering the hens which had broods of chickens—this was one of her daily tasks. She ran towards him with a protesting fowl squawking under her arm.

"Oh, Osmund, I have had such a good idea! Old Job wants you to take his dues to Father Abbot, and it's a hen and sixteen eggs, and they are ever so heavy, so I thought you might ask Mother to let me come too, and I'll carry them—truly I will!"

She added the last words beseechingly, for Osmund was shaking his head.

"You can't," he said firmly. "You're a girl."

"I don't see why that need make any difference," grumbled Hild. "I'm not a bit afraid. I tell you what, Osmund, I'll promise not to argue and to let you decide which path to take."

"I should think so, indeed! But most of the way there won't be any path——"

"And Mother said herself the other day, that a woman with a babe could walk scatheless from somewhere-or-other to the sea—and if we did meet a wolf, I can climb a tree as quickly as you can."

"Oh, the forest is pretty well cleared of wolves if it comes to that——"

"YOU CAN'T," HE SAID FIRMLY. "YOU'RE A GIRL."

"Well, then!" cried Hild, interrupting again. "You know how you hate hens, brother."

"I don't see why I need take Job's, either! Did Mother say I was to?"

"No, she hasn't seen him yet." Hild went back to the clutch of chickens which were lamenting their mother's absence by cheeping with astonishing loudness: tying a string to one of the hen's legs, she fastened the other end to an apple-tree. Osmund looked on, frowning heavily.

"But don't you *see*, Hild, doing service is a man's job. It means the promise to send men armed, all ready to fight, if the overlord goes to war—maidens can't go to war."

"They do!" retorted Hild promptly. "They go to the Crusades and that is a holy war."

"How you do argue!" exclaimed Osmund. "It's really childish—you *know* you can't come. Mother said she was anxious about letting me go—even Eadgar isn't to come with me. I shall have all sorts of hardships!"

He spoke with some pride and Hild, who had not any very clear idea what hardships were, looked at him enviously.

"I think you are very unkind, Osmund," she cried. "Robin Hood isn't like that! He lets Maid Marian roam the greenwood with him, and he spares any train of travellers that has a woman in it for her sake and that of Our Lady St. Mary."

"When I'm a mighty outlaw like Robin Hood, you shall come too," said Osmund consolingly.

He was very fond of his sister, but she vexed him just now. The very idea that one could go on an adventure like a Knight Errant with a little girl of ten, running after one with a hen! Osmund hoped fervently that Mother would not want him to take the hen—it would be so inglorious! Lady Etheldreda was sending a jewel in lieu of fee. It was sewn up in a soft leather bag and hung round Osmund's neck by a string.

Old Job was one of the Royal Warreners and it was his duty to look after that part of the forest which was devoted to the preservation of rabbits, hares and such small game. He was a free man with a little farm of his own which he held from the Abbot. In those days, rent was usually paid in kind, which was sometimes very inconvenient. Osmund began to feel the glory of the day clouded over already.

"It will spoil everything if I have to carry a great fat hen with me," he lamented. "Why can't Job send his grandson with it? It's too bad to ask me."

"Perhaps our mother will say it is too great a burden for such a little boy," returned his sister maliciously. When she saw how vexed he looked, she was sorry, and running to Osmund, she gave him a hug, and said:

"I didn't mean that. Perhaps you could slip off quickly before Job sees you. And I *won't* be cross about not going with you, if you will tell me everything you have seen and heard when you come back."

"I'm sure I wish it was over, Hild," answered Osmund in a burst of confidence. "I hope I shall do everything all right, and not be awkward and bring shame on our mother's training."

"Don't forget to wipe your mouth before you drink at meals," cautioned Hild. "Here is my best kerchief—you may have it, brother. But you needn't be afraid—you have really quite as nice manners as Eadgar—even if you aren't so wise."

At this moment the Lady Etheldreda called and both children raced into the hall where a meal was ready for the young traveller. His mother decided that he need not grant the Warrener's request unless he wished, though she was careful to add that the old man had been kind to them and had kept them supplied with fresh game during the winter.

"Only for Job we should have had nothing but salt meat to make broth for little Sibell when she was ill," put in Eadgar, who had a habit of coming out of his studies quite unexpectedly. Osmund wished his brother had not made this remark. He looked hard at his mother, and then sighed.

"Which would be the knightliest way?" he asked.

"The kindest way is ever the knightliest," said his mother, and she blessed her boy on his broad sunburnt forehead.

Little Stephen ran out, loudly hallooing: "Job! Hi Job! Brother will take thy hen!"

Chapter Two

JOB THE WARRENER accompanied Osmund for the first quarter of a mile, carrying his hen in a sort of sling made of sacking, with a long sacking loop which could be passed over the shoulder. Biddy's feet were tied with a strip of rag and her wings were secured by a strap of the sling so that she could not struggle. The eggs were in a rush basket, neatly packed in moss. Job walked slowly and poured forth good advice at every step.

"Keep to the path, little master," he said. "And if in doubt follow a sheep-track rather than a deer-track: for deer can leap a wide pool, whereas sheep will go round a bog. Dost know the difference 'twixt deer-slot and sheep?"

"Why, of course I do!" cried Osmund impatiently. "But, Job, sheep-tracks will be hard to find now—all the flocks are in fold."

"Ha, ha! young master, you deem yourself wise! And no doubt you think old Job only fit to mark the 'pricks' of a hare or the 'print' of a badger! But wood-lore is many-sided, else 'twere useless. Keep to the sheep-walks and you'll find their tiny paths trodden hard through grass and fern and always on dry land."

"I'll remember, but all the same I'm not afraid of wetting my feet, you know," exclaimed Osmund.

"Aye, but mark you do not sink in a quagmire! 'Tis always quicker to take the long safe road rather than the boggy one which seemeth short!"

"Yes, yes, Job! I promised my mother this."

"Go not so fast, boy! I be passing stiff in the joints. I want to tell you how trees may be your guide. Steer towards oak and beech, avoid alder, and trust not birch for it often——"

"Why, Job, of course! One would think I was town-born! You'll tell me next to remember that willows grow by water," Osmund began hastily, then he remembered courtesy, which one must practise so carefully if one wanted to be a knight, so added humbly: "I ask your pardon, Job, for I know you speak out of kindness, and truly I'll remember what you say."

"Well, then," said the Warrener, "should you be benighted, look upward, not downward to find the road, for you will see the gap between the tree-tops over it, like a white path above you."

"And I know the sailor's star too!" declared Osmund, triumphantly.

"Aye, but you don't know where you are yourself," said Job. "However, remember this." He spun the boy round: "When you are facing North West, you are going towards the Abbey, but home is South East, so you return towards the rising sun. And when you strike the River Maun you must go up it, not down."

"Thank you, Job. And now farewell! I'll give your dues to the Abbot with your loving duty—unless, indeed, Robin Hood should relieve me of them."

"Hush! that is an ill jest, but indeed the great outlaw is like a noble falcon, he preys not on the young and poor!"

With that Job handed over the hen and the basket, and Osmund received them with a sigh. It was very difficult to carry both on the same arm, yet if he did not keep his right hand free, how could he salute those he met, with hand flung high in the air, to prove that though entitled to bear arms—and therefore no serf or slave—his intentions were friendly? He would have to change the basket from hand to hand each time, but no matter! He was glad he had accepted the troublesome commission, for

Mother had been pleased. Osmund glanced back at the top of the slope, and stared until he discerned the thread of blue smoke winding upwards through the trees from the home hearth. As he went on again he began to feel already rather lonely.

The first part of the way was along a well-defined track which led to the mill. Here he could cross the stream, and the next few miles would also be easy going, for there was a path to the Verderer's house. This man was as unpopular with his neighbours as were all the upper officials of the forest. The game laws were harsh and cruel and pressed heavily on all who dwelt within the great enclosure. Prince John, like his father, was passionately devoted to hunting, and ordered the appointment of men as Wardens and Verderers who would not scruple to enforce these laws in full severity. Osmund had often seen one-armed men and poor mutilated hounds—the victims of vindictive punishment for some small transgression. If only his journey had not lain through the Royal forest he could have brought Tray for company—the faithful old hound which had followed the family in their flight from Southwell. Rauf de Mansfield, the Verderer, was quite likely to pry into his wallet and perhaps relieve him of some of his eggs—Osmund resolved to avoid him if possible. In this hope, he stepped off the beaten track and turned into the wood as he drew near the clearing in which the Verderer's house was built. He looked out for traps and snares, though it was scarcely likely that any would be set quite so near the dwelling.

The tough stems of the old dry fern rustled round him as he walked and impeded his steps; in his efforts to avoid the tangled patches, Osmund struck downhill and soon found his feet sinking in the oozy ground.

He laughed to himself, remembering Job's warning, and after splashing and struggling along for half an hour, he admitted to himself that the old man had been right. Another half-hour was lost hunting about for the path again, but at last it was found, and hot and tired, Osmund pressed on towards the sheep-walks with the Verderer's house now safely left behind.

Osmund began to whistle as he walked and his thoughts turned towards that strange hero of the woodland of whom he had spoken to the Warrener: Robin Hood. This man was already celebrated in popular song and ballad, yet no one seemed to know exactly who or what he was. Some folks would have it that he was a wild, badly behaved son of honest Locksley the Yeoman, and others that he was the rightful owner of the Earldom of Huntingdon—which was part of the vast dower which Judith, daughter of the Conqueror, had brought to her husband, Waltheof. The original possessor, Earl Robert of Huntingdon, had been slain at the famous siege of Ely and his faithful steward had fled from Norman vengeance carrying with him his master's son. When he was little, Osmund had imagined that Robin Hood was this very son grown to manhood, but now as he was older and had learned history, he knew this to be impossible. The Conqueror William had landed in 1066, Ely, the last English town to resist his arms, had fallen in 1068, so even if he had then been a baby in arms he would now—in 1193—be one hundred and twenty-five! Whereas it was said that Robin was in the very prime of manhood. The acknowledged Earl of Huntingdon was Prince David, brother to the King of Scots. He was a great and good Knight and had been to the Crusades, but 'twas said that of late there had been a quarrel between him and Prince John. And everyone said that John's friends were all evil men, as cruel and oppressive as himself.

Osmund's present home lay in a small clearing in the forest—for "forest" did not necessarily mean wood, but rather a vast enclosure entirely given up to be a royal hunting-ground. When William had laid waste this land in his terrible expedition against the Northern rising, and had driven out such dwellers as survived the passage of his army, he had excepted a piece of land belonging to the Abbey of Welbeck and on which the Abbot of that day had built a grange or country house. It was convenient to the King to have such a place where he could occasionally stay when on a hunting expedition, and he took care to turn out the existing Abbot and to install a Norman, so that he might be sure of a safe welcome.

The traveller was now passing through a thick wood of oaks and beeches. The path disappeared under dead leaves though Osmund could trace its direction for a time by following Job's plan of looking up to the tree-tops, which were farther apart here where a trail had once been made. But soon he paused in uncertainty. His eye travelling up the rugged grey trunks, tufted with silvery lichen, arrived at the twiggy summit, where burnished rosy buds glowed in the sunlight against the blue sky. The great trees had grown vigorously, their huge arms were interlaced, and saplings had sprung up at their feet to fill in the cleared space. Osmund sat down on a mossy root and considered what to do next. He listened intently hoping to hear the sound of some domestic bird or beast which might proclaim a house; or even the winding of a hunting-horn, but the stillness around him was only broken by the joyous singing of birds.

He carried a horn at his belt and longed to sound it, for the forest seemed very lonely and he suddenly felt very young and inexperienced. It would be too humiliating to be obliged to return and seek a guide, and he made up his mind to press on until he found rising ground from which he could observe the position of the sun and plan his further course. Although it was only March, it was hot down here among the trees, and he began to feel tired and thirsty. There was a thick undergrowth of holly, and presently he smelt peppermint and the ground fell away in an abrupt descent to a grove of shimmering silver birches. Job had warned him only to drink at springs, and not from marshy pools, and peppermint, of course, meant bog. Nevertheless, Osmund went forward. It seemed clearer ahead and he told himself he could walk along the brink of the wet land—it would be easier. A squirrel which was sitting on the ground at the edge of the oakgrove, dashed up a tree with an indignant chatter, and a startled woodpecker flew out, uttering his laughing note.

Osmund stopped abruptly, wondering what had disturbed them. Pigs, most probably, he decided. It was the very place for pigs with oaks on one side and marshy hollows on the other. He walked on, whistling carelessly, and presently heard the noise of a heavy animal crashing through the undergrowth. This was followed a moment later by the sound of hounds in cry, and the boy sprang up the soft green bank and ran towards the trees as fast as he could, still clutching his eggs and hen. He knew at once that the hunted animal was that most savage of all forest denizens—the wild boar.

He climbed on to the low bough of a beech and leaned down eager to see the sport.

Presently the boar burst into view, its little red eyes blazing under its bristling forelock, foam flying from its half-open jaws and its wicked tusks gleaming. Two great hounds were close in pursuit, and just below Osmund's tree, one of them sprang upon its flank. The boar turned with a horrid scream and the second hound rushed in and seized him by the neck. If the first hound had had equal courage, and had closed on the other side, the boar would have been quickly slain, but instead he shrank back from the infuriated beast. The boar now swung round again, its great strength enabling it to dash off its assailant, and to bury its tusks in the poor dog, which rent the air with a desperate cry.

This was more than Osmund could bear. Regardless of his own safety he leaped to the ground, and dancing round the struggling animals until he found his opportunity, drove his dagger full into the boar's throat. Though it had received its death-blow, the ferocious creature endeavoured to rush at Osmund, who sprang back, missing the full force of the onslaught but not escaping a gash in the leg. The monster sank down at his feet next to the quivering hound, and Osmund found himself shaking all over with excitement.

He unhooked his bugle from his belt, but before he could summon up enough breath to blow it, a strange-looking man came leaping out of the wood.

"Who dare stay my hounds? Who dare interfere with my quarry?" he shouted in a fury, and ran down upon the boy, his face scarlet with passion and a great knife gleaming in his hand.

Chapter Three

OSMUND STOOD his ground manfully.

"I did but make in to the help of the gallant hound," he cried. "I fear he's sore hurt."

The big man approached, his heavy steps shaking the ground, like the giant's in the ballad. Osmund began to feel very sick and the hen in the sling on his back suddenly flapped her wings and squawked dismally. The huntsman, who had rushed to his hound, glanced up at the sound, and hurriedly approached the boy.

"Why, thou'rt hurt!" he cried, and pushing him down on the bank he pulled up Osmund's loose chausse, and examined the gash, which was bleeding freely. "'Tis nothing serious," he cried then, "but lie still with thy foot up so, until I bind it for thee."

"Take heed the blood stain not my tunic," gasped Osmund.

"We'll avoid that!" exclaimed the other, and before protest was possible, he had plucked off the hen-sling and had stripped off the boy's tunic as swiftly and unceremoniously as Hild would undress her doll.

Osmund's face which had been rather white, became red with indignation at this treatment, and he expostulated loudly as the hunter picked him up as easily as though he had been little Sibell and strode away with him through the dead fern and rushes to the water's edge.

"Lie still, young fool, till I find a clean pool," he exclaimed. "'Twill smart bravely, I warrant, though 'tis no dangerous wound."

It did indeed hurt a good deal and Osmund set his teeth while his companion washed the gash, laid on a soft cool compress of clean moss and bandaged it neatly with his own kerchief.

"Now I must do the same for poor Fleet," he remarked. The hound had followed them and lay whimpering on the bank.

"Will he die of it?" asked Osmund anxiously.

The huntsman knelt down and examined the dog, which licked his hand and looked up at him trustfully.

"Nay, he'll soon recover," he announced joyfully. "But I vow he owes his life to you, good hen-herd, and that was a shrewd gallant stroke you dealt the boar."

"I'm not a hen-herd!" cried Osmund laughing. "I am but carrying the bird to my lord Abbot of Welbeck, for a neighbour. There were eggs, too! I hope they are not broken. What shall I do if they are? I never thought of them when I saw the boar turn on the brave hound."

Fleet was now bandaged in his turn: he lapped some water and followed his master to where the boar lay dead. The other hound came out of the thicket as they approached, looking very much ashamed of himself. Osmund walked stiffly, but made no complaint; he went in search of his egg-basket while the man wrenched the dagger from the boar's throat and thrust it into the earth to clean it.

"Up to the hilt! Thou art a towardly youth!" he exclaimed approvingly.

"Towardly" meant "extremely promising," but Osmund's pleasure in the huntsman's praise was dashed when he discovered the eggs all broken, yolks and whites in a mingled stream dripping from the basket as he held it up.

"Oh, what shall I do?" he cried in great distress. "Old Job trusted me to bear his dues! I ought to have hung the basket in safety before I jumped down from the tree."

"A fine boar ham will more than make up the loss," returned his new acquaintance heartily. "And that thou shalt have and welcome."

Osmund looked at him doubtfully. The great muscular fellow was no royal huntsman, that was plain enough. He wore a ragged tunic of coarse black serge, girt round his thick waist with a black leather belt, and deerskin leggings bound untidily with straps of untanned leather. Osmund set him down as a poacher, and became filled with misgivings for his own share in the slaughter of the boar. In his desire to save the hound, he had made himself liable to the most horrible penalties. If the Verderer found out, he might be blinded or have his hand cut off! He shuddered inadvertently.

"Plague take the Normans and their cruel game laws!" he cried. "They take all pleasure from the noble sport of hunting. Why, sir, what would my lord Abbot say to such a present, think you?"

The other laughed loudly.

"I wonder indeed!" he cried. "But let me tell you, Sir Saxon, you are now on my land, and under my jurisdiction. And you must therefore obey my law and command, which is that you accompany me home forthwith."

Osmund disapproved strongly of this remark, and snatching up his dagger in one hand and the hen in the other, he took to his heels without more ado. But his bandaged leg hindered him, the hunter caught him up in a few vigorous bounds and laid a huge hand on his shoulder.

"Come, will you walk in friendship at my side or must I truss you up and carry you on my back by the heels?" he enquired.

Osmund's only reply was a determined effort to wrest himself free, but his struggles were vain. He felt himself utterly powerless in the hands of his captor. It was very humiliating and the boy had hard work to keep the tears out of his eyes.

"I'll walk with you, if I must," he said at last. "But I think 'tis scurvy treatment that you use your strength against me so."

The other made no reply, but kept his hand on his prisoner's arm and marched him back towards the water, and along the edge of the pool, which presently widened out into a lake, shut in on every side by tall trees. They went on along the shore until they came to a boat moored in a hidden creek among the rushes. The dogs jumped in, and the hunter lifted Osmund bodily and deposited him beside them, and then pushed off from the bank with the end of an oar.

THE HUNTER CAUGHT HIM UP IN A FEW VIGOROUS BOUNDS.

Osmund made another protest as the boat swung out into deep water, but it seemed to fall on deaf ears. The giant rowed deftly and his powerful strokes sent the boat skimming over the water towards a bushy islet in the centre of the pool. Osmund lay back, feeling very tired and giddy. He said afterwards that he must have fallen asleep—strange though it was—for the next thing he knew was that he was sitting on the huntsman's knee like a baby, drinking something out of a wooden goblet. He stared about him in surprise. They were in a hut, roofed with sod and rushes, and something that smelt uncommonly like venison steak was grilling on sticks over a red, glowing fire.

"Why—why——" he stammered incoherently.

"No need for talk yet," observed the other briskly. "Drink again! And now lie down until supper be ready. You must be my guest tonight, and tomorrow you shall fare onward to the blessed lord Abbot, not a penny the worse for the encounter."

He laid the boy down on a very comfortable bed of dry bracken and added on a less good-humoured note:

"See thou stir not till I return!"

Osmund had not the faintest intention of obeying this order, but hardly had his tired limbs been deposited on the fragrant couch than his eyes closed, and before the hunter quitted the hut he was in a sound sleep.

When he woke, it was nearly dark and the owls were hooting and calling to each other. The hunter had returned and was standing near, with a frizzling steak on a wooden skewer in one hand and a piece of clean dry bark in the other.

"Sit up and eat!" he cried jovially. "But stay where thou art. It will be best not to stir too much tonight."

"But I must get on to Markover!" exclaimed Osmund, accepting the meat nevertheless and the large piece of oatcake which his host held out to him.

"Markover!" he exclaimed. "Why, lad, that is miles away! Nay, thou must be my guest tonight, and tomorrow I'll put thee on a road thou canst not miss."

"Thank you kindly for the supper," rejoined the boy. He was very hungry, and began to eat with good appetite and to reflect at the same time.

This man was evidently an outlaw and a bold one at that, for he perceived that part of the boar meat had been brought home already and was hung up openly on a tree near the hut.

Perhaps he might even rob him of his jewel! Osmund was quite at his mercy here on the island and Lady Etheldreda had warned him not to spend the night anywhere except in a village or monastery. It would be best to try and get away by fair words. This resolution cost him a good deal for it was comfortable in the hut and he was very tired. His host, under the mellowing influence of supper and copious draughts from a leather tankard, had lost his ferocious aspect and looked quite kindly.

"If you please, I would rather go forward tonight," announced Osmund after a pause, "for my mother bid me——" he hesitated a moment—"she bid me lose no time. There's a moon, or there will be shortly and——"

"And you do not greatly relish my company?" concluded the hunter.

Osmund laughed though he felt rather frightened.

"Well, Master," he said stoutly, "anyone must prefer hospitality which is offered rather than enforced."

"Well done! You are a truthful boy and have courage to speak your mind," answered the hunter approvingly. "But if your lady mother were here, she would approve my decision, for I have some skill in healing. I say you must rest that leg tonight, and you are safe enough under my care. Though somewhat rough in my ways, I am not without gratitude, and all I have done has been for your good."

"Give me leave then to release my poor hen and to give her some food," said the boy. He resigned himself to the inevitable.

"The hen has fed, drunk and has gone to roost," returned his host. "Moreover being something of a magician I have restored your eggs."

Osmund stared in astonishment at the basket, where indeed the broken eggs seemed to have been miraculously repaired, then he began to laugh.

"For a moment I believed 'twas sorcery," he cried. "But Job's eggs were brown and these are white! You have kindly replaced them by your own!"

"Well guessed!" replied his host. "And now, as I see you can use your eyes, we'll play a game of guessing. You shall guess what I am, and I will guess what you are. Come, speak out!" he added sharply. "I shall not be offended by frank speech."

"Well, then," said Osmund, gazing at him reflectively, "I should imagine that a person like you—of great strength—might have taken part in some sudden fray and have been obliged to seek sanctuary——"

"Why? How dost thou make that out?" exclaimed the other, evidently very much taken by surprise.

"Oh, I may be quite wrong!" answered Osmund hastily. "I was only seeking to account for your wearing a friar's habit, when you are no friar."

"No friar? How do you know? I might be on a begging journey."

"If you are a monk, I never saw another like you," declared the boy. "You wear chausses, and have no sign of a tonsure, and there is nothing in this dwelling that speaks of a religious calling."

"You have won that throw!" observed the other. "But know that I hold religion in all reverence, though in truth when men call me Friar Tuck 'tis but in jest, though indeed I was once—for a short time—porter in a Convent. But 'twas a life that suited me ill, and all that remains to me is this good stout frock which I have been fain to supplement with boots and breeches. For now I belong to the Free Brotherhood, and trees are the pillars of my cloister."

"It must be a good life if 'twere not for the game laws," Osmund said.

"Oh, laws are for those who live under them," returned Tuck oracularly. "Now 'tis my turn. I guess thou'rt gentle born, and that was easy for there is a fine shirt under thy peasant tunic. And that thou hast a brave knight for father, but that he is far away and your lady mother dwells alone and oppressed by an enemy or unjust relation."

"Why, do you know us then?" cried Osmund, astonished in his turn.

"No, boy, but I use my wits. I judge the father by the son, but if he were alive and at home, he would have sent one of his knaves to carry the dues of a poor churl to the Abbot."

"Nay, but Job is a copy-holder," returned the boy. "His name is written down in great Domesday Book. But as for me I'm just Osmund, at your service."

"Osmund! H'm! There was a certain Dom Osmundus de Bracelonde, brother to a black monk—one Jocelyn, who is the writer of a long and tedious chronicle——"

He paused, but Osmund said nothing.

"But come! Let us to sleep," concluded Tuck, "for we'll start tomorrow with the dawn."

He brought in a bundle of fern from some outer store, and threw himself down on it after having raked out the fire. His deep rumbling voice sounded once again in the darkness.

"And for the jewel in thy bosom, lad, have no fear! Friar Tuck was never known to rob a friend and for thy rescue of Fleet thou wilt ever be friend of mine."

"Thank you, good Master Tuck," rejoined Osmund. He thought the remark rather ominous—would his host scruple to rob an enemy? He must have felt the little bag while pulling off Osmund's tunic, and guessed its contents, for it was still there, safe and sound, under his shirt. The hounds lay across the open doorway of the hut: outside the world was softly lit up by the moon. The dying embers smelt sweet, and all sorts of delicious wood scents drifted in. The light made a silver path across the water like that one heard about in fairy tales. A nixey or water sprite would rise in just such a path; indeed, Job declared he had once seen one. The dogs growled and Tuck stirred and opened his eyes: but Osmund was not seeking to escape: he was only kneeling up in bed to say his night prayers.

.   .   .   .   .

The young traveller slept soundly, but woke early, roused by the chill morning wind. The outlaw was snoring loudly, but he sat up with a prodigious yawn as soon as Osmund stirred.

"Good morning to thee, friend," he cried cheerfully. "Thou'rt a lad after my own heart and I would not have had Fleet slain for a bag of gold. Wilt have my purse in ransom for his life?"

Osmund shook his head.

"I'd rather have the answer to a question," he cried eagerly. "I would dearly like to know if you are a comrade of Robin Hood?"

"Why truly I am! Robin Hood's man, duly seized of my holding by a tuft of the greenest moss in the forest! And now, if thou hast ever a boon to ask of the King of the Wood, I'll be thy surety that it is granted. And meanwhile, up, up! Eat and sup, for thou hast yet a long journey to the Abbey."

Osmund's leg still felt stiff and sore, but Tuck declared that it was healing well. The night mist had been thick, and lay in silvery beads on every twig and every blade of grass. Breakfast consisted of cold venison pie, and a hunch of bread and cheese. As soon as it was swallowed the boat was unmoored and Friar Tuck steered it round the islet with a punt pole and then rowed vigorously to the farther side of the pool. An hour's brisk walking brought them to a well-marked pack-horse track and here the outlaw bid his young friend farewell.

"Job says there's many a good man who has been driven outside the law through no fault of his own," said Osmund.

"True enough, and some step outside for preference," returned the hunter with a grin. "And if you or your friends are ever in search of sanctuary call upon Friar Tuck and I'll promise thee safe harbourage."

"And shall I find you on the island?"

"Nay, there's no certainty! But if you need me, lay three white stones under the beech where the boar was slain. And I'll engage to meet thee there at the next moonrise."

He bounded into the underbrush and vanished, and Osmund walked quickly forward.

He passed over open country presently where shepherd lads piped to their flocks, then through further bands of oakwood where swine were rooting and at length came to well-tilled fields.

The great buildings of the Abbey rose up out of the mist and the sun was only touching the tree-tops when Osmund knocked at the Abbey gate. The adventure was over and he had come safely to his journey's end.

Chapter Four

Lady Etheldreda had warned her son that an important Abbey, such as Welbeck, was likely to be full of strangers and therefore he must bear himself with the greatest discretion lest some amongst the numerous visitors might be friends of Fulk. Osmund pulled the bell-handle, and was startled by the clamour it evoked, the musical notes loudly echoing down the long stone corridors within. The ground about the door was marked with the trampling of many horses and within the enclosure the voices of grooms and servants could be heard, shouting cheerfully to each other.

The Brother Porter presently came to the door—a little thin, fussy man very different from Tuck. Osmund saluted politely and explained that he bore a letter for the Abbot from a noble lady—he dared not mention his mother's name. The porter noted the boy's dusty shoes, the hen, the eggs, the country tunic, and smiled somewhat sarcastically.

"The noble Abbot cannot see thee, nor yet good Father Vicar," he declared. "I think, young man, thou art inclined to presume. One of the good brothers shall relieve thee of thy dues, and thou mayest have hospitality with my Lord's retainers."

Osmund was annoyed to be addressed with "thou" like a child or servant, but pleased to be called "young man."

"Father Abbot will be vexed if he is not told of my coming," he said. "Pray, good Brother, let him have the lady's letter without delay, for it is important. And if he asks the name of the messenger, tell him 'tis Osmund."

"Ask thy name, indeed! You have no small conceit of your-self!" cried the Friar. "But come, I see you have trudged a long way and walk lame, too. I'll send you straight to the kitchen where you shall be instantly refreshed. That's good news, eh?"

He smiled broadly, and Osmund thanked him rather coldly. He felt inclined to protest that he was the son of a knight and not accustomed to be set among kitchen knaves! But then, he reflected, there was no class distinction in an Abbey, and it was unknightly to boast of one's birth, so he swallowed his feelings and followed the porter down a long brick passage to the great vaulted kitchen. It was so large that the whole of the Grange would have fitted inside, and it was full of people, noise and the fumes of food. Great fires crackled and roared all along one side. Before them, all sorts of joints were twirling round and round on a great spit, which two boys were revolving with a handle. Others had game spinning round, each bird on a hook, and the machinery worked by an ingenious clockwork arrangement.

Lay-brothers, with their habits trussed up, were raking batches of loaves out of an enormous oven: they hooked forth the long iron trays, and tipped the crusty rolls into baskets, which were instantly carried off by bare-armed serving men. Osmund was not the only visitor waiting for an audience: there was a whole benchful of peasant folk resting their backs against the wall, with wallets at their feet, passing the time in gossip and jest until Father Procurator and his clerk were free to attend to them. They moved up, sociably making room for the new-comer, and Osmund listened to their chat rather absently for the hot room made him feel sleepy after the long tramp.

"The good monks keep themselves pretty snug here," remarked a fellow, whose lambskin coat and bagpipes proclaimed him a shepherd. "Look yonder at the peacock being dressed for my lord Abbot's table."

"Aye, but 'tis only the guests who will taste it," returned a ploughman from the end of the bench. "Father Abbot keeps the full rule and even doeth extra fasts and penances for the King's weal and for the Prince's repentance—guidance—I should say."

Osmund turned with the rest to stare at the steaming roast peacock, on which one of the cooks was stitching its original skin and gay feathers, while two boys stood by holding ready a large gold dish.

"It is never going to be served feathers and all?" he gasped.

"Aye, marry is it!" a passing scullion paused to answer him. "And there's not many so cunning as our Simon Potstick yonder to sew him up again in his painted shroud without spoiling a feather."

"Ugh, I'm glad I'm not supping with the Abbot!" cried Osmund.

"You'll have your fill at all events," said the man. "But to-day there's a very grand guest in the house. No less than Sir Hugo de St. Lo, who has recently been seized of the Manor of Scarcliffe."

"Oh, a Norman!" Osmund commented.

"Certainly! When have our Kings given Manors to any others? Unless they have pledged them to Jews?"

The scullion hurried away, and Osmund began to nod. He heard the peasants grumbling about Norman oppression and complaining in particular of the Lords who lived in Normandy or Anjou and paid cruel agents to sweat their feudal dues out of the people.

"Why, down our way we have a man who flays the peasants as your wife would skin an eel!" cried one fellow. "You folk are lucky to live under an Abbot, who looks into things himself."

"But we have got to live under forest laws," growled another man. "And see our dogs' claws lopped off at the lawing, aye, and his foot, too, poor beast, unless you can fee the knaves at the lawing leet."

These complaints were familiar enough to Osmund and he listened silently, longing to tell them of his own encounter with the boar. But to do so would he knew be imprudent, for how could he relate the adventure without speaking of the huntsman, and to do this would be equally dangerous to the outlaw and himself. So he held his peace and tucked in the torn leg-covering as well as he could and drowsed, until a monk came into the kitchen in haste and raising his voice above the sounds of clashing knives, bubbling pots and roaring flames, called out:

"Osmund de Brakelonde, ho! Is Master Osmund here?"

The boy got up stiffly and approached the monk, still encumbered with the eggs and hen. His guide led him rapidly through the great parlour where many guests sat at dinner, across the courtyard where grooms were cleaning their horses and children were pouring out of school, into the cloister, where, to Osmund's great surprise, Father Abbot himself was waiting. The golden chain and cross on his breast and the magnificent ring on his finger alone distinguished him from a simple monk. Osmund set down his basket so hastily that the eggs were again in danger, and went down rather awkwardly on his sound knee.

But the Abbot hardly waited for his lips to touch the ring, before he raised him kindly and embraced him.

"Welcome, dear son! But how is this: art thou wounded?"

"It isn't much, my Lord, only I'm sorry to present myself thus unfit—I didn't know I would see you so soon!" stammered Osmund.

The Abbot bent down to examine the bandaged limb.

"Call Brother Paul," he commanded, "and take the boy to the Infirmary forthwith. Is the minstrel healed, who lay there?"

"Sufficiently at least to come down and take part in the feasting, Father Abbot."

"That is well. Bid Brother Paul dress this wound and tend the boy well, and give him a good supper, for I think there is no fever. Canst walk upstairs, my poor child?"

"Oh, yes, Father—my Lord, I mean! I have come four leagues today at the very least."

"Well, Father Cellarer will take thee to Brother Paul, our Infirmarian, and I will visit thee in an hour's time."

Osmund tried to protest that he did not in the least need so great care, but the Abbot checked him with a gesture.

"It is my order, Osmund, and it will enable me to speak with thee privately. My lodging is full of Sir Hugo's friends, and his train occupy all the parlours. Brother John, you will attend to our guest's gear?"

He smiled, as the hen cackled, and with a friendly nod to the boy, walked away.

In spite of his protestations, Osmund sank on to the hard, clean, narrow bed with a sigh of relief. The Infirmarian had washed his leg, and put on some cooling dressing, which smelt sweet and took away the pain. And he had carried off the torn chausses and declared that they would be returned washed and mended at cock-crow next morning. The big basin of broth and bread was very good, and though Osmund regretted that he was missing the feast downstairs, he felt certain that the Abbot's precautions were rather more to keep him out of sight of the other guests than because of his hurt.

Brother Paul set a large beaker beside him, which, he said, contained a cooling drink compounded of herbs and honey, but he warned the boy not to take it till after the Abbot's visit, lest he should find him asleep! Hardly were the words spoken than the boy's quick ears detected the sound of sandals ascending the stairs.

"This is no way for me to receive the Abbot!" he exclaimed in great distress, and made a movement as though to jump out of bed.

An Abbot ranked as a noble and was accorded the greatest deference.

"Stay! Remember 'twas an order!" said Brother Paul, and he pushed Osmund back on the hard little pillow and went out of the room.

At first Osmund felt very shy as the great man came in and sat down beside him on a stool, but he was soon at his ease. The Abbot asked many questions about the Lady Etheldreda and how they fared at the Grange, and whether anyone had been troublesome to them. The lady, in her letter, had stated that there was still no news of Osmund's father. The boy answered readily, and was eager to tell about his brothers and sisters. How clerkly Eadgar was, and how anxious to enter a school, only unfortunately he could not sing, so was of no use for a choir.

"Does he aspire to enter religion then?" enquired the Abbot.

"Oh, no, my Lord! He means to be Lord Chancellor—like St. Thomas of Christchurch, I mean—before he became a bishop," he explained.

"I understand! Like Becket when he rode with a hundred and fifty knights in his train, I suppose?" said the Abbot with an irrepressible smile.

"Yes, Father Abbot," cried Osmund eagerly. "And twelve monkeys in red velvet before kneeling grooms on saddle horses —only I don't think Eadgar would care for the monkeys as much as Hild and I. He would fear they might spoil his book. Alas, poor Eadgar has only one!"

"You shall bear back another as a gift," promised Father Adam, and Osmund was struck silent by the munificence of the offer.

"And now," added the Abbot slyly, "thou art more of a warrior than a budding Chancellor, I think. How came you by that gash on the leg? I am full sure your good mother did not let you leave home in such a state, and 'tis strange for a boy not to speak of an encounter, if thou hadst one in Sherwood?"

Osmund's eyes sparkled with excitement.

"I can tell *you*, my Lord," he cried. "But I thought 'twas wiser to keep silence to all others. I got the gash from the tusk of a boar as I was rescuing a hound—and I reckon the Knight who was hunting pays neither scutage nor soccage!"

The Abbot looked very serious.

"I trust he did not rob thee?" he said.

"No, indeed, he treated me kindly and gave me hospitality. And if truth must out, 'twas I who gave the boar the final blow with my own dagger!"

"Bravely done, but Osmund, you must not act thus on impulse! Do not you know that it is against the forest law, and if 'twere proved against you, the King's men could have you maimed or blinded? What of your poor mother if such a fate had befallen you?"

Osmund shuddered involuntarily, then he said sturdily:

"Is it not very wicked that such things can be done to a free-born man, just for the Prince's pleasure? Must we be true to a bad Prince?"

"Yes, if we have sworn fealty to him through our overlords. Welsh Gerald speaks truth for once, when he says many troubles have come upon us as a scourge for the sin of perjury—Kings, nobles and people are but too willing to forswear themselves."

"But who is forsworn?" enquired Osmund. "Doesn't forswearing mean to take a solemn oath and not to keep it?"

"Aye, and 'tis a great sin. Yet men will do it for ambition or greed for gold, and will plead duress after without due cause."

"It's Normans who do it," cried the boy.

"Nay, English Harold, says Gerald, was the first offender. But sleep now, my son. And be very careful of thy speech before the minstrel who shares this chamber with thee tonight. Such folk are prone to repeat idle words—they are great purveyors of gossip and indeed they make their living by it. Can I trust you to be discreet?"

"Yea, Father Abbot," the reply came in a very crestfallen tone: then Osmund added in an eager whisper, "But Robin Hood isn't a bad man or a perjurer, is he? Folk say he is all for the rights we had under the Old Laws in free England."

The Abbot laughed.

"He is by all accounts a strange personage," he said. "More like the hero of a ballad than a man in real life. But remember this, Osmund, outlaws are dangerous company for a boy who has a mother to protect from a powerful and bitter enemy. And yet," he murmured, as though to himself, "they say he hath a noble nature, and hath never treated maid or woman discourteously. Osmund, be guided by thy mother in all things."

"And shall I see you tomorrow, my Lord, to do service and all?" queried the boy.

"No, child. If fit to travel, I would have thee away at dawn. 'Tis perilous for thee to be here while the house is full of men-at-arms and strangers. Such folk will ever be talking and asking questions, and I would not that any knowledge of thee should come to Fulk's ears. This might easily happen, for Sir Hugo's lands march with the manor of Southwell."

"But I must say the words and deliver my mother's jewel," pleaded Osmund, grievously disappointed.

The Abbot, who was overwhelmed with business, could ill spare further time, but he was very kind.

"Well, so thou shalt," he said briskly, and approached the bed.

But Osmund jumped out and kneeling in his shirt, barefooted on the floor, he solemnly did service, his hands held the while between the Abbot's consecrated hands.

CHAPTER FIVE

O SMUND HAD looked forward to spending several days at the Abbey, and visiting the neighbouring town. It was disappointing to be roused from a sound sleep in the early morning and told that he must take to the road at once.

"But Father Abbot would not have you travel too far," added Brother Paul, when he had made his superior's wishes known. "The Abbey has a mill which is scarcely out of your way home, and he sends this token by you to good Hoddy the miller—that he may entertain you at the Abbot's expense."

The young traveller's downcast face brightened. It might be interesting to stay in a mill! Brother Paul brought him into the special kitchen, adjacent to the Infirmary, where he might break his fast without disturbing the minstrel. Osmund could not help wishing the fellow would wake and perhaps accompany him part of the way; it was dull enough trudging along by oneself. No doubt the monks were right to be so cautious, but it would be a great deal more exciting to take a few risks. Perhaps good Brother Paul guessed at these rebellious thoughts.

"The Lord Abbot considers you a sensible youth for your age," he remarked presently. "But he desired me to warn you once again to be on your guard. It is difficult for a child living in peaceful retirement like you, to realise the boldness and cruelty of such proud barons as Fulk de Brent."

Osmund bolted his mouthful of white bread and asked hastily:

"Has he done any other bad deed since he drove out my mother?"

"Aye, he and his men oppress the whole neighbourhood and that is partly why the Abbot is making a great feast for Sir Hugo de St. Lo, he is glad to welcome a virtuous lord, aye and a powerful one withal! There are a hundred archers below in the great halls and many a gallant knight rides in his train."

"But they are all Normans—I heard nothing but French speech as we passed among them yesterday," grumbled Osmund. "The country is full of Normans. There's hardly a Saxon left in these parts."

"Let me tell you, Master Pert, it is high time such distinctions were forgotten," returned Brother Paul. "Norman and Saxon have been mingled these six generations and so we are good Christians and loyal subjects there is no need to be over-nice about names."

Osmund felt himself rebuked, but he was not convinced.

"There have been such very good Kings in England in old times," he began, but Brother Paul cut him short.

"Hasten, my son, hasten! I would have you away before folk are astir. Here is the Abbot's token, the abbey seal, and here is a book—the Song of Holy Ceadman which he has the great condescension to send to your brother: honour it as it deserves."

Osmund's eyes sparkled and he wiped his hands carefully before he took the gift. It was smaller than other books he had seen—they numbered three or four not counting the great Mass book in Church. This volume was even smaller than his mother's Book of Hours, but it was written out in a most clerkly fashion, and had nice illuminated capital letters with little pictures set inside the gold-leaf scroll. It was bound in sheepskin, tied up with tags. Osmund wrapped it up carefully and tucked it under his tunic. As he did so, he remembered his promise to Hild.

"Brother Paul, may I not pass through the village on my way home? I would fain buy my sister a fairing, and I have some silver pennies to pay for it."

The Infirmarian shook his head decidedly.

"Nay, you must keep out of sight. But I have put up a cake of gingerbread—made with the best spices and sugar—which I daresay you have never tasted before—and if you stay your hunger with bread and cheese, which I will give you also—the maid will doubtless accept the gingerbread as your gift."

Osmund put back his little silk purse with a sigh, and re-fastened his belt, the strap of which ran through a loop in the money-bag. It was a great act of self-denial to refrain from eating the gingerbread and perhaps modern readers will understand this better when they reflect that Osmund had not tasted any sweets or cake for three years. In their present poverty it was quite impossible for the Lady Etheldreda to buy such a luxury as sugar, and honey—the only other substance available for sweetening—was scarce, too in the forest—for bees will not thrive among trees. Osmund could remember the delicious sugar plums and comfits which they had all enjoyed in his father's hall, and he sighed again, wishing the good Knight were at home and their troubles at an end.

He thanked Brother Paul very courteously and remarked that it had been a rare treat to eat white bread again, and then he set out.

This time there was no difficulty about the way, for Brother Paul showed him the stream and said he could follow it to the mill, six or seven miles away.

The brook ran first through wide green meadows, but soon plunged into the thick covert. A little path ran along one bank, and it had been kept clear of briars and encroaching brushwood so that pack-horses could travel easily to and fro. The mill had been built at this unusual distance from the Abbey as there was not a sufficient head of water upon the hill to grind the vast amount of flour which the monks required. The forest trees grew so close together here that nothing could flourish under them: they towered like a great branchy wall high overhead, and when Osmund paused and gazed in between the trunks, he found himself peering into a queer, twilit world. Branches and twigs were interlaced, some trees were dead, but still stood upright, fast fixed between their companions. There were few birds to be heard for birds do not like the dark and coldness of such neglected woodlands. Indeed, Osmund did not like it very much either—there was something unfriendly about that dark wall, quite different to the open glades full of moss, wild flowers and sunlight, which lay about the Grange. He wondered what he should do if he met another infuriated wild boar, charging down the narrow track? The stream was too broad to leap easily and the further bank was marshy; the trees were mostly pines and towered up without a branch within reach which would bear weight. However, Osmund was not one to meet misfortune halfway; he went forward manfully but did not pause to eat his meal until he saw a clearing ahead where another wider forest road joined his pack-horse track. When he reached the spot he found it much trampled by horses' feet. The marks were so fresh that he was convinced a large troop had passed recently: the mill was not far from Sir Hugo's demesne and he jumped to the conclusion that an advance guard of his retinue had been sent to the Castle. They had evidently had dinner here, for there were fragments of food thrown about—sluttishness much disapproved of by a good woodman like Osmund. He made up his mind to go on further or perhaps to eat as he walked, but as he moved on, his eyes fell on a horseman's cloak, forgotten under a tree. Someone would certainly be sent back to look for it presently and Osmund thought it would be kind to carry it with him as the hoof-marks had turned into the narrow track he was to follow himself. He judged that he must be drawing near his destination and, cheered by the thought, began to whistle as he flung the cloak over his arm. But the merry tune broke off in the middle, and the boy remained stockstill, unpleasantly startled. It was customary for a baron's followers to wear his badge, though the science of heraldry was still in its infancy: and this cloak did not bear Sir Hugo de St. Lo's silver ship, but the three fox heads which marked Sir Fulk's livery. Osmund felt inclined to fling it into the mud and, taking to his heels, run back to the Abbey as quickly as he could; he remembered the danger of which Brother Paul had spoken and knew that Fulk's men would have small scruple in slaying the heir of their master's enemy. But it seemed unknightly to run away, and how could they possibly know who he was?

He began to walk slowly forward, looking doubtfully at the cloak: it would be better to take it with him and earn the gratitude of the man to whom it belonged—a spearman evidently by the way it was frayed on the right side.

The stream was much deeper here, and for the last half mile the ground had been sloping downhill: presently the drumming noise of the weir became audible. It was near noon, and a drowsy stillness reigned in the forest, broken only by the humming of insects, and the sound of running water. Osmund's sharp ears could detect no echo of talk or laughter, nor the cheerful jingle of bit and spur, nor the rhythmic beat of hoofs. He heaved a sigh of relief, deeming it probable that the men-at-arms had not paused at the mill. But his satisfaction was short-lived, for a moment later an agonised cry rang through the wood.

"À moi! À moi! Aid, aid in God's name!" followed by confused and pitiful screaming by children's voices, loud men's laughter and the thunder of galloping horses.

Osmund stopped dead, his own danger uppermost in his mind for a moment. But who could refuse help? He began to run down the muddy path as hard as he could towards the shrieks, while men's voices and hoof-beats sounded fainter and fainter as the troop rode away. As Osmund approached, the noise of falling water deadened the human cries. The little river was full, and presently the mill came in view, with its wheel turning merrily. At first Osmund could see no one about and paused in wonder, till a shrill scream came again and the figure of a girl sprang out of the rushes which grew thick and tall beside the tail-race and came running towards him, calling vehemently for help in French.

"Quick, quick! My brother—they're drowning!" she screamed.

Osmund now saw a floating mass, dragged out from the bank by the rushing water; it was the body of a man, bound hand and foot and spinning back and forth in the current. A boy, crouching on the bricked parapet, was clinging desperately to the hood of his tunic, his drenched figure kept dipping into the water and it was plain that he would be drawn down in a few seconds by the weight of the drowning man.

Osmund acted quick as thought. Instead of leaping down to the lower level, he sprang to the sluice-box, poised above the wheel. The sluices were heavy and clogged with moss and slime, but flinging his whole weight against the wooden shutters, the boy succeeded in pushing down first one and then the other. The first stopped the shoot which was turning the wheel, the second, the overflow, wasting into the tail-race. The roar of the falling water ceased, the wheel still revolved slowly, splashing idly, the foam in the pool below drifted away, but the mad impetus of the stream was checked. Osmund scrambled back to the bank and down the steep steps to the lower pool. The girl was leaning over the brink, deadly white, and silent now. The bound man had drifted out into deep water, dragging his would-be rescuer with him; the boy was still striving with ever feebler strokes to swim back towards the bank, but without relinquishing his grip on his companion.

"Catch hold!" shouted Osmund, and he flung one corner of the soldier's cloak towards the pair. The boy grasped it, went under and rose again choking. Osmund had braced his left arm round a stunted willow, but the jerk which came nearly made him loose his hold.

"My horn! Blow my horn," he gasped. "Sonnez, sonnez le cors!"

INSTEAD OF A SILVERY NOTE, ONLY A CHOKED SQUEAL
CAME FORTH.

The girl was quick-witted. He felt her little hands tearing the bugle from his girdle, heard the swift intake of her panting breath. Poor child, instead of a loud silvery note, only a choked squeal came forth, but undaunted, she blew again and again. Osmund set his teeth and held on: as long as that heavy weight dragged at his arm there was hope, but he could not draw the drowning pair any nearer. He gave a great gasp at last and a mighty shout in Saxon.

"Help, for God's love!"

His heart was pounding from the strain, the sweat pouring down his face blinded him. And now the air seemed to be full of bugle notes and the shouting of men's voices. He thought vaguely of his father's tales of mêlées at the jousts, and he shouted again, but faintly this time, for he felt as though he were being pulled in two.

"À Southwell! À Southwell!"

The strain was suddenly relieved and he gasped out again: "Hold on—hold on!"

Then everything seemed to happen at once and presently Osmund found himself sitting up, very wet and shivering, with his head leaning on someone's shoulder and a great noise going on all around. There were a lot of men about, all carrying long bows, but dressed in Lincoln green more like foresters than men-at-arms, for they wore no mail.

The half-drowned peasant had been pulled out of the water and was unbound and drinking out of a horn, and the boy was alive, too, though he looked very white and exhausted. The men were talking angrily and asking: "Which way did they go?"

As soon as Osmund opened his eyes, they put this question to him fiercely. But instead of answering, Osmund said:

"Someone had better see to the sluice."

"What says the youngster?" enquired the hind who had been in the water.

Osmund repeated: "The sluices. I closed them both, so the water is gathering in the pond and 'twill maybe spoil the mill."

"There speaks a shrewd lad!" returned the other. He staggered to his feet, revealing himself to be of small size though tough and muscular. "Open the waste sluice!" he cried. "Nay, the one at the side, thou noddy! I hope those scurvy knaves have not hanged the old man."

"Nay, but they are tied head and heels," cried the little girl. "I pray you, good fellows, go and deliver them and my father will reward you well."

"And who is your father, pretty maiden?" enquired one of the men.

The girl was tall and slim for her twelve years, her long golden hair flowed down over her cotte, which was of rose-coloured silk woven with gold thread. The beautiful stuff was all stained with mud and water, as was the fur-lined cloak which lay in a heap at her feet.

"My father," she said with dignity, "is the noble Hugo de St. Lo, lord of the adjoining manor of Scarcliffe. And Dame Martha of the mill is my dear nurse, and Ivo and I came to visit her. But for all we could say, these wicked men spoiled all the meal and beat and ill-used the miller, and threw Midge, their good son, into the mill-race. Art better, Midge?"

"Midge!" shouted the man supporting Osmund who was distinguished from the rest by his tight-fitting scarlet hose. "Callest thou yonder stout fellow Midge, little lady?"

"It's a joke," she explained seriously. "And, indeed, though short, he is very strong, and would take on any of you stout churls with a quarter staff."

This answer provoked a roar of good-humoured laughter, and Osmund struggled to his feet, struck by a sudden thought.

"Is this Robin Hood's band?" he asked eagerly. "Can it be Robin and his merry men who have come to our help?"

"Who are you, who asks so bold a question?" cried the man in scarlet stockings, who was called Will Scarlet. "And why did you shout 'À Southwell' in your need? 'Twas that cry brought me to your side."

Osmund evaded one question.

"I think Friar Tuck would call me a friend," he said. "At least he bade me claim his friendship at need."

He looked round from one face to another, but they were all strange to him.

"The Captain is not here. Nevertheless thou shalt dine with him today," responded Will. "And you, Miller, too."

The girl led the way to the rude bridge across the leat which gave access to the mill premises. The whole band followed her, Osmund and the boy coming last for they were both stiff and wet. They looked at each other sideways as they went, and the strange boy suddenly smiled.

"Shall we be friends?" he asked. "You saved my life and Midge's life too. You are a brave fellow and I like you."

"You held on like a true man," returned Osmund. "I'm proud to call you friend. Wasn't he monstrous heavy?"

"Aye, truly! But we held him, friend."

His eyes sparkled with triumph. They grasped hands and then both groaned involuntarily as the movement caused darts of pain to run up their aching arms.

Osmund saw a tall dark boy with the Norman's hawk nose, and hair shaved at the nape of the neck as though he bore arms already. Ivo gazed at fair, brown-eyed Osmund, strong and broad for his age, with an upper lip curled for ready laughter, and his hair cut in a shock all round his head.

"I'll love you as a brother be you gentle or simple," cried Ivo. "But come on: we must not lose sight of Petronell."

CHAPTER SIX

THE INTERIOR of the mill showed a scene of wanton destruction: flour and grain had been emptied into the muddy yard, poor Goody Martha's crockery lay smashed upon the hearth, and the very tables bore the marks of sword-cuts. There was no one in the lower chamber and Petronell climbed the ladder into the grist-room. There lay the miller and his wife, with faces as white as curds, quaking in every limb.

"Good cheer, friends!" cried Will heartily. Then his face changed and with a cry of rage he leaped forward drawing out his sharp hunting knife. The unfortunate pair had been tightly bound and running nooses round their necks were attached to the shaft of the grindstones. A few turns of the wheel would have strangled them, had not Petronell severed the cord with Ivo's dagger while the boy strove to rescue his foster-brother.

Midge, who had been stout-hearted enough over his own danger, was nearly overcome by his parents' plight. But Will allowed no time to be lost. The men-at-arms might return and his band was but a small one.

"Come friends," he cried. "We'll hie us away to jolly Robin, and let him deal with this affair. Do not cry, maiden, the folk have taken no hurt and I would pray you courteously to come with us to my master."

"You will be quite safe," whispered Osmund.

"We shall be missed at home," said Ivo, "if we are not back at sunset."

"Fear not, there is time and to spare," returned Will. "Come, every man to horse; our guests shall ride pillion."

In a few moments they were mounted and threading their way rapidly through the trees.

It was not a very comfortable ride as the saddles were not provided with pillions and the sheaf of arrows which each outlaw carried on his back, forced the boys to sit far back grasping the front man's belt with both hands. Petronell was seated in front of her conductor and he held her safely with one sinewy hand while another man carried his bow.

"I wonder why Fulk's men departed so quickly," Osmund remarked to Ivo as they jogged along.

"They hurried off because I told them my father was coming with all his train," returned Ivo. "And true enough so he is, but not until this evening. The mill is not on our land, but any true Knight should take arms when he sees poor folk thus abused."

"Well spoken!" said Will. "Now, hold tight, my merry masters, and we will canter down this glade. Mark! there's the slot of a buck!"

The boys gazed eagerly at the ground, but found it difficult to distinguish the footprints in the grass though the outlaws picked them out unerringly.

After half an hour's brisk riding, they were challenged by someone hidden in the depth of the wood. Will slipped off his horse and murmured something which Osmund did not hear. Then all dismounted and the children and Midge followed Scarlet, while the other men led away the horses.

Treading closely in their leader's footsteps, the children dived under the drooping boughs of a grove of pines and came out into a grassy clearing, in the centre of which stood the largest man they had ever seen.

"'Tis a giant from a travelling show, sure!" gasped Midge.

"It might be Goliath!" returned Osmund.

It was not very mannerly, but they all stood in a row and stared. He was so very big! Petronell thought his waist must be two ells round, and Osmund computed the man's height at seven feet if it was an inch. Ivo was struck speechless.

The giant appeared delighted with their astonishment. He had a round cheerful face, all creased with laughter, and he held out his huge hand welcomingly.

"The King of the forest has fine guests today," he cried. "I bid you welcome in his name."

As he spoke the dark green boughs behind him parted silently and Robin Hood strode into the clearing. His head reached little above the giant's shoulder, yet he stood six foot high in his flat leather buskins and was the most gallant figure you could see in a summer's day. His green tunic fitted close and he wore no cloak or hood. His head was covered with closely curling brown hair, and his beard was of the same colour. His eyes were blue and kindly and though he laughed readily and was of a merry humour, there was a certain dignity about his gait and speech which befitted the title bestowed upon him by the giant. His movements were as sure and silent as those of the wild deer he hunted, no stick had cracked beneath his foot, the leaves scarcely rustled as he passed through the branches.

"Welcome, friend Will," he said. "Who are this noble company of drowned rats? But stay," he added. "First we will eat, and then the adventures shall be told."

Scarlet could not wait and began to pour forth his tale.

"Fulk is at his cruel tricks again," he cried, "and he has made havoc in Langwith Mill, declaring he will allow no mill in the country but his own. The miller and his wife and son would have been in bad case had it not been for these gallant children."

As he listened, Robin's smile died away and his eyes began to glitter. He cut Scarlet short, with a quick gesture of his hand.

"Enough! We'll humble this braggart baron before I break bread. John, I'll leave it to you to see that all my guests here are re-clothed in good dry garments and fed and tended. 'Twere best Fulk's men should not see them."

He unhooked a silver horn from the embroidered baldrick or belt which hung across his shoulder and blew a long joyous call. The silvery notes echoed among the trees, and had scarcely died away when another call rang out near at hand. The bushes were parted by a pair of slim brown hands and a girl bounded into the glade, with two white hounds leaping beside her. She had the grace which comes of perfect health and strength and ran over the rough ground as lightly as a deer. Her abundant brown hair was cut short at the neck like Osmund's own, her sparkling dark eyes were as piercing as those of the falcon on her wrist. She wore buskins of deerskin, or high boots, laced to the knee with silver ribbons, and a short, belted tunic of light leaf-green. Her hair was bound with a silver fillet; in her left hand she carried a man's long-bow, and a sheaf of long, heavy arrows slanted across her shoulder. She stopped abruptly at sight of the men, who all turned towards her, raising hand or bow in respectful salute.

Robin Hood's face had lighted up at sight of her, but quickly clouded again as he began to talk to her in a low voice. The girl interrupted him:

"Well, summon them by force if you will, I'll have no hand in it, for I love not men-at-arms. Meanwhile, these children are shivering—quick, to the treasury, John, and find them dry clothes."

She smiled at the children who had been gazing at her in bewilderment, and Petronell asked impulsively:

"Are you a youth or a lady?"

"I am Maid Marian, sweetheart!" returned she. "Now come with me straight."

The children scampered along after her as she led the way through the undergrowth, so rapidly that the miller and his wife were left behind.

In a few moments they reached rocky ground and the girl paused and motioned Little John forward. Osmund watched him in some surprise. They stood at the foot of an outcrop of rock, down which the small-leaved ivy had grown, covering the vertical face with a dark curtain. The big man strode forward and bending his head appeared to walk straight into the crag. The long ivy fronds closed together behind him, and Osmund guessed truly that they hid the entrance to a cave.

Presently, Little John returned, bearing piles of clothes in his arms. There were rainbow-coloured dresses for the girl— cottes they called them—with light overdresses of blue and scarlet silk, richly embroidered. Marian took them from him and led the girl aside into the bushes, while John offered the boys a choice of gay attire.

"I'd rather wear Robin Hood's livery," said Osmund boldly. "Have you no Lincoln green, Master John?"

John laughed with a touch of scorn.

"None may join our band save such as are brave enough and strong enough to meet our leader in equal combat," he cried. "It is thus that the whole band has been chosen."

"Well, then, by your leave, I'll have this leather jerkin and those chausses which befit a woodman more than this gay attire," answered Osmund, hiding his disappointment and speaking resolutely.

Ivo looked doubtfully at the brilliant garments he had selected: he had an eye for colour, and loved the blending of bright hues.

"That befits a page," remarked John, "but would mark a man in the woodland three bow shots off."

"And why not?" enquired Ivo in muffled tones as he pulled a dry shirt over his head. "I am no man's enemy that I should hide, and when we go a-hunting, I can ride down my quarry—I have no need to slink behind bushes."

Osmund looked vexed and continued his dressing in silence while John went to the assistance of the miller and his family.

After a time Ivo noticed Osmund's silence and he began to wonder if he had been indiscreet. He had told frankly of his own name and parentage, but Osmund had not named his. He noticed, too, that the other boy spoke French with a country accent.

"I meant what I said about our being friends," said Ivo hurriedly. "And I hope I have done nothing to vex you. Do not answer if it is not convenient, but I would dearly like to know your name and where you live. One of the outlaws said you shouted 'À Southwell,' so perhaps you're kin to Fulk?"

"You said you had no enemies," answered Osmund. "But I have a most bitter enemy and Fulk is the man."

"But Christians can't have enemies," interposed Petronell as she came to join the boys.

"Well, I do try not to hate him," answered Osmund. "But he has been very cruel to my mother and my father has taken the Cross, and my uncles are afraid of Fulk because he is the Prince's friend. My name is Osmund and I don't think I ought to tell you any more."

"How exciting!" exclaimed Petronell. "It's just like a ballad! Where were you going, when you came to our aid?"

"Why, the Abbot sent me to the mill. I was to be his guest there for a day or two, for you know it is the Abbey Mill."

"Well now you must come home with us," said Petronell. "Must he not, Ivo? He will be welcome at the Castle for his own sake and for his brave deed."

Osmund wished she would not talk like that.

"Let's just be friends," he proposed. "Anybody would try to pull out a person who was drowning. Ivo here was much the bravest and Midge owes him his life."

"Let's go and see how Midge is," cried Ivo, who felt just as uncomfortable as Osmund.

Petronell rather enjoyed revelling in talk of gallant deeds as she was very romantic; but she respected the boys' feelings and said no more.

Meanwhile, Maid Marian had provided the miller and his family with clothes and was listening to little Midge's plea to join Robin Hood's band.

"If I'm small," he cried hopefully, "I may yet grow for I am but sixteen years old. And I'll engage to shoot an arrow as true to the mark as any of your men though, maybe, a yard or two less far. Let me be your page, lady, to care for your hawk and hound."

"I'll trust to none but myself to do that," she returned. "But thou mayst tarry with us awhile—the miller and his dame shall be carried to the Abbey after nightfall. And what of you?" added Marian, turning to Osmund.

"We want to take him home with us," exclaimed Ivo and his sister in the same breath.

Osmund shook his head.

"Father Abbot said I might bring danger on Mother if I went among people," he explained. "Servants and such-like would ask who I was, and once they started talking, it might come to Fulk's ears that we are still in the neighbourhood."

He stopped and reddened uncomfortably as he thought of Ivo's proud words: "I have no reason to hide."

The Norman remembered it too, and cried out generously:

"Beshrew my silly tongue for speaking so heedlessly. But you know I never thought——"

"Never mind—It's all right," whispered Osmund.

Marian glanced from one to the other.

"One of our brotherhood shall ride home with Osmund," she said with a smile. "And you two—what are you named?"

"Ivo and Petronell FitzHugh," returned the little girl.

"Well, Petronell and Ivo, you shall be returned safely to your own Castle as soon as we have dined. And we must eat swiftly for I would have you away before Fulk's men are brought here prisoners."

"But we want to see them!" exclaimed Ivo.

Osmund wanted this too, but he only looked enquiringly at the huntress. She shook her head decidedly.

"Nay, they will first be surrounded and disarmed and then led about the wood till sunset, and 'tis far better you should know naught of it. Come, we'll dine."

She clapped her hands and Little John appeared with a wooden platter loaded with food, an immense pasty or cold pie having the central place.

The boys sprang up to help him, longing to see the inside of the cave, but though he sent one to the spring for water and gave the other a basket of bread to distribute, nobody was allowed to accompany him behind the ivy curtain.

Marian bade them all to be seated on the mossy grass but after a moment Osmund noticed that Midge was missing.

"Why, we're one short!" he cried. "I hope the young miller has taken no harm from his ducking?"

"Nay, he has his wish and has gone with the band," answered Marian. "Now eat, friends, and be merry! Good John, thou hast already dined, prithee sing to us as we eat."

Little John was proud of his fine voice and obeyed with alacrity. He sat on a fallen tree and trolled forth the following rude ballad in praise of his chief:

"In woodland green, there dwells I ween
A Knight both bold and free;
He pays no jot for tithe or scot
Yet who so rich as he?

His lands are wide full many a hide
His men are brave and true
And he who dare affront him there
Shall soon the insult rue.

His bow is strong, his arrow long
Doth always find its mark.
His bugle-horn shall wake the morn
And sound at edge of dark.

Here poor men find a friend most kind.
Let wrongful rich man quake—
To pass this way he needs must pay
The lordship of the brake!

For Robin Hood is passing good
And passing free of hand
So here's a health to the foe of wealth
And the King of forest land!"

CHAPTER SEVEN

J T WAS A MERRY meal, and Marian made everyone feel at home. Any little jest set her off laughing, and she had the most infectious laugh in the world. Osmund thought that the ladies "bright of hue" who figure in every ballad must be just like Maid Marian, whose teeth were so small and white, whose lips so red and whose eyes so sparkling. The venison pasty was quite delicious and the best bread at the Abbey was not more crisp and white than the manchet which Marian sliced with her hunting knife. No doubt the outlaws lived well and delicately: Osmund wondered from whence came the splendid clothes which filled John's storehouse? He asked no questions, however, and when they had eaten, Marian rose and beckoned Osmund aside.

"It is our custom," she began seriously, "that everyone who partakes of our hospitality be he gentle or simple, should tell us who and what he is. I think if the lady your mother were here, she would wish you to comply with this rule, for you may have confidence that naught will be told again."

Osmund did not answer for a moment while he thought this over, then he nodded in agreement.

"Yes," he said, "that is only courteous. The reason my mother bade me not to speak was because my father, Sir Aelfric, is at the holy wars. He went with the King, and as soon as he had gone, Sir Fulk began to oppress us. First he harried our poor peasants and pastured his cattle on our common lands, and then he swore my father had joined the King's enemies and that his lands were forfeited to Prince John, who had granted them to him. Of course it is all nonsense: my father was never a traitor, never!"

"But there are Courts and Judges to try such causes," said Marian, laying her hand on the boy's shoulder.

"Aye, lady. My mother summoned him to challenge her before the Shire Mote, but his answer was to send his men-at-arms—hirelings from Italy and the Low Countries who have not a word of our speech—and—and——"

Osmund could scarcely bear to speak of that dreadful day.

"They slew our good old gate-keeper," he whispered, clenching his fists. "I saw my mother thrust out into the rain with the baby in her arms. She wept, and they laughed and I drew my dagger and they struck me down and so we fled to Welbeck Abbey."

"Then you are the eldest, Osmund?"

"Nay, Eadgar is older, but he, you see, was at school at Ely. But the monks dared not keep him when they heard of our plight, for fear of Fulk's enmity."

"And now where do you dwell?" asked Marian.

"In the wood—in one of the Abbot's granges, and I have been to pay tribute to him. He is our best friend," declared the boy. "And all will be righted when the King comes home."

"Aye, sure," returned Marian. Her voice was sweet though she used a rustic manner of speech. Osmund believed she chose to do this in order not to seem superior to Robin's comrades, who were apparently drawn from every class. Will Scarlet, for instance, spoke like a yeoman and Tuck like a churl, while one or two of the men had the clipping accent of the Norman and might well have passed their youth as pages in great men's houses.

There was little time to bid farewell to all the new friends, for Marian clapped her hands and instantly a man in green stepped into the clearing and announced that his horse was ready.

"This is for you, Osmund," declared Marian. "Little John tells me you would fain have donned Robin's livery, and that he refused you. Yet you shall wear mine. Never take off this girdle for, as long as you wear it, all our people will render you service. When all goes well with you, wear it under your tunic, but when you are in trouble or seek speech with us, clasp it outside."

As she spoke she held out a narrow belt cunningly worked in green and silver.

"THIS IS FOR YOU, OSMUND," DECLARED MARIAN.

Osmund was delighted, because real Knights always wore some lady's colours and Father had ridden off with Mother's sleeve—embroidered with pearls and decked with fur—bound round his helmet.

"So now I'm your squire!" he cried. "And that is almost as good as being Robin Hood's!"

Marian burst out laughing and clapped him on the shoulder.

"Osmund, thou art a lad after my own heart, and thy mother is a right noble dame who hath not taught thee the mincing ways of Court civility!" she cried.

There was nothing rustic about this speech and though Osmund did not altogether understand it, he was glad she approved of him.

"Now go!" she commanded. "One of the laws of the Greenwood is never to keep others waiting!"

There was not a moment in which to speak to Petronell and Ivo. Osmund girded on his belt and waved his cap to them, and followed his guide forthwith.

The man's name was Gilbert, and he had been a fletcher or arrow-maker by trade until he had taken to the forest. He told Osmund that patteners were all villains and that they had destroyed his livelihood and that none of them was worth a groat.

Osmund knew that there was always great jealousy between fletchers and the makers of the high-heeled wooden sandals which everyone wore in wet weather or snow to raise their shoes of cloth or coloured leather out of contact with the mire. It did not greatly interest him and he began to ask eager questions about Robin Hood and his band. But Gilbert instantly said that it was a foolish custom to talk when faring through the wood, and fatal to good hunting. The right thing was to look, listen and keep silence.

Osmund thought this rather a dull precept as they had such a long ride before them, but he said no more for a time, and then merely enquired which was the best wood for making arrows.

He soon began to feel very tired, the wrenched muscles of arm and side had stiffened painfully, but luckily the outlaw's horse had easy paces. The sun went down and presently the stars came out, and owls began to call deep in the wood. Gilbert was soon obliged to walk his horse as it was impossible to see far enough to risk a swifter pace, and Osmund had some uncomfortable naps, waking with a start, when his face bumped against the outlaw's back.

At last they drew near the Verderer's house and all the dogs began to bark. The Verderer himself came out in a very bad humour.

"Halt! Who rides by so late?" he cried.

"A freeman!" responded Gilbert boldly.

"Stand, I say! Turn back! No one may pass this way after dark!" shouted the Verderer.

"Ho, ho! Owl! Look to thy mice, but do not interfere with the lords of the wood," returned Gilbert tauntingly. He made his bowstring twang with his finger and rode contemptuously on, leaving the Verderer roaring to his varlets to rise and waylay the intruder. No one was in a hurry to obey this order and the outlaw turned into the marked track and cantered down the grass edge for a few minutes and then guided his horse among the thick trees.

"Clasp me close, and bend thy head against me," he whispered. "And sleep not now for we have some delicate riding to do among these close-set trunks."

The horse seemed used to this work and threaded his way between the trees, choosing his path with the greatest cleverness.

"We are coming to Job's warren," said Osmund presently, "and the ground will be full of rabbit holes. There'll be snares, too, in which your horse might catch his foot. Let me run in front—I can show you a safe path."

Gilbert wasted no words, he merely pulled up, and Osmund slipped to the ground and peered about until he found the little grassy path which led from the warren to the grange.

"This way," he cried softly, turning round.

To his surprise, horse and rider had vanished and when he called louder, the only reply was a faint, "Fare ye well!" which drifted to him on the night wind.

Osmund retraced his steps, blundering into trees and catching in low branches, but there was no sign of his late companion.

As he reached the spot where they had halted, the moon came out and poured a flood of soft light down upon the grass. There was the trampled space where Osmund had dismounted, and there—dark marks pricked on the silvery dewy sod—the trail they had made together as they came hither and a second track, facing in another direction, the only trace which Gilbert had left as he vanished into the forest.

A few moments later Osmund was knocking at Job's door. The old man rose to admit him, and seeing that the boy was dog-tired, he asked no question but brought in an armful of dry rushes and a blanket and bid him lie down before the smouldering fire.

Osmund placed his precious wallet in safety, pulled off his shoes, and in five minutes was sound asleep.

.   .   .   .   .

Next morning, Hild was at her daily task of carrying the broody hens out of the barn and tethering them close to the house for fear of foxes. She glanced up at the sky, wondering if it was going to be wet; if so she would have to get one of the boys to help her to carry out the wattle shelters, made of woven hazel-branches, which were too heavy for her to lift by herself. Yes, the sky looked threatening: the children had a special call which they used among themselves—it was rather like the cry of the plover.

"Whoo-ee!" called Hild.

To her surprise there was an answering "whoo-ee" from the wood as well as from the house. In her joy, Hild let all the chickens she was carrying slip out of her apron, and she bounded through the gate and up through the hazel copse with joyful shouts.

"Whoo-ee—whoo-ee, Osmund! Mother! Mother! Osmund has come home!"

In a few minutes they met and Hild's first query was:

"Have you had any adventures?" And the second: "Why, Osmund, where did you get those clothes?"

It would take too long to describe that day and to tell of Eadgar's rapture when his brother gave him the book and Hild's delight over the gingerbread, which was honourably shared among them all. Osmund did not tell about Maid Marian's belt until he was quite alone with his mother. At first the lady started and turned pale, and then she sighed.

"I may keep it, mayn't I, Mother?" pleaded Osmund, alarmed at her expression of dismay.

"Yes," she said at last. "But let it be a secret. Do not speak to anyone about it."

"Oh, Mother! Not to Eadgar and Hild?"

"Nay, my son. 'Twere best for me to keep it. I will lay it aside here in the secret drawer in the aumbry."

She went to the threshold and glanced about but there was no one near. Nevertheless, she closed the door on the inside with its heavy wooden bolt and then opened the aumbry or cupboard which stood near her bed, and beckoned to her son.

"We live in dangerous days," said she, "and you must needs be a man before your time. Under this fifth boss in the carving is the spring which opens the secret drawer—you must press it, so."

Osmund practised with somewhat clumsy fingers but his mother was not content until he could open the drawer easily.

"Now thy belt—I will lay it here among thy father's jewels."

Osmund unfastened the girdle unwillingly, but he noticed that at sight of Sir Aelfric's gold chain, his mother's eyes had filled with tears, so he folded up his treasure and laid it in the drawer in silence.

CHAPTER EIGHT

THE DAYS PASSED so quietly at the Grange for the next few weeks that Osmund's adventures seemed to belong more to the realm of romance than of everyday life. Hild, however, was never tired of questioning her brother, particularly about the Norman girl. Boys, of course, never noticed the most interesting things: Osmund was quite unable to tell her the colour of Petronell's eyes for instance, nor of what her dress was made.

April had been a stormy month of cold winds and lashing showers, but warm weather came in the last week, and all the leaves began to uncurl.

This year the children were not allowed to go to the May Day games at Ollerton, the nearest village, which was about four miles from the Grange. The Lady Etheldreda explained that she feared some of Fulk's followers might be present at the feast and the children must dress their own maypole, which should be set up in front of the house. This was a very disappointing announcement, for with the exception of Job's three stupid, fat grandsons there were no children in that part of the forest.

Nevertheless it was exciting and delightful to rise at dawn and go out into the dewy forest where all the bird choirs were in full song, and to see who could find the best flowers. The wild cherry was ablow still and there were primroses, anemones and violets in the glades. The daffodils were over, but Hild had once found wild lily-of-the-valley and she always hoped to come upon it again.

The grown-up people went a-maying too, but the children thought it much more fun to wander by themselves, especially as Mother remained with baby Sibell within sight of the house. The four elder children started out with baskets and Eadgar suggested that they should each go in a different direction and meet at a certain birch-tree in about an hour.

"How shall we know the time?" demanded Stephen, "we haven't a sand-glass with us."

"We'll just have to guess," replied Hild briskly. "The one who arrives first must whoo-ee for the others. You had better come with me, Stephen—you're too little to go by yourself."

"I'll go with the boys, then," said Stephen, much offended.

"Come with me," proposed Osmund. "You can find your own flowers, only stay within call. I'm going to look for marigolds by the brook."

Hild waited, hoping Eadgar would offer to accompany her, but he was looking for a hedge-sparrow's nest. The parent birds fluttered near with anxious cries.

"Do come, brother," called Hild, plaintively.

"I want to see if there are eggs—of course I shan't touch them. We settled all to go separately, didn't we?" returned he. "You can come with me if you promise not to look at the nest without me," he answered.

Hild accepted the bargain.

"I promise! And let's go to Primrose Hill, shall we? It's so sunny, there will be heaps of flowers out there."

The part of the forest she named was some way off, and they ran and dawdled by turns until they reached the rising ground.

"I see it—I see it! Just behind that piece of dead fern!" cried the little girl. She pointed out the tiny, beautifully shaped little nest which had two eggs in it just the same colour as the bright blue sky. Hild longed to take one in her hand.

"I'd be ever so careful," she pleaded as Eadgar pulled her away.

"Yes, but the mother bird always knows if it's been touched and then she deserts, and just think what days and days and *days* of work she has had building that lovely little nest." He pushed the tall bracken frond carefully into its original place, and walked away, Hild following uncertainly.

"Where are you going? I think it's very dull, each to go alone," she grumbled.

The blossoms were faded in the open spaces, where the sun smote them, but in shady nooks under the hazels, there were plenty of buds still, and newly-opened flowers. Hild began to fill her basket, making tidy little bunches, surrounded by leaves and tied up with grass. A cuckoo was shouting his joyful song not far off, and just overhead Mrs. Cuckoo was flying heavily about, making a noise like running water while all the birds followed scolding and twittering.

"I hope she won't find our hedge-sparrow's nest," cried Hild, looking up at the golden oak leaves uncurling against the deep blue sky. But there was no answer for Eadgar had wandered on out of earshot.

The lower branches of beeches showed a sprinkling of green: their heads were still covered with masses of burnished buds. But there were more birches than any other kind of tree just there, and their new leaves smelt faintly of roses.

By the time that Hild had filled her basket with primroses and wild violets she judged that the hour must nearly have passed and she was just about to shout for Eadgar when he came flying back towards her.

"Hush, hush!" he whispered urgently. "There are men hiding in the bushes: they are Sheriff's men, for I saw the silver badge under the dark cloak."

"But they won't hurt us—we aren't doing any harm," said Hild in surprise. "They are looking for a thief most probably."

Eadgar seemed doubtful.

"If the Sheriff is good, I suppose his men would be good," he murmured, "but the Sheriff of Nottingham is bad and so 'tis the other way about. Here are more coming!"

He darted into the undergrowth pulling Hild after him. The little girl squeezed herself under a rock which was covered with bilberry bushes and made room for Eadgar beside her. They pressed together, their hearts beating violently with excitement.

The first band of men came out into the open upon their comrade's approach. There were about twenty stout fellows all told, well armed with cross-bows, clubs and daggers.

"Well, found you aught?" cried the leader of the second band.

"Not a thing, Ancient," returned one of the others. "There's not a house hereabouts except the Warrener's and a tumbledown grange full of women and children."

"Our master will be wonderful wroth if we have no one to show," grumbled the man addressed as "Ancient" or Corporal. "He is riding through the lower wood with eighty men, but our spies tell us that Robin Hood is dwelling somewhere in these parts by himself—his band have ridden over the Yorkshire border and the Sheriff will never have such a chance again."

"Let him come and tackle the bold outlaw himself then," grumbled another man. "They say he has the strength of ten."

"Aye, but the Sheriff has called out Baron Fulk's fierce Flemings—there is a ring of swords round the wood, you may say," remarked the Corporal. "And there's a good reward, Dick Pottle—a rich reward! Three hundred pounds of gold for Robin Hood's head!"

"We can set at him all together," rejoined the valiant Dick. "Or perhaps slay him in his sleep! That was a fresh-killed buck we found, comrades, and I'll wager Robin Hood was hunting last night for the moon was full."

They moved away, still talking, while the children cowered down holding their breath.

"I like not to see men slain—oh, 'tis terrible!" whispered Hild at last. "But we must find Osmund and warn Robin Hood! Mother says he is not wicked, and brother's heart will break if his friend is betrayed."

"But it's dangerous!" declared the boy. "And first I must take you home."

"Come on, then."

Hild left the shelter of the rock and began to move softly from bush to bush as she had seen Job do when in pursuit of game. But this method was too slow and they soon began to run towards the trysting-tree as fast as they could set foot to the ground.

Osmund was waiting for them impatiently. "Where *have* you been?" he called as they drew near. "We have been shouting for you all over the wood."

"Never mind that now, brother!" exclaimed Eadgar. "There is something much more important——"

"You're to come home at once, Mother says," interrupted Osmund. "There are men-at-arms about, and Goody Alice is in a terrible taking, Hild—she's mad wroth with you!"

"I don't care!" exclaimed his sister, twisting her arm out of Osmund's grasp as he tried to hurry her along. "The Sheriff has surrounded this part of the forest and he means to take Robin Hood and cut off his head! And we overheard the men say that Robin is alone! Can't we find him—can't we save him?"

Osmund's flushed face turned pale with horror.

"First we must go to Mother," he declared.

The maypole was half-dressed when they came into the clearing in which the Grange stood, but Lady Etheldreda was gazing anxiously about while Stephen wove a garland on the grass. She listened in great perturbation to the children's news, and at first declared that they could do nothing but pray for Robin's safety. The two elder boys implored her leave to scour the thickets and warn Osmund's friend, and at last she consented. Hild begged hard to accompany them, but her mother thought her safer at home.

Osmund and Eadgar pushed their way through the undergrowth without any idea of which direction to choose.

At last Eadgar stopped.

"We are not likely to find Robin Hood like this," he declared. "He is a past master of wood-craft, and will no doubt hear us afar off and keep out of our way. If we only had some means of letting him know we are friends! The outlaws must have ways of signalling to each other."

Eadgar was popularly supposed not to be practical, but he often thought of things which shrewder people neglected. Osmund instantly appreciated the sense of this suggestion.

"I'll try and remember," he said. "Was there any call or password? Nay, I am sure I only heard Friar Tuck hallooing to his hounds."

"But when Will Scarlet came to thy rescue at the Mill did he not wind his horn? Or what cry did he use to gather his friends?"

"There was no cry," answered Osmund. "But the bugle notes—if I could remember how they went—something like this—Tantivy, tantivy, tan-tallo! Wait a minute!"

He flung himself down on a bank and unhooked the horn which he had worn continually since his meeting with the outlaws. Drawing a long breath, he put the mouthpiece to his lips and blew at first tremulously, then full and true. Between each stave he paused, and both boys listened eagerly, but there was no sound except the alarm notes of the birds who resented the intrusion into their songs. Four times did Osmund sound the same call: then Eadgar caught him by the arm.

"Hist! If thou hast learnt the call, will not the Sheriff's men know it too?" he asked anxiously. "We do not want to draw down trouble on our mother!"

"True!" agreed Osmund. "Let us keep under covert."

He moved swiftly into the shadow of an ancient yew, tripped over something in the long grass and fell sprawling.

"Where's your vaunted wood-craft?" began Eadgar laughing, but he stopped suddenly for his laugh was echoed in a deep, manly tone from under the dark boughs.

Osmund sprang up, ready to take to his heels when another bugle rang out, deep in the recesses of the forest: it made a series of angry brassy notes unlike the forester's gay call.

"Down, down!" ordered the voice from under the tree. "Friends of the Merry Brotherhood, hide or fly!"

"Master Robin, is it you?" asked Osmund eagerly. "Can we hide here too? But, no—that won't do," he corrected himself. "Surely a low-growing yew is just the tree that folk would search."

"You are right, lad," remarked the outlaw, for it was indeed he. "But I am going to show these townsmen some play and 'twill be safe enough for you two to lie here while I lead the dance. Hast never heard of my namesake Robin Goodfellow?"

"The tricksy elf for whom Joan sets a bowl of cream? A truce to jest, Master Robin, for you are in grave danger," declared Eadgar. "The Sheriff has called out a hundred of his men and the followers of Fulk de Brent are with him—the whole wood is surrounded. And Mother let us come to warn you."

There was no answer: Eadgar dived down under one side of the tree, Osmund under the other; they found themselves face to face on the bare patch of ground round the trunk, but there was no one else there.

"Where has he gone?" gasped Eadgar.

"Here is the mark of his body in the soft dead yew leaves," whispered Osmund. "And he certainly was here, for I fell over his leg! Let's wait and listen. Anyone could trace us by the trampled grass out there, but Robin won't let them come this way."

Eadgar did not feel quite the same happy confidence.

"I think we had better run home," he suggested.

But hardly were the words out of his mouth than Robin's bugle sounded the identical call which Osmund had endeavoured to copy.

"Tantivy—tantivy, tan-tallo!"

The silvery cadences echoed among the trees at some distance from where the boys lay.

"He went from us just like a shadow," whispered Osmund admiringly. The outburst of cries and shouts which followed indicated the position of the Sheriff's men, and some of them were unpleasantly near.

A horse neighed, and they heard the thunder of galloping hoofs tearing down a ride. Osmund could not resist the temptation of taking part; lying flat under the drooping fringes of the yew he winded his horn—faintly, loudly and faintly again.

"Hark, they are coming this way! We must run," he murmured. "Let's hide in the hollow oak we found last summer."

He slipped out at the further side of the tree and paused to locate the nearest group of pursuers. Eadgar was aware that he had no talent for sport of this kind, so he said: "You lead," and loyally followed the younger brother.

It was indeed a highly dangerous game of hide-and-seek. If the Sheriff or any of his followers had laid hands on either of the boys, they would have put him to death without a second thought. Robin Hood's bugle sounded mockingly every now and again. It was his aim to draw all his pursuers together and when they thought themselves hot on his trail, to tempt them into the thickest part of the wood, where horses could not penetrate. Osmund soon realised this and stopped blowing his horn.

"They haven't any dogs with them, I think," he murmured, as he swarmed up a sycamore tree and scrambled thence on to the mighty branch of an oak. "Come on! If we get into the centre of this tree, its great limbs will hide us, though it isn't in full leaf yet. Look, there they go! You can see the saplings moving where they force their way through."

Eadgar climbed up more slowly.

"We had better not talk," he said, peering down rather anxiously. "Look, there's a man with Fulk's badge!"

"Keep quite still," returned Osmund.

They flattened themselves against the rough bark of the tree, watching breathlessly. They could see the man so plainly that it seemed impossible that he should not see them. But the Fleming was watching the ground for his quarry and though he presently passed so close to their hiding-place that they could hear his panting breath, he did not look up.

"That was a narrow escape!" whispered Osmund, without moving. "Now it is in my mind that Robin will lead them into the fir-wood where the boughs interlace so closely that one can scarce pass between the trees. But we have only seen one Fleming, and perhaps he is a spy and the others are still ringing the wood."

"If Robin doubles round behind them he will return to the yew," answered Eadgar, "and it behoves us as true men to go back and await him there, danger or no danger."

Osmund nodded.

"Yes. And then let us take him home. We could hide him somewhere—under the woodpile perhaps. But don't move yet, brother! We shall hear Robin's bugle again."

The boys had often watched a hunt, organised for the amusement of one or other of the great lords of the neighbourhood. Prince John had led the chase over this part of the forest only a year ago. It was a brave sight to see gallant men and gaily caparisoned horses, and beautiful ladies galloping along the forest glades, though like a true woodman, Osmund was convinced that the best sport was to be had by following the deer a-foot. But never before had they witnessed a man-hunt and there was something peculiarly terrifying in this display of force and craft to do a human being to death. Both boys were pale and silent as they presently climbed down and made their way back to their first hiding-place, taking care to walk on dead leaves or moss, and to keep in shelter all the way.

To their amazement Robin had reached the yew before them. He was breathing quickly for he had been running hard, but he sat up with a pleased laugh as the boys crept in, and made their report and suggestion.

"Fulk is a bad enemy of mine," he said, "and of yours too, by all I hear. Now hark ye—is there any old woman in your house who would lend me her kirtle and stomacher?"

"But you couldn't pass as an old woman," protested Osmund. "You're full six feet tall and more—and you've a beard!"

"Why so I have, but none the less I'll contrive to turn into as good a gammer as you'll find on May Day. Bring me cap and wimple and gown—and go forward with your merry-making—an old pedlar dame will come and grace your feast."

"Are we to go home now and leave you here?" said Eadgar.

"Job's house is nearer," interrupted Osmund. "And his good dame lies ill a-bed of the rheumatism. What if I got you her things? Job is true, and loves not the Verderer over well. And there's no one else there, for the lads have gone to the village, I know."

"I'll wait here then," said Eadgar.

Osmund agreed and tried to slip away as silently as Robin Hood had done, and to run as swiftly.

Chapter Nine

I T WAS LONG past dinner-time though the Lady of the Grange kept Saxon hours, and gave her household four meals a day instead of two as was the Norman custom. Sibell and Stephen had partaken of cakes and syllabub, but Hild begged leave to await her brothers' return.

Goody Alice had got over her anger at what she considered Hild's wild ways, and had set out a great bowl of curds and cream, with honey-cakes, and a jar of the preserved wild-strawberries which were only brought forth on great occasions. She had placed a large tray on a stool in the shade of a lilac bush, for the sun was hot as it was in the year.

The children were making cowslip balls when at last the old hound who was lying on the sunny steps below the door, barked and wagged his tail.

"Here they are!" screamed Hild, jumping up in great excitement: "and they've brought Gammer Moggy, Job's wife, with them."

"She steps very lightsome for an old woman," observed Etheldreda. "But ask no questions, children," she added quickly. She gazed attentively at the boys' companion as they approached together. "You are welcome, good dame," she said courteously. "Stephen, run and ask Alice for a measure of murat wine to refresh our neighbour. And do you sit in the shade by me, Gammer, while I continue my work."

"Aye, sure I'll rest me right willingly," returned the old lady, in a thin, cracked voice. She hobbled up to the bench and sat down and Lady Etheldreda moved her spinning wheel so that the bundle of wool hid the newcomer's face from any chance passer-by.

THE STRANGER DRANK IT AT A DRAUGHT, MUCH TO THE LITTLE
BOY'S ASTONISHMENT.

Hild dared not disobey her mother's command, but she saw that the boys were as excited as she. She stole up under pretext of offering a dish of wastel cakes, and had a good look at the old lady. It certainly was not Mrs. Job, and she noticed as she leaned against her knee, that her mother was trembling. The stranger had a brown face which was so closely wrapped in a wimple that only nose and eyes were uncovered; a large hooded cloak was drawn over the broad shoulders, and Hild's sharp eyes detected a broad gap between the full skirt and the sleeved woollen jacket, through which an under-garment of well-worn buckskin could be seen.

She backed away hastily before the supposed old lady could help herself from the dish and met Osmund's warning eyes.

"Oh, brother," whispered Hild. "His jerkin is showing under the mantle! Is it really——"

Osmund nodded vigorously and then went on hastily with his meal.

"Mother says if anyone comes we are to be very busy with the maypole," he muttered. "Now, Hild, don't keep looking round—we must just behave as if it *were* Gammer Moggy!"

Stephen had returned carefully carrying the tall beaker of murat—a kind of wine made from mulberry juice and honey. The stranger drank it at a draught, much to the little boy's astonishment. Old Moggy generally sipped and mumbled for ever so long.

As soon as they had finished eating, the Lady Etheldreda bade the children finish dressing the maypole. She fetched her lute from the hall and tuned it while they proceeded gaily with their work.

The "dressing," as it was called, of the pole consisted in winding long garlands of greenery down all its length and crowning it with a wreath of primroses. Other spring flowers in circlets and posies were heaped at the base, and branches of cherry and green leaves were hung on either side of the house door. Then the lady played a sprightly air on her lute and the older servants came out to see the fun. The younger ones had gone off to Ollerton and would not be back till after nightfall. As there were only four children to dance the maypole, they had to take three ribbons each, and the plaiting was soon in a tangle; they thought it great fun to reverse their steps, turn backwards and begin again, and soon their happy laughter almost drowned the tune. Little Sibell capered about getting in everyone's way until the disguised outlaw caught her up on his knee, jumping her up and down in time to the music.

The Lady Etheldreda could not forget the danger which threatened. Her gaze constantly strayed to the thickets only a bow shot from the sunny garden and she was the first to hear approaching footsteps.

"Get some perry, good Walter," she said quickly to the serving-man, "for I think there is little murat left and here come——"

Her voice trailed away in terror, and the lute almost slipped from her grasp, for she recognised the man who had just ridden through her gate as Fulk de Brent—her arch enemy. He was accompanied by the Verderer who had charge of that portion of the forest, and a strong guard of his own foreign mercenaries.

Eadgar and Osmund flew to their mother's side, and Hild ran to Sibell who was struggling on the outlaw's knee.

"Don't cry, baby, we'll stay with old Nanny," exclaimed Hild loudly, and she leaned up against the stranger so as to hide the tell-tale jerkin.

Fulk showed the marks of the hard fighting in which he had passed his youth. His face bore an ugly scar, and was further disfigured by an habitually malignant expression.

"So here is where you have gone to ground with your brats," he remarked. "The Abbot of Welbeck owes me a reckoning for this."

"Do not blame the monks," answered Etheldreda, with dignity. "I flung myself upon their charity with my little children, and they allow me to inhabit this house and till the holding, unseen and forgotten by men."

"I cannot conceive of a better place in which to harbour my enemies, and plot against me," exclaimed Fulk. He had ridden on to the grassplot, regardless of the havoc wrought by his horse's hoofs on the sward. "I daresay it was with your connivance that my men were ambushed only a few weeks ago," he added in a bullying tone.

"No one was ambushed in this part of the forest, that we heard tell of," cried Osmund indignantly. "And you see all my mother's followers here," he added boldly, "save two hinds who have gone to the May Day games."

"Who gave you leave to speak?" roared the knight, and he aimed a buffet at the boy with his heavy mailed glove. Osmund flung up his arm to protect his face, but did not step back, though the blow made him stagger.

"You are rearing two young traitors there to defy me," continued Fulk. "Aye, they were as well as in my care, unless indeed I spit them both on my sword, out of hand, as were wisest."

"My children have done you no harm, nor have I," said Etheldreda. She folded an arm about each of her sons and drew them close to her. Her piteous terror softened the hard heart of the Verderer and he remarked gruffly:

"You forget, Sir Fulk, that I have jurisdiction over this wood, and be sure if there is anything done or plotted against your honour or dignity, I shall arrest the perpetrators instantly. Madam here is a quiet neighbour enough, and I keep a vigilant eye on all that goes on."

Hild was quite breathless with fright and she clutched the outlaw and hid her face in his cloak. He sat quite still, every muscle as tense as a taut bow-string, waiting to see if the danger would blow over.

One of the woodwards now came forward and announced that he had searched the house and croft thoroughly that very morning and found nothing amiss.

"The Warrener's wife is often here," he added, "and there are no other neighbours for three miles about."

Fulk nodded. He was pleased at having discovered Etheldreda's retreat, for he feared she might have sought refuge with powerful relatives who would dispute his ill-gotten possession of Southwell Manor.

"Take heed you keep within the confines of this wood, then," he said. "There must be no trafficking with the monks, mind, woman! If I hear of you or any of your household appearing at town or market, I shall protect myself by taking those brats of yours into safe keeping."

"Aye, safe is the word," remarked the woodward to a forester with a jarring laugh. "For not a breath of air, a ray of light, a crumb of food nor a drop of water penetrates into Fulk's new dungeon, they say."

He pronounced this speech loud enough to be heard by all. Fulk nodded again, in approval, and turning his horse rode away again, followed by his men.

"Base, discourteous churl, to speak so to my mother!" exclaimed Osmund, clenching his fists.

"When we're old enough we will avenge you, lady," said Eadgar.

He did not generally use this title, though it was customary for children to address parents thus respectfully. But now it seemed he could not show his mother enough deference to make up for Fulk's insulting tone.

"Alas, my sons, I have no wish for vengeance. But I fear the Lord of Brent has heard ill-tidings of your father," she sighed. "Else he would not dare to treat me so despitefully."

"Fulk will never be nearer to death until he comes to his last hour," observed a deep, man's voice.

Hild jumped. She had only heard high, womanish tones coming from beneath the folded wimple, and it was alarming to see an angry man's face, fierce and bearded, emerge as Robin pushed aside the drapery as though it choked him.

"Lady," he added earnestly. "Call when you need upon a Knight of the forest. Rude and unpolished I may be, but you shall find me a true man, and one who wields a sharp sword withal."

"I thank you, friend," returned Etheldreda. "I would have no blood shed for me, but some day I may indeed call upon you to do me another service. And, meanwhile, pray you, should you meet any palmer from the Holy Land or any returned crusader question if he knows anything of my dear Lord Aelfric de Southwell."

"Aye, marry will I!" returned Robin emphatically. "Indeed, I always make it my duty to question any traveller I may meet!"

A merry look succeeded the angry one on his face, and putting the little girl gently from his knee, he stepped behind the woodpile. The children ran eagerly after him from either side, but they only met each other: Robin Hood had melted into the greenwood as a leaping fish disappears into its native element.

CHAPTER TEN

ULK'S UNEXPECTED appearance and his threats had cast a blight on the simple feast; the children helped Dame Alice to carry in the empty bowls and dishes, and Walter fetched away the spinning-wheel.

The Lady Etheldreda issued orders that no one was to go beyond the garden without leave. Men-at-arms could still be heard, blowing their horns and shouting rallying cries far away in the wood, and it was dangerous for any to be abroad.

The sun went in and a cold wind rushed through the trees, sending the petals flying from the cherry-blossom garlands and withering the primroses. The children for once were quite ready to come into the house; the little ones were tired after the early morning, while the three elder had much to talk about. They all sat in the big chamber which ran across the full width of the house and combined the usual summer parlour and the winter one or "solar" in one room. The roof was wooden-vaulted and there were deep window seats, on one of which Eadgar, Hild and Osmund sat in a row.

"Now!" cried Hild eagerly, "tell me your adventures."

"Well, Eadgar thought of sounding the horn," cried Osmund, nothing loth, but beginning in the middle of the story.

The Lady Etheldreda sat by the newly-kindled fire, with her wheel beside her and Stephen lying at her feet, playing with his jointed wooden knight—a favourite toy. She looked across at her three elder children: they were so happy together, and she herself hated the thought of separating them, but Fulk's threats made her blood run cold. The Baron of Brent was a follower of Prince John, who had the name of having committed countless cruelties. She lived in terror of being declared a widow and being forced by the Prince to marry again or pay an immense fine, such as had been extorted from Eustace de Balliol, when he had wed the widow of Robert Fitz-Piers. Widows were equally oppressed in these days whether they wanted to re-marry or not. The Regent assumed a right to dispose of the hand of any woman, and practically put heiresses up to auction, handing them over without mercy to the man who paid him most for the possession of their lands. She herself might not have submitted so meekly to be driven out of her husband's manor, had she not feared that resistance would have spurred on John to force a second marriage on her.

Fulk had recently announced that her beloved lord was dead, but had brought no proof of it, nor would he permit the lady's cause to be tried at the Sheriff's Court. It was common knowledge that the Sheriff of Nottingham allowed justice to be bought and sold, that is to say, that only those persons who offered him a fat bribe could get their pleas presented at the Shire Court. Poor men, who did not happen to have a friend among the powerful barons of the county, found their causes continually set back and subjected to heart-breaking delays, while Fulk and such folk who were hand-in-glove with the Prince, could always triumph by unjust means.

The Lady Etheldreda longed to consult the Abbot. She even thought of sending the boys by stealth to her brothers in the far North, but it seemed too dangerous to make any move for the moment.

"Children, children!" she called suddenly. "Come here—come gather round me and we will pray for your father's safety. Our Father—God *is* our Father—God will bring your earthly father safe home."

.　　　.　　　.　　　.　　　.

That night, when the boys went up to their room, Eadgar came over and sat on the end of Osmund's bed. Stephen was already asleep and there was no light in the room, save a glimmer from the open window.

"I have been thinking," began Eadgar, and then he made such a long pause that Osmund became impatient.

"You always are thinking," he retorted. "It is time we were doing! It was dreadful that Fulk should come and insult our mother as he did, and that we should not have been able to defend her."

"I know," agreed his brother. "That is just what troubles me. I want you to rouse me early tomorrow and let us both go out and practise shooting at a mark."

"Yes, let us practise every morning!" exclaimed Osmund eagerly. "What a pity we have only two real arrows. Do you think we could make any for ourselves?"

"Good enough to practise with, I daresay, but they would be no use as weapons. We might get some from the fletcher at Ollerton if we could pay for them—but how can we do that? And even if we were the best marksmen in the world, it would make little difference," went on Eadgar despondently. "We are only boys still, and if we killed Fulk, his folk would slay our mother and all of us."

"I have another idea. I think we should go to seek Father ourselves!" said Osmund. "But we couldn't leave Mother here alone; one of us must go, and one stay."

"I shall go then," declared Eadgar. "I am the eldest and it is for me to go."

Osmund felt inclined to dispute this. He could not help thinking that he was more fit than Eadgar to act the part of knight errant. It would seem very tame to stay behind, feeding the calves and doing such odd jobs on the little farm as any peasant lad might accomplish. Churning, for instance! Tomorrow was churning morning and it would be his duty to work the churn for Joan instead of shooting at a target! Eadgar had crossed over to his own bed, but he was still sitting up, hugging his knees and thinking of his plans.

"We would have to wait until Fulk has stopped watching us," he remarked presently.

There was no answer for Osmund was already asleep.

.   .   .   .   .

In those days the lack of money was not as urgently felt as it would be now. Barter or exchange of goods was more frequent than payment by cash. There were no shops in the village, though travelling traders came to the yearly fair at Martinmas and set up their booths on the green. Country people did a great many things for themselves, but if it was necessary to send the churn to the cooper's for repair for instance, you asked him if he would accept a couple of bundles of pea-sticks in exchange for the job. Peas were an important crop, as they were not only eaten green but dried for winter use, and of course the cooper had his garden as well as everybody else. Peddlers and tinmen wandered about the country selling their wares or exchanging them for a night's lodging. If you wanted a pair of leather shoes, you had to order them from the cobbler and sometimes wait for weeks before the order was executed. But the family at the Grange only wore leather shoes for feast days—clogs, pattens, and cloth shoes were good enough for every day. Etheldreda, Dame Alice and Joan the dairymaid spun and wove the wool of the tiny flock of sheep: then it was washed in the stream and shrunk and dyed to make the family clothing. There was no room to grow flax, so the lady was obliged to obtain her linen thread in hanks from a draper in Nottingham, who was fain to accept country produce for his wares.

As Osmund rocked the churn on the morrow of May Day, he made plans, and reproached himself for not having been more diligent in the past. He wished now that he had paid attention when Walter tried to show him how to use a bill-hook last Autumn, when the men were making hurdles in the hazel copse. Job's grandsons were quite handy with an axe though the youngest was only a year older than himself.

"If I could get some wood of the right kind for the fletcher, maybe he would give me some arrows in exchange," he thought. There were plenty of goose-feathers to be had—the strong grey quills from the wings—the soft downy feathers were sorted into bags, carefully cleansed and kept for the re-filling of feather-beds, though never for pillows—Alice held this to be unlucky!

"Take care, thou'rt slopping the milk on my clean flagstones!" called Joan angrily.

"It won't hurt your flagstones," grumbled Osmund.

"'Twill make a greasy patch and more work for me, and I'll thank thee to be more heedful!" exclaimed the girl. "I've got enough for three pair of hands as 'tis."

"I'm very sorry, Joan, and I'll wipe it up myself as soon as the butter comes," answered Osmund contritely. "Do see if it *has* come," he added, "for my arms are aching."

Joan took off the lid and gazed into the depths of the churn.

"Not a sign," she remarked. "It must be bewitched. I wish I had a good charm to say over it."

"Mother says we shouldn't use charms," remarked Osmund, setting the churn rocking again. "She says it's better to say a prayer."

"Ah, sure, the lady is too good altogether," returned Joan, clattering about in her pattens. "They tell me she had some old beldame sitting at your maypole yesterday—aye, and feasting out of our own cups and platters—never tell me 'twasn't a witch! There'll be no butter today and so I tell you!"

Osmund shouted with laughter. "But it's come, Joan! I'm sure it has! I can tell by the sound—slap, slap against the side of the churn—the old woman must have been a *good* fairy!"

Joan looked under the lid again and found that the boy had guessed right. She was quite annoyed to find that her prophecy had been false.

"Come! I should think it had come!" she grumbled. "I have a good mind to box thy ears! How often must I tell thee to stop at the first little grains? There'll be no flavour in it now."

Osmund was tempted to leave her to mop up the floor herself, but a promise is a promise and if you are practising to be a knight, you must always be ready to do a kindness to a woman, be she gentle or simple. So he cleaned the flags and then carried the pails of buttermilk into the shed where the pigs' food was mixed, before he ran off to find Eadgar and Hild. He was eager to tell them that Joan had mistaken Robin Hood for a witch, which he thought a great joke, but the Lady Etheldreda looked grave when she heard of it.

"You see, children, how quickly news flies about," she said. "I was hoping that no one had realised the presence of a stranger."

"Job was very discreet when he was here this morning," remarked Eadgar. "Alice questioned him about his wife, but he would give her no answer—he pretended to be in one of his surly fits. But he told me——"

"Oh, Eadgar, what? Do say what he told you!" begged Hild, devoured with curiosity.

"He said he found the clothes at his door this morning," said Eadgar. "They were neatly folded in a basket with a haunch of fat venison underneath, and a gold piece on top!"

They were in Lady Etheldreda's room; unlike the other chambers it had a door which Osmund now carefully closed, before he divulged the thoughts which had occupied him during the churning.

"Dear Mother," he began, "I have a plan which is, I think, a good one for us all. Let me go to the procession at Southwell and seek speech with Sir Hugo—he is bound to be there. I can ask Ivo to bring me to his father."

"Alas, son, I dare not beg even such a gallant knight as this Norman to espouse our quarrel," she answered sadly.

"No, but he could perhaps tell us something of the King," persisted Osmund. "Eadgar thinks one of us should seek news of my father, and perhaps Sir Hugo would know where the King tarries. Is it not over a year since we heard that noble Richard had been falsely taken prisoner by the Duke of Austria?"

"And what is worse, sold by him to the Emperor of Germany!" chimed in Eadgar. "How can such traitors call themselves Christian princes, Mother?"

"We must not judge others, my son," she returned with a sigh. "But I am very anxious. One rumour had it that the King had been captured with one only knight in attendance: yet, surely had that knight been your father, he would have contrived to send me word?"

"Then, dearest Mother, let us get speech privately with Sir Hugo. The Abbot said he had just returned from his estates in Normandy," cried Osmund. "Perhaps people speak more freely there than here in England—perhaps he could at least find out the name or arms of that one faithful knight."

"Fulk forbade me to let any of you leave this retreat," she faltered. "But it is over a month to Whitsuntide—we will take no decision yet."

CHAPTER ELEVEN

WHEN WILLIAM of Normandy established his rule in England and parcelled out the country among his own adherents, he introduced also his well-known enthusiasm for hunting. His genuine love of this sport was reinforced by its utility: it ensured that his lords should be men of action and keep good horses in their stables, and that the King would therefore have picked cavalry at hand in case of war. The feudal system was designed to keep the barons in due subjection, and as long as there was a strong man and a tolerably just one on the throne, the plan worked well enough. But since the Conqueror's time the country had been rent by civil wars; Henry II, the father of the present King, had looked upon England as an appendage of his French possessions. Richard had gained the people's love by his deeds of individual prowess, but there were those of high station, and even Church dignitaries who held that a King's duty was to rule and guard his own country, rather than ride forth on adventures, even if the Holy Wars were his excuse. There were those who murmured that the King had no right to extort money by unfair means, so that England was stripped of her last penny, and the flower of knighthood was summoned to accompany him to the East, while lands and families were left unprotected to become the prey of less virtuous neighbours.

"If Prince John had only gone to the Crusades and left King Richard at home!" the good folk would sigh.

Gentle and simple agreed in this fruitless wish, and the excitement produced in the neighbourhood by the announcement of the Prince's arrival at Clipstone was inspired as much by fear as loyalty.

Henry the Sheriff of Nottingham—Hal Hardfist was his nickname—thought this a favourable opportunity for ingratiating himself with the Prince. John's favour could always be bought and it was essential for Hal to retain his post and to be upheld against Hugo de Scarcliffe who was making himself exceedingly troublesome by raising questions anent recent doings in the shire. The Sheriff could count on Fulk and on the partisanship of certain great nobles who dwelt on the border. The Lord of Gisborne and even the mighty Hugh de Balliol had accepted large presents of money from him. It would be inconvenient if Sir Hugo began to call attention to the means by which these sums had been raised. Folk were already murmuring that justice was bought and sold in the shire, and that Mansfield's charter had been infringed and the wardship of orphan heirs seized by Hal Hardfist in defiance of ancient custom.

King Richard's ransom had been made to serve the ends of all the rogues who called themselves the Prince's friends. Heavy taxes were extracted from all and sundry and the Sheriff of Nottingham and his like soon discovered that no very close reckoning would be made of the funds collected for the King's deliverance, as long as a good portion of them were passed into the hands of the Prince and his adherents.

John was too cunning to remove all the officers of the Exchequer whom Richard had left in charge, but before the extra taxes or "aids" could reach the royal treasury they had to pass through the hands of the Reeves of each town and the Sheriffs of each county.

John continued to lament in public the poor response of the country, and to intrigue in private with the King's enemies. He did not, however, even pretend to curtail his own luxurious style of living and his arrival at Clipstone was the occasion of a great display of magnificence, though as days went by, the faces of local merchants and tradesmen became more and more gloomy.

The English had always resisted aggression and songs began to be hummed round the village anvil and in the ale-houses, with choruses which declared that:

"Kings wot not how it cripples husbandry,
Farmers to tax and fleece outrageously."

HE WAS DICTATING TO A PAGE WHO SAT ON A STOOL AT HIS FEET.

John pretended to be cynically amused at such things, and even composed verses himself with satirical allusions to the "lion in chains." He was dictating some such couplets one day to a page who sat on a stool at his feet, as he reclined on a carved chair in the great hall at Clipstone Castle. It was more of a palace than a castle really, as the fortifications were but slight, and John, who had built it for himself, had concentrated on comfort and beauty, confident that he could fly to the neighbouring fortress of Nottingham should danger threaten. The walls of the hall had been newly wainscoted to please him and the said wainscot painted in a trellis pattern, for John believed that twisted lines defeated "the evil eye" and he was very superstitious. The windows were filled with painted glass which it was whispered that he had carried off from a monastery under pretence of receiving it as a present. The pictured saints and angels looked out of place and seemed to gaze down in astonished displeasure at the revelries of the Court. The hearth was at the end of the room with a vent-hole through the wall, instead of being placed in the centre of the hall as was usual. The Prince wore a rich robe and a carcanet of gems round his head, and refreshed himself from a goblet studded with precious stones. If the page stumbled over a word, he was promptly stimulated by a blow, but he laughed assiduously at the right places, knowing that if he showed sufficient appreciation he would be rewarded by one of the gold pieces which ought by rights to have been paid to the clamouring tradespeople.

"Ha, Fulk, how do you like this?" enquired John unceremoniously as the Baron entered in state to pay his addresses at Whitsuntide.

The Norman instantly fell in with the Prince's mood. He waved away his attendants and acknowledging John with a graceful bow, he took the paper from the boy's hand and read it aloud with a shout of laughter.

"A hit! By my troth, in the gold!" he exclaimed. "A sharp jest indeed, but I trust, my liege, it comes not to the cat's ears."

"The cat?" queried John.

"Aye, your Grace. The cat—a small thing of the lion tribe but sharp of claw withal."

John's face clouded over, and he darted an angry look at his companion.

"Sir Fulk, you forget your duty!" he exclaimed haughtily.

"Nay, Sire—your Grace, I mean, but duty is overruled by love," returned Fulk boldly.

John smiled, well pleased. He understood, as he was meant to do, that the lord of Brent would gladly see him upon the throne in his brother's place. Flinging his arm round Fulk's neck he conducted him thus affectionately embraced into his private room, the walls of which were hung with the richest silks, woven with threads of gold in the Eastern manner. Here they found a man called Hugh, whom the Prince had thrust into the See of Coventry in spite of the resistance of the Canons. The Bishop was seated at a table, perusing the Prince's correspondence, and wearing a somewhat portentous face.

"How now, whence these grave looks, my lord?" enquired John.

"Perchance, at the poor yield of gold from the archdeacons for our beloved King's deliverance," suggested Fulk in a sanctimonious tone.

"This is no time for levity, my lord," exclaimed the Bishop. "Here are grave news—at least 'tis new to me, though I perceive the letters reached your Grace's hands some six weeks since."

"Aye, or even earlier," agreed the Prince indifferently. "I tell you, Coventry, we should have made sure of Longchamp before he left this country—the folk would hardly have sainted him, I think, as they did our poor father's enemy—the Becket. But now he has returned as our brother's envoy and we dare not touch him."

"The Chancellor is not a man of nobly austere life as was Thomas of Canterbury," returned the Bishop. "But he possesses at least one sterling virtue, my liege, which is somewhat scarce among your followers—loyalty to his King."

John's hand flew to his dagger, but unlike his parent, he could always contain his rage when it suited his purpose, though he was apt to take a shameful revenge at some more convenient time.

"Good my lord, I did not tell you out of love, lest it disturb your rest," he answered smoothly; "And thou, Dan Fulk, must also be told—know then that William Longchamp, our brother's pestilent Chancellor whom we banished from his See and from the realm, searched the continent of Europe until he has smelt out our brother's prison."

"That is sore news," faltered Fulk.

"There is worse to come," continued John. "He has actually persuaded the Emperor to let Richard plead his cause before the Diet of Hagenau. Our mother's clamours to the Pope have achieved that no doubt: Henry of Germany is afraid of the Holy See."

"But the Emperor will do anything for money," exclaimed Fulk quickly. "If things go well for the Lionheart at the Diet, the Emperor can but come to definite terms for his ransom, and you, my liege, must offer him a greater sum—nay even a yearly or monthly payment—to retain him in prison."

"Yes, that is a good thought, sweet Fulk! A yearly payment might well tempt his imperial highness, and thou hadst best bestir thyself to raise a goodly sum. Thou art like to prove a savoury mouthful of cat's meat else," said John, narrowing his eyes and glancing obliquely at his friend.

"And meanwhile, your Grace must show yourself often and pleasantly to the people," urged the Bishop, ignoring this byplay. "The Whitsun games at Southwell would be a good occasion. Summon such staunch supporters of the Crown as still lurk in these parts to attend you."

"I suppose so," agreed John with a sigh. "I would I could pay Longchamp what I owe him. I would I had him safe in my dungeons at Corfe Castle to starve to death as I did the wife and children of de Braose! Ha, they had best beware who think they can play fast and loose with John."

He darted an evil look at Fulk and then on Hugh. The Norman shrank back, but the Bishop faced him boldly.

"Of two evils 'tis wise to choose the lesser, my lord Earl," he remarked, stressing the title. "Once your royal brother had named your nephew Arthur as his heir to the Pope, the King of Sicily and who knows what others, it would have been wise to proceed warily."

"Yes, you fool," retorted John. "But if you and your fellows had not overruled me, William of Longchamp would have had an accident—or an illness—just as my dear nephew will soon have an accident or illness—just as——"

He broke off and went to the window humming his little scurrilous song.

Hugh listened unmoved. He was a politician and had obtained his bishopric through John's connivance in order to enjoy its power and revenues. He intended to use John for his own ends—if he could—but at all costs to preserve the position he had won, menaced as it was by the disapproval of such churchmen as Hugh of Lincoln and his like. The majority of folk disapproved of soldiers and administrators being given the Sees which of right belonged to priests and spiritual pastors. In his heart, Hugh agreed with them, and even planned that when he had succeeded in ousting Longchamp completely and becoming Chancellor himself, he would obtain the appointment of some holy man who would minister to his neglected flock. He might also continue the erection of the Cathedral, and show Hugh of Lincoln that others could build as well as he.

"Ah, sweet Coventry," murmured John, "that was a good day when we heard of the Emperor's letter to Philip wherein he declared that their joint enemy, our bold Richard, was lodged in a strong castle kept by trusty guards who surrounded him with their naked swords by day and watched his bed at night! And he, the Lionheart, in chains—there's a sweet jest!"

He laughed heartily and the other two joined in his brutal mirth.

"If only the Pope had not interfered," concluded John querulously.

"H'm, yes, the Holy Father must needs hold the balance between his Christian sons," commented Hugh. "But even so, my lord Earl, you must remember how men took occasion to renew their oaths of allegiance to Richard—aye, all over this country."

"I need no reminder," declared John sharply. "Nor yet your repetition of 'lord Earl.'"

"I fain would address you by a nobler title," declared Coventry boldly. "The country is too much disturbed to accept of a child of six as a ruler—and at any moment an accident might happen to our noble liege, Richard."

"Plague on it, it can't happen!" cried John with a grin. "Those naked swords may curb our dear brother's pride, but they also render barren any attempts my friends may make to assist me. But we have had enough of wise talking," concluded John, thus lightly alluding to two desired murders of his next of kin. "Let us away to the merry-making at Southwell. Fulk, summon my gentlemen, I will wear the cloth of silver—or must I go armed?"

"Nay, all are your friends here, my gracious lord," declared Fulk. "The silver, and the embroidered mantle of white samite become you vastly well."

John smiled sweetly, but as soon as the curtain had fallen into place behind Fulk's retreating form, he remarked:

"There goes a snake in the grass, Hugh."

The Bishop started in genuine surprise, but John added petulantly:

"He knows the cloth of silver will not become me, now that I am somewhat sunburnt. I shall wear the green robe sewn with pearls."

Hugh sighed impatiently. This man had not sufficient persistence in any cause, good or bad, to make him reliable for a moment.

John began to hum:

"Smiter of Saracens see what may hap!
  Lion turned cat is now fast in the trap!
  Pride hath a fall I trow
  Richard lies crushed and low!"

His voice rose jubilantly at the last words.

CHAPTER TWELVE

OSMUND HAD NOT given up his project of meeting Sir Hugo of Scarcliffe, but he resolved to wait until the last moment before pressing his mother to consent to the expedition. On the Friday before Whitsun in the early morning, he announced that he had something special to ask her, and the lady withdrew into her bower, followed by all the children.

"Dearest Mother," began Osmund at once. "Give me your leave to wait upon Sir Hugo. The Sheriff will be busy merrymaking at Nottingham, and the roads will be full of travellers going to their homes for the feast. No one will notice me."

At this moment the heavy footfall of Alice was heard, stumping across the hall outside. Her voice, as usual, preceded her.

"Are you there, my lady? There is a pestilent ill fellow at the door—a peddler he calls himself—on his way to the procession at Southwell. He is wooing all the maids' pennies out of their pockets. 'Tis true he sells at a marvellous low rate, but to my mind that proves his wares are naught but rubbish——"

"Wait, children," bade the lady and she went hastily to the door. The housekeeper, though faithful, was inquisitive and somewhat of a gossip, and Etheldreda did not wish to be found in conclave with her children—good old Alice would want to know what was being talked about.

The lady reached the door first, passed through and shut it behind her.

"What is the procession at Southwell?" enquired Stephen, as soon as they were alone.

"Don't you know?" cried Hild. "There is a feast held at Whitsun every year—processions from different parishes and High Mass and a fair on the green."

"Why?" asked Stephen. "Why is it, Hild? Why is it at Southwell and not at Ollerton?"

"I don't know," she answered, adding hastily, "I don't suppose *anybody* knows."

"Of course they do—*I* know," declared Eadgar. "It is a very, very old custom dating from Paulinus——"

"Who——" began Stephen, but Osmund clapped a hand over his mouth.

"Oh, Stevie, *don't* interrupt! I do so want to settle about going——"

"And it was confirmed by a bull of Pope Alexander in 1171," continued Eadgar, raising his voice to dominate the other's talk. "Every parish and hamlet has to bring a gift for Pentecost to the Minster of St. Mary."

"What's a Pope's bull? Is it a prize beast?" demanded Stephen.

Osmund gave a shout of laughter, but Eadgar answered gravely:

"No, little brother. It is a letter from the Pope with his own seal attached."

Stephen subsided—he disliked being called "little brother," being easily offended by any allusion to his youth.

Osmund had, meanwhile, gone to the window and, mounted on the step in the embrasure, was craning his head out between the vertical bars. Down below in the paved courtyard, the peddler was sitting with his pack lying open on the top of the covered well. Joan and Dolly were turning over its contents and the peddler was whistling as he looked on. Osmund uttered an exclamation.

"Do come and listen—I think—I'm sure—oh, I wish he would look up!"

"That's the ballad the travelling minstrel sang," cried Hild, poking her yellow head through the next pair of bars, and she began to pipe up in her clear little voice:

> "I'm Robin Hood of the gay green wood
> And I wander from sea to sea
> And never have I met a traveller yet
> Who has not paid me his fee!"

"Hush, Hild! Be quiet!" cried Osmund, drawing in his head and thumping his sister on the back.

"Alice says little ladies should not look forth at casements," observed Stephen.

Hild had opened her mouth with an indignant cry at Osmund's blow, and it remained open in astonishment as the peddler glanced up and his merry eyes met hers. There was something very familiar about that laughing look, but this was an old man's face—his beard and hair were quite white.

The Lady Etheldreda came slowly down the steps into the yard. She waited until the maids had concluded their purchases and then beckoned to the children to join her. They did not lose a moment but scampered through the hall and down the stairs as quickly as they could. Osmund only paused to say to Hild:

"I'm sorry if I hurt you, but you really must be more careful!"

"But he whistled the tune!" she urged.

"I know, but you needn't sing out his name for all that!"

"But brother, how could Robin turn himself into an old man?"

Osmund's only answer was an emphatic "Hush!"

Little Sibell who had been asleep in her cot by the great hall hearth was awakened by the children's noisy passage through the room and began to cry. Alice hastened off to her beloved charge, driving the maids before her, and the lady found herself alone with the peddler and her family.

"I pray you have a care, friend," she murmured anxiously, for she too had recognised Robin Hood in his disguise.

"Nay, lady, 'tis safe enough I promise you," he answered. "I am on my way to the Whitsun Fair at Southwell, and thought I could not do better than change clothes with a peddler for the nonce."

"But you will soon be suspected if you ask such small prices—scarce half what your wares are worth!" protested the lady.

Here Osmund interposed eagerly:

"Mother, pray ask Robin if he will not take me with him. Dear Master Robin, do but let me come too and I will carry the pack!"

"What! Wouldst thou fain take part in the junketing?" enquired the peddler.

"Aye, that would I!" returned the boy emphatically. "But 'tis not only for that—I thought we might hear news of the King and hence of my father, for surely all the knights in the shire will be at the Whitsun games and I might get speech with Sir Hugo de Scarcliffe."

Eadgar interrupted indignantly:

"Now Osmund, that is not fair! I told you that it is my right to seek our father."

"I know—I only thought I might have gone first to Southwell," muttered Osmund. "And you would try Wakefield Fair."

The lady's breath had been quite taken away, but she now spoke rebukingly:

"Hold your peace, both of you. You are become strangely forward now since there is no lord in our hall. And I think," she added with a slight smile, "that you have been listening to too many ballads and songs: children do not go to seek brave knights in jeopardy: they learn their book and strive to be humble and meek."

"But, dearest lady, we may not bide with folded hands while Fulk threatens you!" said Eadgar. "Ever since May Day we youths have been more eager than ever to seek protection for you."

"Youths!" murmured the lady. "Troth, you are but babes!"

"Nay, lady, the boys have a right spirit," interposed Robin Hood. "The elder indeed looks somewhat pale and over-slender to be my pack-boy, but I am willing to take this bold fellow with me and to return him to you unharmed, if he promise to obey me in every particular."

As he spoke, the outlaw smote Osmund a jovial blow on the shoulder, which sent him head-over-heels into the long grass.

"You mustn't hurt him, Robin," cried Hild anxiously.

Osmund jumped up laughing, though rather ashamed of being knocked over so easily. The outlaw nodded approvingly, and then turned to the lady of the house.

"I must have time to consider," she murmured hastily.

"No time like the present, lady," he returned cheerfully. "Come—a swift yea or nay."

"Do say 'yea,' Mother!" besought Osmund. "I will obey Robin in everything, I promise you. And Eadgar, maybe Sir Hugo will take you as his page and then you will soon be able to challenge Fulk yourself."

Eadgar said nothing. He waited until his mother had uttered a reluctant consent and then turned away and walked into the house. He felt both hurt and indignant at Osmund being chosen, though his sense of justice made him own that his brother's devotion to outdoor life and field sports made him more fitted for carrying the pack than himself. Since his return from Ely—bearing the first two books of Roger de Howden's Annals bound together in vellum—he had spent his time in study, in dreaming and in trying his hand at writing. He had quite made up his mind to be a chronicler and practised on a piece of sheepskin, as he had no paper. But it was his *right* to go in search of news of their father, and he had thought of it first—it was not fair that Osmund should take his place.

Eadgar kept his two precious volumes in a little cupboard in the wall near one of the window embrasures in the hall. He sometimes pretended that he was a monk and that the hall was the cloister at Ely and the windows were the "carrels" or alcoves, to which the monks carried their books for study. He had got out one of his treasures and curled himself up on the stone window seat, when Osmund came running in with two new arrows in his hand.

"Eadgar, Eadgar!" he shouted. "Oh, there you are! Here are some arrows out of Robin's pack for you—real ones, look at the lead and the good goose pens! And, brother, I told Master Robin you were the eldest and all that, but he said it had better be me this time, as I know Ivo by sight, and Mother says she would rather you stayed behind to protect her."

"Of course," said Eadgar, rather ungraciously. "It's all settled. You always do get your own way."

"I don't," retorted Osmund gruffly. "Go, if you want to— but go quickly or perhaps Master Robin will think we have both turned craven."

Eadgar glanced up and suddenly the hard, ungenerous feelings melted away.

"No, you must go," he said decidedly. "I am sorry I was wrathful and self-seeking. Go, Osmund—and thank you for the arrows. Perhaps Fulk will come here again and if so I can let fly at him."

Osmund glanced through the window and saw that the peddler was already leaving the yard. He waited for no further speech, but rushed out of the room, down the stairs and after him, only pausing for a few seconds to kneel for his mother's blessing.

Robin heard the boy scampering in his wake, but he did not slacken his stride or turn his head until they were deep in the wood.

"Thou goest not gaily enough for a peddler's boy," he said then, throwing down his pack under a tree. "Open that, and do on a pair of scarlet hose. There's a small embroidered cap, too, that will look better than that darned hood of thine."

"It is such as pages wear," remarked Osmund doubtfully; and mindful of Little John's words, he added: "Won't red stockings be seen afar?"

"And why not? We want to be seen! We're going to sell our wares. I am Dick the peddler and thou art my lad, Martin."

"Alice said you sold your stuff too cheap," observed the boy as he pulled on the bright-hued stockings, and hid his own discarded chausses in the dead leaves under a log.

"Aye, 'Robin Hood's pennies' will pass into proverb, I dare say," answered the outlaw, watching with approval as Osmund fastened the pack neatly and slung it over his shoulder by its leather strap.

"We travel by the main track and shall offer our goods to all and sundry. Canst sing a merry lay to shorten the way, 'prentice Martin?"

"I know a song about the bold outlaw Robin Hood, if that would suit," answered Osmund blithely.

"Tune up then, so it has a jolly chorus. We'll buy a tabor and pipe at the fair, if we can come by them."

"So blithe as the linnet sings in the green wood,"

sang Osmund,

"So blithe we'll wake, we'll wake the morn!"

"So blithe we'll wake, we'll wake the morn!"

chimed in Robin.

"And through the wide forest of merry Sherwood
We'll wind the bugle horn.
We'll wind the bugle horn.

With Will Scarlet and John, who was never subdued,
Robin Hood and his band so bold
Will reign in the forest of merry Sherwood
What say ye, my hearts of gold?
What say ye, my hearts of gold?"

CHAPTER THIRTEEN

"**N**OW HARK THEE, Osmund!" cried Robin Hood, as they marched gaily along. "I and my band are brothers, and thou shalt be as one of us and shalt have a woodland name as befits our company!"

"What shall it be? What will you call me?" asked the boy eagerly.

"Why, marry, I'll call thee 'Blackbird' for thou hast a sweet tuneful note in thy bill not too much unlike his. Also 'tis our whim to nickname by contraries——"

"Oh, yes, Little John is so big and Much—as you now term him—so little!" chimed in Osmund.

"Aye, and thou being yellow as a ripe oatfield, we'll e'en dub thee after the swart songster!"

"Thank you, Robin!" exclaimed Osmund fervently. "I do love to hear about your life," he added. "Is all true that the ballads tell?"

"Nay, by my faith!"

"What! Not Little John's love for you and his being your sworn man?"

"Aye, that much is true, but all those tales of combats in which I am for ever flying like a craven or calling for Little John's aid—those are inventions framed to pleasure the Sheriff and his ilk."

"That's just what we thought," agreed Osmund. "But Robin—what is the true tale of Little John and you?"

"Why, then, Blackbird—but come, give me the pack—I'll e'en carry it the next mile or two. Well, Blackbird, you must know that the ballad is part truth and part lies, like all ballads. Can you sing it?"

Osmund instantly began:

> "In summer when the shaws be sheen
> And leaves be large and long
> It is full merry in fair forèst
> To hear the birdys song.
>
> To see the deer draw to the mead
> And leave their hillis hee,
> And shelter them in the leavès green
> Under the greenwood tree.
>
> It befel on Whitsuntide
> Early on a May morning——"

"Stay!" interrupted Robin, "thou shouldst sing rather: 'Early on a *June* morning,' so will it fit with this very day." He took up the air himself:

> "This is a merry morning, said Little John
> I vow by the greenwood tree
> And more merry men than I am one
> Are not in Christianity.
>
> There's one thing grieves me, said Robin
> And doth my heart much woe
> That I may not, no solemn day
> To Mass nor matins go."

"And *did* you go?" exclaimed Osmund. "Did you really go to St. Mary's Church at Nottingham, where everyone knew there was a price of three hundred pounds on your head?"

Robin nodded and sang the next verse:

"It is a fortnight and more, said Robin
　　Since I my Saviour see
　　And I will with him intercede
　　By the might of mild Mary.

"So, then," he went on, striding easily in front of Osmund through the serried ranks of young beech, "you must know that I was recognised by some under-strapper of Hal Hardfist, as the folk call him. Straight, he jumps from his knees and away with him hot-foot to his master, for he dared not stay me himself. I came out of church therefore, fearing naught, and fell into the armed band before I had time to lay a finger on my trusty bow, which I had left at the church door, as was but seemly."

"Oh, what danger you were in!" cried Osmund breathlessly.

"Aye, but mark you, for all the price on my head the Sheriff could not get one of the honest townsfolk to witness against me! Nay, they all declared as one man that I was an honest yeoman of Yorkshire, by name, William Locksley——"

"And *are* you?" asked the boy as he paused.

Robin did not answer the question.

"So not having the hardihood to slay me out of hand, the craven Sheriff flung me into gaol. They bound me with fetters and chains enough, I warrant you, and then the Sheriff called in his friends and fell to drinking for glee, and ordered the gallows to be got ready for my hanging the next morning. Once he had me safe in the Castle, he cared little whether I were Locksley or Robin Hood and he planned to send my head to London and claim the reward."

"And how *did* you get out?" enquired Osmund.

"Why, though they had disarmed me, they had not troubled to take my horn away, and in the early dawn, so fettered as I was, I made shift to hold it to my lips and to blow four blasts which means 'Robin is in dire danger'——" He began to sing again:

"The porter rose anon certain
As soon as he heard John call——

"For Little John had followed me to the town and was prowling about, trying to find out where I was. He did not slay the porter as the ballad says, but felled him with a blow of his fist, stole the keys from his girdle, opened the door of my dungeon and unlocked my chains. The rest of the song is true enough."

"He gave him a good sword in his hand,"

sang Osmund,

"His head therewith for to keep.
And there, where the walls were lowest
Anon down there they leap——"

"And so we did," agreed Robin. "And we didn't let grass grow under our steeds I promise you, on our way back to the forest."

"I have done thee a good turn, said Little John
Quit me when thou may,"

chanted Osmund,

"I have done thee a good turn,
Forsooth as I thee say.
I have brought thee under the greenwood tree
Fairwell and have good day."

"Nay, by my troth,"

trolled Robin,

"So shall it never be,
Beshrew me for a false yeoman
If I ever part from thee——

"There is someone ahead of us, blundering about among the trees. Ho, friend! Take the pack, Blackbird!"

He slung the bundle over the boy's arm and ran lightly forward. Osmund followed as quickly as he could and found the supposed peddler in talk with a man, whose gay apparel and lutecase, proclaimed his calling of jongleur or strolling gleeman.

"Faith, Master Peddler!" he exclaimed, "I am glad to meet with you, for I see you are armed and I must say I go in terror of meeting that rogue Robin Hood, who is the pest of this countryside they say—he you were singing of just now."

"If you have money in your pouch, you run some risk," agreed the peddler. "Though 'tis said he never robs poor man nor harms woman. Art thou for Southwell Wake?"

"Yes," admitted the minstrel, glancing rather doubtfully at his interlocutor. Then his eyes fell on Osmund and he started. "Why, I know this lad," said he.

Osmund had instantly recognised the fellow as the minstrel with whom he had shared the infirmary at Welbeck, but he thought it wiser to make no admission. So he stood behind his master, looking as stolid as possible and began humming under his breath the rhyme with which Goody Alice was wont to rock Sibell to sleep.

> "Robin Hood, Robin Hood,
>   Wends in the mickle wood;
> Little John, Little John,
>   He to the town is gone!"

"Come, Martin," cried the peddler. "Show not thyself thus unmannerly. Sawest thou this good fellow at the Abbey, when thou wentest to have thy leg dressed?"

"Aye, master, maybe 'tis the same. There was a gleeman there, but I scarce set eyes on more than his top-knot for he lay asleep withal."

"Go to, thou art a saucy lad!" exclaimed Robin. "But let us go forward together—for your company must needs be merry. What art called, Master Minstrel?"

"Wido, an't please you, honest peddler. But know you a fair way, for beshrew my heart if I do! And these plaguey branches and briars are making havoc of my coat."

"Follow me, we'll soon come to the path," cried Robin.

The musician was much reassured by his recognition of Osmund, for surely, he thought, a youth who was in the good graces of the Abbey could scarcely be in league with thieves or footpads. He was rather a conceited person and a great gossip, as Father Adam had prophesied. Osmund wondered how anyone could talk about himself for so long without ever pausing to draw breath. Robin listened attentively: he was always ready to study a new character and pick up terms which might serve him in one of his many masquerades.

To hear Wido prate, you would certainly have thought him the sweetest songster, the most excellent lutist and the most shrewd chapman in the world, for he had ballads to sell as well as to sing. And he was also, by his own proclamation, the most marvellous of story-tellers.

"Do you but listen to me, my masters, tomorrow night and you shall see me draw tears from rocks and sighs from jagged stones when I narrate the life and death of Earl Waltheof!" he declared. "Tonight, indeed, you may hear me, too—I'll tell a merry tale or two at the tavern to earn my supper and, if I can gain so much—for your suppers likewise."

"I thank you, friend," answered Robin, raising his voice and laying his hand on the musician's cloak, for the man's tongue was still going like a clapper. "But I and my boy wend not into Mansfield. We lie in the woods tonight, as 'tis fine and dry, but we'll join you willingly enough upon the road tomorrow."

.   .   .   .   .

It was a warm night and Osmund thought it a great adventure to sleep out under the trees. Robin Hood had first made his way to a little river and showed Osmund how to lie flat in the grass and tickle trout under the bank. When they had four or five nice fish, they went back to the woods, kindled a fire, cleaned the fish and roasted them on twigs over the hot embers. Robin had cheese and oatcake in his wallet, and plucked young dandelion leaves and tender sorrel for salad and he warned the boy that the practised wayfarer always carries a little salt in his bag.

Osmund thought he had never tasted anything so delicious as the hot trout, and made bold to ask some questions as they munched their supper.

"Where is Little John now, Master Robin? And indeed where are they all?"

"Why, the Sheriff became over anxious to pursue us, and also we have slain all the best buck in this county," returned Robin. "I sent my folk over into Barnsleydale, and I mean to follow them as soon as I have had my frolic."

The outlaw was very careful to pour water on the ashes and to cover all traces of the fire, and he also insisted on walking some distance further before choosing a place in which to spend the night. He showed the boy how to scrape a hole for his hip-bone as they lay on the mossy ground and moreover lent him his own mantle as coverlet.

Osmund lay long awake, watching the last rays of sun wash over the tree-tops like a golden wave, the gleams shoot downwards picking out here and there a slender trunk, a quivering leaf, and then vanish as suddenly as though the warm blue shadows leaping up from the ground had swept them away. In the early morning he waked with cramped limbs to hear the first blackbird proclaiming the new day; it was soon followed by the cuckoo. In half an hour the air was full of a medley of bird-notes, but Osmund had fallen asleep again by that time and did not stir until Robin roused him, bidding him go wash at the stream before they resumed their journey.

Had he been alone, Robin Hood would certainly have covered the whole distance in a day for the hardy forester thought little of walking thirty miles at a stretch. As it was he had a vigilant eye to his young companion and ordered a rest at regular intervals. A second night was to be spent in the woods within scent of the wood-smoke arising from the village hearths, and when they had supped, Robin proposed that they should go to the gorsy bank overhanging the high road and watch the folk riding into Southwell.

"I might see Ivo," said Osmund, "and get speech with his father thus."

"Aye, you might," agreed Robin Hood. "But we will sit where no one can see us, and you must not speak or stir until I give you leave."

Osmund agreed, and as he was more tired than he would have cared to confess, he fell asleep soon after they had ensconced themselves in the warm, sweet-scented shade of the golden bushes.

When Robin roused him by pressing his hand upon his knee, he thought he was still dreaming. It was nearly dark, the stars showed faintly white in the soft blue sky, and craning forward his head, Osmund smelt horses, and perceived two riders drawn up in the sandy road below.

"They must come this way," said one man in French.

"Listen well," murmured Robin Hood in Osmund's ear.

"If it be not soon we may as well go on," returned the other. "I have not yet quaffed my evening draught, and Fulk will wonder why we tarry."

"No matter," declared the other. "We are agreed that we must be sure of Bernard de Balliol before we attempt to gain Hugo tomorrow."

"And if the Knight of Scarcliffe denies us—what then? We are scarce strong enough even with the Balliol's Picards. Though their father Lord Eustace, is said to be a man of peace, he owes a mighty sum for scutage, and will not be averse to a delay of payment. We can judge by the strength of their following whether Bernard means to join us or no."

"Once all the castles are in our hands we can proclaim John as King, and Richard may whistle for his ransom! France will stick by John," said the other. "Philip fears the Lionheart since his cowardly desertion almost in sight of Jerusalem—he trembles at the thought of Richard's vengeance. But if Sir Hugo fails us, 'twill spoil all, for he'll raise the King's party."

"Oh, the Prince is preparing a jest against Lord Hugo's refusal! He will hasten him away abroad to our beloved King Richard, to carry over the paltry sum which the country has raised for his ransom——"

"And what becomes of Richard's knight? Him thou wottest of——"

"Hush—he is Fulk's prey when he comes—aye, that is Fulk's price—else he fears he will not have quiet possession."

"Scarcliffe is a good manor, Alberic, and if you have no special fancy for it—but soft—this must be the Balliol's out-rider."

They moved forward, and Osmund turned a white face towards his friend.

"Robin! They were talking treason! Did you understand?"

"Not one word! Think it over carefully so as to forget naught. We must not speak here."

It seemed to Osmund that they sat there for an age, while greetings were called out below, and Norman pages with lanterns at their saddlebows, lighted their masters slowly along the track. The light gleamed on the shining chain mail of more armed men than it was usual to bring to a church festival. But at last the dust settled into the ruts behind the last rider and Robin drew Osmund away. When they were safely in the woods, the boy related all that he had overheard, helped out by Robin's questions.

"We must warn Lord Hugo," said Osmund. "But what do you think they mean to do, Robin? Will they rise against the Council?"

"H'm, more likely they will win the members over, by fair promises, to put John on the throne forthwith. Go to sleep, Blackbird, we can do nothing tonight."

"But Robin, who can be the man they called King Richard's knight?"

"No more talk tonight," ordered the other. "We must sleep for we'll need bright wits tomorrow."

Osmund was silent for a little, then he whispered:

"The Balliols are very powerful folk, aren't they? They own half Northumberland and hold lands also of the King of Scots?"

"I know naught of courts or courtiers," declared Robin. "But we'll stand by our friends, lad, and warn the gentle knight of Scarcliffe of the toils prepared for him."

"What if the 'King's knight' were my father?" queried Osmund.

But Robin returned no answer: the same idea had occurred to him.

CHAPTER FOURTEEN

THE GREY STONE Minster of St. Mary's at Southwell towered above the little town which clustered round it. The place had only half emerged from the forest, great beeches stretched away behind the church as though their green and silver columns were a continuation of the stone aisles within. The monks had planted orchards and the people only felled such trees as were needed for their dwellings and to clear the communal fields. So that Southwell was a leafy town and the booth-keepers set up their stalls, each under a tree-trunk in the shady marketplace. Bird songs could be heard undisturbed in any pause in the shouting and noise which were deemed the necessary accompaniments of every festivity. Osmund, who was unaccustomed to crowds and jollity of this kind, was quite bewildered. The village, which he had not seen for three years, was so greatly changed that he hardly knew it again. Weeds sprouted between the cobbles, the houses were ill-thatched and the people's holiday attire was patched and mended. For while the Council of Regency quarrelled among themselves, the taxes they imposed were extorted from the people by some unjust overlords, who made the peasantry pay their own share and their lords' as well.

The Minster bells made all the air tremble with their joyous clamour as the peddler and his boy joined the procession streaming in to Mass.

Osmund was mechanically making his way to his own family bench, with the carved lions decorating the end of the seat, but Robin gripped him by the elbow, and he hurriedly retraced his steps to a shadowy corner by the font. The monks filed into choir, the husbandmen, or farmers, knelt in groups with their families, and the merchants who had come from all around to attend the Fair, gathered near the door. The great church with its low heavy vaulting, was cool and smelt of incense and the damask roses which decked the altar. The gift-bearing processions from the neighbouring villages would begin later, when the Sheriff of Nottingham rode in in state and there would be a great High Mass.

At the present moment the usual low Mass was being celebrated, with the best red vestments the Community possessed to do honour to the glorious feast.

As they came out of church presently, Osmund plucked Robin by the sleeve.

"Abbot Adam from Welbeck may be here," he announced. "What shall I do if he comes near?"

"Nothing," said Robin. "He won't recognise you because he won't look at you closely. Townspeople see little or nothing unless they study to do so."

"But Robin—Master, I mean—the Abbot is a good friend of ours and spoke very kindly of you."

"Remember what I told you. You are not to greet any acquaintance without first asking my leave," declared Robin sternly.

"What, not Ivo? I see him yonder," cried Osmund. "And there is Petronell on her palfrey and a lady with them and an old Knight."

"Follow me," bade the outlaw abruptly.

Osmund obeyed reluctantly and Robin led the way to a sheltered nook where a country lass was milking a flock of goats. She was delighted to fill a horn cup for each of them, and Robin pulled a hunch of bread out of his pouch and divided it with the boy.

"We can't have goats at our place because they spoil the young trees, so we forest folk have milch ewes instead," remarked Osmund, between hearty bites. Then, when the girl had fallen to her work again, he added:

"Am I not to speak to Ivo at all, Master?"

"Aye, surely. Presently we will go and offer our wares but not while they are in the midst of the market place and might cry out thy name and cause folk to recognise thee."

Osmund nodded comprehendingly: he saw that this was very wise and admired Robin's foresight.

As soon as they had finished their meal they went back to the green, where the chapmen had already begun to trade.

ACCOMPANYING THE SALE WITH MERRY JESTS AND LAUGHTER.

The forester's prudence was not of long duration and he soon became tired of trying to find purchasers for his stock at reasonable prices and began to cheapen his wares at an amazing rate. There were a good many other peddlers who had for years included Southwell Games in their annual round, and these became more and more angry as their customers forsook them to rush after the newcomer. Osmund thought it great fun: the pack was unrolled on the grass, and he handed up one object after another to Robin, who yielded it to the first offer at a tenth of its value, accompanying the sale with merry jests and laughter.

He did not, however, neglect Osmund's affairs but presently stooped down and whispered in his ear:

"Slip away through the crowd: Ivo stands alone near the church. Take some riding whips and fish floats and flies and make as though you would offer them for sale."

Osmund obeyed, nothing loth.

The Scarcliffe children had dismounted and stood on the Minster steps watching the antics of a man on stilts who was dancing on the trodden grass.

"Wilt buy a choice whip or a pair of spurs, my gallant lord?" enquired Osmund, adding in a lower tone: "Hist! Don't you know me?"

The young Norman stared at him in surprise, but his sister leaned forward eagerly.

"It is the nice forest boy," she said. "The boy who rescued Midge—it's Osmund."

"So it is!" exclaimed Ivo. "Why, friend, I am right glad to see you. Won't you come home with us to the Castle?" he went on eagerly, anxious to prove that he considered Osmund's apparent poverty no bar to their friendship.

"I'm only pretending to be a peddler," declared Osmund quickly. "Master Robin is here too and we want you to contrive that we may have speech with your noble father, without anyone knowing about it."

"Sir Hugo has been summoned to attend the Prince," said Petronell, "and my mother has just carried our gifts to the Monastery."

"I trow my business must be with the Knight," rejoined Osmund. "Is Prince John coming today? I have never seen him close. Fulk will be with him doubtless and the Sheriff also, so Master Robin and I must keep well in the background. I would we could have seen your father before he joined the Prince."

"We leave early, for we must lie at Mansfield tonight on our way home, and that is fifteen miles off," said Ivo. "Could you wait for us on the road—perhaps at the bridge over the River Greet——"

"That may be too late," interrupted Osmund. "There is a plot contrived against your noble father's faith and honour! When did he leave you?"

"Only an hour ago," rejoined Ivo. "He was to meet the Prince a mile or two out of Southwell."

Osmund heaved a sigh of relief.

"There's still time then," he cried. "For they'll not broach such a subject on the highway, I'll warrant you."

"But Osmund, what has the outlaw to do with this?" asked Ivo. "You are quite sure Robin Hood *is* a friend? You do not think he would mislead you and lay a trap for my father?"

"How can you have such a thought?" exclaimed Osmund indignantly. "If Robin be an outlaw he is a noble one withal! For he has never slain anyone unless first attacked and has never harmed any company in which a woman travelled, and has never laid hand on any husbandman or labourer. I cannot say but that he slays a fat buck when he has need, but that is his worst sin."

"I've heard tell that he comes of yeoman stock and that King William the Red drove his folk off their land when he made forest here," cried Petronell. "But howsoe'er it be, we trust you and your friend too, Osmund. I do wish you could come home with us for I do want to hear more about your sisters——"

"Oh, Petronell, do stop chattering!" exclaimed her brother. "This isn't child's play, for Robin's men told me that Osmund would be in great danger if he quitted the forest. So you see it must be some truly grave matter that brings him hither."

"I'm sorry!" said the little girl. "And now, dear Osmund, let me buy all your fish floats, though indeed I hate fishing and seeing the poor pretty creatures gasping out their life on the grass. Here, take my purse!" she urged, trying to press it into his hand.

"Why maiden! there is a golden mark in it!" exclaimed Osmund laughing, "and I'll wager my master has sold his whole stock in trade for two or three shillings."

"Nay, but do take it—out of friendship," she pleaded, "and buy yourself what you need."

"I have everything I need, but I thank you very kindly," said Osmund. "And when I'm a grown-up knight I'll wear your sleeve on my helmet. Now give me a tester for this little whip. I'm sure your lovely white pony doesn't need a touch of it, but I must pretend to be selling you something."

"But how are we to warn my father?" asked Ivo anxiously.

Osmund thought hard. Robin had impressed upon him that he was only to give the message to the Knight himself, for he feared the children might chatter indiscreetly.

"Make your way to Sir Hugo the very *instant* he appears," he said at last. "And tell him this secret word: 'Remember the late Earl Waltheof. The tale repeats itself.'"

Ivo and Petronell repeated the phrases after him.

"You must get him to believe it is mighty serious," urged Osmund; then he suddenly broke off with the exclamation:

"Look! There come the Morris dancers!"

People ran up the steps to get a good view, as the merry monotonous music of the pipe and tabor broke on their ears. Robin had finished his traffic and came pushing his way through the crowd, with a harp on his shoulder which he had somehow acquired since Osmund had left him. The Morris dancers came in single file, leaping and capering down a narrow woodland path, each waving a coloured handkerchief in either hand; their gay clothing decorated with jingling bells according to custom. A mob of peasant children ran along beside them, shrieking the name of each traditional character as it came into view. The dancers were brilliantly dressed in gilt leather and silver paper with streamers of many coloured ribbons.

The leader was so tall that the stilt-walker was heard to grumble that he must be raised on pegs; he was followed by the Fool, in cap, bells and parti-coloured clothing, armed with a ladle with which to collect contributions at a later hour. Next came the Lady, prettily tricked out in green and silver, and at her appearance Osmund felt his master's hand grasp his shoulder as he uttered an exclamation of astonishment. Osmund stared too: surely he had seen that laughing face before and that tall, slender form? There was something familiar about the leader, too, and the hobby-horse, who capered and pranced in vermilion stockings:

"Why, I'm sure that's Will Scarlet!" whispered Osmund in Petronell's ear.

"Of course it is!" she whispered back in delight. "And Maid Marian, as fresh as a May morning! And little Midge as the Fool, all out of time—they should have made him the colt!"

"Peace, children, or you will hang us all!" declared Robin, in a low voice. "Come, lad, the tinkers and peddlers are lying in wait for us with ash staves. So we'll do a magic change and reappear as a blind harper and his boy."

Seeing that everyone's attention was bracketed on the Morris dancers, Robin strode away to a secluded copse. Osmund told what had passed between him and Ivo and awaited further orders.

"Here's a trial of thy courage and humility," said Robin, looking somewhat questioningly at his young friend. "I am going into the crowd apparelled as an ancient beggar in a tattered old cloak, a burst hood and chausses more holes than stuff. I have a disguise of the same kind for you, and it might be none too clean."

Osmund could not control the disgusted look which passed into his face, but he managed to prevent himself from speaking.

"Well," concluded Robin, "are you too dainty and nice to put them on?"

Osmund got very red and answered frankly: "If it is only for a frolic, Master Robin, I'd rather not wear dirty clouts. But if it stands to your safety or advantage—or—or if you wish it," he added with a great effort—"I'll wear them like your true man."

Robin's face which had been wearing an unwontedly grave expression, now lit up with his usual laughing look.

"Well spoken, i' faith!" he declared. "The question was put to try thee and I know now I can trust thee at a pinch. Off with thy gay stockings and on with these humble grey weeds. They are well-worn indeed but fresh washed and as clean as soap and water can make them. Tuck thy yellow locks under the hood and with this bit of charcoal I'll darken thine eyebrows—so!"

Having disguised Osmund to his satisfaction, the outlaw shook some of the white powder out of his own hair and beard, frizzed them up with his fingers and twisted his whimsical face into a dolorous expression. He seemed to turn into a whining beggar under Osmund's astonished gaze.

"That was a good thought of thine about Earl Waltheof," he said. "But lest Hugo forget the tale, Wido must tell it again. Remember, I shall have my eyes closed, and you must lead me. When a man acts a part he must live the part—else he is soon discovered."

"But won't Wido know us?"

"Aye, but we'll tell him 'tis but a counterfeiting trick, such as beggars often use. Watch your friends when the Prince arrives. If they cannot come near their father, thou or I must contrive to do so."

"I marvel how you manage always to have a change of clothes at hand just when you need it!" said Osmund wonderingly. His new outfit consisted of a long tunic, girded with a belt, leather shoes, worn over bare feet, and separate hood. Robin pointed out that this could be easily doffed when craving alms, and enjoined a humble demeanour.

"Why, I spent all the peddler's gains and dipped in my private store as well. Now lead me back to the fair," cried Robin, "and place me in the centre of the green if we can find space there. When the last processions have come in, the Prince will arrive and then the feasting and dancing will begin, and I shall be called on to play."

"And can you harp, Master Robin?"

"Certainly, I can harp, Sir Pert! Now make no sign that thou hast ever set eyes on those merry maskers before—I thought they were all safe in Barnsleydale!"

CHAPTER FIFTEEN

THE JOLLY ATMOSPHERE of merrymaking on the green seemed to have changed as the blind harper was led back through the crowd. The chiming of the bells had ceased, and though processions from the neighbouring townships were still marching in, vigorously singing, discontented muttering round the booths formed an unpleasant undertone to the hymning voices.

Wido the gleeman was seated on the root of an ash-tree, near the village well, and Osmund imparted this fact to the harper.

"There is a music-maker here already, master," he added aloud, "perhaps we had better try the other side of the green, near the armourer's forge; there will be nothing doing there today as 'tis Sunday."

"Nay, brother, sit you here!" cried the minstrel, jumping up and showing his recognition by a sly wink. "'Tis easier for me to fare through the crowd, and thou wouldst get sorely jostled, sightless as thou art."

"I thank you kindly," returned Robin, sinking down with Osmund's help. "But stay here too, friend, if so be thy voice and instrument will accord with mine—we'll divide the takings an thou wilt."

"They are likely to be small then," grumbled the other. "You two are but just come, but do you know that Earl John is here, and what do you think was his very first act—before he had so much as entered the Minster?"

"Why, did he perhaps offer his gift at the Monastery door?" quavered Robin, in the old man's voice, which he assumed with such ease.

"Nay, beshrew me if he did! He went to the Monastery certainly, and out came the Prior, and bowed, full of courtesy, and what says the Earl, think you?"

"Have a care!" urged Osmund, touching his arm.

The minstrel continued unheeding:

"Forsooth he laid claim to a 'free loving gift' as he calls it, and demanded a sum from the monks which they will have to pledge their lands to pay—let alone the profit from the Whitsun gifts, which they counted on to rebuild their tower."

"Master, Fulk's men are about us," whispered Osmund. "I know his badge, and I think that must be Sir Hugo yonder on the bay horse. Those knights we saw in the lane keep close to his side, and Ivo cannot come to him, try as he will."

"How now, brother? Hast thou no gallant tale to tell?" enquired the harper, jerking the gentleman by the sleeve. "Strike up the story of Earl Waltheof!"

"'Tis too early in the day," objected Wido.

"Nay, nay! Let's have the tale. 'Twill bridge the gap to dinner!" exclaimed one of the bystanders, a buxom matron with a flock of children clinging to her wide skirts.

"I'll get a hearing for thee!" murmured Robin; he struck a chord on his harp.

Wido leaped upon the top of the well and called in a clear ringing voice:

"Listen to the story of a noble knight and of how his death was compassed by false traitors! You must know, lords, ladies, gentles and good people all, that in the days when the proud Norman first ruled this land, there was a noble earl, one who fought bravely and was marvellous fair to look upon. Waltheof was his name, and his ancestor was Siward, that hero of renown.

Now Waltheof was lord of great possessions and when King William was crowned, he gave fealty to him, and the King loved him wondrous well and gave back to him the lands he had surrendered and gave him his own niece, Judith, to wife, a marvellous fair lady on whom he had bestowed many manors, rich possessions and jewels without number. The lady was fair to look upon—aye me! but she was black of heart."

"Has Ivo reached his father?" whispered the harper in Osmund's ear.

"Nay—they will not let him by."

"Then mark—at the end of the story, I will make a diversion and you must strive to get him from this side. Tell him only to beware lest Waltheof's tale be repeated."

Osmund pressed his hand on the outlaw's knee in token that he had understood.

The Prince was still in the Monastery, but his followers were waiting on their horses at the gate.

Wido continued his lay, and told in a mixture of prose, verse and song, how the great happiness and prosperity of Earl Waltheof grew from hour to hour. And then a cloud appeared in the sky. The fierce Norman barons became swollen with pride and chafed under the King's rule.

"Stark he was to men that withstood him," declaimed Wido, "but mild to those that loved God!"

"Hurrah!" interrupted a wayfarer, who bore the appearance of a discharged soldier. "Hurrah! Like our Richard! God bless him!"

The cry was taken up and Wido refreshed himself from a large leather beaker while the crowd proclaimed their loyalty.

"If a man would live and hold his land needs it were that he followed the King's will," continued Wido as soon as he could make himself heard. "But there were those who nourished black treason in their breasts. Alas, woe is me for Rolf de Guader, the treacherous lord from Bretagne, Roger Fitz-Osbern and the King's brother the Earl of Kent."

More and more people gathered round Wido as he related how the plot was formed and the wicked earls resolved to gain the help of Earl Waltheof in their revolt against the King. And to call in the Danes—England's traditional enemies—to harry the coasts with their fleet and prevent William's return from Normandy. Earl Rolf seized the occasion of his own wedding feast at Norwich while the King was in France: he gathered all his friends round him, and invited Waltheof who held more possessions than any other. Then when the loving-cup had gone about the table many times, they bound the unsuspecting Waltheof by a terrible oath not to reveal the secret they were about to declare to him. All thoughtlessly he took the oath, and forthwith they declared their villany.

"'Join with us,' said the Earls, 'and the third part of England shall be yours by equal division.'

"'Nay,' quoth Waltheof. 'In all nations fealty sworn by every subject to his liege lord should be faithfully kept, King William has received mine. Has he not given me his niece in marriage, a rich earldom and his familiar friendship to boot? Shall I be faithless to my King?'"

"Nay!" exclaimed the crowd, hanging on Wido's words.

"Nay!" repeated the gleeman dramatically. "And so said noble Waltheof. 'Far be it from me,' quoth he. 'There never was song sweet enough to charm away the disgrace of treason.' And so he departed from them, sorely troubled and grieved because of his oath. At length he betook himself to Lanfranc, Archbishop of Canterbury, a holy and enlightened man, and confessed unto him, and the priest bid him tell all to the King in spite of his oath, and the great danger to himself. Waltheof's wife counselled him the other way——"

"They always do!" interjected the smith, who was the village wag.

"Aye, Judith was not content with the riches she possessed, but would fain have been mistress of the third part of England, and free of the strong hand of her uncle. Nevertheless the Earl obeyed his conscience rather than his wife and this the woman could not forgive. Waltheof then went to Normandy, bearing rich presents and told all to the King, and William received him graciously and carried him to England with his court. Meanwhile, the wicked earls broke into revolt but were crushed after hard fighting by the King's forces. The Danes who had been summoned by the rebels and promised rich booty, sailed into the Humber. King William was greatly wroth, and the traitors being fled, seized Waltheof and cast him into prison, and then came to him his niece Judith, maligning her husband, for as the chronicler has it 'she most wickedly hurried on his destruction.'

"Now William the King, though he was stark in war would never have blood shed by law, and in all his reign there was only one man condemned by law to die—and this one the good and virtuous Waltheof. For the Norman earls hated him and full of envy they poisoned the King's mind and prevailed with him to sign his death warrant. Waltheof, meanwhile, lay in prison, spending all his day in prayer, bewailing his sins and chanting the psalms of David which he had learned in childhood. Priests, Abbots and Bishops went to visit him, knowing of his holy life and the people of Norwich town greatly loved him. The Normans therefore——"

"Take care," murmured the harper, for though his lids seemed closed, he noted that the Prince's followers had turned their horses so as to face the story-teller.

"The envious Barons therefore," Wido hastily corrected himself, "coming down at sunset with the warrant, gave orders that Waltheof was to be slain ere daylight next day, before any of his friends were 'ware what was toward. So they led him forth, strong, tall and beautiful in the prime of his manhood, on to a hill outside the town gate, and here when he had distributed all he had to the poor, he craved leave to kneel him down to pray.

"'Rise, Sir,' cried the cruel executioner, 'that we may execute our lord's command.'

"'Stay, friend,' quoth Waltheof, 'at least until I have said a Pater Noster.'

"So he began his prayer, with great devotion, and his enemies were filled with fear. 'Strike,' cried they privily unto the executioner. And so as Waltheof came unto the words 'Lead us not into temptation,' the executioner drew his sword and smote off his head at one stroke. And now, mark the marvel! God willed to proclaim his innocence by a miracle, for the poor dishonoured head continued the prayer and all present clearly heard the words: 'But deliver us from evil, Amen.'"

"Alas, for the goodly Earl!" exclaimed the stout matron. "Nay, but that is a sad tale, gleeman!"

"Alas, for our goodly King!" exclaimed the harper, and he nudged Osmund. "Alas, our noble Richard, pent in prison! Is he not the lustiest knight that ever saw the day? Form a ring, fair ladies, and rally to me my roaring lads and I'll sing you a song of our own Lionheart."

Osmund slipped through the crowd on the pretext of collecting contributions. He ducked under the girth of Balliol's horse and held out his hood to the Lord of Scarcliffe. As the knight bent to drop in a coin, Osmund uttered his warning: "'Ware Waltheof's fate——"

He could get no further for Fulk pushed his horse between them, nearly riding the boy down.

"Hurrah for Richard!" shouted the harper. "God save our noble Cœur de Lion!"

Wido sprang up on the covered top of the well again and leaning gracefully against the bar from which hung the chain and bucket, he began to troll out a song popular with royal archers on the march:

"King Richard I understande
When he went out of Engelande
Let make an axe for the nones
To break therewith the Saracens' bones."

"A ring—make a ring!" called out the country folk laughing. "Who'll join the ballad? Come, Jenny, come Meg!"

Girls and women gathered round as eagerly as fine ladies in their great castles were wont to do. They held hands and swung back and forth vigorously in time to the rhythm, so that every part of them was in movement except their feet.

"God save King Richard!" exclaimed the smith. He had been drinking rather freely of strong heady mead. "And may he soon come home! Meanwhile there'll be a sad toll of all hard-won money ere we leave Southwell tomorrow or I'm mistaken in our Lackland."

"Who dare call Prince John by so foul a name?" exclaimed a harsh voice, and Hal the Sheriff pushed his horse so violently through the crowd that a gingerbread stall was overturned and women fled shrieking.

Osmund had struggled back towards the harper. The Sheriff's horse was coming unpleasantly near, and planting himself in front of Robin, he called out anxiously:

"Have a care for my master, my lords, he's blind!"

"Clear the ground for my lord Prince!" exclaimed the Sheriff.

Osmund gazing past him saw the Prince sitting a few paces away on his coal-black charger. At first he thought him the noblest figure he had ever beheld. John was clad in a long tunic woven of green and gold, with gold lions all over the skirt where it divided at the saddle. It was girt round his waist with a zone or belt studded with flashing emeralds, and a buckle brooch of the same stones clasped his golden cloak on his shoulder. His eyes were golden too under proudly arched brows and when Osmund met their hard gaze he did not think John noble any more. The handsome face had clouded over, the full mouth was set in an evil sneer, and Osmund became aware that the minstrel was still lustily singing:

> "The Saracens away they rapped
> All that he hit he also strapped——"

The people standing near now paused and fell silent, but those in the background shouted the chorus with a new meaning.

> "All that he hit he also strapped!"

John was not slow in guessing they applied the words to him and warmly desired that the Lionheart should return and strap (or crush) his disloyal brother. His smile tightened into a grimace.

> "And the prison when he came to
> With his axe he smote right through,"

carolled Wido.

> "Doors, bars, iron chains
> The King will burst them all amain.
> His ship is nearing fast the strand
> Welcome King Richard of Engelande!"

The last line was greeted with a cheer, which withered away under John's menacing silence.

"Lead me off, boy," said Robin, but it was rather he who thrust Osmund before him, round the well, past the sugar-plum stalls until they stood in the sweet-smelling bean rows at the rear of the houses.

John's voice pursued them:

"Clap me that rascal in the stocks!" he said. "Master Sheriff, you should keep better order."

Robin swept Osmund behind him, laid down the harp carefully, and grasped his stout staff in both muscular hands. But no one followed them: the Sheriff's men laid hands on poor Wido, who made no resistance, and dragged him off.

"They'll break his lute!" exclaimed Osmund, and darting under Robin's arm, he ran back to the market-place and snatched up the instrument which had fallen into the dust. It filled him with anger to see how roughly the minstrel was being handled. The peasants had fled from the green and armed men filled all the space—followers of Prince John, the Sheriff and Fulk de Brent. Hal Hardfist was very much to the fore and ordered his henchmen to clap poor Wido into the stocks forthwith.

Fairs always attracted a certain number of sturdy vagrants and folk who lived by their wits. These were anxious to curry favour with the Prince, so they not only cheered loudly, but thought to please him by abusing the minstrel who was alleged to have shown him disrespect. From words they quickly proceeded to deeds, and pelted the unfortunate man with mud, stones and sticks, as he sat fixed wrist and foot in the stocks, unable even to raise a hand to shield his face.

Osmund laid the lute in safety inside the fence of one of the cottage gardens, and waited until the Prince had moved on, accompanied by the disorderly element of the fair. The village people emerged again and the booth-keepers began to replace their wares, which had been tossed over by the mob.

Meanwhile Wido sat in the blazing sun, his hat had been knocked off and trampled underfoot. A stone had cut his cheek and it was bleeding and he was all bedaubed with mud and grime. The village folk clicked their tongues commiseratingly but dared not go near him. The monks were all in choir, their sweet solemn chant came drifting faintly from the Church.

Osmund glanced back doubtfully, but Robin was not in sight, so he went across to the stocks, and wiped poor whimpering Wido's face with his handkerchief. The day was scorchingly hot, and it sickened the boy to see the unfortunate prisoner writhing about in his efforts to get shelter from the cruel glare. If he bent forward the fierce heat smote his neck: if he tilted his head back the sun fell on his eyes. Osmund whipped off his own hood and placed it on Wido, and then ran to the well to get him a drink of water. The cup was fastened to the well post by a chain, but a compassionate woman came out of a cottage near by and handed him a bowl.

THE POOR FELLOW DRANK EAGERLY.

"Why," she cried wonderingly—"Aren't you—you look like——"

"Nay, nay," exclaimed Osmund hastily. "I be the blind harper's boy and naught akin to yon poor fellow."

"'Twas our dear lady I thought thou wast akin to," retorted the matron. "But thou hast a right country tongue and I was a fool to take thee for our little gentleman."

Osmund turned away so hastily that he spilt the water and had to refill his bowl at the bucket. This done, he carried it carefully across to the stocks and held it to Wido's lips. The poor fellow drank eagerly, he was nearly frantic with pain and fear.

"He'll hang me," he muttered. "He'll hang me the same as he hung John o' Lincoln. I'll swing for this—and all my bairns will go lacking bread."

"But you didn't do anything!" cried Osmund indignantly. "A man can't be slain in free England for singing in praise of England's King."

Hardly were the words out of his mouth when a heavy hand fell on his own shoulder and the poor woman's bowl flew out of his grasp and was shattered on the iron band of the stocks.

"Ha, you young rogue!" exclaimed the rough voice of one of the Sheriff's pikemen. "I have you! Where's your rascally harper? I dare swear he is no more blind than I am!"

"He has left the fair long since," declared Osmund promptly. He saw that it was useless to struggle, as his captor was accompanied by three or four of Fulk's Flemings. He prayed with all his might that the man might not have been with his master on May Day.

"Thou'lt know his hole and must declare it, else 'twill be the worse for you," exclaimed the fellow. "The Sheriff has given orders that he is to be arrested and the Prince swears he won't dine till he sees you all swinging from the rafters in the great hall."

Wido greeted this unpleasant statement with a melancholy yell, which caused the heartless soldiers to explode with laughter.

"I expect that was only a jest," said Osmund, in rather a quavering voice. "Because surely the Sheriff has no jurisdiction on Church land."

With a sudden effort he wrenched himself free, and dodging the men-at-arms, flew across the green and into the porch of the Abbey, shrieking as he ran:

"Sanctuary! Father Prior, Father Prior, sanctuary!"

There was a sound of clattering sandals and movement inside the Church, but before the monks could get to the door, the pikeman had fallen on the boy, and shouted to his mates.

In a moment he was bound hand and foot, and carried off bodily, his outcry brutally stifled by a handful of sand pressed into his mouth. At one moment he had giddy visions of blue sky and tree-tops, at another of trampling feet and bruised grass, as the soldiers tossed him uncomfortably about between them in their haste.

"We want no trouble with the monks—haste away to the Manor," cried the leader. "You can set the rogue on his legs as soon as we are out of sight of the Church."

Osmund presently felt the cold steel of a knife slid between his shins and cutting his bonds. His legs would hardly support him and he was dragged along by two men, more uncomfortably than ever. He was still coughing and choking, but as he was hauled through the gateway of his own old home, he raised his eyes, looking round wildly for help. His glance fell on the horrified face of Petronell who was mounted on her white pony: he did not know if she had recognised him or not, and there was no time to think. Before he could even breathe freely, he found himself in the presence of the Ancient of the Sheriff's troop, and the question about the harper was being repeated.

At first Osmund feigned stupidity and stared dumbly, but when the pikeman repeated his superior's query with a blow, he made shift to answer:

"I never served the blind man till today. He hired me on the village green to carry his harp."

"Ha, as I said, he cannot be blind at all!" exclaimed the man. "Who led him to the fair, answer me that? Was it the minstrel?"

"I know naught of it," declared Osmund. "I came from Mansfield to see the fun, and thought no harm to give yon poor lad in the stocks a sup of water. We're kindlier folk our ways than you be here," he added boldly.

"I think the churl speaks truth, Ancient," said another man. "I saw him at Mass this morning, and neither harper nor minstrel was with him. He's but a silly shepherd lad, to my thinking."

"And whose man art thou, forsooth?" demanded the Ancient. "One of the Scarcliffe folk, I see. Well, thou'rt a fool, I tell thee. If Prince John wants to see three folk hang before supper he'll have his way, and if we haven't the harper and this wretch to string up, he'll slip the noose on thee and me!"

A dead silence followed this sally, for the Prince's grim notions of jest were well known.

"Can't you give the boy a taste of hot iron, Ancient?" asked another fellow discontentedly. "To look for a beggar on a fair day is like hunting for a needle in a bundle of hay. I and my mates had expected a little pleasure and junketing while the Prince and Sheriff are at the chase."

"Why, 'tis useless to torture the boy," interposed Lord Hugo's man. "For I myself saw the grey duffle cloak of the harper flying into the forest while the lad was demanding sanctuary. 'Twill be an awkward thing for my lord Fulk, if men who have claimed sanctuary are hanged in this hall."

"Plague on the monks and their sanctuary," grumbled the Ancient. "Well, men, they say there's no dungeon in this house, so you must e'en clap the prisoner into the guard-room in the turret—that is safe enough—and we'll to our game, and the Sheriff can do as he lists when he comes in."

Osmund had often played hide and seek with his brothers and sister up and down the spiral stairs, up which he was now hurried, a captive. The little room in which he was to be confined had been used to store arms for use on the battlement tower.

The men thrust him in so roughly that he fell forward on his face.

Chapter Sixteen

Southwell Manor had been fortified like eleven hundred and twenty-five other houses and castles, during the troubled reign of Stephen, but with more peaceful times its outer defences had fallen into disuse, the moat had silted up and the bailey had been turned into a terraced garden.

The unquiet conscience of Fulk the interloper had caused him to dread the sudden vengeance of his enemies, and one of his reasons for seizing upon Southwell was its aptitude for military defence. The house stood upon a little eminence, scarped on one side: Fulk caused the drawbridge chains to be renewed and repaired the portcullis, or heavy iron barrier, made to slide in stone grooves to cover the great door. The keep or castle, stood within a battlemented wall, which was entered by a gatehouse flanked by two towers, and it was in the upper room of one of these that Osmund had been imprisoned.

For some time the boy lay as he had fallen, face downwards in the dust, then he tried to struggle into a sitting position. This was no easy matter for his arms were tightly tied behind his back, but at last he managed to draw his knees under him and get up. His legs were shaking and he crouched down again, looking round desperately at the stone walls and the one small iron-barred window too high to see through. He thought of his mother and her tears when she bade him farewell, and he burst out sobbing. Perhaps he had done wrong in rushing to Wido's aid in that self-willed way instead of waiting for Robin's consent and assistance.

"Most dear and loving Saviour," prayed Osmund earnestly. "Let me suffer for this but not my mother. St. Peter and all holy poor men, pray for me. My holy patron, come to my aid!"

As though in answer, he heard a voice say "Osmund!" and for a moment he was much too startled to reply.

"Osmund!" came again, in a more urgent tone.

"Yes," he gasped. And then he realised that the sound came from the door, though he had heard no approaching footfall.

"Osmund—it is I—Petronell. My father and Ivo are hunting with the Prince. Tell me quickly where I may find Robin Hood, for I reckon we'll need him, in case Sir Hugo's plea for you should fail."

"Petronell!" exclaimed Osmund. "Go back quickly, for heaven's sake. It is very dangerous for you to come here. Ask Sir Hugo to take no risks for *me*—Pray him to defend my mother. Robin will tell you who she is——"

"I can hardly hear a word you say," interrupted the little girl impatiently. "No one knows I am here, and you are quite safe till after dinner. Sir Wilfred the priest has been clamouring at the gate and demanding that you and the lute-player should be delivered to him——"

"There isn't any right of sanctuary at Southwell really," interrupted Osmund in his turn. "And of course the Sheriff will declare that as soon as he returns. But hearken, maiden! Don't you hear the Morris Dancers?"

"Oh, Osmund, do be serious! Prince John is a cruel beast and 'tis but an hour to supper-time!" she began, and then broke off and sprang to her feet. "The maskers! Of course, how dull of wit I am! Good-bye, dear Osmund—keep up a brave heart."

"Be careful, Petronell. Don't get into danger!" begged Osmund anxiously, but there was no answer. The little girl had already flitted lightly down the spiral stairs. She had gone up shoes in hand, for they were new ones of scarlet leather and might have made a sound. The men-at-arms were drinking inside the courtyard and Petronell slipped out unperceived and ran like the wind down the long ferny glade at the far end of which lay the village.

The fun on the green was now fast and furious, for Vespers were over, the folk had come out of Church and the Prince and his myrmidons were far away, pursuing the buck in the forest. The booths were all displaying their wares for though no sales were permitted on Sunday, would-be buyers might examine and price, and future exchanges might be arranged. All the woodland industries were represented, and every man carried the insignia of his trade. Labourers who wished to be hired wore knots of white ribbon in their capuchins or straw hats, the haymaker carried his scythe, the shepherd his crook and pipe, the charcoal burner his bag of sulphur. There were booths with a great display of latten plates and dishes, and fletchers or arrow-makers with bunches of grey goose feathers at their belts and patten-makers eager to pick quarrels with them. Petronell had never been in such a crowd by herself, but she pushed her way through them with determination, in her effort to get near the Morris Dancers who were threading their way in and out among the low houses. At last the mob became so thick that it was impossible to advance another inch, and tears of despair rushed to her eyes. But a moment later the music ceased, and she saw the wooden ladle, with which it was customary for the Fool to collect contributions, waving about over the heads of the spectators.

"Let me through, I want to give the Morris Dancers some money," she cried.

A good-natured person in front who had no intention of making any donation himself, but was most willing that others should do so, turned round and caught the little girl up in his arms.

"Here, Sir Fool!" he shouted. "Hither with thy spoon!"

Instead of dropping in a piece of money, Petronell clutched hold of the ladle:

"Midge!" she cried. "Oh, Midge, I must speak with you! Good folk, let me by, I have a message for my foster-brother yonder!"

Before the Fool could answer, the huge leader of the Morris leant over the intervening people and plucked Petronell bodily from the other man's arms.

"Get me to Robin! They are going to hang Osmund!" she whispered in his ear.

"Trust me!" returned the giant, and he began to caper again, holding Petronell on his shoulder with one hand and waving his kerchief in the other. Poor Petronell felt extremely embarrassed as she was jogged along, the people all clapping and applauding, convinced that the Morris Dancer was carrying his own child. No one dreamed that the flushed, shy maiden was the daughter of the noblest knight of the county, and she trembled lest any of the Scarcliffe folk should recognise her.

As soon as Little John had danced out of the press, he began to run, Maid Marian lightly keeping pace with him, while the Fool, the hobby-horse and the rest spread themselves across the path to intercept any inconvenient followers. Hardly were they within the verge of the wood when John paused and gave his own peculiar whistle three times.

Almost immediately Robin Hood stepped out of the thicket, a freshly-killed deer over his shoulder. He wore a woodman's jerkin.

"What news?" he asked abruptly.

"They're going to hang Osmund!" exclaimed Petronell bursting into tears. "Osmund and the minstrel and the blind harper are to be hung before Prince John will sup."

"Ho, ho! Is that the way the wind blows! And I suppose Master Osmund thinks himself a fine fellow now he has got into trouble! He promised his mother to obey me and not to act without my counsel. Tuck, my trusty brother, take my best horse which Pinder George has yonder in the thicket, and go drive the deer so that the Prince gets little sport till late in the day."

"Aye, master. My hounds are here in leash, but I'll need a score of our band."

"They are within call. Mark you, friend, the Prince must not sup till nightfall. Go with him, Will, and you too, Stutely."

"Where is the boy?" asked Marian. "Fear not, little maid, Robin Hood will find a way to save him."

"He doesn't deserve it," said the outlaw.

"Yea, but he does!" exclaimed Petronell indignantly. "A craven would have had a thousand reasons for leaving the poor minstrel to his fate. But Osmund thought only of knightly compassion: how could anyone expect to be hanged for showing mercy to a poor creature in pain?"

"Master," cried Much, stepping forward. "I'se go hang in Osmund's stead if that will do. Don't thou take on, my little lady. I'd be drowned dead if it wasn't for him, and I reckon I can hang as well as my betters."

Much was a simple youth, but he had his own notions of honour and gratitude. At the same time he was by no means anxious to die, and could not forbear a snuffle.

"You'll not forget the owd folk, I know," he concluded, wiping his nose ungracefully with the back of his hand.

"Well spoken, my midget!" exclaimed Robin. "But thy neck is in no peril for the nonce. Go you with Brother Tuck. As for you, little maiden, you know nothing of courts I see, where *right* is always the Prince's wishes and *wrong* what the Prince dislikes! However, we'll finish this merry day with a final jest: aye, the last laugh will be ours."

"Now do not go running into peril without necessity," began Maid Marian anxiously, for there was a wild gleam in Robin's eye which she knew portended fearful rashness.

"Trust me, sweetheart! And do thou ride home to thy bower in Fountaindale and prepare a goodly feast, for we shall be hungry enough, I warrant you, and I know not if the meal will be supper or breakfast."

"But, Robin——"

"We'll be with you soon after midnight, I trow," he concluded. "And now, John, I need you, and you, too, Arthur à Bland."

"Have you a plan?" asked Petronell.

"Aye, and a good one! 'Tis best that no one should know who Osmund is, and therefore 'twill appear as though that rascal Robin Hood was but rescuing one of his own knaves. Go back to Lady Roheisa, my lass, and bid her not trust the Prince—Who comes? Down, all!"

The outlaws dropped flat with scarce a rustle of the tall bracken. Petronell lay down, too, creeping close to Maid Marian and gazing terror-stricken through the green stems towards the path.

"It sounds like Ivo's pony," she whispered presently in great relief.

"Lie still, till we know who may be with him," returned Marian.

"Scarcliffe folk," declared Robin. "Go forth, Petronell, and stay him in the path."

The girl obeyed, quite expecting the others to rise likewise, but as she waited for the riders to come up to her, she noted that not one had stirred. Indeed had she not proved it herself she could never have believed that ten men and a maid could vanish so completely.

Ivo it was, who presently drew near, urging on a tired horse all lathered with sweat. He was followed by five men—a lance, the group was called when they accompanied their lord to war. He reined up in astonishment at the sight of his sister.

"Petronell! What has happened?"

"Your news first!" she cried.

"My father bids us all return to Scarcliffe. He wishes my mother to go ahead with us, for the Prince has commanded our attendance at Southwell tonight, and he fears this portends no good. Osmund was right."

"Oh, brother, poor Osmund is a prisoner at the Castle——"

Ivo glanced anxiously over his shoulder.

"Tom Long-arm," he called. "Give Lady Petronell your horse, and lead on to the lychgate. Sister, you and my mother must be out of reach ere the Prince returns, for he means to seize us as hostages."

"And you? Ride on, Ivo, I'll run beside you. Fall back there, Tom, a moment!"

"I can't abandon Osmund," said Ivo. "I'll see you and my mother safe on the Mansfield road and then perhaps I could bribe the porter."

"I tried that," she returned. "But he was too much afraid. The Prince and Sheriff are determined to wreak their spite on those who seemed to uphold King Richard."

"Leave Osmund to me, young folk," said a voice from the grass. "And obey your father strictly for he is in mortal danger. Stay not in Mansfield either, but away to your own folk. Aye, ride right on to the Minster where your mother is still at her prayer."

At the first words Ivo swung his horse round, so as to interpose himself between Petronell and possible danger. But she whispered "Robin," and Ivo understood and listened with bent head.

"Osmund is my friend," he murmured as Robin paused.

"Mine also," returned the outlaw. "For he saved Tuck's hound, and I'll answer for his head with my own. A knight's duty is to protect the women first."

Ivo bit his lip and bowed his head in assent. He could not trust himself to speak. Petronell was white and silent too as she mounted the trooper's horse and the little band passed out of sight.

Far away in the woods the royal bugles rang out merrily.

"They are over near," said Robin. "Off with you, Tuck, and you too, sweetheart."

"What are you going to do?" enquired she.

"Marry, sit here in the fern with my two mates. Whereabouts in the market stands the armourer's stall?"

"Near the forge, I should think," returned John incautiously.

"It does not, then!" cried Robin, rewarding his follower with a buffet which made his head ring. It was the rough-and-ready means by which a faulty shot or an error in observation was punished by their code and Robin submitted to it as well as his followers. "Mark you, the armourer is over against the woodstapler. Now listen! I had thought to have had a merry evening playing the blind harper before the Prince, but that is all spoiled now. Hark to my instructions, friends, and see ye follow them."

He whispered earnestly for some moments, and Arthur, the fair-haired tanner chuckled, but Little John objected.

"There's no need for you to go, Robin. I've broken a prison before this and can do so again. Or we can stand by the gallows and put an arrow through the hangman's head."

"You deserve another box on the ear," declared his leader. "Have I not said that Prince John wants to string me, Osmund and the lute-player up in the hall? We can't all get in there, through a double bailey, save by open riot against the Prince's grace and there is no reason for that. Nay, we'll wait till sundown. Have you the air, Arthur?"

"*Three merry men, and three merry men!*" began the tanner, quite out of tune.

"Beshrew me, thou'rt flat, Arthur," cried Robin. "But 'twill serve. Meet me here in an hour."

He glided away, made a loop through the trees and strolled towards the Castle.

.   .   .   .   .

A bonfire had been lighted in the centre of the open space at the cross-roads and the merry-makers were dancing on the level ground round it, when three men reeled out of the dusk, linked arm-in-arm and loudly singing:

> "Three merry men and three merry men
> And three merry men are we!
> We dance and sing, hey ding-a-ding ding
> All under the greenwood tree!"

"As drunk as lords, I declare," exclaimed a village matron indignantly. "Look where they go—alack, they'll knock over neighbour Trot's table of whitepot pies."

The revellers indeed rolled up against the old lady's board, and set her shrieking, but rolled away again without causing any damage, and next moment cannoned against the armourer's stall and sent swords, bucklers and helmets clashing to the ground. They continued their devious way, heedless of the man's abuse, and he was reduced to venting his indignation on his hapless 'prentice.

"Pick up all the smallwares, thou dolt!" he cried.

"I've got everything, master, save only two files," returned the lad, dodging the blow aimed at him as he groped about on the turf.

The three merry men were still proclaiming their presence at the far end of the village, but a diversion was created by the note of a hunting-horn ringing out down the darkening glade.

"The Prince, the Prince is returning!" was the cry.

"Oh, Lord, save me! Oh, I'm going to be hanged!" wailed Wido, waking up from an uneasy doze. "Oh——"

His outcry ceased abruptly, but a low voice in his ear declared:

"Go on! Shout and howl, you fool! Deaden the sound all thou canst!"

Wido began to lament again with the full strength of his lungs in order to drown the comforting sound of a gnawing rat which had begun stealthily beside him. It was no rodent, however, but the rasp of a file rapidly eating through the iron pin which locked the bar over two slots through which his wrists were thrust.

"Once thy hands are free thou canst loose thy legs thyself," whispered his unknown friend. Huge as he was he managed to crouch behind the prisoner so that Wido's form hid him from all but a close observer.

The village folk crowded down to the road to see the Prince ride past; a spectacle was always worth looking at, and John and his followers made a fine display. Some of the women murmured that the Knight of Scarcliffe looked pale and troubled and that the Sheriff's sworn woodwards rode as close on either side as though he were a prisoner. But this was dangerous talk, and the good dames cheered loudly immediately after the words, for fear of being suspected of disloyalty.

After the royal hunter and his friends, came the henchmen carrying the spoils of the chase. A lymer, or tracker, counted them aloud.

"Four buck, two does, another buck! Seven pardi! I could have taken my oath there were but six slain!"

"Then thou would'st have forsworn thyself friend!" remarked a voice from under the seventh deer. The other carcases were carried by two men, with some labour, slung between them on a staff, but this last stout fellow bore his load on his head and strode along so valiantly that he passed his fellows and was the first to reach the porter's lodge behind the clattering horses.

The Sheriff's men met their master at the gate.

"We've searched the country far and near for the harper in vain. We found the harp but the man hath fled out of reach," they confessed.

"Have a care, thou clumsy dolt! Canst not see his Worship the Sheriff?"

"Your pardon, my lord," besought the churl, pausing a moment with the deer still poised on his head: its dappled limbs drooped on his shoulders and obscured his face.

"You must say he resisted you and you smote him dead!" exclaimed the Sheriff. He heard a stifled laugh and glanced about him angrily, but the game-bearers had moved on and his own men surrounded him, all looking as fierce and grim as he did himself.

Chapter Seventeen

The little window of the turret room was partly obscured by ivy, and spiders had built their webs across the corners. Bats flitted in and out, untroubled by the presence of a prisoner. Osmund crouched on the floor, trying to say his prayers, but sorely distracted by his aching arms and troubled thoughts. There was a great deal of noise going on in the house, but it came dull and muffled to his ears: here in the dark, musty cell all was still save for the tiny squeak of the bats, and a queer scraping sound on the roof, which Osmund could not identify. Then something moved at the window, the ivy was drawn away and a hand grasped the bars.

"Blackbird, art here?" whispered Robin Hood's welcome voice, and the small aperture was darkened as he strove to look in.

"Robin!" exclaimed the prisoner. In the intensity of his relief, he felt girlish tears rush to his eyes and he was glad they could not be seen.

Robin was lying full length on the roof, and craning down his head to peer into the cell.

"Have they bound you?" he asked.

"Yes—my hands! Oh, Robin, go before they see you! You can't get me out—but tell my mother——"

"Hush! There's no time for talk. Turn thy back to me and stand tip-toe!"

Robin swung himself down, holding by the bars, and thrust one leg into the cell: thus perched astride of the sill, he reached down and severed Osmund's bonds with his knife.

"Stand away and let me see if I can force out the bars—nay, we must file them! Now, Blackbird, rub the feeling back into thy arms. Move about—get rid of all cramp, because everything depends on our activity, and the fleetness of our steps."

BATS FLITTED IN AND OUT.

"Robin, won't they hear you filing and shoot from the court-yard?" asked Osmund anxiously.

"A life without risks were a dull one," answered Robin, working away in a very frenzy of haste, and pausing every now and then to try if he could heave out the bars by force. "Off with your jerkin, child, it will be hard enough to get you through."

144

At last the iron rods gave away under the impact of Robin's knee, and he stood up, poised on the sill, and delicately stretched his limbs as a cat might do.

"Now, Blackbird—hop forth! Do not become afraid if thou stickest in the midst, there is room enough, so thou manage right. Pull thyself up, hold by my belt—nay, get thy knee on the sill."

Osmund struggled to obey, but the sweat poured down his face as he writhed in the narrow aperture. Robin Hood placed his own body as a bulwark and instructed Osmund to turn himself face to the wall, and pull himself out by holding to the edge of the roof. When this was accomplished at last he spoke again.

"Promise me not to look down and do exactly what I say— soft—there is someone below—don't move or speak."

Osmund held his breath, acutely conscious that Robin was protecting him like a living shield. The light of a lantern wheeled waveringly across the dark buildings.

"Hullo, Sandy Break-barrel, art there?"

"Ou aye," returned Robin, assuming a Scotch accent.

"Must I come help you bring forth your prisoner?"

"Nay, marry, I can make shift to kick the churl downstairs myself. Are they ready for him?"

"Pretty well, the French lads are twisting the halter."

He went back to the Keep and Robin whispered:

"Go on up over the roof—set thy foot on my knee so—cannily, Osmund!"

The boy scrambled up, feeling horribly helpless as he sprawled on the slippery lead of the sloping roof, his toes braced against the narrow moulding at the edge. He lay without moving by Robin's command until the outlaw had climbed past him on to the battlements, where there was standing for an archer at the top of the tower. Then he undid his leather belt and hauled the boy up by it until he could grasp the parapet and help himself.

"Now," said Robin, "what next, I wonder? They'll find the cell empty in a moment and then the hunt will be up!"

"I wedged a bit of broken iron under the door," said Osmund. "They won't be able to open it easily."

"Now that was truly well thought of! We'll lift the trap-door so—and draw up the ladder, but we won't go down this way."

"The wall used to be broken round by the East tower, I remember," whispered Osmund. "But perhaps they have had it repaired."

"Aye, and we would be bound to meet the archers on the wall. Nay, Osmund, we must climb over and down the portcullis—and that right quickly, while they are still busy with the wine."

.   .   .   .   .

Osmund had many a nightmare in after life in which that wild climb was re-acted. He could never have accomplished it alone, but Robin Hood's agility was second only to his great strength.

Southwell Manor was a fortified house, rather than a Castle proper, the gate-house was therefore only two stories high and it was possible for Robin to lower Osmund by the wrists until he could find a precarious footing on the iron spikes of the portcullis. This well-known defence was in the shape of a barbed slab of iron, which was raised by a chain and wheel, and slid down stone grooves in the gate pillars when closed. There was a horrible moment when Osmund had to release one hand, and stoop to grasp the ornate tooth-moulding of the cornice. He was so engrossed in the task of finding hand and footholds that he never noticed how Robin managed to get down unaided, and was surprised to find his friend hanging beside him and laughing as good-humouredly as though they were both on a bird's-nesting frolic.

"By my troth, Blackbird, here we are, spread out on a door for all the world like a couple of dead rats nailed up by friend Job on his poultry house! The lazy wretches have not raised the drawbridge so we can slip down in the dark——"

"Hold! Who goes there?" interrupted a voice from the wall above.

Osmund twisted his head anxiously to look over his shoulder but it was a misty night and he could see nothing below him. Nevertheless he heard the ring of pike-staffs striking on stone and knew that there must be at least two sentries.

"A friend," called a deep voice out of the night.

"Little John," whispered Robin. "Don't move for your life, boy."

"Friend, pass the word!" challenged the man-at-arms.

"Richard!" shouted Little John at the full pitch of his lungs.

Instantly this name was repeated by a hundred voices, shouting out of the forest on every side of the castle. The startled sentries flung down their pikes and loosed off arrows at random and there was a sound of running feet and a hub-bub of voices inside the courtyard.

"Quick, Blackbird, down and jump into the moat!" whispered Robin Hood.

At the first alarum the Captain of the Guard had given the order to raise the drawbridge and the two fugitives were in danger of being pinned between the rising platform and the gate. Osmund dropped into the moat feet first and bobbed up and down in the brackish water most uncomfortably, until Robin joined him and seized him by the shirt.

"Canst swim?"

"Aye," spluttered Osmund, kicking himself into a horizontal position.

"Keep close along the wall—no—on the castle side. Hark at my men!"

"I feel like a tickled trout!" exclaimed Osmund.

The cry rang round again, this time taken up singly by one post after another.

"Ho, Richard! Richard! Richard!"

A shower of arrows from the wall pattered among the leaves and then an anxious voice called to the archers to stay their shots.

"They think it is the King!" muttered Robin, raising himself half out of the water. "Come, now's the time to cross the moat while they talk within."

He struck out, Osmund followed, and they both scrambled on to the further brink without being detected. Robin pushed the boy quickly before him, until they were within the forest border. Then he shouted lustily:

"St. George for England!"

There came a rustling and rapid steps.

"Is it you, Master? What orders now?" panted Little John.

"Where are the horses? We'll ride to Haywood Oakes and then to Kirkby Forest after this night's play."

"Arthur can lead you to them straight. Must we stay here?"

"Nay, bid the band withdraw silently. Is Wido safe away?"

"Aye, master—I reckon he won't stop shaking with fright till Christmas comes round!"

Robin laughed.

"This lad is of better metal," he said. And Osmund's heart swelled with joy at praise from Robin Hood.

"Faugh, I'm all over evil-smelling slime," he said.

"No matter! There are fair streams in Sherwood—we'll not draw rein till we're over the River Greet."

"But Robin Hood, what of Petronell—and Ivo, too?"

"Nay, thou'st risked enough. Up, in the saddle! Will, do thou ride behind the youngster for he is ready to drop. Where is Maid Marian?"

"She waits at Friar Tuck's well," answered Scarlet.

The horses were already in motion, moving swiftly and silently for they were unshod. As they reached a broad woodland track, the pace increased to a gallop.

Osmund suddenly felt very limp and exhausted and was glad of Scarlet's strong arms clasped round him.

He was only half awake when an hour or two later, he found himself lying on the ground being stripped of his wet clothes, rubbed with dry fern, and hurriedly thrust into garments of the coveted Lincoln Green.

But there was no rest for any of the company that night. Osmund was soon on a horse again and hurried forward until dawn found them on an open moorside, whipped by the chill tart breeze of the uplands.

The boy slept soundly in the improvised hut of sods and heather-bushes which had been reared by the men for Maid Marian. She despised it, however, and after a few hours' rest was ready to take her part in shooting at a mark with the rest of the band. It was customary for every bad shot to be punished by a heavy blow, Marian being exempt, though her skill at archery was so great, it was said she had never earned the penalty.

It was a hot summer noon, when Osmund emerged, feeling none the worse for his adventures. The warm air could be seen shimmering over the wide expanse of moorland, and the noise of running water told of a neighbouring stream. It was delightful to bathe in a clear pool and to get rid of the last nauseous flavour of the moat.

Having seen the mighty tanner, Arthur à Bland felled to the ground in reward of a careless shaft, Osmund felt rather anxious when Robin called him to come and try his skill. He was allowed to approach much nearer to the peeled hazel-wand than any of the others, and managed to hit it with one arrow out of four. The failures were duly penanced with a light tap, for Robin said a novice must be schooled not banged. Osmund was glad he had not cried off the contest as he had been tempted to do.

Osmund had never been to the southern end of the forest before and the country was quite new to him. The outlaw's camp had been made on the further side of Robin Hood's Hills, on rolling limestone pasture land where horses and riders could find cover in the long grassy hollows, yet where a sentry at a well-chosen look-out post could give early warning of the approach of any armed band.

Robin's intention was to wait until his scouts brought in tidings of the movements of Prince John and the Sheriff, and the two men he had appointed for this office rejoined the main party in the afternoon. They reported that Sir Hugo had been dispatched with a letter from John to the prisoner-King, that his lady and children had not been pursued, and that, though the Prince had soon discovered that he had been tricked, he was nevertheless in a panic and had ridden south with his retinue with all speed.

As a matter of fact, John was convinced that the secret of his plot had leaked out and was sure to come to Richard's ears. His first idea was to get Hugo de Scarcliffe out of the country before he could get speech with the King's adherents. His letter to his brother was couched in the most loving terms, for he was an expert in the art of dissimulation. Having, as he hoped, made an appeal to Richard's warm heart which would act as an antidote to any rumours of disaffection, his next anxiety was to consolidate his alliance with Philip of France, so that he might strike for the crown of England at a convenient moment, secure of the assistance of his brother's arch-enemy. He summoned Fulk to accompany him and dismissed Gisborne and the Balliols to their Castles in Yorkshire and Northumberland.

Hal Hardfist too was an embittered and disappointed man. He had spent his ill-gotten gains like water in the entertainment of the Prince, and now John had departed without making him any recompense. His wife never ceased upbraiding him for managing so badly; she had had vast expectations from the Prince's visit and thought the Sheriff would have been given a couple of rich manors, or the monopoly of pannage dues in Clipstone, or some other such prize by which extravagant princes were apt to reward their friends—at someone else's expense! Robin Hood had escaped him after defying him openly, for he was now convinced that the troop which had caused the Prince so much alarm at Southwell, was none other than Robin's band. The Sheriff did not propose to spend any more money on a fruitless pursuit of the outlaw, so he disbanded his hired soldiers and retired to Nottingham in great dudgeon.

When Robin had talked things over with Maid Marian, he decided that it would be safe for Osmund to go back to his home and ordered Scarlet to accompany him. They were to start immediately, going round to the west of Mansfield and passing Woodhouses before turning towards the Grange.

As Osmund and Scarlet rode along through lanes and uplands, the whole air was sweet with the smell of cut grass and the rhythmic sweep of the scythe made music till the edge of dusk. The wild honeysuckle hung in great bunches of bloom on every bush, and when they drew near Sherwood, the fragrance of the lime trees in flower met them on the breeze. No one hindered or stayed them, though they had to turn aside into the forest to avoid the Verderer on his rounds.

Scarlet knew every coppice and covert far better than the King's paid servants: he knew where the neglected trees had grown so thickly that no man could pass between them afoot, and where there were narrow ways through which horsemen could go single-file if they stooped their heads warily.

"The Verderer will keep to the road," declared Will scornfully, as they stood holding their horses' bridles. The outlaws' mounts had no jingling bits or stirrups to betray them, all metal parts being wrapped in bands of plaited grass.

It was approaching sunset when they drew near the Grange. Osmund begged his friend to stay with his mother for a day or two, but he shook his head.

"At least sup with us and spend the night," urged the boy, but the outlaw again refused.

"There is no roof for me but the starry heaven," he declared. "But I thank you kindly, and pray you practise your shooting: we'll have some merry days in the forest before the summer is out. And now farewell, for I smell the smoke of your mother's kitchen fire."

"Farewell, dear Will, and thank you!" cried Osmund.

There was no answer and a moment later Job came grumbling out of the undergrowth, with a bunch of rabbit snares in his hand.

"So you're home again!" he remarked. "And who were you talking to at the top of your voice—scaring all the game?"

Will had disappeared and Osmund thought it discreet to answer one question with another.

"Art going home, Job? Won't you get up behind me, my horse will carry us both well enough as far as the Grange."

Job scrambled up, well-pleased to get a ride.

"And where did the horse come from?" he enquired.

"He is not mine—only borrowed," returned Osmund, and he made his tired steed trot the rest of the way, so that Job was kept busy holding on and asked no more questions.

Chapter Eighteen

J T WAS STRANGE after the excitement of the past few days to settle back into ordinary life again. Yet soon the daily round of little tasks and duties made recent adventures seem like a dream.

Eadgar was soon as busy with his chronicling, as though no such persons as Robin Hood and Fulk de Brent were in existence. Osmund faithfully practised his archery, and little Stephen also learnt how to shoot with a light bow. They were not allowed to aim at the King's deer, but good-natured Job permitted them to slay rabbits and Osmund soon became an adept at watching his quarry. Old Alice dressed the skins and lined all the children's winter garments with coney-fur, so that every one was busy and contented all through the long summer.

Osmund would have liked to go to Scarcliffe, to enquire for Ivo and Petronell, but the Lady Etheldreda was too much alarmed by the danger he had already been in to allow him out of her sight.

Robin Hood came once to visit them and to fetch his horse. He did not come to the house but blew his bugle to summon them to him in the deep thicket. He reported that Sir Hugo was still away and that the lady and her children were dwelling in the manor house in apparent peace and security.

"As long as Earl John keeps abroad there is nothing to fear," he remarked. "And even if Dan Hugo has been sent on a fool's errand to the King, it will do him no harm, beyond the wastage of money."

"Are you going to stay here for a bit now?" asked Stephen. "Osmund and I will slay some rabbits for you, if you'll stop."

"Thank you, my bold archer—'tis a courteous offer, but my game is dapple-coated, and I go northward again to seek it."

"Master Robin!" exclaimed Eadgar, suddenly emerging from deep thought. "If King Richard does not return soon, will Prince John be crowned King? Because, if he comes back here in power it may go hard with our mother."

"Aye, truly it would be safer for her to dwell awhile with her brother in Cumberland," agreed Robin. "Do you ask the lady to write a letter and I will see it delivered."

But when she was consulted, the lady refused to make any move though she was glad enough to send news of her present plight to her brothers in the north. She was convinced that her husband still lived and would return, but she was anxious that Eadgar should be trained up in a knight's household and finally agreed that he might accompany Robin when he went to hunt in the forest of Geltsdale whence it was easy to reach Greystock Castle. It was all arranged in a hurry and Osmund felt very sad and lonely as he watched Eadgar depart. Hild marched up to Robin at the last moment and announced that she had a secret to impart to him. He was mounted, and he stooped and lifted her on to his horse.

"Now, my maid! Nay, do not whisper—thou dost but tickle my ear and I hear nothing! We'll draw apart a little from the others. Now!"

"Well," said Hild, feeling rather shy. "It is only that I wanted to tell you that perhaps you won't find Eadgar quite such a good outlaw as Osmund. You see he is rather law-y really—I think he was born like that."

"But we have rules in our band, too, sweetheart. I am an outlaw only because my enemies have pushed me forth of the pale. I have a great respect for the law of England."

"Really?" asked Hild. She studied Robin's face to see if he were laughing at her: he was quite grave, but his eyes were twinkling.

"I am very glad," said Hild, with a sigh of relief. "You won't tell Eadgar what I said, will you? And you will not lose patience if he should be somewhat dreamy? I wish I were going with you, too, Robin."

"Perhaps I will carry you all off some day," he said. "But meanwhile run back to your mother."

He swung her down, waved his hand to Osmund and calling Eadgar rode away. Other members of the band came out of the bushes to join him, forming up behind and riding two abreast, like a procession. Maid Marian was not among them this time, much to Hild's disappointment.

"Let us go and play in the wood," suggested Hild, as they walked back through the paddock.

"It does not seem worth while without Eadgar," rejoined Osmund. "And I think our mother is sad: I will stay with her today."

"What shall we do if the Sheriff comes?" enquired Stephen dismally. "I suppose he'll hang us all when he finds out that brother has gone."

"Oh, but he won't find out!" cried Osmund, forcing himself to speak cheerfully. "We'll dress up Hild to represent him. Hild will have to practise looking wise and carrying a book about, and of course we'll have to cut her hair off."

"I'd just as lief!" she cried. "I have always wanted to be a boy! Do ask mother if I may dress in Eadgar's things and represent him while he is away! It would be fun! I'd be the eldest then and you'd all have to obey me."

"But you aren't taller than Osmund," objected Stephen, disapprovingly. "And I shan't obey you, I am a boy and you're a girl and you can't ever be a knight or a monk and I can."

"I could be a queen," answered Hild. "But I think I'd rather be an abbess and rule over a large monastery and ride about on a milk-white mule."

"You would have to be very good first," said Stephen doubtfully. "I think you had better marry Prince Arthur and then you would be Queen of England if you lived to be very old."

Osmund left them to continue this discussion, for he knew they would talk on these subjects for hours at a time. He went to rejoin his mother and she felt comfort in his presence and let him help her with her manifold occupations for the rest of the day.

In the evening when Lady Etheldreda sat at her spinning-wheel the children gathered about her and she began to tell them of the great joust at which she had first seen her husband, Sir Aelfric. He carried all before him that day, and was the best Knight and most gallant in the lists. She described her anxiety as she leaned over the edge of the ladies' balcony, trying to distinguish his flame-coloured crest in the dust-filled arena.

Besides being strong, beautiful and of dauntless courage, he was very courteous to all and could make songs.

"I want my sons to grow up just like him," said Etheldreda. Her hand trembled and she broke her thread, but she would not weep before the children for she did not want to make them sad.

.   .   .   .   .

It was strange to think of Christmas without Eadgar, and Hild cried at the thought that for the first time in her memory she could not give him a Christmas gift. However, her mother suggested that it should be prepared all the same and given later; so Osmund and Hild went on with the rather unpleasant work of scraping down sheepskin, rubbing it with pumice and cutting it into neat sheets which were afterwards to be sewn up into a book for Eadgar to write in. Hild sometimes scrubbed too hard and made holes, which Osmund had to mend by putting on neat patches, glued with white of egg, and carefully smoothed at the edges.

At the beginning of winter all the animals on the farm, except a minimum reserved for stock, had to be slaughtered and their flesh salted down for winter use. Turnips and mangolds were unknown and in the forest holdings it was not possible to save enough hay and corn to feed many beasts. The plough-oxen of course had to be preserved and a small ewe flock and a couple of milch goats.

The children hated this period: there was extra churning to do and great crocks of butter were salted down. Job came to assist in pickling the meat and storing it in kegs and in return Stephen and Osmund went round his rabbit traps for him, frequently letting the prisoners loose if they found any alive and uninjured. In order that Job might not be the loser they felt obliged to collect bags of fir cones for his fire, as make-weight.

Christmas passed quietly. The Waits did not penetrate so far into the forest, and the family went to an early Mass at Ollerton, returning home before any of the customary festivities had begun.

The Verderer met them as they were coming back from church: the lady holding little Sibell in front of her on her mule, and the other children and servants trudging sturdily beside her. Osmund flung his own hooded cloak over Hild's more feminine headgear and she ran forward to lead the mule, taking big strides in imitation of Osmund.

"The peace of this holy season be with you, Verderer," cried the lady as they passed each other.

"Greeting," he returned in a surly tone. His glance swept the little party and seeing three boys, as he thought, his suspicions were not aroused. They all breathed more freely when they turned off the highway into the friendly woodland path. The few persons they met called out Christmas wishes: they all wore happy smiling faces, and were going to or from Mass in family groups. Later on there would be wassailing and Christmas games in all the farms and the Mummers would go their rounds from house to house.

Hild had a sudden inspiration.

"Osmund," she whispered. "Couldn't we be the Mummers? Let's act St. George and the Dragon—you can be St. George and——" She was just going to choose the part of the Princess, when she remembered not to be selfish. "Sibell shall be Princess," she said, "and Stephen the dragon, and I'll be the old King."

"Isn't Sibbie too young?" objected her brother.

"Oh, no," cried Hild, "she would look so sweet—we could crown her with that gilt paper that came off the gingerbread. And you and I could be King and Queen as well as the Saint and the Dragon."

"We had better tell Mother and she will let us have things to dress up with," cried Osmund.

So after dinner, a small band of Mummers thumped on the hall-door. Everyone professed great surprise and delight at their appearance. The audience consisted of the Lady Etheldreda, Walter, Alice, Joan, and two farm boys. It was unexpectedly swelled by the arrival of Job, with his wife and grandsons, who came to present their Christmas duty. The Princess won great applause by executing an impromptu dance, with her gilt paper coronet tilted over one eye. The dragon roared shrilly and writhed about, tightly swathed in an old bit of green tapestry and St. George speared him in gallant style. There was a good deal more action than dialogue about the Mumming, which was quite according to antique tradition, and at the end both actors and audience stood up together and sang carols. And thus ended a happy day.

CHAPTER NINETEEN

As the short winter days succeeded each other un-eventfully the impression of impending danger faded altogether from Osmund's mind. Job told him that a big herd of deer had come into the neighbourhood, and the boy rejoiced, knowing that his friend Robin was sure to get the news and come in due course to hunt them. But January and February passed without further excitement, April Fool Day arrived and the children played jokes upon each other as usual. Osmund was so wary that when Hild ran to the barn to tell him that a monk was in the hall, he did not believe her.

"I think such jests are stupid," Osmund declared. "They make people wroth and there is little wit in them."

"But it isn't a jest," exclaimed Hild. "I was to tell you to come at once."

She ran away, and Osmund flung down the flail he had been balancing uncertainly in his hands, and slowly followed her.

A fresh wind was stripping the blossom from the pear trees in the garden, and when he opened the house door it rustled the sedges on the floor and set the window hangings flapping. The lady was in the inner room and directly Osmund entered he knew by her face that the monk had brought bad news. The poor man looked very tired; his frock was worn into fringes at the hem by hard walking, and splashed by the deep mud of the roads. While he talked, his thin hands held fast to the crucifix on the rosary which hung from his leather girdle.

"This is my son, good Friar," said Etheldreda, as Osmund

paused in the doorway. "He is but a child in years as you see, but discreet and brave, as becomes his father's son."

The tears rushed to her eyes as she spoke and she added in a lower tone: "Tell him, I pray you."

"Is my father dead?" asked the boy bluntly.

"Not yet dead, but like to die," answered the friar. "Unless God save him by His power."

"This good kind Brother David has risked his life to bring us thy father's letter," went on Etheldreda. "Prince John has seized his person on some lying charge of treason, and for months he has held him captive here close at hand in Nottingham Castle."

"At Nottingham!" exclaimed Osmund. "Why we passed within a few miles of the town when I fled from Southwell with—with our friend."

"Aye—my good, dear lord! No wonder I felt I could not leave this country. But that is not all, my son."

"I learned that Sir Fulk has been pressing for your noble father's death," continued the friar. "And none dared act without the consent of the Council of Regency. But now Prince John has returned and has signed the warrant to pleasure him and Fulk himself is riding from Westminster with it, hard upon my heels. Father Superior, grieving greatly that such an injustice should be done, gave me leave to seek the knight's friends, lest perchance they might purchase his release."

"My brothers—the Knight of Scarcliffe——" exclaimed the lady brokenly. "But, alas! There is no time!"

Osmund felt as though he were in a bad dream. A death warrant for his father, condemning him as a traitor! How could this be—was not his father the very pattern of chivalry—had he not sacrificed everything to serve the King?

He bit his lip hard and clenched his hands, determined not to give way. Hild, who had been standing by her mother, slipped out of the room.

"When does Fulk leave London, good Friar?" asked Osmund at length; he drew near his mother as he spoke, as though to give her courage.

"I know not, my son, but I rode in haste and was greatly mocked at on my journey, for, indeed such a mode of travelling ill suits our order. But think, Lady—have you no friends at hand?"

The lady slowly shook her head, but Osmund spoke eagerly.

"Aye, good mother—one friend!"

As she glanced up at him in surprise, he stooped to her ear and murmured "Robin!"

Her face flushed with a wild hope, then the colour ebbed again.

"My poor Osmund—we do not even know where he is—it may be a hundred miles away in Cumberland, or in the sea caves of Yorkshire."

"It is our only chance," declared the boy.

"I know not what to advise," declared Brother David. "For to fight against the Regent is certainly treasonable and yet to let the noble knight be done to death unaided were a sin indeed! If you could get some great person to protest—but then," he added confidently, "of course your friend must be a powerful noble!"

"Alas, Friar, he is but a poor outlaw—Robin Hood."

The monk's face fell in spite of himself, and he grew pale with dismay. The lady rose quickly and upbraided herself for not having provided him with food and drink.

"Come and warm yourself by the hall fire, while I bring forth some refreshment," she cried. "And, Osmund, take the horse and ride to Father Adam at Welbeck with all speed."

"Alack, Lady—I come from there. The Abbot is away on a journey, the Vicar ill abed, and the Novice-Master could but give me directions to find you here."

They had passed into the solar as they were speaking and Osmund only waited to bolt the door before flying to the secret drawer. His fingers shook so much in his impatience that he could not at first touch the spring, but a second attempt was successful, and a moment later he was clasping Maid Marian's green belt across his shoulder. He went rapidly through the hall, overtaking his mother as she went down the steps to the buttery, whither Dame Alice had already preceded her.

"Stay, my son, you will need money," she cried. "And you will have to take one of the horses from the plough. But you are so young—what can you do—where will you go?"

"First I'll leave a signal for Friar Tuck, Mother, and then I'll ride on and find Robin and his men."

"But we know not where to seek——"

"You must pray, Mother, and God will show me the way."

The lady looked at him anxiously, but making no further demur she took her long silken purse from her girdle and put it into his hand. Osmund secured it under his tunic and seizing his hood and cloak ran down into the courtyard. To his surprise the better of the two horses was already there, tied to a ring and steaming with heat after his labour in the field: Hild came staggering out of the stable carrying the saddle.

"Where's Tom?" asked the boy in surprise, as he took the harness from her, placed it on the horse and began to tighten the girths.

Hild tossed her head.

"Oh, he's ploughing with old Bess. I didn't know if our mother was going to say aught to the servants, but I knew you would need a horse, brother, so I thought I would get it ready."

"All praise to thy quick wit, Hild!" exclaimed her brother, his voice slightly muffled by the saddle-flap which he held up with his head, while he strained at the girth.

"And I've got the pony here, too," continued Hild eagerly. "For it would surely be wise for you to show me where Friar Tuck lies——"

"You!" interrupted Osmund in amazement.

Hild stamped her foot.

"Oh, brother, do not waste time! You know I am good at remembering a path. My mother cannot rush out of the house at a moment's notice without having all the folk a-gog. I'll be back before I'm missed and then I can guide my mother to meet Tuck tomorrow. What's that belt?" she added.

Osmund explained as they rode, the little pony jogging along beside the dapple-grey, which had begun life gloriously as my lady's palfrey and was now of service to till her scanty fields. Hild was quite accustomed to riding and Osmund had no fear of her being unable to manage her mount, but he was anxious lest she might fall in with other perils as she rode home alone. The forest was full of dangers and the girl might meet thieves or rogues of a very different type to Robin and his men. There were wild beasts to be reckoned with, too, and the Verderer might stay her or frighten her. Hild was quite aware of Osmund's thoughts and shared his fears, but she determined to be brave.

"We must not think of 'lets' and 'buts,'" she declared resolutely. "But only of our noble father and how best to save him."

But after all her valour was not to be put to the test, for as they presently rode down a little glade where a forester was at work, the man glanced at Osmund, stared for a moment, and then dropped his axe and ran after the riders.

"Ho, you with the belt!" he shouted. "Stay a moment—I'm your man."

Osmund hastily wheeled his horse between his sister and the woodman who was quite unknown to him.

The forester saluted civilly.

"I must take orders from anyone wearing my mistress's belt," he declared. "What errand has Maid Marian for me?"

"Robin has need of a strong band armed," declared Osmund promptly. "Know you where any of his men lie?"

"Aye, I can find three—maybe more," returned the other. "Where are we to meet—at Friar Tuck's great beech by the three——"

He broke off, waiting to see if the boy would complete the phrase.

Osmund held out his hand which had three white pebbles in it.

"I would you could do me another service," he cried. "'Tis to see my sister here safe home after I have shown her the beech. We come from the Grange yonder—a little further than the warren."

"Gladly will I do so," rejoined the woodman. "And you, young Master with the belt—whither are you going?"

"I'm searching for Robin Hood himself," confessed Osmund frankly. "Maid Marian bade me use this girdle in case of need, and now my father is in dire peril and I know that Robin will help us if I can only reach him in time."

"A word in your ear, young master. Speak to the blind beggar at the four cross-roads on the way towards Watling Street. The beggar can send a message almost as fast as a homing pigeon."

"But he won't know who Osmund is, and if he can't see the belt how will he recognise it?" asked Hild.

The woodman winked.

"Oh, the beggar is not so blind as all that!" he cried with a jovial laugh. "And all that company are sworn to serve Robin, who is a good friend to every vagrant. You can trust him, young master, once he has set his blind eyes on your belt. Ho! Ho!"

"Do you mean he's a cheat?" asked Hild greatly surprised and shocked. "Isn't he blind at all?"

"Not too blind to find Robin at all events," declared the woodman. "But go you on—the cross-roads are fifteen miles away. I'll go get my axe and follow towards the beech. And I be to meet you yonder at moon-rise tomorrow, as usual, I suppose?"

"Yes," said Osmund. "And let those who can come mounted, for we have far to go. Farewell, good friend."

Hild had already trotted on, for she knew Osmund's larger horse could easily overtake her. The beech was soon reached, and the stones placed. Osmund blew a long blast on his horn, in the hope that Friar Tuck might be on the island. But there was no reply and no smoke was going up from the reed-thatched hut.

"If I cannot get home tonight I will return here or send a messenger to meet you here tomorrow," said Osmund. "My plan is to beg Robin to intercept the death warrant—yes, if necessary to attack Fulk on the march."

"There's very little time," rejoined Hild, sadly. "Men can ride post from London in less than two days to Nottingham. But God speed you, brother. Do not get into more danger than you can help."

She held down her head so that he should not see the tears in her eyes, called out rather chokingly: "God be with you, brother," and wheeling her pony, rode back along the way she had come.

Osmund waved his hand and went forward in the opposite direction, following the margin of the pool until he came to the path which Friar Tuck had shown him. It was a long ride, mostly through forest tracks. Watling Street was reached at last—not the real Watling Street, Eadgar always insisted, but the main road which country people called by this name.

The blind beggar was certainly a fraud for he jumped up as soon as Osmund turned the corner of the road and came towards him, balancing his great staff in his hand in a threatening manner.

He usually stooped and limped and pretended to be very infirm, but now he stood upright and challenged Osmund loudly.

"Where stole you that belt? I declare you came not by it honestly!"

"The lady to whom it belongs gave it to me with her own hands, and I seek her now with great urgency, hoping through her to find——" Osmund stopped, wondering if it were safe to name Robin Hood.

The beggar's angry look was instantly replaced by a broad smile.

"What, are you one of Robin's men? Beshrew me, but I thought you somewhat young! Why, Robin was here, but an hour ago and left us to ride towards the Peak country. But your horse is tired—I'll lend you a better one."

He put his fingers into his mouth and gave a very loud whistle. There was evidently some special meaning in its modulations for in a few moments a ragged boy came running out of a lane leading a stout cob saddled and bridled.

It was no moment to stand upon ceremony and though Osmund wondered if the beast had been honestly come by, he said nothing, but changed horses with all speed. The pretended blind man ordered the lad to show him a short cut by which he could catch up Robin Hood, and promised to collect such followers of the outlaw who lived in the neighbourhood and march them down to Tuck's beech.

It was growing late in the afternoon before Osmund heard at last the faint notes of Robin Hood's bugle. He sounded his own horn as loudly as he could and to his joy the outlaw heard and answered it.

They met at last in a little clearing in a ring of blackthorn bushes and Osmund scarcely paused to salute Robin before pouring out his story.

The outlaw decided swiftly.

"We have thirty men here," he said. "Our best hope is to ride to Nottingham with all speed and strive to waylay Fulk before he reaches the town. You, George-the-Pinder, go bear this token to Friar Tuck and bid him follow us to the secret cavern under the Castle rock at Nottingham. And you, Arthur à Bland, must take a good horse and ride forthwith into Yorkshire."

As Robin spoke he took the gold chain from his neck and gave it to the Pinder while Arthur was entrusted with his ring. Osmund could not hear the instructions which accompanied the token for Robin led his man aside and spoke to him low and urgently.

"And now to horse!" he shouted at last, vaulting lightly into the saddle. "Ride, men, ride for the honour of Sherwood and for the life of noble Aelfric."

"And my mother! Dear Master Robin, will you not bid Friar Tuck to have my mother in his care? She was to meet him at the beech tomorrow," explained Osmund.

"I will e'en go with George and see that the lady has proper protection," said Marian. "And then I'll ride on to the cavern and await you there. God speed thee, Robin!"

Osmund glanced over his shoulder as they moved off and marked that the beautiful girl was gazing after them: the smile had faded from her lips and she looked sad and anxious: it made him realise the desperate peril of their enterprise.

CHAPTER TWENTY

Jt must not be imagined that Abbot Adam and his Community had forgotten their friends at the Grange or had been careless of their welfare all this time. Though the Abbot had many anxieties both general and particular, he had never ceased to importune the leading Churchmen of the country for tidings of his friend, Sir Aelfric de Southwell. The gallant knight had accompanied King Richard on his glorious crusade and had last been heard of when the English Army had been deserted by Philip of France and his followers, as they lay in camp, almost in sight of Jerusalem. The Prior had sent a messenger to Longchamp, before he fell from power, but the Chancellor's reply was negative: he had not heard any rumours of Aelfric's death, save those circulated by Prince John. As these rumours coincided with Fulk's lawless seizure of Southwell Manor and demesne, Father Adam was not inclined to believe them. His Abbey had been brought into direct conflict with Fulk by the destruction of the Mill and the monks might not have borne the insult so meekly had they not been anxious to avoid any feud which might involve the defenceless lady at the Grange.

Now things were going from bad to worse. If John seized the throne, the horrible disorders and bloodshed of Stephen's reign might be repeated. It was above all necessary to save the English people from a similar period of civil war and anarchy, and all loyal churchmen were agreed in their effort to raise the King's ransom and to re-establish him in his realm.

Father Adam had received alarming tidings that the Prince had seized all the Channel ports, and that he was making such stores of arms and provisions as he could.

The country had been drained by Richard's levies to provide supplies for his crusade: Gloucestershire alone had provided fifty thousand horseshoes, and Northampton sixty thousand "pens" (or goose quills) for feathering arrows. The Abbot reflected on these things as he rode along, followed by two monks and a short baggage train. He was on his way to Ely to visit William de Longchamp, who was in retirement in his own See. The Chancellor's retinue of a thousand knights had melted away after his fall from power and ignominious attempt to fly from England in 1191. Though he had patched up his quarrel with Prince John and had courageously returned to England on Richard's business, he was fully aware that he was surrounded by enemies of whom John was the most dangerous, though outwardly professing affection. Even his friends looked upon the Bishop of Ely as a doomed man and held aloof from him, and Father Adam had pondered long before venturing on the present step. He had no very high opinion of Longchamp, but realised that he was perhaps the only man in England of the King's party who could give true tidings of Richard's plight. The Abbot carried with him a letter from saintly Hugh of Lincoln.

The Spring floods had not yet subsided and it was more than likely that the whole fenland would be under water, in spite of the many drains and dykes which traversed Cambridgeshire.

The Abbot had determined to travel by Stamford and Peterborough, but he now regretted that he had not taken boat at Boston, crossed the Wash in spite of tidal dangers, and sailed up the Ouse to Ely. He and his followers had managed to traverse the River Trent at Nottingham, but had now lost the road in a waste of shallow flood-water some ten miles further on. The horses were wet and exhausted, Brother Daniel's mule showed an alarming desire to lie down and roll in the muddy pools, and the guide whom they had hired at Nottingham admitted that he had lost the way.

It would have been disagreeable enough to spend the night shivering in the wet pastures, for there was no village in sight, but there were other and more pressing dangers. A troop of horsemen had been hanging on their flanks for the last half-hour—never coming near enough to hail—and now another band was discernible, advancing from the south.

Father Adam's baggage contained little money or articles of tempting value, but he was acutely conscious of Hugh of Lincoln's letter which he carried in his breast. There were some plain statements in it which would be anything but pleasant to Lackland's party, and which might cost the bearer his life if it fell into the wrong hands. Yet Adam was determined not to destroy it save as a very last resource, as he relied upon it to strengthen his plea that the Church must set her face implacably against any attempt at usurpation. Hugh agreed that prelates must encourage their flocks to stand firm for their righteous King and just Government—the oath of fealty and the reign of law and order here went hand in hand.

"They are knights yonder," remarked Brother Leonard, pointing ahead.

"They are not knights behind us then," retorted Brother Daniel, dragging up his mule's head for the hundredth time, "for when they passed that causeway a while ago, there was scarce a sound, nor yet a spark from the flintstones—and who rides in large companies with unshod horses? Not honest merchants!"

"Outlaws, probably," admitted Father Adam. "We must risk the dykes and push forward while there is still a gleam of light in the west. Take my staff, good knave, and probe the ground. See thou lead us not into a quagmire."

As the little band went slowly on a light twinkled out in mid-air ahead of them. It was a frequent custom in this dangerous country to set a lantern in a Church tower as a guide to travellers, and many good Christians left bequests for this charitable purpose.

"God be praised!" exclaimed the Abbot fervently.

"I told you my holy patron St. Leonard would lead us safe!" cried the brother on the horse.

"St. Leonard is the patron of all travellers," agreed Father Adam.

The guide shouted that his feet were on a good made road, and the tired wayfarers hurried after him and were soon advancing at a round trot.

Presently faint glimmers from cottage windows were seen and in a few minutes the monks came to a village with a comfortable inn. The host was delighted to receive so honourable a guest as the Abbot of Welbeck: he led him into his best guest-chamber, kindled a fire, and brought out his finest flitch of bacon.

Monks and servants sat down to table together, as was their humble custom, but hardly had they set hands to the dish, when the little street outside was filled with the clatter of horses and lancers.

"'Tis the Prince's men!" exclaimed mine host. "They passed here at noon and have been turned back by the water."

"I shall invoke the holy prophet," said Brother Daniel, who never could refrain from a jest. "Oh, by thy bowl of pulse and bread, good patron, save our supper!"

The Abbot rose up and went to the window. One hand was thrust into his breast and played with the seal of the letter which lay under his white cassock: his rochet was drying before the fire.

"It is Fulk de Brent!" he murmured, after one hasty glance, and stooping down as though to fling a log on to the hearth, he pushed his letter under the rushes.

A moment later the knight bent his towering casque to enter the low-ceiled room. He was out of temper at the delay in his journey, for he was in a great hurry to accomplish his evil mission. He recognised the Abbot of Welbeck with a rude stare, to which the courageous son of St. Norbert returned a courteous salutation.

"What dost thou here, beggarly monk?" enquired the Norman. "Out of my sight and back to thy Abbey! I have here the death-warrant of thy friend and patron, and if thou dost not wring from thy fat lands a rich gift to allay the Prince's anger, thou and thy monks shall participate in his fate."

It was very discourteous of the Baron to use the familiar "thou" in addressing a dignitary of the Church, but Father Adam answered quietly.

"If you speak of Sir Aelfric de Southwell or Sir Hugo de Scarcliffe, you must be under grave error, for I declare neither of these noble and Christian knights would ever do deed unworthy of his vows."

Fulk coloured furiously for he knew well that no one could truthfully say the same of him.

"How long can a man live without his head?" he asked brutally. "So long has Aelfric to live after I reach Nottingham and no longer. So begone to thy Abbey and chant his requiem forthwith for I require thy lodging here."

So saying he seated himself in the Abbot's chair and shouted to the host to bring him wine.

The man knew his danger but was of the obstinate English type which declines to be brow-beaten.

"We've no wine here," he said, stumping into the room and setting his dish of frizzling rashers on the table. "And we're honest folk—and fair is fair. The monks ordered the supper and the sleeping chamber and I'll not have 'em turned out, unless 'tis King's orders."

"I'll have thee flogged at thy own cart-tail, thou presuming rogue!" exclaimed Fulk. "Here men! Away with the churl!"

Honest Jerry was hustled out of the room by a couple of squires, who had to call men-at-arms to their aid. During the scuffle, the Abbot protested vigorously, but vainly. He and his party were rudely pushed into the street while the Norman and his men took possession of the whole lodging.

The Abbot paused irresolute. He was so filled with grief and horror on his friend's account that he hardly appreciated his own peril.

"Aelfric to die! If the Prince hath so far prevailed with the Council against the King's friend, things are bad indeed!" he muttered.

"Father Abbot, here are the other folk down on us now!" exclaimed Wat, the serf.

It was now nearly night and the village people could be heard hastily barring themselves into their houses for word had flown round that there was a riot at the tavern.

There was a warm smell of horses in the air, but only a light tapping of unshod hoofs as two or three men rode down the centre of the cobbled street. The Prior, whose eyes were getting accustomed to the dim light, discerned a series of curved points moving up behind the foremost rider.

"What, are ye honest archers?" he exclaimed.

"Free yeomen, be we," returned a voice. "Knights of the road and lords of the forest glade."

"Master," cried another voice. "Is it the Abbot? It sounds like the tone of dear Father Adam."

"Who is that?" exclaimed the Abbot.

In answer he found his hand seized and respectfully kissed by someone who was kneeling on the wet stones before him.

"Father Prior—it is I—Osmund Fitz Aelfric. What are you doing here? We thought there was a brawl going forward!"

"Is there any honest Englishman here who will stand by me and prevent a crime?" exclaimed the Abbot. His head swam with fatigue and anxiety; he felt he was losing grip of his usual sound judgment.

"FATHER PRIOR—IT IS I—OSMUND FITZ
AELFRIC."

"'Tis outlaws and if they attack the bearer of a Warrant 'tis felony!" gasped Brother Daniel.

The light from an open door fell on the riders and showed their green liveries and long-bows for a moment.

"Soft!" whispered someone close beside the Abbot. "It is Fulk de Brent and his men who lie in the tavern yonder, and brings he a warrant——"

"Aye, indeed, and that for the death of good Sir Aelfric!" interrupted Brother Daniel.

"Fear nothing, dear Father Prior," said Osmund. "Here is brave Robin Hood and thirty stout bow-men, and he declares the warrant for my father's death shall never cross the river as long as he breathes."

"But Fulk has fifty men and acts by Prince John's orders!" gasped the monk.

"We mustn't bring Father Adam into it, Robin," urged Osmund. "Should he not go forward on his journey before we attack?"

"Be wary, cousin," urged Scarlet. "If Fulk has fifty men to our thirty, it were best to waylay them at the ford, where our bows can have full play. They have the advantage of us now, as a boar in covert."

"The poor tavern-keeper is to be whipped for befriending me," said Adam. "Yet I scruple that ye should bring your heads in peril in drawing bows against the Prince's man."

"We're on our own business," declared Robin Hood, "and will make honest Jerry part of it. Have they your baggage within?"

"Aye, and four sumpter horses, a mule and the Prior's palfrey," cried Wat.

"And a most private paper, which I hid beneath the rushes near the hearth," confessed the Prior. "I would that I had burnt it."

They were interrupted by an outcry in the tavern yard.

"Hist! What is that?" whispered one of the outlaws.

The whole band retreated up the street and shrank back into the shadow of the churchyard yews, seeming to move as silently as though they were shadows themselves.

A group of young men came out of the inn carrying lanterns and a farm cart was dragged forth and placed in the road. Two or three sheaves of straw were piled on the green and set on fire to the great danger of neighbouring thatched roofs, and then the watchers saw the stout, burly figure of the host, and that of a thin, tall, gaily-dressed man, dragged out. Both were kicking and struggling vainly.

"Oh, look, Robin, look, that is Wido! Fulk must have captured him on the road. Please don't let him be flogged!" begged Osmund.

"Away, Sir Monk! 'Twere better you were no witness to this," whispered Robin. "Two of my men shall escort you to the next village, and there your horses and belongings shall be brought to you tomorrow. Away, Sir!"

The Abbot would fain have urged Osmund to accompany him, but the boy seemed to have disappeared, and Robin's men, having received their orders, were deaf to any other suggestions. The Monk and his followers were mounted half against their wills, and led off into the darkness at a rapid pace, for their two guides were anxious to land them in safety and get back before the fun was over.

It was Osmund's first fight and he was trembling with excitement as he tightened his bow-string and loosened the arrows in his quiver as the other men were doing.

Robin spoke his orders.

"We will shoot by name," he said. "I will call the names and ye will each send an arrow first at those men-at-arms standing by with whips, and then at the folk who will come tumbling out of the inn to their help. Tie up horses. Is 't in bowshot, Will?"

Scarlet, who could slay a buck at forty yards, decided that they would have to advance a hundred paces.

"No bow for you, Blackbird!" declared Robin Hood, plucking away the boy's cherished weapon. "Take this knife and when I give the word, run in, cut the prisoners' bonds and bring them here. Lie low all, until I cry 'À Robin.'"

He stepped out of the shadows into the flickering glare of the burning straw and marching rapidly down to the green, he cried commandingly:

"Halt! By whose orders is this done?"

"What's that to you! Stand back, rogue, or we'll make thee a third!" cried the Captain of Fulk's band. "Lay on, I say, and spare not!"

The troopers raised their whips, and were about to strike when Robin called:

"Scarlet!"

An arrow came singing through the dusk and transfixed the upraised arm.

The man fell over his prisoner, shrieking with pain and fright.

Robin had drawn back out of sight, but continued to name his men: a well-aimed arrow was the prompt response to each call and soon the tavern roared like a hive of bees, and men came pouring out, some carrying arms and some the pint pots in which they had been drinking.

Fulk was no coward and was one of the first to reach the street.

"To me, men!" he shouted. "Out pikes, and charge! Clear me the street, ho! À Brent! À Brent!"

"Run round behind the houses!" whispered Robin in Osmund's ear. "Be quick! Else those two bound men will be slain!"

As soon as the boy was safe out of the street, Robin gave a low whistle.

Fulk's men charged valiantly, but they met with no resistance, and their war-cry echoed foolishly over the flooded fields: the foe had disappeared!

The pikemen stamped about, shouting to each other and rattling their spear-shafts against closed doors. There was dead silence inside the houses and dead silence in the yew-trees though thirty tall young men were clinging to their branches, or standing motionless against the trunks with their hoods pulled round their faces.

Osmund found a great many obstacles in the rear of the little houses; he fell over fences and roused all the dogs that were not already barking. At last he scrambled out breathless and scratched over the last wash-house on to the village green. The bonfire was burning out, but there was sufficient light left to show that the prisoners were unguarded. Osmund cut their bonds, wielding the keen knife with great care, and Wido instantly threw himself underneath the cart, where he thought he would be safe from flying arrows.

Jerry rushed into the stables for his stout quarter-staff, and Osmund, his heart pounding, hurried to the tavern and looked in through the window from which Fulk had been leaning a moment ago. The room was all in disorder, with the food still on the table and the lamp flaring in the draught.

There lay Fulk's saddlebags with his crimson cloak tossed across them. The enemy must return directly, Osmund knew, and his mouth went dry. He did not hesitate, but scrambled through the window, and crept across to the door. He was well aware that he held his life in his hand, but he moved deliberately—any noise might wreck his enterprise. First he closed the door, securing it on the inside with the wooden bolt, and then flew to the saddlebags, and sliced at the straps with his dagger, there was no time to undo buckles for the foe was already returning: they were almost at the door.

"Beware, Osmund, beware!" shrieked Wido from under the cart.

The boy left his task and ran to close the window, though it was but a frail protection against fifty armed men.

"Put out the fire," he called. And then, as he cut and tore at the heavy wallet, he prayed aloud:

"Oh, sweet Lord Saviour! Oh, Mary, blessed Lady, help me to destroy the warrant even if it costs me my life!"

Chapter Twenty-One

Fulk de Brent was tired, wet, cold, hungry and furious. An inglorious struggle in the dark with robbers added the last touch of misfortune to an unpleasant day. He was determined they should pay dearly for their attack.

"To me, Captain!" he shouted. "Rally your men! Form in line there, and do not let the rogues escape! Hanging is too good for them! Who is on guard at the tavern?"

The Captain did not answer but continued to call up his men by name. He had not appointed either guards or sentries, not deeming that there was any likelihood of attack.

"The warrant!" exclaimed Fulk. "Dog! thou shalt answer with thy life if my wallet hath been touched!"

"Back to the Inn, the lances of St. Lo!" bawled the Captain.

Twenty men, armed with lances struggled towards him. They were horse-soldiers, accustomed to fighting mounted, in broad daylight, and they were bewildered by this skirmish in the dark.

The Captain's casque gleamed as he swung round and instantly two arrows struck it. He fell headlong in the road, but the well-tempered steel saved his head.

"Back to the Inn!" ordered Fulk and there was a rush forward, men stumbling against each other and swearing aloud as their arms clashed together.

Meanwhile, Osmund had scattered the contents of the wallet on the floor; the first bag yielded nothing, but the second held the great parchment square with heavy seals upon it, carefully wrapped in a strip of lambskin.

The fire was burning brightly and Osmund thrust in the warrant, but the parchment would not catch. The men-at-arms were battering at door and window and Osmund picked out the scorched warrant and slit it desperately with his dagger. The strips crackled wildly and curled up—the words "Death" and "Aelfric" leaped out in fiery letters and Osmund desperately piled on the embers. He could hear showers of blows striking the wall, but owing to Wido's promptitude in quenching the straw, they could not immediately find the window.

Osmund made sure that his last hour had come, but there was still time to serve Father Adam. He groped about on the floor under the soiled rushes, and just as the shutter fell in and hung shattered from its hinge, his fingers grasped the rolled letter and he flung it on the flames.

He swung round then towards the window, determined to die facing the enemy.

A man stood just outside, grinning with triumph as he aimed a mighty lance thrust at the boy. But the lance fell clattering to the ground and he sank down across the sill with a yell of pain, a long arrow quivering in his shoulder.

It was little Much's shot. He had followed Osmund and when the boy climbed into the house, the miller's son established himself on top of an adjacent haystack. He waited until the light from the broken window enabled him to make good aim and then quickly fitting another arrow, he loosed it off at the next man.

Osmund stood stockstill, stunned with surprise at his own escape. The door still held, but the upper panel cracked ominously. Then he looked round and, spying another shuttered window at the far end of the room, ran towards it. The parchment flared and then died down leaving the room in semi-darkness and opening the window cautiously, Osmund dropped down on to a woodpile. Much's low whistle guided him to the stack, but his knees shook under him and he had great difficulty in scrambling up.

"They are in the room! Look how they run to and fro between door and window!" whispered Much with a chuckle. "Let's have another shot and then back to the Master."

He aimed high and his bolt struck the house and glanced off into the street. Osmund lay flat beside him trying to get his breath, while Much emptied his quiver.

The outlaws had evidently attacked Fulk in the rear to judge by the noise, but it was impossible to see what was happening.

At length a bugle note rang out, sweet and shrill behind the Church.

"Come on," murmured Much.

They slid down on the far side of the stack and making a wide cast behind the backyards and gardens of the straggling street, they came up with Robin's men, just as they were leading out their horses.

A line of picked archers knelt behind the churchyard wall, keeping attack at bay, until all the horses were out of the enclosure. Meanwhile Robin was calling over his men and Much and Osmund came panting up just in time to answer to their names.

"Good!" cried Robin. "Now mount and away, my merry men! Scatter all! To Sherwood!"

Horses and men were both used to moving at night. The men-at-arms heard a splash or two coming from different directions and loosed off their cross-bows blindly. No bolt found its mark, and mocking voices called back, now right, now left:

"Sherwood! Sherwood!"

The foresters made their way through the flooded country as easily as Jack-o'-Lanterns, or so it appeared. Robin had previously appointed a meeting-place at a lonely farm, standing on rising ground a mile or two north of the village.

By degrees the whole band came in and made themselves very comfortable for the night in the hay-loft. Foragers had provided bread and cheese and a flagon of ale, which was dispatched in the dark.

Robin appointed six men to watch in pairs through the night and then settled himself down in the sweet-scented bedding:

"Rest first and a council at dawn," he declared.

He seemed to fall asleep directly judging by his soft even breathing, but Osmund lay awake. His father's danger haunted him, for though the warrant was destroyed, the hapless knight was still fast in prison. When Osmund dropped off to sleep it was only to wake with a start, with the outlandish cries of Fulk's Free Lances echoing in his ears, or the nightmare vision of the threatening spear fading in the darkness.

He knelt up at last and tried to repeat such parts of the psalter as he knew by heart, and though this reminded him of the mournful tale of Waltheof, the beautiful verses soothed and comforted him, and presently he sank back into the hay and slept.

When Osmund woke, Robin Hood was nowhere to be seen. Much and Scarlet were cleaning their horses when he came out of the barn, but the other outlaws had vanished.

The farmer thought it wiser to take no notice of the strangers in green livery, and was rewarded by a gold piece glittering at the bottom of a milking pail.

"Why didn't you wake me? Where is Robin?" shouted Osmund as he ran down to join his friends.

"Robin's orders," returned Scarlet laconically. "Get thy steed, Blackbird, we'll eat breakfast as we ride."

"But where's the chief?" demanded the boy again.

Scarlet merely shook his head, and Osmund's heart sank.

It was a fresh spring morning and sheltered banks were already showing celandines in flower. A pair of great hawks were quartering the flooded fields as the outlaws went along. Scarlet said they were Marsh Harriers, and Osmund, as he watched the great birds now beating slowly above the reedy expanse, now soaring high in the air, or sailing on strong upraised wings, thought what sport it would be to rear and train a young bird and match it against his father's falcons. But with the thought his sorrow came back upon him, and he urged his horse on and again begged Scarlet to tell him where Robin Hood had gone.

"Why, to gather the band, Blackbird, and to find out if there is any chance of gaining the Castle."

"Oh, Will, you know that could never be! How could archers, even the noblest and bravest, take a strong place such as Nottingham? They have mangonels, habergeons and all sorts of siege-engines there, and a picked garrison!"

"There is small chance of success as thou sayest, Blackbird," rejoined Will with a sigh. "But if Robin makes an attempt, be it never so desperate, be sure we will die for him to the last man."

Osmund could not speak, but he held out his hand and Scarlet stooped down and wrung it.

"We have gained a few days at least," he said encouragingly. "And who knows what may happen in a few days? I doubt not our Robin hath some trick up his sleeve."

The water was going down and the river was crossed without much difficulty about noon. Scarlet led the way close up to the town and behind some thick bushes at the foot of the escarpment which was crowned by the Castle wall. Here was the hidden mouth of one of those strange caverns with which the district abounded, and here they found Maid Marian awaiting them and food prepared.

Marian was unwontedly serious.

"We have strange news," she said presently. "I have been in the town this morning, selling heather brooms—there was no danger, Will—who should know me here? The town-crier was going his rounds and he proclaimed a sad, strange thing."

"My father's execution, I suppose?" faltered Osmund as she paused.

"Yes, Blackbird, I must needs tell you. He proclaimed your father as a traitor to the King, announced that he lay bound in the deepest dungeon, and must die as soon as the Council sent down the warrant—but that is not all."

"Sir Aelfric is no traitor—'tis a foul lie!" cried Osmund. "Do they threaten my mother's life also?"

"Nay, but they invite all relations and whilom friends of the condemned man to come—under a safe conduct—to bid him farewell."

"I'll go!" cried Osmund, starting up.

"Oh, no, you must not! It means certain death!" exclaimed Marian. "'Tis the most open trap—sure no one could walk into it. There is not one man among them one can trust—Hal Sheriff, Guy de Gisborne, Hugh de——"

"Nevertheless I must go," repeated Osmund with determination. "My mother will have Eadgar to comfort her, and I cannot let my father die alone."

"But you must be guided by Robin, Blackbird," declared Marian. "He bid me wait him here and surely he will be with us soon."

"And so I will be guided! But you'll see—Robin will agree with me."

Marian announced that Robin had gone to hasten some friends from Yorkshire. He had sent George of Wakefield to summon them after first hearing Osmund's tale. There was also a big gathering of outlaws in Sherwood ready to protect Etheldreda and the children.

It was the most tedious day that Osmund had ever spent and it seemed strange to him that everything around should go on just as usual: birds singing and building their nests, women washing linen in the stream, sheep driven in to the fair, and wool-merchants chaffering on the bridge just as if there were no horrible tragedy impending.

"Perhaps before the sun goes down tomorrow I shall be dead," thought Osmund, for he had no illusions about the danger of the part he proposed to play.

At length about an hour before sunset Robin Hood came in, so quietly that no one saw him until he greeted Marian.

"Good e'en, sweet maid!"

"Robin! I trow you startled me. Well, are they come?"

"Aye, they are but a mile or two behind me. Yet unless we can get a message to our man——"

"Listen, Robin," interrupted Marian. "Blackbird has a request to make." She told quickly of the proclamation and Osmund's resolve to answer it.

"Everyone says it is but the sorriest plot to capture all the poor knight's family and slay them," she added.

"Aye, doubtless. Nevertheless it is Osmund's right to stand by his father in this sore strait if he so desires. But ponder well, Blackbird! No one can think the worse of your honour or courage if you do not take this desperate risk."

"But will it do the knight any good?" asked Marian. "Nay, if boy die too, it will be the last drop of bitterness in his cup of sorrow."

Osmund stood stock still, considering: then he looked up at Robin.

"I can never be happy again if I do not go. I must stand by my father even—even if I cannot help him."

Marian began to murmur something, but Robin Hood shook his head.

"Nay, maid, the lad speaks truth. And Blackbird, there's just a chance that thou mayst yet save Sir Aelfric. We dare not attempt to wrap a rope round thee for they will certainly search thee, and in any case the knight will be in fetters. But if thou canst reach his cell and by sign or sound show us where thou art, 'twill be strange if I win not to thee."

"I owe you my life already," began the boy.

"Where's my flageole?" interrupted Robin. "Stick this in thy belt, Blackbird. I'll explain as we go for they'll close the gates at sunset and there's not a moment to lose. Get me a disguise, Marian—a tinker's—a charm-vender's——"

"Nay, Robin, I have little here. These white weeds which Friar Tuck plucked from Hal Hardfist's head cook and——"

"That will do! I'll be a cook!" cried Robin, bursting into a peal of laughter which echoed strangely round the rocky walls. "Fit me out a basket as though I were returning in haste from a late marketing. I'll discourse you so cookishly of crust and capon that——"

"But master, you cannot bear a bow if you go dressed as a cook!" exclaimed Scarlet.

"I'll go armed with spit and ladle!" cried Robin, jovially. "Fear not, Marian. Stay you here till our friends arrive. I'll return ere the gates are closed."

Marian stepped forward impulsively as though about to make a further appeal: but she checked herself with a great effort.

"We have our part," she whispered. "All is not lost yet. God be with you, Blackbird! Trust Robin!"

Osmund asked Marian to keep his purse and then went up the slope to the town gate: Robin followed a few minutes later and they both disappeared into the crowded street.

The town-crier's bell presently began to toll: and after a time his strident tones were faintly audible:

"Oyez, oyez, oyez! Good people!"

Marian stopped her ears and turned back into the cavern.

Chapter Twenty-Two

Nottingham Castle had been rebuilt by William the Conqueror on the remains of a previous fortress. It stood in a commanding position, perched on crags of soft sandstone rock. The whole town was of ancient origin; tradition said that it dated from the time when folk dwelt in the caves with which the river cliffs were honeycombed, and that its name was a corruption of Snottingha-ham or 'town of caverns.'

The Great Hall was a gloomy place: the floor rushes had been so long unchanged that they had darkened almost to blackness and exhaled a dismal odour. The universal custom of flinging all bones, gristle and the unpalatable portions of a dish under the table for the dogs to dispose of, did not tend to improve the condition of the floor. The Castle had for years been used merely as a military post, and there was no lady in residence to see to the cleanliness of the rooms or to the renewal of hangings or rushes. True, Richard had held a parliament there, before departing for the Crusade, but he was accustomed to rough camp ways, and it had been considered sufficient preparation to scatter a few fresh rushes on top of the old mouldy ones. When Prince John came to hunt, he avoided the Castle altogether and installed himself in the utmost luxury at Clipstone.

To add to its unattractiveness the Castle had twice been burnt in the civil wars of the last hundred years, and the roof of the great hall still bore traces of the flames in blackened timbers and charred vault. The wind whistled shrilly through the arrow-slits in the walls, and drew round the edges of the great screens set on either side of the hearth.

Baron Guy de Gisborne and his cronies Hugh de Balliol and Alberic Fitz Warren were keeping up their spirits by copious potations from the great black leather flagon which was the only vessel the Castle provided for carrying wine. When the Sheriff was presently announced, they had already imbibed pretty freely, and hailing him familiarly as a kindred spirit, they filled up the mazer, or large bowl, from which they were drinking turn and turn about, and invited him to propose a toast.

Hal Hardfist glanced over his shoulder and marking that the men-at-arms were out of earshot, he said boldly:

"I drink to the crowning of our good friend, Prince John, and to the downfall of all who stand between him and the throne."

"That is a bold toast," announced Guy, seizing the bowl as Hal set it down after a prolonged draught. "But I think we may quaff it in safety!"

"Has thy jest of the town-crier produced any result, Hal?" enquired the Balliol.

"Aye, a young lad has presented himself and doubtless through him we can discover the rest of them," returned the Sheriff. "As soon as the warrant comes we can put the boy to the question—I have brought my torturer, who is very efficient, though I say it and he is my own man."

"I cannot think why Fulk tarries," grumbled Guy. "'Tis but a hundred and twenty-four miles to London—he should be here by now."

"Aye, but the roads are flooded," put in Alberic.

"There's another thing!" cried Hal Hardfist gleefully. "This boy who has walked so confidingly into the trap is the very same who slipped through our fingers at Southwell last Whitsuntide—I'm pretty sure of it, though he seems stubborn and stupid and admits nothing."

"Why, then, he was captured in flagrant rebellion against our Prince and was rescued by the vile robber, Robin Hood!" returned Guy. "We'll get all needful information from him and hang him with his sire."

"No, that won't do," declared Hugh. "The English people are strange folk and don't relish the murder of children."

"Very well then, he can die in prison," said the Sheriff soothingly, for the other barons had turned furious faces on the Northumbrian. "It is always foolish to fly in the face of popular prejudice. We'll behead the knight, or hang him as a traitor, and after the boy has told all he knows, we had best drop him down again into the deepest dungeon, and forget all about him. He will simply disappear."

"Shall we have him in?" asked Guy. "I long to hear news of Robin Hood, for I cannot relish food or drink while he cumbereth the ground."

The others agreed and Osmund was presently marched in between two soldiers. He had made up his mind that it was safer to say nothing at all for fear any imprudent speech might betray his friends. So to all questions, even when accompanied by blows, he replied in Saxon that he did not understand. The Sheriff then addressed him in the native tongue, but still Osmund shook his head and said: "I don't know."

"His wits are astray from shock and fright. Heave him down into the dungeon, men, and see he gets no food. When he begins to feel the pinch of hunger, he'll speak fast enough. Had he letters or money on him?"

"Nay, Sir—naught but a child's toy pipe! 'Tis my belief the creature is but a natural!"

"My torturer will extract some sense from him, I'll go warrant," murmured Hal, watching Osmund closely.

The boy strove to look perfectly vacant as he was led away, through the guard-room, across a court, down endless greasy damp steps, to a narrow stone passage lit only by a flickering lantern. Here one of the soldiers lifted a trapdoor and two others seized Osmund by the arms and thrust him down into a dark cell which struck cold for all its close airlessness. For a moment he hung dangling in the air and then was dropped on a heap of mouldy straw. The shock of the fall took his breath away but when the heavy steps of the men-at-arms had retreated he presently called out:

"Sir Aelfric! Father! Are you here?"

"Who speaks?" returned a faint voice, which Osmund thought to recognise. He got up and walked forward slowly, feeling his way with his foot.

The cell was quite dark. Its only aperture was a hole some ten inches square pierced through six feet of stone wall. No light came in and a painfully small supply of fresh air.

A narrow stone bench lay along one side of the cell and on this a man was sitting.

"Father! Is it you? I am Osmund Fitz-Aelfric."

The prisoner rose with a cry.

"My mother is safe, and the others," said the boy quickly. "And, with God's help, our friends will save us too."

Aelfric seized his son in his arms. He had resigned himself to die and had been buoyed up by the thought that he would suffer alone and that neither friends nor kindred would share his fate. And now at the eleventh hour his child had been captured by his enemies! Aelfric did not believe that there was the slightest chance of succour for either of them: he listened to Osmund's eager whispers dully and sank back on the bench with a groan.

"It is Robin Hood's plan," the boy repeated. "And when we hear the bell ringing for the Night Office at the Monastery, I am to begin to play."

"It is useless," returned his father heavily. "Brave men will throw away their lives in vain."

Osmund found it strangely difficult to keep awake until the appointed time. He talked to his father, and walked about the narrow space; he felt along the floor in the hope of finding a loose flag-stone, but all seemed as firm as the blocks of which the Castle was built. Finally he twisted a thin rope of straw and attaching his white scarf to one end, pushed it carefully along the air-hole until it hung out over the wall. Far away beneath rolled the river and Robin's cave, but it hardly seemed possible that even the woodlander's sharp eyes could distinguish his signal in the deep windy night.

Osmund had actually dropped asleep, his head resting on his father's knee when Sir Aelfric roused him.

"Listen, son, is not that the Monastery bell?"

Osmund rubbed his eyes, quite bewildered for the moment. Then he remembered his part, and pulled out his pipe. He was an indifferent performer at the best of times and could never introduce the merry trills and grace-notes which Robin used. He felt for the stops and blew into the pipe, and the reed gave out a shrill sharp note, which sounded painfully thin and small in the silence of the night.

At first the boy played wildly, but presently he settled down to such popular songs as he was able to render. When Osmund's breath failed from exhaustion the knight took the instrument and blew away valiantly, at first attempting noble chants, but soon declining to the popular marching-songs and the queer little Eastern airs which his men had sung on the Crusade. From time to time, Osmund would gaze earnestly through the tiny window. Sometimes there were stars to be seen, sometimes dark clouds hid them, but at last to his dismay, he saw the sky lightening with the grey glimmer that preludes dawn.

"Oh, Father," he cried, dropping the pipe. "'Tis almost day, and no one has come."

"Nevertheless we'll continue our music until it is fully light and all attempts at rescue must be abandoned," declared Aelfric. "'Tis better to die for the King than to live a traitor, Osmund, and I would not change places with Prince John."

"Aye, Father. And I'm not afraid to die with you."

In spite of his brave words, Osmund suddenly felt very cold. He wondered if Robin Hood had been discovered and slain and what would happen to Maid Marian. It was like being dead already to be shut up in this horrible dark cell where one could scarcely breathe and could neither hear nor see!

"This is the air which Blondel, the King's minstrel, played when he went from castle to castle in the Tyrol with William de Longchamps, seeking for Richard," said Aelfric. He put the pipe to his lips, but before a note sounded, Osmund grasped his arm.

"Listen, Father, listen! Hearest thou aught, or is it only the knocking of my own heartbeats?"

They both held their breath: down below their feet a pulsing noise was audible, as regular as the muffled ticking of a great clock.

Boom, bang! Boom! Boom! Boom!

Osmund picked up a broken iron fetter and pounded on the floor as hard as he could, while Sir Aelfric piped with all his might and main.

It was a race against the growing light, but every minute the sound of the pick-axes came nearer, and the prisoners were devoutly thankful for a heavy storm of rain, which darkened the sky, and doubtless pattered deafeningly on the leaden roof of the guard-room. At length the very floor began to quake under heavy blows from below and Aelfric and his son stood on the stone bench. This last hour seemed far longer than the whole night of anguish. Far overhead, they heard buglers sounding the réveillé and a second later the floor cracked and a shower of stone splinters flew up into the room.

Chapter Twenty-Two

"Robin!" cried Osmund eagerly, leaping down and tearing away the broken edges.

"Hold!" answered a strange voice. "Thou'rt clodding me in the eyes, lad. Stand back till we wield our picks. Art thou he they call Blackbird, and is feyther there?"

"Aye!" returned Osmund, wondering to hear a broad Yorkshire accent.

"Stand back then, lad. Steady, mates!" The man withdrew his head and working in an almost incredibly small space, quickly enlarged the hole.

"Get the boy out as soon as you can," besought Aelfric. "The guard may enter at any moment."

"Nay, we'll go together!" insisted Osmund boldly.

He withdrew his scarf from the window, and waited with what patience he could until the tunnel was wide enough to allow of Sir Aelfric's passage.

He prayed his father to go first and while the prisoner lowered himself with difficulty, helped from beneath, Osmund gathered the refuse under the straw and dragged the whole bundle over the top of the hole as he slipped into it in his turn.

.   .   .   .   .

"Master Robin," said Aelfric courteously as they all stood breathless and dusty in the cave at the end of the tunnel, "we owe you great thanks."

"We're not safe yet," replied the outlaw. "Come, will you accept my guidance, Sir Knight, and be our guest in our noble palace of Greenleaf?"

"He means go with him to Sherwood Forest," murmured Osmund.

"Aye, right willingly. But first give me arms, for I think we shall scarce get out of the borough without a fray," returned Aelfric.

Two men had been busily filing through his fetters and he now stretched forth his arms with a sigh of relief.

The outlaws began to slip out of the cave in groups of twos and threes. Some of them climbed the rocks so as to command the road, others faced the gate and were drawn up defiantly, each with bow bent and arrow fixed, in case there should be a sortie from the Castle. It was a warm Spring morning and the white mist rising in swathes from the water meadows on either side of the river obscured their moments. The whole party crossed the bridge and horses were brought for Aelfric, Maid Marian and Osmund. Robin mounted too and led them forward at a brisk trot. His plan was to ride in a southerly direction for a few miles, then to turn in a half-circle round the town, and regain the forest by crossing the sheep-walks.

Hardly had they started when the Castle bugles sounded the alarum. The great bell began to toll and the roll of drums throbbed through the air.

"They have discovered our flight," said Aelfric, rising in his stirrups to look back.

Osmund did the same. The river shone pale and full between its flowery borders, where the kingcups were opening; streamers of mist filled the air, through which the pinnacles of the Church towers and the battlements of the town wall pierced fantastically. Osmund could see little black figures running to and fro, and gathering in excited groups on the towers.

"Master Robin," said the Knight. "They will certainly pursue, and 'tis my opinion that we may give battle and raise the country against the dastardly usurper, John."

This suggestion suited well with Robin's humour, and the two hurried on to choose suitable ground. Some cover for the archers was needed and sufficient space for the horsemen to manœuvre. The sodden meadow-land about them was most unsuitable for the swift action that Aelfric advised.

"I will first defy them and summon them to yield," he suggested. "Then if they refuse, the mounted party will charge and your archers will pour in their arrows."

Scarlet had ridden ahead and now sent Much flying back to announce that a large party were advancing upon them from the south.

"Their dust is rising as far as eye can see," reported Much, "and Will thinks 'tis Fulk de Brent with at least two hundred horsemen."

Robin's face fell.

"If that is so, we shall have to retreat to the woods, without striking a blow, which is a sad pity," he said.

Scarlet came galloping back.

"We are caught between the river and the town, Master, for there's a strong party marching out of the Castle."

Robin glanced from left to right. On one side was a wide arm of the river, on the other a marshy wood.

"Then we'll have a brush with Fulk!" he said. "Into the wood all—Little John, stay by Marian. Now, Sir Knight, this is a bad place for horses, will you be guided by me? Aye? Then Alan-a-dale, take the steeds behind the wood, and archers, up with you into the willow trees! Brace your feet well and make sure you have full room to draw your bows."

There was a great splashing and plunging as the horses were ridden off, then Osmund found himself standing with his father on the outskirts of the thin wood. At their feet thousands of delicate wild anemones were opening their purple-tipped petals, and birds were singing rapturously.

"My son, I command you stay with Robin Hood, and obey him as you would me," said Sir Aelfric suddenly. "And you, good forester, harken. Thirty men cannot hope to win against two hundred. I will challenge this false Knight Fulk to single combat, for I will not have you risk your lives on my account. The King will need you when he lands."

The Knight was bareheaded and wore only a light mail shirt over his green tunic, but his dignity of carriage marked him out anywhere as a man of importance.

As he went back to the road, he made his horse caracole and leap in the air, and finally drew up in the centre of the causeway, with his lance drooping till the sharp point rested in the dust.

As the advance guard of the approaching battalion came up, Robin blew his bugle, and the echoes fell back mockingly from the Castle rock half a mile away.

"Halt! In the King's name!" cried Sir Aelfric.

Chapter Twenty-Three

T HE TROOP of armed men, advancing briskly from the south, were already on the alert, for they carried their lances in rest. The first lines halted on being summoned by the solitary Knight, but succeeding ranks moved up quietly behind and spread out on each side of the road.

Osmund stood holding by Robin's stirrup; it was all he could do not to disobey and rush after his father. His eyes travelled anxiously down the long rows of glittering spears. There was small hope that the rules of chivalry would prevail against such a host of enemies! In another moment the gallant Knight would be done to death, only a miracle could save him!

But even with the thought Osmund's eyes fell on a gay silken pennon, fluttering from the lances of a troop which was just coming round the bend of the road.

He uttered a strangled cry and rushed from under Robin's restraining hand.

"They are friends, they are friends!" he shouted. "Sir Hugo of Scarcliffe! Aid, aid!"

.   .   .   .   .

Osmund could never give a clear account of what happened next. He had a confused vision of archers and knights mingling, of Sir Hugo and Aelfric grasping hands, and of the King's standard fluttering above them.

Then he was in the midst of the outlaws again and everyone was shouting:

"Richard has landed! Hurrah, for Cœur de Lion!"

Before he had got his breath he heard the shock of mailed men, meeting in a charge. Alberic Fitz Warren had borne down upon them and had insolently refused to give way to the advance guard of the King's own army. Sir Hugo instantly charged, with Aelfric riding at his side, and struck Fitz Warren with such force that the lance pierced his breastplate and he fell dead to the ground. Many of his men were also slain; the remainder fled back towards the Castle, but were overtaken and routed before they could reach the stronghold.

The town surrendered, the Castle was given up to the King's men and the whilom prisoner Aelfric returned in triumph.

Robin rode with him to the barbican and there drew up.

"No further, Sir Knight! I and my men love not the air that is breathed behind walls."

"Friend, you need fear no wrong——" began the Knight eagerly, but Robin Hood stopped him with a gesture.

"I am an outlaw," he said.

"We're all outlaws if it comes to that," grumbled Little John.

"But you all fought bravely for the King this day," said Aelfric. "Is outlawry your choice, Master Forester, or has it been imposed on you by your enemies?"

"I am under a ban, certainly by my enemies' contrivance," answered Robin, laughing. "But I must admit that I have waged war without intermission—against the King's deer."

"I would fain detain you, Master Robin," declared Aelfric. "But since you will not stay, at least promise you will come if the King himself summons you."

"Right gladly," returned the outlaw heartily. "And now, leaving you your son, I will, with your leave, go and escort your lady hither."

"Richard landed at Sandwich yesterday," broke in one of Sir Hugo's followers, "and follows us closely. He should reach

Nottingham tonight. We are bidden to seize Pickhill, which is now the only Castle in this district holding out for John. 'Tis said the Prince hath fled to France."

"Aye," chimed in another. "When word was brought that John had raised an army and defied his brother and lawful King, Richard said these very words: 'John will never face force!' he said, and he laughed."

"Aye, but bitterly withal," said the first knight. "For he had always treated John as a most loving brother and had showered benefits upon him."

Sir Hugo had fallen in with Fulk on the previous day and the recreant knight had fled with all speed when he heard that Cœur de Lion had actually landed. The fortress of Pickhill surrendered without a blow, and knights and yeomen came trooping in from all the countryside to proclaim their loyalty to Richard and to offer their services.

The weeks that followed were happy indeed. Eadgar and his uncles hurried down from the north and the Ladies Etheldreda and Roheisa rode into Nottingham accompanied by their children, and all were invited to be the King's guests in Nottingham Castle.

Richard's enemies fled, for they feared him exceedingly and in course of time they made abject submission and were suitably punished.

Osmund's only remaining anxiety was as to Robin Hood's future. Sir Aelfric arranged a meeting in a woodland glade, where the King paused to rest after hunting.

Richard was primed with the full story and gave Robin his hand to kiss very graciously. Then he looked him squarely in the face and asked:

"Outlaw, will you serve me, if I requite you and your band with all courtesy? How many be ye?"

"Three hundred," said Robin Hood, leaving the first part of the question unanswered.

"That is over much for a forester," returned the King. "Mark you, Robin, I like to hunt myself and such a retinue as yours will leave small game for me. Hark you, fellow, wilt be in-lawed again?"

Robin glanced at Maid Marian who was standing beside him.

"Aye, so I lose not my freedom," he answered sturdily.

"Then 'Robin' thou must die!"

The outlaw was surrounded by the King's men, but he did not blench.

"Let it be with a sword in my hand then!" he exclaimed.

The King laughed and struck him a hearty blow on the shoulder.

"Go to! Thou'rt the lad I'd like at my shoulder when storming a breach! Hark ye, Sir Aelfric—is the Abbot of Welbeck here as I ordered?"

"Aye, good Sir King," the Abbot answered for himself, and hurried forward very much perturbed at the turn affairs seemed to be taking.

"Come then, friends, we'll be merry! Robin Hood shall die indeed, for I here and now proclaim that bold outlaw is no more and here in his shoes stands the King's friend. What is the name of that Manor, erstwhile Prince John's? Everingham? Then the Abbot shall be sponsor to you: Kneel down, Robin: and now rise up, Sir Adam de Everingham, hereditary forester of this our royal forest of Sherwood! Thou shalt be properly seized of the Manor this very day, and look to it that thou hast always good hunting for me here."

Robin grasped the King's extended hand and then remembered, and kissed it respectfully.

"If you'll be guided by me, Sire, I'll put you on the track of the noblest hart in the whole forest—aye, or in England either," he cried.

Robin was as good as his word and the quarry he found provided so fine a chase that its fame has gone down to history.

Richard followed the hart right over the Yorkshire border into Barnsleydale and there lost him, but in gratitude for the sport which the beast had given him, the King ordered a proclamation to be made at Gisborne, Tickhill and other places "that no person should kill, hunt or chase the said hart, but that he might safely return into forest again."

"Which hart," says the ancient record, "was afterwards called a 'hart royal proclaimed.'"

Robin Hood—or Sir Adam, as he was now styled, at least in public—had achieved the same enviable security. Hal Hard-fist and his crew fled the country and Robin installed his own followers in the place of Verderer, Woodwards and Keepers. Much's parents returned in triumph to the Mill.

The good Knights, Sir Hugo and Sir Aelfric, became fast friends as did their ladies.

Eadgar was made one of the King's pages, but as he showed more talent for learning than for the arts of war, Richard passed him on to the household of the Bishop of Ely. There the boy forgot his chronicle in the delight of studying architecture, and though you may not find his name in any record, Eadgar helped to draw the first rough draft of the wondrous nave of Ely Cathedral.

The children of the Grange had many other adventures, but all that can be told here is that they all remained friends.

On May-Day Sir Aelfric invited the new-made Sir Adam and his followers to dine with him at the Grange: Sir Hugo, Roheisa and their children were there too.

The maypole was gaily dressed and after the children had danced round it, they dragged Robin into the seat of honour, and pelted him with cowslip balls. They had prepared a present for him which they now offered in triumph: a new bow, bound with green velvet and gold thread, and a sheaf of arrows in a silver-laced quiver "penned" with peacock feathers.

The gift was inscribed: "To our good friend Sir Adam de Everingham," but as the children joined hands and danced round him they all began to sing:

> "With Will Scarlet and John, who was never subdued,
> Robin Hood and his band so bold
> Will reign in the forest of merry Sherwood,
> What say ye, my hearts of Gold?"

The answer was a hearty cheer in which knights, ladies and foresters joined lustily.

> "God save Robin Hood! Long live our jolly Robin!
> And merry merry men, and merry merry men
> And merry merry men be we!"

The End

WIDO . . . BEGAN HIS ENTERTAINMENT WITH A BALLAD

(See page 211)

Robin Hood to the Rescue!

Contents

Robin Hood to the Rescue!

CHAPTER ONE

J N THE MERRY days of old, there was no merrier place than Sherwood Forest, for though the jolly outlaw, Robin Hood, was a reformed character and had been rechristened and knighted by King Richard, he hunted the royal forests as blithely as ever. True, he no longer emptied travellers' pockets, nor made them pay toll, willy-nilly, when they crossed his domain, but he befriended the poor as stoutly as ever, and challenged any rich baron or tax-gatherer who dared to act unjustly.

Robin only used his title of Sir Adam de Everingham on state occasions, and though his headquarters were supposed to be in Barnsleydale where the King had granted him land, he was more often to be found in Sherwood, under a lodge of green boughs, or sleeping out on the open hill-side. His band of followers had followed his fortunes and had added the badges of Royal Rangers and Woodwards to their old uniforms of Lincoln Green. They were still the best bowmen in the countryside, and popular with all who had not evil deeds on their consciences.

The chief friends of Robin Hood and his lady, Maid Marian, were the noble Sir Aelfric de Southwell and his family. The Knight indeed was seldom at home, as he was one of Cœur de Lion's most trusted leaders, and was now busy in Normandy assisting his master to construct the new Castle Gaillard, or Saucy Castle, to overawe the French. His wife Etheldreda meanwhile looked after the demesne, and her five children: Eadgar, who was page to the Bishop of Ely, Osmund, his junior by a year and now nearly thirteen, Hild, who would be twelve next birthday, Stephen, eight, and Sibell, four. They lived in a fortified Manor House next to Southwell Minster, and Eadgar was still at home because he was always given leave to return to Southwell for the great celebrations at Whitsuntide, the Minster having special privileges for this feast.

It was glorious June weather, and the Castle children were allowed to ramble at their will about the forest which covered the higher part of the country. The ground surrounding South-well itself was extremely watery, for not only did the district boast at least seven wells, patronized since Roman times, but was traversed by the mighty River Trent and its tributary brooks. Etheldreda fondly imagined that she might at last enjoy a little peace, for her three great enemies, Guy de Gisburn, Hal of Not-tingham, and Fulk de Brent, were now dead, and it seemed as though no one were likely to trouble her during her husband's absence, as had been the case on previous occasions. There had been many guests at the Manor during Whitsuntide, but all had now departed to their homes. Wido, the travelling minstrel, lingered behind and came up one evening to give a last enter-tainment before he took to the road again.

He was a great friend of the children, and his arrival was a delight to the whole Castle. Eadgar was never tired of listen-ing to the immense romances which Wido could relate, partly in prose and partly in verse. Perhaps his favourite of all was the Romaunt of Arthur, a medley of thrilling tales, which Wido had picked up in Wales. Each separate story somehow hooked into three or four more, and there seemed no reason why the romaunt should ever come to an end.

Osmund loved the parts about jousts and fighting, but he thought the tales of magic very foolish.

"I'd much rather the knight just won by courage, Wido," he declared. "Magic is too easy—besides, it isn't real."

"I wouldn't be sure, young master," Wido always replied.

Soon everyone gathered in the Great Hall; the lady Etheldreda took her place near the hearth but with her chair turned round to face the room. Wido was tuning his lute as he paced about in front of her; the ladies of the household and the children sat in a semicircle on either side, while the maids, farmservants and men-at-arms assembled at the back. The Seneschal posted himself opposite the lady, as was his right, and the hinds and villeins crowded in at the far end of the hall.

Wido had a fine baritone voice, and began his entertainment with a ballad. Everyone clasped hands and swung arms and body in time to the tune, rather in the way people do when they sing Auld Lang Syne nowadays. It was a new ballad all about a knight who parted from the lady he loved to go to the Holy Wars, and of how he came back long years afterwards disguised as a pilgrim to find out if his lady had kept faith with him. He met a false friend, who declared that his Adeliza had forgotten him and married the Lord of Castles Three, so the pilgrim rushed into the forest wide and became a hermit. After that the children rather lost the thread of the tale, but it ended tragically as such ballads always did. The lady dismissed the wicked lord and began to pine away, and somehow or other she wandered into the forest glade and died of grief just outside the hermitage while the hermit was at his orisons within.

"It's not a bit like what would really happen," muttered Eadgar. "Hermits retire from the world to think about God—not about faithless ladies."

"He ought to have slain the Lord of Castles Three," declared Osmund, "didn't he, Wido? Didn't he slay the false knight?"

"The ballad does not say so," replied Wido, twanging his lute crossly. He disliked any interruption and could not bear to be criticized. "Maybe the spectre cold of the hermit bold that night to him appeared——"

This time it was Stephen who interrupted. "I don't like it," he cried loudly.

The lady Etheldreda shook her head at the gleeman. She had warned him beforehand not to mention either spectres or witches as she did not want Stephen and Sibell to be frightened.

A minstrel had to please the lady of the Manor at all costs, so he smiled, asked a riddle which had a punning answer and began another tale.

"Once upon a time," he said, "there was a hill shepherd in Wales. He was so poor that he had nothing at all of his own. One day his master called him and bid him drive his flock to London town and sell it there as the price of wool in Wales had fallen. So the shepherd cut a stout hazel staff from the thicket and went his way. 'Twas a long journey, but he beguiled the time by singing the old ballads with which the Welsh entertain each other when they meet in the warm farmhouses and make merry, when the snow is on the hill." Here Wido burst into song:

> "King Arthur of the Table Round
> A mighty man was he
> With his Knights so bold
> And his crown of gold
> And his Kingdom from sea to sea."

"It wasn't really from sea to sea," began Eadgar, but everyone else said:

"Hush!"

"Well, you know all about King Arthur, it seems," cried Wido quickly dropping into prose again. "Suffice it then to say that under his rule the Cymri were a great and valiant nation. When Arthur fell in battle, he was mourned by mortals and all in the land of faerie, but a rumour grew that Arthur was not dead, but would return when the times were ripe and rule over his land again in peace and glory. 'Twas the prophecy, too, of Merlin the magician, who wrote hundreds of prophecies in mystic verses called triads, which the Welsh preserve with great reverence."

"Have any of them come true?" inquired Eadgar.

"Of course, or they wouldn't have been prophecies," retorted Wido, and passed rapidly on, lest the young scholar should be inclined to argue the point.

> "The shepherd left his mountains
> In the land of singing streams,
> In the land of night-born fountains,
> In the land of radiant gleams;
> And he came to London town,
> And on London bridge stood he,
> And he gazed up-river and down
> In bewildered reverie—

"That is to say, he was so astounded, poor, simple fellow, at the array of shops and booths on each side of the bridge, and at all the boats of merchandise and the wherries plying for hire down below, and at the bawling of the merchants' varlets, proclaiming their wares, and all the bustle of town, that he was as one stunned. More than one rogue slipped a hand in his pocket, but 'twas empty. He had sold the sheep, lodged the money with a merchant, as his master had bid him, and slipped the luck-penny into his shoe. Presently as he stood still, craning his neck over the parapet, a hand fell on his shoulder, and a voice asked him a question. The shepherd whirled round and saw a stranger in a big cloak with a large book under his arm. 'I have no English,' he said, very respectfully, for he saw at once that his questioner was a wise man.

"'Where got you yon speckled staff?' said he, in very good North-country Welsh.

"'In my own land,' said the shepherd.

"'Take me to the place and your fortune is made,' said the wise man. 'For I can tell by the look of your staff, that under the roots of that hazel lies buried a vast treasure of gold and silver.'"

At this point the lady turned the hour sand-glass, which stood on a stool beside her. Wido took the hint and condensed his story.

"In a week and a day, the two men were standing on the sheep-walk at the very spot," he went on. "The stranger said some queer words out of his book, and moved a stone at the root of the hazel. A big hole opened out before them and steps leading down into a vast cavern. 'Follow me,' said the magician. 'But mind how you go. We shall pass three great bells and if you touch any of them, we are both dead men.' So saying, he stepped briskly down the stairs and the shepherd followed him into a huge subterranean chamber. In the centre was a circular table round which lay knights in armour with their weapons beside them. The shepherd marked one taller than the rest, with a crown of gold on his head and a red dragon on his shield. The table was piled with gold and silver dishes, bags of coin and bowls of precious stones. 'Take what you like but make no noise,' said the wise man.

"Now the shepherd had never seen such riches in his life, and he seized the biggest and heaviest he could and hurried to the stairs, meaning to put his treasure in a safe place and come back for more. He was in such haste that he forgot to be careful, and a long bar of gold struck against one of the bells as he staggered by. Oh! what a noise it made, like all the thunderstorms you have heard, rolled into one. The shepherd nearly died of fright! The warriors in the cave leaped up from sleep and seized their arms, but when the wise man shouted above the tumult: 'The time is not yet!' they all sank down again, and the shepherd and the magician dropped their treasure and fled into the open air. 'You fool,' said the magician, 'you did not heed my warning, and now you have broken the spell. Whoever looks upon Arthur again until his hour comes, is doomed to wither away and die.'

"With that, he pushed back the stone and stamped it down. The shepherd ran home, meaning to come back some other day, but search as he might, he never found the place again and never again set eyes on the wise man. The few jewels which he had slipped into his pocket, made him rich enough to buy a farm on which he lived happily ever after."

As soon as Wido finished the lady Etheldreda made a sign to the Seneschal who made a sign to the steward who made a sign to the pantrymen. Everyone got up, the shepherd, the swineherd, and the hayward withdrew into a group, as behoved freemen, while the grooms and villeins lifted out the trestle tables which had been laid against the wall, and the cook and his underlings hurried away to send in supper.

Hild remained dreamily sitting in the rushes, and Alice had to call her three times before she could get her attention.

The elder children were expected to help in the serving and then to take their places next their mother at the high table, where the lady kept a watchful eye on all that was going on, and noted any waste or slovenliness with a prompt reproof. Stephen and Sibell were carried off to bed where they were regaled with honey possets as a treat. Wido tucked into boar's ham with a good appetite, and Hild set a dish of dried plums near him, for she knew his fondness for this form of dessert. Dried fruit and sugar plums were only served on special occasions.

Chapter Two

SOUTHWELL VILLAGE was built on low-lying land, but on the north and west rose a series of wooded hills interspersed with marshy valleys, known locally as 'dumbles.' Besides discovering the springs of salubrious water, the Romans had built roads and villas in the neighbourhood; the remains of one of these houses, sunk deep in a cleft in the woodland, was the children's favourite place, and this summer they were determined to trace out the course of the paved road which had once run past it, but which had long since been lost and forgotten.

Eadgar was a dreamy, studious boy, who could be happy for hours writing a chronicle in a sheepskin book which Osmund and Hild had made for him as a Christmas present. Even when he was not illuminating initial letters, or poring over the carefully written page, he was thinking about it and composing the bit he would write next in the stiffest and most solemn style he could invent. The chronicle was written in English, at Hild's request, and Eadgar was rather ashamed of a composition in the vernacular, and felt bound to make it as dignified as he could to atone for not writing in Latin or even French. The discovery of the remains of the Roman villa and their adventures of the previous year made an interesting chapter, for Eadgar's work was exclusively concerned with the happenings of his own time.

"We must find out exactly where the old road goes," he remarked one day. "I could make a map of it, if we once traced it out."

"It can't go very far," said Osmund, "we have ridden or walked all through the country and there is no road which corresponds to this one."

"We know the southern end goes through the marsh and joins the lane," pursued Eadgar. "But we don't know exactly about the other direction—it was lost under the brambles."

Eadgar sat down on a fallen tree staring unseeingly at the fluttering leaves, among which warblers and titmice were busily seeking provender for the young birds whose lisping notes sounded loudly from hidden nests. Presently Hild approached, and planted herself before him.

"Eadgar, do let us do something interesting," she pleaded. "Osmund and Stephen are practising with their bows, and I've scraped my finger—look!—and it is too sore to shoot any more."

"You should use your glove," said Eadgar. "You might skin your wrist badly."

"I know, but I didn't," retorted Hild. "It is nothing much and I have washed it in the brook. Do come for a walk," she added coaxingly. "Perhaps if you and I went softly together, without any loud talking, we might discover the way the road goes when it leaves the cleft."

"You speak as if the road made a noise like a stream," said her brother, laughing. "Come on then, let us go and listen for the road."

Having gained her point Hild did not mind a little teasing.

Curiously enough the villa was hidden in a deep valley—the Romans had evidently made use of an existing road, and built their dwelling beside it. It lay some twenty feet below the level of the surrounding land.

Hild led the way up the bank at a brisk pace and, forgetting all about the wise and solemn exploring she had suggested, she began to run along the edge of the ravine, laughing, singing and talking, sometimes dodging into the wood or pausing in a clearing to pluck wild roses.

Eadgar followed and soon the walk became a race. Hild tucked her long plaits into her tunic that they might not catch in the branches, and bounded ahead, pushing her way through bushes and briars with an impatience which recked nothing of the damage done to clothes and stocking, until at length they came out of the wood into an open space of unfenced pasture.

Isolated groups of nut bushes were dotted about near the edge of the wood: they looked like islands in the rippling sea of flowery grass. As Eadgar gazed he became aware of a strip of turf, darker green than the rest and raised a foot or two above the meadow surface. It stretched away before them, five yards broad, almost from their very feet to the top of the grassy hill which bounded the horizon.

"It's as straight as if it had been drawn with a ruler," said the boy in an awed voice.

"What?" asked Hild. "Where?" she added wonderingly.

"Don't you see?" he answered. "The road—the Roman road."

"Does it go all the way to Rome, do you suppose?" inquired Hild, wading through the grass towards it.

"Well, it couldn't go across the sea, of course, and we have our backs to Rome now—we are looking north," said Eadgar dreamily.

Hild whirled round as though she expected to see the pinnacles of the Eternal City behind her; but there was only the wood, with the deepening glow of June sunlight gilding the top-most boughs.

"This old track must be our road," she whispered. "Do let us see where it goes to! Come quick—let's run along the Roman road!"

Her excitement infected Eadgar. He could not tell how it was that the road should show so plainly now as though it had risen up through the bosom of the meadow. Hild clutched his hand and together they went solemnly forward through the tall buttercups until their feet left the spongy ground and struck upon a hardness which told of buried pavements. Then they began to run, enchanted by the discovery and the magic of the hour. The secret, buried road had risen into the open and lured them on. Half-laughing, half-awed they sped up it together, slowing down sometimes for a few paces to get their breath, and then flying onward once more.

Eadgar had only meant to go a little way, but, once started, an irresistible fascination drew him on. If only they could get to the top of the hill and find out if the Road was still discernible on the further slope! Hild had at first been as eager as he, but at length her steps began to flag, and she stopped with a little cry of dismay.

"It's getting dark!"

Eadgar felt as though wakened with a jolt from a delicious dream. The sun had sunk behind the tall trees and, when they turned and stared backwards, the straight ribbon of the road had vanished. It was some special effect of the evening rays which had made its course appear so plain; now that they were withdrawn the whole surface of the grassy plain seemed even.

"It's gone!" faltered Hild in terror.

"No, it hasn't. You can feel it underfoot." Eadgar stamped on the sod. "Come, we must go back quickly. There's no reason to be afraid—we can see the wood from here—and anyhow the country is quiet enough."

"I'm not afraid," declared the girl, but her pale face belied the words. "'Tis passing strange though—almost as though we had been bewitched. Let's run!"

They started off at a brisk pace but in a few minutes Hild was floundering in a marsh.

"I've stepped off the path somehow," she called in alarm.

As Eadgar came to help she noted that his stockings, too, were wet and muddy.

"We must go back to where we were standing," he said cheerfully, "just over there—see where our feet have crushed down the grass."

They tried to retrace their steps, both concealing their anxiety.

"We didn't come through this patch of sedges," declared Hild. "Try and think where the nearest road is, Eadgar. You have ridden over all this country with Osmund."

"Yes, we'll find a road, of course," answered Eadgar. "But I haven't been much at home these last three years. If we find our own Roman road again it will take us straight back."

"You said we were facing north when we started," said his sister. "But if we had been wouldn't the setting sun have been on our left—'twas behind us surely?"

They debated this point for some minutes, their feet sinking meanwhile in the spongy soil.

"I think we had better go on to the top of the hill," Eadgar decided at last. "We are sure to see some house from there—perhaps we shall be able to see the Manor—or we'll find a shepherd or someone who can guide us."

"I'm afraid of falling into a bog," said Hild.

"Take my hand, I'll go first," answered Eadgar.

He went forward uphill, and the girl pattered after him. It no longer seemed a glorious and dazzling adventure, and Hild kept thinking of the lady Etheldreda and of what her feelings would be when the other two boys came home alone.

"Now you really are a distressed maiden," cried Eadgar, laughing to cheer her. "And I'm a Knight Errant—rather more errant than I could wish at this moment; but we're really not far from home."

"I smell wood-smoke," whispered Hild. "What if it should be——"

"Why, it might be our good friend, Robin Hood!" cried Eadgar joyfully. He sprang ahead and was pushing eagerly through the low bushes of dwarf willow and hazel which covered the hill top, when he was sharply challenged, and heard the warning click of a cross-bow.

"Hold, friend!" cried the boy. "I bear no arms, and only seek to be directed to Southwell."

Instead of the friendly group of jolly foresters, shepherds or charcoal-burners whom he expected to see, a grim little band of men rose up silently out of the grass.

Eadgar recoiled, thrusting Hild behind him, but it was too late. There was a muttered order, and the children were roughly seized.

A fire was smouldering in the centre of a ring of trampled grass, but there was no roasting venison such as Robin Hood would have provided. The figures that surrounded them looked more like those of sea-faring men: they had red, weather-beaten faces and gold rings in their ears, and wore heavy woollen tunics. They spoke with a South-country accent, strange to Eadgar's ears.

"They two will be better nor nothing," said one fellow. "They be gentle nurtured, I do allow, and that do always fetch its price."

"We come from Southwell Castle," said Hild eagerly. "The lady will give you a good reward if you take us home in safety."

"Yes, sure," answered the fellow. "A crown piece and a drink o' sour ale and all the monks' minions will be set on our heels after. What will this one fetch, think 'ee?" he asked, and catching Eadgar suddenly by the back of the neck, he flung him sprawling on the grass before his fellows. They all laughed brutally, and the boy sprang up, scarlet with anger.

"Beware how you touch me, churls that you are! I have been the King's page and now serve the Lord Bishop of Ely!" he cried.

"He be worth a fair pound o' weighed silver in Ireland," declared the leader of the band. "But the wench is over young though she is fair-favoured."

He was about to catch Hild by the hair in order to drag her forward into the firelight, but Eadgar rushed between and pushed away the villain's hand. He was instantly felled to the ground again, and Hild shrieked for help with all her might. Her voice had no more effect than the cry of a frightened bird, and the ugly threats with which she was assailed quickly reduced her to silence. The young prisoners were now bound and gagged and forced to sit down on the grass while their captors decided on their fate. The children gathered from what they heard that the men were a band of slavers from Bristol where the horrid trade was still carried on in secret in spite of the vigorous disapproval of the Church. Chieftains in the wilder parts of Ireland were always ready to purchase slaves, especially those who had been gently reared, but the chief of the slavers, whose name was Eli, was of opinion that it would not be possible to get so far across country with their prey.

"It will be safer to get rid of them in Wales," he declared. "E'en if we have to return to the ship empty-handed. Saddle the beasts, boys—we must start at once."

On this point they were all agreed. It would not do to linger in the neighbourhood. While they argued together Eadgar managed to pull off his woollen garter and tie it round a hazel twig. Presently a string of horses were led out of the bushes and saddled, bundles were re-distributed and Eadgar and Hild were each mounted in front of one of the seamen.

The horses were good and had been well rested. The men seemed to know the country and set off at a round pace. They crossed the rivers at lonely fords and avoided every village and group of houses clustered round a Manor or Abbey.

Eadgar prayed desperately that they might be waylaid and questioned or overtaken by his mother's men-at-arms. He reproached himself bitterly for his folly, though he could not have foreseen the danger into which they had fallen headlong. No one had ever heard of slavers in their quiet, settled part of the country, though there were horrid rumours of their raids in Northumberland and on the turbulent border. It was said the chieftains there sold the prisoners they had captured in their forays, though it was against the law and severely punished by the lord Marchers if the guilt could be brought home.

But no one met or stayed them. The scouts who rode ahead were much too clever, and though the captives saw twinkling lights afar off in comfortable houses, they could do nothing to make their plight known and felt themselves carried every hour further and further from home and safety.

CHAPTER THREE

THE FITZ-AELFRICS were a very united family and liked doing things together, and Osmund was annoyed when he discovered that Eadgar and Hild had disappeared.

"The other two have gone off exploring without us," he grumbled to Stephen. "I don't think it's fair."

Stephen was angry too.

"That's too bad!" he cried. "Why didn't you stop them? And now we'll have to go home because I've got my sleeves wet in the brook."

Stephen came slowly stumping up to his brother: he was rather tired with his exertions and not averse to going home a little earlier than usual, but he would have died rather than admit it.

"Oh, bother!" cried Osmund, and he threw down the chisel, with which he had been shaping tesseræ, with such violence that several of the neat little red sandstone squares were broken.

"I wanted to explore the road! Why couldn't we have gone too?" protested Stephen.

"They can't have got very far as they haven't taken the bill-hook," cried Osmund. "The brambles are much thicker and stronger now than they were when we scrambled through in the spring, and it only leads to an old land-slide, anyhow. Let's run home—if the others don't find us here it's their own fault."

"I suppose they will go straight to the Manor if they are late," answered Stephen. "We can give a call or two presently."

They scrambled into the wood, and Osmund blew the little hunting-horn he carried slung on his belt. Then they both gave their own particular family rallying cry: "Whoo-whoo-ee!" but there was no answer.

When they reached the Manor there was no sign of the others, and Dame Alice, the old nurse, was very angry about Stephen's wet sleeves. When she discovered that Eadgar and Hild were missing, she informed the lady at once, following up with the story of Stephen's plight and ending with the demand that all playing in the wood should be forbidden. Then she drew a long breath and began all over again, but the lady did not seem to be listening very attentively. She chid herself for being over-fearful, but all the same her face grew pale and she stepped hurriedly to the window and pushed back the shutter.

"They will return before long," Osmund assured her. "No doubt Eadgar has lost his way—and Hild does not know the wood as well as I do."

Etheldreda leaned out, looking anxiously towards the dark trees.

"Nothing could happen to them," repeated Osmund.

"Son, go and call my lieutenant," said the lady. "Why do you hesitate? Do my bidding this instant!"

"I was only thinking that all the men are up on the pastures at the shearing," said the boy. "But I'll call Master Algar—and, mother—may I ride with him?"

"It's my belief nothing but trouble comes of this wandering outside the garden," broke in Dame Alice. "Dirty chausses, children staying out late, and now my poor little lad with his arms soaked——"

"Go, dame, go hence—put Stephen to bed. Nay, wait—Stephen, I must know when and where you saw Hild last? Had you quarrelled that you were not all together?"

Osmund had departed on his message, and Stephen was alone with his mother.

"We hadn't quarrelled at all," he declared. "I should have been angry though, if I had known they were going without us," he added honestly.

"Eadgar should know better than to stay out after sunset," said the lady, moving restlessly to the window again.

Stephen did not feel at all alarmed, but he knew that both Eadgar and Hild would be penanced for their heedlessness. They would probably be forbidden to go outside the garth for two or three days, and of course this would stop all the fun in the wood. He stood quite still listening to the distant tramp of the lieutenant's heavy jack-boots as he slowly mounted the stone stairs. Osmund's flying footsteps were soon heard and he came panting in, made the scantiest bow as he held up the door-curtain and then rushed up to his mother.

"Lady, Mott the forester is below, saddling his horse. May I go too and show him which way they went on leaving us? We'll soon find them, never fear!"

Etheldreda gave her consent and Osmund dashed away again. Stephen was ordered to bed to his great disappointment; he went slowly up the spiral stairs which led to the children's room, and on the way peeped into the lady's bower where Hild slept on a little pallet bed at the foot of the lady's big one. The floor of the bower was strewn with scented rushes and Stephen paused in the doorway to sniff appreciatively.

Osmund thought it fine fun to go out riding after sunset, and he hurried with the forester to a clearing not far from the secret road. Here they tied their horses to trees and Osmund guided Mott to the place where trampled grass and bramble showed that the children had passed. It was still light enough for the quick-eyed woodman to descry sundry threads of wool clinging to the briars, which Osmund identified as belonging to Eadgar's clothing. It was quite easy to follow their track and Mott shook his head over the bad woodcraft and was inclined to chide Osmund for his desire to hurry.

"Nay, nay, we'll not go back for the beasts," he declared. "Fair and softly, fair and softly, young master! No tracker will gallop over the slot of the deer."

The boy left him before the phrase was finished and ran and walked by turns until he broke through the bushes at the edge of the wood and came panting to the open pasture. There he shouted and shouted again, but there was no reply, only a startled owl flew out of a fir tree and sailed away over the grassy plain as silently as though his wings had been clothed with wool instead of feathers. Osmund soon found tracks through the grass, and he went forward, heedless of danger, at a rapid pace.

The wind had died down, and the tinkling of a stream could be heard in the stillness. Overhead the sky was serene and blue, with green bars on the western horizon. Every now and then the fragrance of meadow-sweet was wafted to Osmund's nostrils. He followed a false trail where Hild had blundered off the road and came back again, and presently summoned Mott with a shrill halloo.

The woodman found the boy standing in the coppice where the ashes of a recent fire were still smouldering.

"They had horses," he said breathlessly. "Quick—Mott—say how many horses there may have been here?"

"Not so fast, young master!" began the man as usual. "Why, who is to say yet that is aught but a tinkers' camp? *Pardi*, 'tis like enough our Eadgar is at home by now——"

"Nay, look!"

Osmund held up his brother's woollen garter, which he had found tied round a hazel twig.

THERE HE SHOUTED . . . BUT THERE WAS NO REPLY; ONLY A STARTLED
OWL FLEW OUT

(See page 227)

"He left that as a sign. It must mean they are in danger and we must act at once. Do thou follow the trail and I will go and call out our men. How old is the trail, Mott, say? Listen, maybe they are near still."

They sank down behind a bush, holding their breath. Osmund could hear nothing but the loud beating of his own heart. After a moment or two Mott began to move about on his hands and knees. After a careful examination of the charred wood he opined that the brands had been quenched two hours agone. While he was still deliberating as to whether it was right for him to let Osmund return alone, the boy left him and pushed his way through the bushes.

It is difficult to hurry when one is breathless and in great anxiety and when one's tired legs begin to feel like bars of lead. The ground was soft too—water welled up round Osmund's feet at each step, but presently something wonderful happened. As he was staring ahead, trying to gauge the distance to the dark border of the wood, he perceived a path outlined before him, straight as an arrow, darker in shade than the surrounding grass. He made towards it, scrambled up the steep side and went forward, marvelling, along the secret road that seemed to have risen out of the meadow at his need.

When the wood was reached, Osmund kept along the outer edge until he reached the ox-drove. He was about to leap the low hedge, when the sound of angry voices and the noise of stout blows made him pause. On the other side of the fence two men were struggling fiercely. The quarter-staffs with which they had at first been fighting had been flung aside and they were now using their fists. Though one man was decidedly larger and heavier than the other, the battle seemed to be equal and terrific blows were exchanged without either champion showing any signs of yielding. One was clad in archer's green, the other in tattered rags, and his beggar's bundles were lying at the wayside.

Osmund was about to continue his way—prudently keeping the hedge between himself and the disputants—when the larger of the two suddenly shouted for mercy.

"Hold thy hand—I yield!" he cried.

The other instantly stepped back, dropping his hands. His foe, who had feigned to sink to the ground, sprang up with a huge stone in his hands which he dashed down on his opponent's head.

"Shame!" shouted Osmund.

"A Robin!" roared the archer, as he reeled back.

The boy jumped over the hedge, ripping his tunic on the way. There was no time to pick and choose prudently, and though there were many Robins in the world besides Robin Hood, there was a likelihood that the reformed outlaw might be at his tricks once more.

The huge beggar picked up his stone again, and was lifting it high with the intention of crushing his adversary's skull, when Osmund put down his head and ran at him. It was not a knightly mode of attack, but it was successful. Boy and beggar fell together and rolled in the dust, and as he struggled to free himself Osmund heard the well-known, sweet bugle-notes ringing gaily through the evening air.

Tantivy—tantivy—tan-tallo!

The beggar had dropped the stone in his fall, and now began thumping Osmund with all his strength, but a strong hand soon plucked the boy out of his grasp, and Osmund found himself panting for breath, with Robin Hood on one side and his huge henchman, Little-John, on the other. Yes, it was Robin Hood sure enough, though he was disguised as a common archer and his brow was dripping with blood.

"Thou'rt well a-paid, Robin!" cried Little-John indignantly. "Why must thou ever go brawling without friends at thy back? But I'll pay this rogue his score—full measure, too!"

Little-John brandished a fist nearly the size of a leg of mutton in the astonished beggar's face, and then whipping a huge cudgel from his belt, he prepared to administer a terrific beating.

Robin Hood interfered.

"Nay, nay! Little-John! The man is a stout, hardy fellow and will make a good henchman when he has learnt fair play——"

Osmund interrupted:

"Robin, you came in the nick of time. Eadgar and Hild have been carried away and we never needed your help more sorely."

The forester shot a keen glance at him. He knew Osmund of old and judged that this was no childish false alarm. He held up his hand to still the clamour of his comrades who had gathered round, furiously demanding leave to punish the beggar for his insolence. Then he questioned Osmund in quick, sharp, phrases.

"Have you searched the woods? Our Eadgar hath no great sense of direction."

"Yes, we have searched and called. But, Robin—Mott, our woodman, and I traced them to a thicket yonder, and the ground is all trampled by horses, and we found the embers of a fire, which have been quenched these two hours, Mott says."

"Has there been any talk of slavers being seen hereabouts?" asked Robin—he was still Robin Hood to all his friends and only used his title 'Sir Adam of Everingham' on state occasions.

"Slavers!" repeated Osmund in amazement.

"Aye, those sea-faring villains from Bristol have been abroad again. We have traced them down from Barnsleydale, but they gave us the slip in the Peak country. Hark ye, friend," he added, turning to his late antagonist. "Canst tell us aught of this?"

The beggar was crouching over his bundles, and now raised a bruised and surly face.

"An I could I wouldn't," he declared vengefully; then, as he caught Little-John's angry eyes, he added hastily: "I'm an honest beggar and would scorn to hold any traffic with such base folk."

"Nevertheless, you might have heard news among the travelling community," said Robin. "And you'll be no loser if you help us. There'll be a hue and cry raised for this lad, for he is the son of a noble knight and the King's page withal!"

"Thou hast broken my head," growled the beggar, "but I have broken thine also, and bear no malice," he added, cheering up. "I did meet a party of queer folk this very noon, watering their horses at the old ford up yonder—but they had no prisoners with them or young folk of any kind."

"That news hath called out the first and last angel thou'rt ever likely to meet!" cried Robin, tossing a gold coin to him as he spoke. "How many men? Good horses?"

"A dozen or fifteen—I did not count, and all on good beasts," replied the beggar, a beaming smile lighting up his face as he caught the gold piece and tested it in his strong teeth before thrusting it into his stocking.

"We've two horses tied in the wood," said Osmund eagerly. "And I was running home to send word to our men, who are all up on the pastures, while Mott tries to make out the trail."

"Our cattle are tired," returned the forester. "Go you, Tuck, to the lady and tell her Osmund is with me. Bid her send her men down the western road towards Cannock Chase, and call out the Verderer and his folk. Beggar, we shall meet again—thou didst deal me a foul blow and I'll be venged of it in fair fight. John, I leave you in charge of the band—get fresh horses and follow me."

"Where?" demanded the giant, planting himself in his chief's path with his huge arms akimbo.

"Why, thou must follow my track! Blackbird, lead on to thy horses. Fear not, we'll overtake them—if not tonight, by dawn."

Osmund was glad when his friend called him by his old nickname, bestowed upon him in jest, and going by contrary like all the nicknames of Robin's band. He glanced up at his friend anxiously as they hurried along, but could make nothing of the forester's expression. It was impossible to ask questions—all he could do was to answer Robin's queries as they ran.

"Thou'rt leading me astray, Blackbird—the horses are to the left of us," interrupted Robin suddenly.

He strode ahead, and led the way unerringly to the spot where the tethered beasts were stamping and fretting at the flies. Robin vaulted into the saddle without touching it with his hand, and stooped his green-hooded head as he guided his steed rapidly between the close-growing trees. Soon they were galloping single-file across the pasture-land, startling the water-birds, which rose up with a clatter of wings from the pools where they were feeding. Mott was overtaken about half a mile from the slavers' camp. The track of hoof-marks on the turf was fresh enough and could be seen even in the dim light. Robin sat still for a good five minutes, silently reflecting. Then he smote his knee angrily with his hand.

"They turned due west, mark ye, master, at this cross-roads," announced Mott. "They had some bit of a parley, I reckon, by the way the marks are set—the horses must have been reined up and fidgeting, as I make out, for I——"

"Blackbird—it will be a long night-ride, and maybe a skirmish at the finish. I'll leave thee here with Mott."

"Nay, Master Robin, nay! This is my quest! Let me come with you," begged Osmund.

"Follow, then," said the forester, and his heel touched the horse, which instantly moved off at a sharp trot.

Mott had not time to finish drawing the long breath he had begun to inhale preparatory to giving an immense exposition of his deductions from the marks in the grass, when he found himself alone again with only the gentle night-sounds for company. Robin was galloping his horse now, though the track was ill-paved and dangerous—yes, Mott decided, they had left the grass lane for a paved road.

"Where do you think they have gone, Master Robin?" asked Osmund, as they walked their horses down a stony incline.

"To the Welsh border," returned Robin briefly. "Eighty miles if 'tis an inch."

Osmund found it all he could do to keep up, and later in the night all he could do to stick in the saddle, leaving his horse to follow Robin's as best it could.

But fast as they rode, the slavers went faster yet. Robin paused sometimes at little taverns and lonely homesteads, and learned that mounted men had passed, clad like seafarers and armed like bandits. Sometimes they seemed hard on their heels, sometimes to have lost their traces altogether, and when dawn came they found themselves on a wide, trackless moor, out of sight of all human habitation.

Chapter Four

THE FUTURE LOOKED black enough as Robin Hood and Osmund led their horses across the waste, going afoot to ease their cramped limbs and to save the tired beasts.

"Master Robin, have you any friends in Wales?" queried the boy.

"Nay, and I know nought about the Welsh save a rude rhyme," returned the forester, and he began to sing:

> "Taffy was a Welshman,
> Taffy was a thief,
> Taffy came to my house
> And stole a leg of beef!"

"That would cost thee thy life were it the other side of the marches," cried a strange voice.

Osmund gazed about but could see no one. Robin leaped to the ground and had his bow in hand at the first word: he kept his fingers on the quiver, though he did not draw forth a bolt—he laughed.

"You are right, friend," he answered. "But in truth I would not be so uncourteous. I pray your pardon if you belong to that valiant nation."

"Who spoke and where is he?" asked Osmund. He could not help thinking of Wido's accounts of magic—invisible knights bent on evil abounded in the minstrel's tales.

"Yonder, in the thick reeds," said Robin in a low voice.

They were near a marshy stream, and some tall sedges were

growing in the water. The rustling, grey-green leaves seemed too sparse to hide a man, yet when Osmund followed the direction of Robin's eyes he saw something stirring among them, and presently a small, dwarfish creature came creeping out and advanced towards them.

He saluted with both hands flung high in the air, to show that he intended no attack.

Osmund rubbed his eyes and stared and stared again, for the Welshman—if such he was—seemed to belong to a fairy-tale rather than real life. He was under five foot in height and somewhat misshapen. His beard and hair were matted and his eyes glared feverishly. He wore a tarnished shirt of chain mail over leather breeches, and his bow-legs were defended by 'rusty banded chausses,' or hosen as the Saxons called them. But if his armour was neglected his arms were bright enough: a sword trailed in the wet grass, and two bright, naked daggers were thrust through his belt.

"Well met," said Robin. "Can'st thou tell us, honest comrade, where we may break our fast? We have ridden far, and my young friend here is sore weary."

The stranger fixed his dark-blue eyes on Osmund and addressed him without noticing Robin's query.

"Why dost thou seek friends in Wales, young Saxon?"

Osmund glanced at Robin for leave to answer, and his friend nodded.

"We're on the track of a party of false slavers who have carried off my brother and sister," he said.

"You are twenty miles from the border," said the dwarf. "But perhaps we can help each other. I have bread in my wallet, and I was cleaning the fish I have taken in the brook when I heard your voices. Will you eat with me? We can kindle a fire without much fear, for there is not likely to be anyone astir for another two hours."

"We must take heed where we light fire, though," said Robin. "For the earth of these turbaries, once set a-glow, will burn for six months at a stretch."

"I've no friends hereabouts, and care not if the whole kingdom burns," said the stranger vengefully. "I did but cross the dyke in arms to pursue my private enemy, and the whole country came out like a swarm of bees."

As he went grumbling back to the stream, Robin murmured to Osmund:

"He speaks of the great earthwork which King Offa built of old to hem in the Welshmen. They say it ran from sea to sea, or at any rate from the Dee to the Wye. And my rhyme is true enough, for it means the Welsh are constantly bursting out and seizing their neighbours' cattle."

"Is he a border cattle-thief, then?" asked the boy.

"Beshrew me, no! I take it he is a free-lance of sorts," said Robin, "and any Welshman found in arms on this side of Offa's Dyke is condemned to death without trial by Harold's ancient law."

"Then if we help him to get back in our company——"

Robin silenced him by a touch: the little Welshman was coming towards them with two or three small fish dangling from his hand.

"Eat, and then try and sleep," went on the forester as he took out the horses' bits, slackened the girths without removing the saddles—for the beasts were warm—and tethered each to a tough ground-willow bush. "We must go softly here and trust to gather knowledge which will save time later. Trust me, Osmund."

"Indeed I do, Robin," cried the boy.

"I would Little-John and our knaves would come up, for I am lightly provisioned both for arms and money," continued Robin. "Nevertheless, I'll stake a hundred crowns to one that within three days we'll have our birds safe out of the fowler's snare."

Three days seemed a long time to Osmund.

"Hild will be frightened," he said in a low voice. "And our mother will be wild with anxiety. Could we not call out the nearest Lord Marcher, Robin? You are Sir Adam de Everingham now and a Royal Forester to boot."

"Aye, but I don't look it," said Robin, with a grin; he glanced down at his well-worn green tunic, which had been badly torn in his combat with the beggar. "Yet have no fear—Robin's wit is a match for them all."

The Welshman generously divided his small supply of food in three portions, but Osmund could hardly eat his share of bread for yawning. It was a warm, misty morning and all the grasses and bushes were spread with gossamer threads. Long before the trout were cooked, the boy had curled himself up in the heather and was sound asleep.

There was no rest for Robin Hood, for he well knew that he was engaged in a race against time, with only his shrewd brain to aid him. With his usual impetuosity he had started off armed only with his long-bow and without followers or money. He glanced impatiently at the horizon from time to time, hoping to see the dust raised by the advance of Little-John and his men. The Welshman asked many questions but was chary of answering any in return. Robin watched him without seeming to do so, and noted that though his accoutrements were so dilapidated, the creature's manners were courtly. He excused himself for providing no richer drink than spring water and took out a fair kerchief to wipe the horn after he had quaffed. He had undone his sword-belt for greater ease, and Robin marked that he flung his weapon down carelessly on his right side where he could not readily draw it without bungling.

"By my faith, I'll hazard a guess that 'tis not the bow-string which has hardened thy middle fingers," he cried suddenly.

As he spoke Robin Hood laid his hand playfully on the

scabbard and twitched it out of its owner's reach. It was well that his eyes were on the man's face and that he was as wary as a cat and as quick in movement, for in an instant the Welshman was upon him with drawn dagger.

Robin leaped up and back and parried the blow with the hood which he had taken off for coolness.

"I have eaten your bread," he cried, grasping the little man's wrist in his strong fingers, "and mean you no wrong. But I'm a harpist myself—at times—and think no harm to recognize a brother in the craft."

"Miserable churl—dost rank thyself with me, in whose veins runs the blood of princes?" screamed the dwarf, struggling helplessly in Robin's grip.

"Do not wake the boy," said the forester calmly. "I also may be of quality above my habit, but I make no boast of it, and give you kindly thanks for your courteous hospitality. Sit down again, my lord, and tell me on which day do the folk from either side of the march traffic in Offa's Dyke?"

"Tomorrow," said the Welshman, sulkily belting on his weapon as Robin released him.

"Then if you will come with us, we'll ride forward as soon as the horses are rested, and my boy can sit behind you on the crupper. If my friends have rejoined me I can lend you peaceable garments—if not——"

He broke off—measured the dwarf with his eye and then the sleeping boy.

"Osmund is almost——"

He was going to say 'of Welshman's stature,' but suppressed the phrase as uncivil.

"Do you agree, my Lord Taliesen?" he concluded respectfully, but with a twinkle in his eyes.

"I see thou art an intelligent fellow and not unacquainted with our literature," observed the little man condescendingly.

"Tradition says that Prince Elphin netted the great bard and musician Taliesen from his weir, whereas you have found me by a foul, muddy, Saxon stream! I'll tell thee the tale anon, but I cannot sing it to my harp, as were worthy, for it has been stolen from me by an insolent dog, whose blood shall wash out the injury. My name is Elian-ap-Gruffydd—ap Conan——"

Robin's eyes closed involuntarily as words continued to pour in a torrent from the Welshman's lips. Between dozes, he made the right exclamations of scandalized amazement, pity and horror, as Elian told in more words than the forester would have conceived possible, the tale of his enmity with a Norman baron. To make a very long story short, Elian, who was a noble bard, had won a musical contest and had been rewarded by the late Prince David with the gift of a golden harp. This harp had been stolen by his enemy during a raid, and the Welshman, riding across the march in pursuit, had been attacked by the English, his men had been slain or scattered and he himself had been forced to fly on the English side. The Lord Marchers and their men were on the *qui vive* all along the border, and if taken with arms upon him a Welshman would have short shrift.

"The alternative would be to doff your armour—and return in some other guise," said Robin, amazed that such a simple expedient had not already occurred to the Welshman.

"Thou sayst I am no fighting man," returned Elian, drawing himself up to his full, insignificant height. "But thou knowest nought of the Welshman's spirit of fire! Besides," he added candidly, "I have no acquaintance in this base country who would dare aid me in my present state."

"Say nought against my bonny England," cried the forester, "and I will see you safely back across the border. But I will pray you in return to speak for me to any Welsh chieftain who may purchase this pair of hapless children, and I will undertake to pay thrice the fee they cost him."

Elian replied—with a dozen anecdotes to illustrate his tale—that it was by no means easy to trace folk sold into slavery, especially children. Merchants of such commodities did not work in the open, and were chary of replying to any inquiries.

"Well, then, we'll sleep a couple of hours," interrupted Robin at length, "and ride to the march as soon as may be."

CHAPTER FIVE

THE GROUND BETWEEN the two great earthworks, Wat's Dyke and Offa's Dyke, which wound along the Welsh border, had long been considered neutral territory. The folk of each nation agreed to come here on certain days to barter their wares, and that a perpetual truce should be maintained in this No Man's Land for the convenience of trade. The Welsh brought ewes'-milk cheese, young cattle, strips of salt beef, hogsheads of grease, and kegs of butter. The English had wool, corn and leather to offer, as well as cloth, shoes, armour, and every kind of article beloved of women—combs, scarves, girdles, beauty philtres, and quack remedies.

A Jew or two would be there with a pack on his back, scorned by all, but doing good business nevertheless.

Osmund protested vigorously when Robin informed him that he was to sham sick and lie hid in a hay-mow while the Welshman borrowed his clothes. There was no sign of Little-John, and Robin Hood explained that Elian would be of great use to him at Offa's Dyke, as he—Robin—knew no word of Welsh. They had ridden within half a mile of the dyke and had turned their horses out to graze and seized a few hours' sleep. Also they had eaten well, for Robin had bought provisions and a flask of wine which they shared with their new comrade. The Welshman, who had seemed quite satisfied with a handful of oatcake and a tiny fish and had sought no further meal during the day, now put away such an astonishing amount of food that the others—who had extremely good appetites—were astonished.

"'Tis a habit of our nation," observed Elian complacently as he caught Robin's eye. "In times of shortage we can subsist on next to nothing."

The three comrades were seated on heaps of hay in a loft which formed the upper part of a lonely grange, when Robin announced his plan. The building stood on high pasture-lands, out of sight of any house. A wide extent of country could be seen from it and no one could approach without being marked at a distance. A rough grass track led up to it and meandered away beyond it towards the Welsh border. Osmund was very indignant at his friend's proposal, but the forester was firm.

"I have need of Sir Elian," he said, "and if he rode with me in armour through the English side of the march, he would not stand a dog's chance. The life of any Welshman in arms is forfeit directly he steps over the boundary. 'Tis a cruel law and may date from King Offa's time, for all I know."

"But—but"—Osmund vainly sought for arguments.

"Play the man!" exclaimed Robin. "'Tis thy brother's rescue I am thinking about. This is no merry-making adventure. If Little-John comes up with our party, do you send a man to find me."

Osmund jerked his tunic over his head in sulky silence, and then pulled off his boots of soft leather—much-worn and scratched—and sat down in his shirt.

"Fie, there's a big rent in the tunic, indeed!" exclaimed Elian. "And is there to be no surcoat? I understood the surcoat was now worn in England, whatever."

"Take it or leave it," quoth Robin. "But in courtesy, add a word of thanks to my young friend who has stripped the very clothes off his back for your service."

"The Welsh are a very polite nation," began the little man indignantly, but the forester cut him short.

"However, whatever, and soever!" he cried gaily. "We start forthwith, so you must e'en keep your courteous speeches for the next meeting!"

With that he seized the indignant Sir Elian in his arms and leapt lightly down to the barn floor, disdaining the ladder. Osmund was obliged to press his face into the hay to smother his laughter as Robin ran down the green path between the hay-fields, towing the Welshman after him by the wrist in a way most upsetting to his dignity.

The sight quite restored the boy's good humour, and as soon as the ill-assorted pair were out of view he cast about for an occupation.

Elian's suit of mail lay half-buried in the hay, and what boy could have resisted trying it on? It was dirty, covered with mud and horse hair, but made by a smith who was past-master at his craft. The leg-pieces were chausses of banded mail, and were composed of rows of flat steel rings overlapping each other and sewn on crimson velvet. There was a little tuck between each row, through which ran a cord, so that when the wearer moved the velvet gleamed between the silvery rings. Osmund pulled them on, after a cursory cleaning with bunches of hay. The sleeved tunic, made of the same materials, was too tight, and Osmund was obliged to leave it open in front, almost as wide as the white leather lacing-thong allowed. The inlaid steel cap was a little too large, but Osmund managed to pad it with a bit of hay-rope. It was great fun to be dressed as a knight, and he sought about until he found Sir Elian's sword-belt. The sword was shorter than those used by English knights, who preferred the heavy two-edged blade of Norman design. Elian's scabbard was beautifully inlaid and encrusted with jewels, and the hilt was blazoned with his arms. Osmund girded on the belt, drew the sword and balanced it as his father had taught him. He tried a few sword exercises—thrust and cut, lunge and recover—but his feet slipped in the hay. Perhaps there might be a level space outside where he could practise while still keeping a look-out. Osmund pushed open the wooden shutter which covered the window and gazed round. There was no one to be seen, but far away, at the foot of the slope, a faint spiral of smoke went curling up beyond an oakwood—it might be rising from a farmhouse chimney, or merely from a fire casually kindled by some swine-herd in the wood. Why should he not go and see, Osmund asked himself? If Little-John came he would recognize the horses and await his return there, and Osmund was the son of an English knight on English soil, so surely there could be no harm or danger in seeking speech with his countrymen? Sir Elian had repeated the story of his misfortunes as they rode together across the barren moors, which presently gave way to watery pastures where they had crossed the River Dee, south of Chester town. On reflection, Osmund went back to the loft and hid the sword under the dusty hay, left over from the previous summer.

He took off the broad belt too and replaced it with his own green girdle. This was one of his greatest treasures, for it had been given him by Maid Marian herself—she who was now the Lady of Everingham, but who, until last year, had presided as queen of the outlaws who gathered round Robin Hood in Sherwood Forest.

In England the haymakers were at work already, but on these border uplands the grass was still unripe.

He held Elian's steel cap in his hand as he presently went down the green path, with the tall wild-flowers brushing against his mail-clad legs. Most Welshmen, he had heard, were black- or red-haired, so for safety's sake he uncovered his thick, fair hair. Osmund glanced back from time to time, but there was no sign of Little-John and the horses were grazing quietly. Presently he came to the top of a narrow valley or cwm as the Welsh call it—a hollow in the mountain slope. At the farther end a little grey farmhouse nestled in a group of trees. Osmund had a few coins in the silk purse slung round his neck, and he now hauled it up by its twisted cord, extracted a fourpenny bit and went forward with it in his hand.

There was a great barking of dogs as the boy approached the reed-thatched house and he called out to them in Saxon in a friendly tone. A woman came to the door but rushed in again when she saw that the stranger wore armour. Two men came running from the barn with flails in their hands, which they raised threateningly. Osmund called out again.

"Good morrow, friends! I am alone and unarmed!"

He held up his hands as Elian had done and began to feel that he had been very foolish. Tales of border lawlessness and cruelty crowded into his mind, but he forced himself to walk forward.

"I am page to an English knight," he called. "And seek but to buy bread and cheese, for my lord has gone away and left me unprovided."

"He speaks not like a Welshman," said one of the men, lowering his flail.

"Why, 'tis but a boy," cried a girl's voice, and a buxom milkmaid came out of the byre with a wooden pail of milk on her arm. "Why, what's all the pother about? I'll wager the fellow has but lost his way to the fairing-grounds."

"Indeed, damsel, you say truly," Osmund answered for himself. He spoke very politely, and though the milkmaid shouted with laughter at being addressed like a 'gentle,' she was pleased all the same.

"Thou'rt welcome to break thy fast and keep thy four-penny," she went on as Osmund made his request. "We look not so closely to the store but that we can spare bite and sup to a wayfarer. Come, sit you on the bench at the dairy door and tell me who thy master is while I turn my cheeses."

She spoke a strange dialect, which Osmund could only partly understand, for there were words of Danish origin mixed with the Saxon. He was unwilling to talk of himself, for though he might truly call himself page to a knight, he did not wish to give away further information to strangers. The milkmaid, however, was quite ready to talk herself—she told him that she was the farmer's daughter and that her father had gone to sell some lambs at the Dyke Fair—she was just handing a heavy slice of barley bread and cheese to the boy, when one of the men drew near.

"Doll, take heed! Best send the brat packing! You'll have the whole swarm down upon us else," he muttered.

Sir Elian had talked about the country folk coming out like a swarm of bees: Osmund pricked up his ears.

"My master does not come from these parts," he said. "He is a great man in the Eastern Counties, and has but gone to look at the fair out of curiosity. He is a stranger from Yorkshire."

"Well, we want no strangers here," persisted the man. "So begone, Sir Page, before the dogs are loosed at your heels."

Doll tossed her head:

"'Tis I who give orders here," she declared, "and I say the lad shall sit and eat and pass the time for me. Go about your business, Tom ploughman, and leave me to manage mine."

"You were glad enough to call for my protection when you thought the Welsh were coming t'other day," retorted the man. "And there's a Welshman abroad yet, and likely to be a fierce one, too."

"But surely you are five or six miles from the border here?" cried Osmund.

"Scarce one; and the Welsh will go twenty or more—curse them—to get our cattle," said Doll. "And our young men match them! There's bad blood in these parts ever since the King's army was cut to pieces in grandfather's time. Over there, 'twas—where the Welsh have a stronghold above the Dee—Ewloe Castle, they call it."

"But surely English folk have no need to raid Welsh cattle?" asked Osmund. "I've always thought the Lord Marchers kept stern rule here."

"Aye, but the lads was vexed, see you. The Welsh have been crowing ever since the Victory of Ewloe, as they call it—and the ale had gone round too often at the Midsummer Feast. However 'twas, the lads went across the dyke on a dark night and did some mischief, I believe, and carried off some of the Welshmen's gear——"

"And broke the Taffies' heads when they came after 'em," put in the hind with a grin.

"There was three men killed," said the girl. "But they made less stir over that than over a fiddle, or harp, or some such thing as the lads ran off with for a marlock. I would it were safe back, for I know the Welsh better than these folk do—they put their pride above the lives of men, and will have vengeance."

Osmund had emptied the wooden bowl of milk and eaten a good portion of bread and cheese during this discourse.

"Farewell, kind damsel," he said, putting on his steel cap in order to doff it as he got up. "And here, churl, is fourpence to mend thy manners to strangers."

He tossed the battered silver coin to the labourer, who stood rubbing his beard and staring uncertainly at him, and then walked out of the yard with all the dignity he could muster.

He had just passed the angle of the lane when he heard running footsteps crossing the field on his left.

A moment later there was a rustling in the hedge, the untrimmed growths of hazel and wild-rose were parted and Doll's large, round, rosy face peered through.

"Hist! Quiet now!" she whispered, and paused to look over her shoulder.

HE GAZED ANXIOUSLY AT HER BROAD, HONEST FACE AND THEN
CLAMBERED UP THE BANK

(See page 250)

Osmund halted and looked round too. The lane was empty, but he heard one of the horses neigh far above at the grange.

"Maybe I'm wrong," said Doll, in a hoarse, reedy whisper. "But maybe it was the Welsh harp you had in your mind when you came to our place?"

"The Welsh harp!" repeated Osmund eagerly. "No—yes—wait a minute, Doll." He gazed anxiously at her broad, honest face, and then clambered up the bank. "Listen, the Welsh hold my young brother and sister prisoners—and if only I could lay hands on the harp I'd have something to bargain with."

"You must promise to give it back though, if I tell you where it is hid—and not bring the Welsh seeking it," she insisted. "You must swear you'll not bring the Welsh about our ears."

"I promise, as I'm a Christian," declared Osmund.

He stretched his head upwards among the green leaves. Doll bent down and whispered:

"In the monks' rush-stack at Haordin Castle."

"But where *is* Haordin?" demanded Osmund.

There was no answer. The branches flew up again as Doll jumped down into the field. Someone was coming along the mountain track—a huge man dressed in green. He walked bent in two and kept moving from one hedgerow to the other, grumbling and exclaiming all the time as he hurried along.

"Little-John!" shouted Osmund joyfully.

CHAPTER SIX

ITTLE-JOHN returned Osmund's greeting with equal
heartiness. He stood upright, his great arms stretched
from hedge to hedge.

"Well met, Blackbird, well met! Beshrew me if Robin hath
not forgotten how to lay a patteran! My back is nearly broken
searching for signs of his track—but where is he, and what
news? Why, I scarce knew you in yon mailed gear!"

Osmund made no mention of Elian's harp as they went back
up the hill. Honest Little-John was not as fine-witted as his
friend and comrade Robin Hood, and Osmund felt that the
affair must be carefully handled.

Little-John and his men were very tired—and Osmund suggested that he should go and find Robin, while they took a little
rest. The Castle men-at-arms were anxious to accompany their
young master, but he declared that he was safer alone. He promised faithfully not to approach the Welsh side of the earthwork,
and then, mounting his horse, cantered down the hill and into
the bridle-track which led to Offa's Dyke. As he drew near he
could hear the lowing of cattle and the shouts of the vendors,
and now and then a snatch of music. The road was churned into
mud and marked with the feet of sheep and unshod country
horses. Osmund thought it prudent to turn aside and tie up his
steed in a little wood before he plunged into the throng.

Welsh and English voices vied with each other, frightened
heifers charged through the crowds, tumblers beat drums to attract attention to their show, and earnest housewives bargained

for Welsh cheeses and hams. The fair, though not large, was so animated and noisy that Osmund almost despaired of finding his friend. As he passed anxiously about from group to group, he was more closely remarked than he himself was aware of.

The Welsh, both gentle and simple, shaved the hair on their faces, save that on the upper lip. All young men, even nobles, went barefoot, and wore only a light tunic to the knee and a mantle of thin silk or coarse homespun according to their quality. They were easily distinguishable among the bearded English peasantry, and first one man began to follow Osmund, then another joined him, and presently five or six moved after him.

Osmund began to feel very hot and uncomfortable. He turned round and spoke to the best-dressed of the group in English: the man responded in vehement Welsh, which, of course, Osmund could not understand. He endeavoured to turn back towards the English side of the dyke, but immediately the Welshmen ringed him round and began to hustle him in the opposite direction.

"Robin! Robin! Come to my help!" shouted Osmund, resisting as best he could. No doubt the men had recognized the little Welshman's armour. "Sir Elian, Sir Elian, Sir Elian!" he now called. "Does any Englishman here speak Welsh? Will no one explain for me?"

Two or three stout English drovers hurried up, staves in hand; the Welshmen paused, puzzled by Osmund's cries for the very man whom they imagined he had robbed, if not murdered. Osmund hardly knew how to explain the situation without bringing the dwarf knight into danger, but while he struggled and stammered, Robin Hood came upon the scene, and with a thrust or two of his powerful arms passed through the crowd and stood at Osmund's side. The Welsh, seeing themselves hopelessly outnumbered, released him, and running into the bushes which flanked the base of Offa's Dyke, they were out of sight in a moment, seeming to melt into the landscape like running deer.

"How now, Osmund, what do you here?" inquired the forester gravely. "I thank you, friends, for your timely help," he added to the drovers. "This page belongs to a patron of mine and has taken French leave to follow me, as the archers say."

"It is ill meddling with the Welsh, though," said one drover. "They have been hardly treated in the past and are of vengeful nature. That young knave of thine might well have caused a riot."

They hurried back to their beasts and Robin stood still, looking sternly at Osmund.

"Little-John has come," said the boy. "I never thought the armour would be recognized, Robin. Our folk are resting at the grange, for they are mighty weary, and you did not forbid me to follow you—so I came."

"Blackbird, thou must learn to obey the wish as well as the word, else canst thou not be counted a member of our fellowship," quoth the forester. "Come, we must find Elian, who is lingering at the soothsayer's booth. So far we have discovered nothing."

"Is there no news of Hild and Eadgar?" asked Osmund anxiously.

Robin Hood shook his head.

This was a grievous disappointment. Osmund's faith in his friend was so great that he had hitherto had no real fear as to the final outcome. But if Robin Hood, the invincible, had failed to track the slavers, or if they had vanished with their prey across the lawless Welsh border, what hope was left? It was but a day's ride to the sea, and were there not always Irish pirates cruising off the coast of Wales, ready to aid evil-doers for a share in the booty?

"They tell me the border barons will not raise a finger to help any wrong," went on Robin Hood. "Their following is greatly weakened by the King's French war, and men are scarcely to be had to reap the corn, archers' wages are so high-risen. So I am of a mind——"

He paused, looking down at Osmund with that laughing light in his eyes which always betokened a dangerous errand.

"I'll come too!" said Osmund quickly.

"And so thou shalt," agreed the forester approvingly. A brave spirit pleased him, and he was of opinion that a likely youth could not serve his apprenticeship to perilous deeds too early. Maid Marian might not have agreed with him, and it was very certain that the Lady Etheldreda would not have done so. But Robin felt confident that his own strength, shrewdness and proficiency in arms would serve to preserve the boy's life, and he recked little of difficulties and perils which fell short of death itself.

"It was a foolish notion to don the Welshman's armour, Blackbird," said Robin Hood. "But I fear thou takest after me and art inclined to leap before looking. Seest thou, these Welshmen are ticklish as to points of honour and so forth—they are easily offended."

"They don't like being carried off by force, in fact," rejoined Osmund slyly.

"Well, it seems I cannot blame you without blaming myself," cried Robin Hood cheerfully. "Between us we have offended the goblin knight, and he is not disposed to do more to help us. He advises us to apply direct to the Prince, a noble and most gracious youth, by his telling and his special patron."

"Then Sir Elian will plead our cause himself?" exclaimed Osmund hopefully.

But the forester shook his head. "That is just what he will not do. Either the man is just drawing the long-bow about his noble lineage and grand acquaintance or else——"

"Or else what, good Master Robin?"

"Or else he has given the Prince a cause of anger against him. I am mighty unlearned in these ways, Osmund, so sit down on this knoll and let us divide this gingerbread cake while you tell me all you know about the Princes and governance of Wales."

"Oh, that we had Eadgar here!" said the boy, and then he kept silence for a moment while he wondered anxiously in what plight poor Eadgar and Hild might be at this very moment. It seemed as though they were wasting time, yet he knew that Robin Hood's ways were to be trusted and he racked his brains as to what he knew.

"The Welsh are always at war among themselves, I've heard," he said at last. "They had a great prince called Owen who ruled over them all, but he died ages ago—before our King came to the throne."

"More than five years ago then?" said Robin, smiling.

"Nay, when my father was a little boy—at least twenty-five years ago. And ever since all the Welsh princes have been fighting each other and the Lord Marchers."

"H'm—difficult to keep out of brawls if you're a marcher," commented the forester. "If you are friendly with your Welsh neighbour his enemies attack you, and if you are unfriendly he attacks you himself! Who is King of Wales now?"

"They don't have a king—they just have princes—and the Prince of Gwynedd is their overlord. He has just succeeded to the throne, and he is quite, quite young—only sixteen or seventeen. Wido had a song about him."

"A green sapling makes an uncertain shot; he's over-young," said Robin. "What else?"

"That is all I know," confessed Osmund, "except that the Welsh are always raiding across the border, and, of course, the English raid back——"

"And perhaps the other way about," interrupted Robin, "But go on."

"A girl at the farm over yonder told me that in this last raid—at Sir Elian's place, I suppose, a harp had been stolen—she said the Welsh would set the whole country in a blaze for a mere harp."

"Easy to be seen thou art no minstrel! But I have a notion—above all things we have time to beat. Maybe that was why Elian refused to go to his Prince. What was it he said about the harp? Oh, plague upon it, but the fool's long tales made me slumber."

"He said that a bard must never part with the harp which is the Prince's gift," repeated Osmund; "and so I thought if we could find the harp we would have something to bargain with—but if we can't save Hild and Eadgar soon, they may be carried off to Ireland——"

Robin Hood gave his young friend a playful blow which sent him rolling on the grass.

"Aye, but you foolish fellow, we're only *waiting* for a harp!" he declared. "Where said the girl that the instrument lay hid?"

"In the monks' rush-stack at Haordin Castle," repeated Osmund. "But how shall we find that?"

"By using our wits, to be sure! For it will be a brave shot in our quiver. Ride quickly to the grange—doff that suit of mail, and if Elian has not yet sent back thy tunic take Much's, and push the overflow under thy belt. Tell Tuck I have need of his friar's gown, and bid them all await my coming——"

"When—where?" asked Osmund breathlessly.

Robin Hood reflected for a moment.

"Wherever they find good hunting," he decided carelessly at length. "They must keep a man on watch at the grange, so that I can find them if need arise. But you and I will try peaceful methods first. Hold a moment, Blackbird!"

Osmund had already sprung up.

"Bid Little-John brew a mess of the brown moss that clings about the roots of heather—and say he must put in lumps of pine gum and make a thick mixture, strong enough to dye gold. And now begone, for I must find Elian and make some inquiries ere we get to business."

There were a dozen questions at the tip of Osmund's tongue, but he only asked:

"Is there anything more, Master Robin? And will the Merry Men take your orders from my mouth?"

"Well thought of! Show them this." The forester stooped and plucked a long grass-blade, which he wound in a knot about two leaves which he took from his pouch.

"Was it by such a sign that Little-John and our folk followed you hither?" inquired Osmund.

"Ask no question to which you can find the answer yourself—that is a greenwood law," returned Robin. "You know very well we of the greenwood have each a patteran like the gipsy folk, and leave a sign when we travel by which our friends may follow us. Now haste away, but do not run in sight of the folk or they will take thee for a thief."

Osmund followed this advice, but nevertheless made good speed. He had fully hoped to get to the knoll before Robin Hood's return, but as he came out of the bushes and advanced sideways down the steep grassy slope of the earthwork, he saw his friend's figure seated on the same spot as though he had never moved.

"Little-John is waiting in the copse with the two best horses," announced Osmund, panting a little as he came up the mound.

"Elian has fled," said Robin. "No doubt he was afraid when his men began to hustle you. I doubt he won't send his folk to return thy tunic, either."

"There has been no sign of them yet," agreed Osmund. "Little-John is monstrous discontent, and he bid me say——"

"I can guess the whole tale, but we have no time to listen to it. Hark ye, Osmund, 'tis a big pity that we know no Welsh, but fortune serves us, nevertheless. I have fallen in with some of the Welsh Prince's men, who were buying wine and provisions for his table. And we'll e'en follow them back to his Court tonight—at least, the harper and his boy will."

"And will the harper be blind, Master Robin?"

"Nay, lad, this time the harper has need of his eyes."

"And where are we going now?" inquired Osmund.

He was forced to adopt a sort of trotting pace, for the forester was covering the ground with huge strides, as he passed rapidly through the crowd and hastened towards the group of ash trees where Little-John was awaiting them.

"I'll tell you when I know myself," answered Robin cheerfully.

Chapter Seven

Osmund could not restrain his mirth as he watched Robin Hood endeavouring to fold Friar Tuck's immense frock about his tall, sinewy frame. Tuck had once spent a few penitential months as porter to a monastery, and had fled thence wearing the garment which had been bestowed upon him in all charity. He had an absurd fondness for it—patched and ragged though it was—and refused to part from it. Only Robin's command could have induced him even to lend it for a few hours.

The whilom outlaw, serious for once, struggled to arrange the vast folds, and then girded himself with the worn leather belt, in which he drilled a new hole with his knife, tucking in the long end.

"Well, lad? With that black hood I have bought me, shall I not pass as a brother?"

"Perhaps—at a goodly distance," agreed Osmund. "A monk would have a rosary in his belt—not a hunting-knife, though."

"This is a knife for cutting rushes," declared Robin with a grin. "But perhaps a hook were better. We'll buy one as we go along."

So saying, he stuck his knife into his stocking and sprang upon his horse. Osmund mounted the other and they moved cautiously to the edge of the thicket.

"We'll go back to the Fair and choose a hook," said Robin.

"And mind you look lowly and humble, Blackbird, as befits a youth trained in the cloister."

259

He touched his horse with his heel and cantered along the top of the embankment until he came to a cattle-track slanting down it. A little below them in the bright sunshine were a couple of very beautiful horses of that noble Spanish breed introduced into the border country by the famous Norman, Robert of Belesme, the builder of a score of strongholds on Welsh land. The horse couper kept them disdainfully apart from the thick-set country steeds, and though many came to admire, there seemed to be no buyers.

The men saluted the shabby monk respectfully.

"I fear this fair will hardly attract folk of sufficient quality to buy your fine beasts," said Robin, speaking in a feigned voice which made Osmund jump.

"If truth be told, we've had no offer as yet, brother," returned the dealer.

Robin pulled a few coins from his pouch and bade Osmund go and buy a reaping-knife such as was used for gathering rushes. When he returned, Robin was still talking to the horse-dealers; he kept his serious expression and shook his head mournfully from time to time, but when Osmund came within earshot, he found the conversation did not match the expression at all.

"I'll look for thee at next Martinmas and we'll have a merry time," Robin was saying. "But just now I have need of those two horses—if they are as good as they look, which, indeed, I think they are, the price is not too high. Gold I have none for the moment, but meet me at the church yonder—I see the tower above the elm-trees—tonight at six, and I'll come purse in hand."

"What do we now?" asked Osmund.

"Why, gather rushes, to be sure," rejoined Robin.

He turned his horse's head and rode up the dyke again. Osmund checked his pace in passing the Spanish horses. They were stamping their slender feet at the flies, tossing their proud little heads and switching their long, silky tails. Osmund had never in his life bestridden such a creature, and, of course, longed to do so.

Robin beguiled the way by instructing Osmund on how to lay a 'patteran'; he had acquired the art from the gipsies, each of whom have a personal and a tribal patteran, which consists in twisting certain leaves and grasses together and laying them under the hedge at intervals so as to form a trail which only the initiated can find and follow.

They rode over pasture-land for some way till Robin said: "We'll strike into the wood here, Blackbird, and I'll ride first. Look, yonder flies the flag on the Castle turret!"

Osmund's eyes followed Robin's pointing finger, and he saw the warm, red sandstone of the Castle wall rising through trees high above them. The country they had traversed formed a series of wooded ridges, with marshy valleys between. There were many streams, and now, as they halted their horses, the sound of running water filled the air. The Castle stood on an artificial eminence which crowned a cone-shaped hillock. Robin Hood rode down through the untrimmed oakwoods, crossing some abandoned out-works fast falling into decay. At the bottom of the ferny slope ran a wide, sluggish stream, broadening here and there into long pools.

"A good place for water-fowl," quoth Robin. "And there are certainly rushes a-plenty. If thou canst see the rush-stack before I do, Blackbird, I'll give thee a silver penny."

There was no one about, and they went on, glancing keenly from side to side. Osmund was the first to call out that he saw swathes of cut rushes drying on the grass. Robin had seen them some minutes earlier, but he said nothing, and presently dismounted and tied his horse to a tree. A moment later he made an exclamation of annoyance and pointed to the stack on the further side of the stream.

"Hide the knife," he said peremptorily. "No, give it to me."

"LOOK, YONDER FLIES THE FLAG ON THE CASTLE TURRET!"

(See page 261)

Osmund watched the long chopper disappear through the hole in Friar Tuck's gown—rent wider for the purpose—and waited orders in silence.

"Yesterday thou wert careless enough to lose the reaping-knife," announced the forester severely, "and holy poverty demands that we find our tool again. It may even have been built into the rush-stack, for I call to mind that thou hadst it in hand when we laid on the last sheaf. Truss up thy chausses—take off thy shoes, and we'll e'en ford the stream and search for it."

The bottom of the stream was deep in mud, and Osmund was obliged to clutch the man's strong arm as he slipped and stumbled in the water. They were hailed by a dissipated-looking man-at-arms with a hawk on his wrist as they scrambled up the opposite bank. The mock-friar shouted up the story of the reaping-knife, and the other bawled down his advice to give the boy a sound thrashing. He watched for a moment to see if the brother intended to put his counsel into immediate execution, but seeing the pair merely begin their work at the stack he strolled off and took no more interest.

In a very few minutes Osmund's fingers touched something hard and then a melancholy, muted note sounded as he grazed a harp-string. Robin drew out the knife, and also a coil of rope with which he bound up a large bundle of rush sheaves with the harp in the centre.

"We'll carry it between us," he said. "Pull up the reeds on thy side to cover that gleam of gold." He rebuilt the stack swiftly and they hastened back across the water. When the horses were reached Robin slung the bundle across his back, with a great fringe of rushes sticking up over his head.

Chapter Eight

THE RETURN JOURNEY to the dyke was very wearisome. Though it was downhill the going was bad, and the horses tripped and stumbled continually. Osmund was terribly hungry: the sun was going down and he could not help hoping that Little-John would have a meal ready for them and that they would be able to sleep in the hay-mow before riding further. But he was determined to utter no complaint.

Little-John met them half a mile below the grange. He was full of complaints and discontent, and implored Robin Hood to let him take part in the adventure. But Robin was adamant.

"I have other work for you to do," he declared. "For, look you, as Elian would say, I believe we can spit two birds with one bolt."

"Which two birds?" inquired Little-John. "Speak plain words, as befits an honest yeoman," exclaimed John. "For truly I am in no mood to follow flights of fancy."

"First, then, we must rescue Eadgar and the little maid, secondly, we must punish the slavers; and I want you to watch for them at this side of the border."

"It seems we are to be at the beck and call of every brat in the country," grumbled John, trying to force his good-humoured features into a scowl.

"Blackbird and I will undertake to find the captives, and you, Little-John, must trace and punish the slavers," Robin ordered. "Is the beggar still in our company?"

"He is up above at the grange, and anxious to join our band."

"We will try him first—is he trusty, think you? Would he serve to get speech with the slavers in case they have already sold their prisoners?"

"H'm, that is a ticklish errand—one I had best undertake myself," said John, his face clearing at the idea of a dangerous adventure. "And hark ye, Robin—it will be strange if Maid Marian be not soon upon thy track."

"Just what I think," agreed Robin. "We have no time to lose. Have you any money upon you, friend? I have need of a score of gold pieces."

"The beggar's wallet is well-lined," said John, coolly. "And I brought it along—was not that well thought of?"

"So that accounts for your bruised lip and swollen nose," cried Robin, much amused. "Cut a tally stick, Little-John, and Osmund shall count the coins. As the fellow is only a novice—so to speak—we must be prepared to hand him back his purse, if he leaves our company."

While he was talking, Robin Hood had unbound the big bundle of rushes and disclosed a small golden harp. He plucked the strings critically and then, taking from John a smoking pot of some sticky, dark compound, he proceeded to dab it all over the frame of the instrument until every glint of gold was hidden.

"'Tis real gold, not gold-leaf," declared Little-John admiringly. "And I doubt if the dye will ever stick to it, though I put in the pine-gum as you bid me."

"It will dry in half-an-hour," declared Robin. "And I'll go bail thou hast a slice or two of venison frying for us, which we can eat while we wait."

He sniffed the air, and then strode behind a thick bush where a low wood fire was burning, and thin collops of meat were frizzling on wooden skewers on the hot stones in the centre. A leather bottle of wine hung from an adjacent bough.

Little-John produced flat loaves, like large bread-buns, which were used both for plate and nourishment. The custom was to cut your loaf in two with the knife which everyone carried, scoop out the lower portion and lay on it a copious helping of meat and gravy. Then, having eaten one's meat—throwing any bits of bone or gristle which it might contain under the table—one finished up by eating the 'plate' itself, now agreeably soaked with gravy.

On this occasion the three friends sat down close to the fire, slit their loaves in two and helped themselves by digging the points of their knives into the sizzling collops. It was the best meal Osmund had had for three days, and he did ample justice to it. Robin Hood managed to dispose of two collops to Osmund's one, and John twitted him with having put on Friar Tuck's appetite at the same time as his frock. Robin retorted with one of his playful blows which made even the gigantic Little-John reel. He wasted no time on words, but rose directly he had finished eating, pulled off his monkish disguise and slung the harp across his back.

"Take my horse," he said then. "Ride down to the market and buy a couple of gay cloaks and a pink feather for Osmund's cap. Thou'lt meet us on the road that goes from the church yonder into Wales."

Little-John did his commission well and the horse-coupers were prompt at the tryst. The beggar's purse was considerably lightened as Robin paid without bargaining. The 'luck-penny' which the dealer handed back Robin tossed to the stable-boy, and springing into the saddle, he rode gaily away. No one could have recognized the toil-worn monk and his henchman in the somewhat raffish-looking pair who rode over the bridge into Wales a few minutes later. They bestrode princely horses and their mantles vied with the rainbow, but anyone could mark mud-stained hose and worn sleeves protruding from under the silken folds.

"Followers of the gay science," said the folk, looking after them. Anyone could have guessed them to be travelling gleemen without even seeing the harp.

Robin Hood led the way at a brisk pace for about five miles, then he pulled up and looked keenly about him. They had just reached the top of a long rise and were surrounded by bleak moorland, with patches of pasture broken by marshy pools and groups of wind-dashed thorn-trees. A stormy sunset flamed in yellow and orange to their right and behind, the border hills, magnified by the evening mist, showed rose-coloured where the light shone on sandstone and wet, brown bracken.

Osmund insensibly drew closer to his leader and Robin's long-bow, which he was carrying, rattled, and made his horse so restive that he could hardly control it.

"What are we waiting for, Master Robin? Steady! Whoa there, stand!" cried Osmund breathlessly.

Robin made a queer sound—a low, prolonged whistle and then said a string of still queerer words in a strange, chanting tone.

The restless horse stood quite still, trembling a little and pricking its ears.

"We're waiting for the retinue of the Prince of Gwynedd. They were down at the fair buying provisions, and their lord is camped somewhere about fifteen miles off. He is the head Prince, as you told me very truly, and the Prince of Powys has done him homage, but he has an uncle at Oswaldstree that he is none too sure of, and a cousin in the next contref or commote, or whatever they call it—Merry something—hark, I hear horses!"

"What about the cousin?" queried Osmund.

"Well, it seems he thinks he has a chance of being overlord himself and is in no hurry to do homage to his kinsman."

"Oh," said Osmund.

It all sounded very complicated and warlike. The popular impression of the Welsh was that they were always murdering each other in family feuds, and there were horrid stories of their cruelties. But then there were horrid stories about English cruelties too! King Henry put child hostages to death and Prince John starved his enemies in underground dungeons.

"What language was that in which you spoke to the horses?" he asked, trying to make his voice sound quite casual and self-assured.

"Fairy language—or phœnician, as they call it in Ireland," rejoined his friend. "I learnt it from the gipsies. Now, when these people come up, make your horse curvet—show him to advantage."

The wet road twisted away behind them like a grey snake, and Osmund could see no one, nor hear a sound save the sharp stabbing note of flitting moorland finches. But a few minutes after Robin had spoken a little procession of men and laden ponies came into view, laboriously climbing the hill.

Two riders, armed with light lances, detached themselves from the main body and advanced at a rapid trot. They drew rein when they reached Robin Hood and his companion and saluted courteously, calling some question in Welsh.

Robin returned the salute with studied grace.

"Alas, I have no Welsh," he said. "But I journey to the court of the noble Llewelyn, to seek a boon, offer a gift and sing a lay."

"The Prince would love you better if you put the last first," answered one of the men in a sing-song tone. He was nicknamed 'the Sassenach' on account of his proficiency in the language. "But he is always glad to greet a fellow-musician, therefore, I pray you, ride on in our company."

The Welshmen were young and ill-mounted, and their glances kept returning admiringly to the strangers' horses.

"Those are no merlins from Llanfyllin horse-fair," remarked Gwyllim Sassenach. "Where got you those choice bits of horse-flesh, Master Harper?"

"By honest purchase," returned Robin. "But truly they are over-fine for a poor minstrel and his boy—they are more meet for a prince."

"I thought Merlin was a Welsh prophet," put in Osmund. "Or did you mean the hawk—" He added hastily: "Fair sir," realizing that a gleeman's servant would be unlikely to take part in the conversation unbidden, as a knight's son might do.

"Nay, the merlin is a special breed of pony, strong and handsome little beasts fit for mountain-riding."

"Like yours?" suggested Osmund.

"Yes, indeed, like mine," repeated the Sassenach, but he sighed and cast envious looks at the Spanish horses.

Presently a wall of mountains came into view on the left, while the ground fell away in front, and Gwyllim led the way across a wild, untracked moor.

"The main way goes by a steep pass, or notch, as we call it, down the mountain," explained the Welshman. "But as our beasts are heavy-laden we shall strike across by the oak woods, avoiding the defile—and pass out of Powysland," he added in a lower tone.

He called something to his companion, who pressed forward and led the way over country which Osmund had never seen matched save in nightmare sleep. Now they were splashing through a boggy morass, where the Spanish horses plunged and slithered and nearly unseated at least one of their riders. A few minutes later the sumpter-ponies, who were shod, were striking sparks out of the flinty ridges of rock which broke through the thin crust of earth. Next, in the failing light, there was a woodland valley to be traversed, and Robin groaned, fearing their precious mounts would do themselves a mischief.

"Hold hard! Master Sassenach," he cried. "This may be good merlin country, but beshrew me if it will not maim a gift for a prince!"

"Fearest thou to follow us? Is it as my comrades say, then, art thou a spy?" exclaimed Sassenach, pulling up.

In a moment the two strangers were surrounded by a ring of angry faces, and the dying light glittered on the long knives which every man had drawn from his stocking.

"My master is no spy," cried Osmund indignantly. "He is a——"

"Harmless musician, seeking his fortune," interrupted Robin. "Take my weapons if you will, but in honesty admit that I am only in your company by your own invitation. In my country we fling not evil words at our guests."

This remark cut Gwyllim to the soul. If there is one thing upon which a Welshman prides himself more than another it is in courtesy to strangers.

"I crave your pardon most humbly," exclaimed the young man, crimsoning down to the collar of his scarlet mantle. He poured forth some excited phrases in Welsh, and then leaping to the ground he begged Robin's leave to lead his horse himself until they should regain a road.

As they wound their way along the narrow track Robin Hood began to sing, half under his breath.

"Childe Roland to the dark tower came——"

Osmund felt an eerie sensation rush through him. The wind howled down the valley, and as they at length emerged from the shadow of the trees a cold rainstorm dashed against their faces.

CHAPTER NINE

THE WELSH WERE not as yet great castle builders, they preferred the ancient hall, presided over by the tribal chief. Their favourite methods of warfare were by swift attack or by ambush—sitting down for three or four months to starve out a fortress did not appeal to them in the least.

As the travellers drew near the dwelling where the young Prince was staying, they could see its long outline high on the hillside. A strong column of smoke rose above the roof and soft, ruddy light streamed from the wide-open doors.

"You know our custom, doubtless," said Gwyllim, riding up to Robin Hood. "The door is always open to the guest, and when he comes in the maidens of the house will hasten forward to offer him water to wash his feet. If he refuses, it is a sign that he is journeying farther that night, but if he accepts it means that he wishes to stay."

"I thank you, fair sir," replied Robin, "and will accept the Prince's hospitality in the generous spirit in which he offers it."

"Any Welsh house would do the same, were it but a wattle hut," returned the other proudly.

They toiled up the ascent, and Osmund was surprised to find that there was no attempt at cultivation in the neighbourhood of the hall—no garth, nor ploughed fields, only wild pasture thickly studded with clumps of wild-rose and seedling thorns. As they drew near the door four or five youths ran out to take their horses, while maidens in garments of thin silk came to the doorway to light them in with torches. Gwyllim had hurried on ahead and had already dismounted, he was endeavouring to talk two languages at once—to introduce the strangers, to bid them welcome, and to tell the news he had gleaned during the day, all at the same time.

The apartment into which they entered reminded Osmund of nothing so much as the abbey tithe-barn. Clouds of smoke from the large wood fire in the middle, hung about the roof, making it look higher than it actually was. The vast space was full of people, some at chess, some eating and drinking, some playing with beautiful hounds—Osmund counted ten or twelve of these—and some calmly sleeping on the broad bench which ran all round the wall.

The maidens led the strangers in courteously by the hand, brought seats for them—stools with low arms and no backs—and offered them water for their feet, which they duly accepted. One girl wheeled up a large harp and prepared to entertain the new guests with music and song, a second gracefully presented a gilded horn, filled to the brim with wine, and a third knelt down to unlace the travellers' muddy buskins.

Robin would have protested had he not been afraid his action would be misunderstood, but Osmund saved his embarrassment by plumping down on the floor, ducking his head in what was intended for a polite salute to the kneeling maiden, and undoing Robin's buskins himself.

"'Tis my duty to serve my master," he observed.

To his surprise the girl answered him in English, though with a pretty lilt in her tones which betrayed her origin.

"In Gwynedd we think no shame to serve a guest, be he gentle or simple."

"A right noble custom," cried Robin, giving Osmund a push with his knee as a warning that he was to be discreet. "Pray tell me, is the most noble Llewelyn in residence, fair maiden? For we have ridden over the border to beg a boon which admits no delay."

"My cousin is but now returned from hunting," said she. "And he will soon be here to bid you welcome. Supper will be served in less than half an hour, but if you be hungry, food shall be brought forthwith."

"We'll await supper, I thank you," said Robin. "But meanwhile I would gladly empty this horn to the glorious customs of ancient Wales."

While Robin drank, Osmund washed and dried his feet and fitted on a beautiful pair of deerskin shoes from the selection which the girl brought him.

"Do let me do your feet," she whispered to him. "And then I can stay and talk to you. Otherwise I shall be sent away and you will be entertained by Eluned and Essylt."

"All right—you pour out the water," agreed Osmund. "How did you learn to speak English so well? Have you talked to any other English boy lately?"

"What a strange question!" said she.

Osmund looked up eagerly. The girl was quite young—not very much older than himself, and very pretty.

"I did not mean to be over-curious or rude," he urged. "But we are in search of my brother and sister, who have been carried off by slavers into Wales, and I hoped—I wondered—if you could have seen them?"

"We can't talk now," she answered, hastily dragging a shoe on to his foot. "But I'll send my brother Rhun to you at supper. My name is Gwenllian and that is my sister Eluned at the harp."

The lady with the drinking-horn made her a sign and Gwenllian rose immediately and beckoned a serf-woman to remove the basin. She herself gathered up the towel and went out of the room by a curtained doorway behind the dais at the far end.

Servants now began to set up trestle tables with long oak benches on either side and the Welsh took their places, the better-born in groups of three, and the others in indiscriminate rows. When the huge dishes of smoking meat were carried in, the curtains parted behind the dais and a young man of striking beauty came in and uttered some courteous phrase of greeting.

Osmund had posted himself behind Robin Hood in the customary position of a page, but the Prince observed this and sent one of his own suite to lead him to a seat. There were evidently many other guests besides the Harper and his boy, and the Prince and members of his family waited on some themselves and kept issuing orders for the care and comfort of all. They walked round the hall, seeing that everyone was served, speaking kindly welcome to high and low and making sure that all wants were attended to before they withdrew to the dais and began their own meal.

Meanwhile musicians sang, played, cracked jokes and asked riddles which provoked shouts of laughter. Osmund's neighbours spoke only Welsh, so he could hold no conversation with them, and presently turned his attention to Llewelyn. The Prince was about eighteen years old at this time. He was tall and well-developed, with a broad brow and dark, chestnut hair cut below the ears, instead of flowing to the shoulders according to the new fashion. His eyes were keen and penetrating, set rather deep, under straight, finely pencilled brows: at first sight he might be set down as a fighter, at a second glance divined to be a dreamer: in fact, brain and body were equally matched in this noblest of Welshmen. A garland of golden oakleaves fitted closely round his head and he wore a wide-sleeved tunic, with a woven border of green and gold.

Osmund watched, fascinated, and was startled when a voice suddenly whispered in his ear:

"I am Rhun."

A boy stepped over the bench and sat down beside him.

"Are you a harper, too?" he inquired. "The Prince is going to ask your father to play as soon as supper is finished."

"He is not my father," began Osmund—and stopped abruptly.

"I have been sent to entertain you and bid you welcome," went on the Welsh boy. "My sister tells me you have come to look for a lost brother. What is he like? Because yesterday we saw some men from Meirionydd—they are wild, fierce folk from the mountains, and their overlord has not yet done homage to Llewelyn as he ought to do——"

"Well, go on!" urged Osmund breathlessly.

"They had some folk with them, bound—a youth and maiden—and they said they were villeins who had run away—but we don't have villeins in Wales."

"Eadgar is a little taller than me and dark and much more Norman-looking," declared Osmund. "He has a curved nose——"

"I didn't look at his nose," interrupted Rhun excitedly. "But he called out: '*Ad adjuvandum me festina.*' No serf would shout for help in Latin."

"It's just what Eadgar would do, though," cried Osmund. "Which way did they go? Perhaps we can overtake them."

He rose, but Rhun pulled him down again.

"'Twere better the Harper should ask the Prince. See, he has sent Gwyllim Sassenach to invite him to play."

Osmund watched in a fever of impatience while Robin Hood strode up to the dais, saluted the company, and, sitting down, stretched out his strong, brown hand to the harp-strings.

"Will you not come up among us, friend?" said the Prince.

The knights and ladies courteously made room and Robin sprang lightly upon the dais, and in his jolly, ringing tones began to sing the ballad of *The Nut-Brown Maid*, strumming an accompaniment with rather more force than art.

After a moment Llewelyn laughed and laid a hand on the player's wrist.

"I think, friend, thy fingers are more accustomed to twang a bow-string than touch a harp," he cried. "Speak truth! Whose man art thou, and what doth an archer disguised as a minstrel?"

His young face became suddenly stern, and Osmund found himself trembling for his friend's safety.

"My lord, we came to beseech your help," he called, and pushed his way forward to Robin Hood's side.

The forester was no whit abashed.

"I am an archer first and foremost, as you truly guessed," he replied coolly. "But my business is with fleeing deer rather than armies. I am no man of war, but I can spin a quarter-staff, if need arise, and wrestle withal."

"I have no doubt thou canst," replied the Prince. "But speak to the point—tell me thy business and what brings thee into my country?"

"I came in pursuit of slavers who have carried off two children—the brother and sister of this lad here, and the boy a royal page to boot. We fear they are being taken through your dominions to Ireland, and are come to beg your aid."

Llewelyn turned to Gwyllim and asked a question and Rhun said something vehemently in Welsh. Two or three young men in the hall started up and, seizing their weapons, came forward, but the Prince shook his head.

"I am telling them we want peace, not war," he declared impatiently. "When will these hot-heads understand that everything cannot be settled by the sword! My grandfather Owen struggled with them for fifty years."

"Nevertheless, thy own sword has not slept in the scabbard!" exclaimed Gwyllim.

Llewelyn's eyes shone with a sudden angry light.

"Our swords and bright spears shall keep our country's boundaries," he said. "But are not to be used to slay our own kin. I have sent a youth to the courts of all the chieftains of Powys and Meirionydd: they must needs come here to do homage and pay the customary dues. Also we will send word that our ports shall be watched."

"But the men with whom these slavers deal will not use the King's ports like honourable sailors," said Robin bluntly. "There's many a lonely bit of coast-line where they can ship a cargo. Why, I have often—" He paused as he caught the young Prince's glance.

"It is the utmost I can promise at the present time," Llewelyn declared. "But tomorrow, when the chiefs arrive, I hope we may find means to allay your anxiety."

He then took leave of the company in a few courteous words, recommended the Saxon guests to the care of Gwyllim and Rhun, and withdrew to his private apartment.

While they had been on the dais the hall had been prepared for the night. Slaves had scattered fresh rushes and had carried in pillows and blankets to be distributed all along the wide sleeping-bench which lined the walls. The fire was carefully built up, and three young men sat down near it, wrapped in cloaks. It was their duty to tend it by turns all night.

Osmund took the first opportunity to repeat Rhun's information to Robin, but he was so dead-tired that he could not keep awake to talk things over as he had intended. As they lay down, the most heavenly strains of music sounded softly from the inner room. Never had either of them heard the harp touched by such a mighty hand.

"By my soul, I'll never call myself a harpist more!" exclaimed Robin softly as the sound died away. "Gwyllim, who plays? 'Tis never the same man who entertained us after supper!"

"'Tis the Prince himself," returned Gwyllim. "Young as he is there is no musician to touch him. And if you saw him leading his men in the field you would say the like—he has no peer."

CHAPTER TEN

"WAKE UP, WAKE UP! It is broad day and your master is abroad this hour!"

"What—where?" muttered Osmund. He opened his heavy eyes and saw a long ray of amber light striking the smoke-blackened beams of the roof far above him. For an instant he was quite bewildered and stared and blinked at Rhun, who was kneeling beside him.

"Are they found?" he cried at last, sitting up and throwing off the coverings.

"Not yet, I fear. But we thought perhaps you would like to come and see the place where Gwen and I saw them—at least if it was them."

"Yes. Wait a moment till I say my prayer," cried Osmund, jumping up. "And then we must find Master Robin."

"The men are all gone out to the horses," said Rhun. "But do you come with me—we can be back in twenty minutes, and by that time the cows will be milked and the folk will be serving out food and drink in the hall."

Osmund tightened his garters, slipped on his shoes and followed his new friend.

The hall was empty, but outside men and women were hard at work. Gwenllian was waiting for them on her pony, which she rode astride.

"Eluned won't come," she remarked. "Ever since little Sir Elian addressed an ode to her she thinks she is a beauty, and gives herself airs, and he only did it because he thought it would please Llewelyn."

She led the way down the hillside, through a steep birch-wood: a river gleamed below, winding between lush meadows.

"We'll have to cross by the ford," said Rhun. "What a bother it must be to wear hosen! But you can ride the pony. I'll bring him back to you after Gwen has crossed."

"No, I thank you. It's easy to manage unless the water is very deep."

So saying Osmund kicked off his shoes, dragged up his chausses over the knee, and tied them to his belt with the strings provided for the purpose. He was glad to be wearing Much's peasant clothes instead of his own.

The sparkling water was quite warm though it was so early. The river was low and the rocks over which it flowed had been heated by the long hours of sunshine on the previous day. The three young people climbed up the opposite bank and followed the valley a little way until they came to a stream, spanned by an ancient, crumbling bridge.

"The country folk say the Romans built that," said Rhun. "Now here we climb up on the right of the stream, keeping to the edge of the great beech-wood."

"Peasants will not come here at night," remarked Gwenllian. "At least they won't go higher than the farm yonder. There are some strange heathen stones at the top, and it mightn't be lucky to meddle with them. But I'm not afraid," she added, and striking the pony with the green hazel-switch she held in her hand, she sent it scampering and scrambling up the hillside.

The boys ran after her, but soon slowed their pace to a walk. Osmund wanted to ask about Elian, and Rhun said he believed the little man hoped to be Llewelyn's family bard, but he did not think that the Prince would grant the appointment.

"Why," he added, "Gwen has gone right on to the head of the cwm! But this is the place where we saw the party. We were nutting, you see—though of course the hazels are not ripe yet. They were resting in this clump of hazels."

Osmund pushed aside the long, mottled rods and peered into the little clearing—then he made an exclamation and rushed forward. Something had caught his eyes, fixed into the fork of a bush. It was a long strip of gold-embroidered silk.

"Hild's girdle!" he exclaimed. "They have been here. Rhun, be careful—don't trample the ground—let's see which way the track goes."

"Why, that is plain enough. There were seven or eight horses, so it won't be difficult to follow them——"

"Seven or eight!" interrupted Osmund. "Look, there are the tracks of two or three score at least—the turf is cut up and trampled half a furlong wide."

"It may be the track of one of the chiefs riding down with his men to do fealty," suggested Rhun. "We had better find Gwen and go back at once to tell the Prince. See here—the traces of a group of horsemen mingles with the big troop—or maybe they have just followed the broad track."

He called his sister's name: "Gwenth—lian! Gwen!" but there was no answer.

"How far would she go? Is that the top of the hill?" asked Osmund, as they plodded up the steep path and noted that though the hoof-marks went in the same direction they kept to a little distance from the bridle-track.

"It is a couple of miles to the top," answered Rhun. "I expect she has only gone as far as the standing stones to prove she is not afraid of bogies."

"Let's run," said Osmund.

They hurried on and came out on a wind-blown grass-land which sloped upward to the horizon. Osmund noticed a raised green track in the turf, but before he had time to comment on it

Rhun pointed to a mound which rose out of the hillside against the sky.

"There, can you see the stones?" he was beginning when Gwen and her pony shot out from behind the hillock and galloped towards them. The pony plunged and struggled through the heather bushes and arrived with heaving flanks and lathered chest. Gwen too, looked scared.

"Let's get home, quick!" she cried.

"Did you see anything of the slavers?" asked Osmund as he and Rhun ran panting on either side of the pony.

"No—I saw nobody—I mean—oh, do let us get home!"

Gwen burst into tears, and then pretended that she was only coughing.

Rhun began to gasp out remarks in Welsh, and Osmund tried to tell of the finding of the girdle in English, but the girl seemed too much frightened and bewildered to take in what they were saying.

At last, half-way down the lane, Rhun laid his hand on the bridle and halted the pony.

"No one is following us, sister," he declared. "You know I have hearing as keen as a mountain roe's, and there is no step of man or steed in our wake."

Gwenllian shuddered and turned paler than ever.

"I fear not those whose footfall makes an echo," she whispered.

"What did you see?" demanded Osmund. "Witches, or fairies, or what?"

"God keep us from all harm!" exclaimed Gwen in Welsh. Then she added in English: "I will not tell you what I have seen, lest if there be evil it fall on you as well as me."

"Mother says ill-wishes can't hurt good Christians," declared Osmund cheerfully. "So tell *me*, maiden, if you fear to tell your brother."

He tried to speak consolingly, but Gwenllian jumped to the conclusion that he did not believe she had seen anything alarming at all, and she was greatly offended.

"Very well, Sassenach, be it as you wish!" she cried haughtily, and pushing Rhun violently aside she leant down and whispered in Osmund's ear. "The pony shied at something bright, and I jumped down and looked into a crack between the rocks. And I saw Arthur and all his Court!"

Osmund stared at her open-mouthed for a moment, then he grew angry in his turn.

"I see you are only playing!" he cried. "You do not understand that my sister's and brother's safety is more to me than life! I thought you had been frightened by robbers, and you begin a childish tale about Arthur, who has been dead five hundred years."

"But I saw them," protested Gwen. "How could I be deceived in broad daylight? And those who see Arthur before his time to return as King pine away and die."

"Anybody might pine away, if they neglect to break their fast!" exclaimed a cheerful voice, and Osmund shouted "Robin!" with great joy and relief.

The forester was sitting on the bank only a yard or two away, but hidden from the children by a holly bush. He got up in one swift, graceful movement and stepped forward.

"The maid is afraid," he said quickly. "Her hands are as cold as icicles. You are safe with me, child, I will not let any danger nigh you."

Gwen sobbed uncomforted.

"She thinks she has seen something unreal," said Rhun.

"Face a fear and it is halved," said Robin. "March boldly upon it and 'twill melt away. I fear nobody, for no good man has cause of grief against me."

"She says she saw Arthur and all his Court," remarked Osmund.

"Oh," returned Robin thoughtfully. "That were a wondrous sight, *pardi*! And did they bear bows like me, maiden, or were they unarmed?"

"They were all in greaves and breastplates," answered Gwen. "And their helms lay beside them, and a spear was at each man's knee."

"Oh," said Robin again. He turned his head and glanced steadily up the mountain behind them. He watched the trees and bushes and the movements of the wild birds, all intent on their own business; then he listened. They all listened, but there was no sound but the sweet, inconclusive babble of the stream.

"Master Robin, look—we found this," cried Osmund, showing the girdle. "It is Hild's—I am sure of it."

Robin nodded but did not answer. He began to lead the pony forward, while Osmund went on eagerly talking. When the bridge came in sight, Robin stopped.

"Listen," he said solemnly. "Can you keep counsel? Will you, Rhun, take your sister home and tell this strange tale to none until I rejoin you?"

"Fair sir, you are a stranger," said the Welsh boy bluntly. "Is it not against my duty to hide anything from my patron, the Prince?"

"Tell him in private then," agreed Robin, "and add this word: When the wind is in the heather, but the tree is still, let the Chief gather his friends, and the deer sleep on the hill."

"We'll go swiftly," cried Rhun. "Youth," he added, turning to Osmund, "jump up behind Gwen: I'll run."

"Nay, I'll stay with Robin Hood," declared Osmund.

Rhun wasted no more words but scrambled on to the pony and started it towards the river at a gallop.

Osmund whirled round, prepared to run straight up the hillside again, but Robin stood quite still, his feet apart, his brown, curly head thrown back, absorbed in gazing first in one direction then in another. At last he began to walk slowly upstream.

"Passing strange," he muttered. "Perhaps the little lass was inventing after all. Or could she have been right? If there was aught human astir up there the birds would give us tidings."

"Could there be anything *not* human?" inquired Osmund, with a most unpleasant, creepy feeling running up and down his spine.

"We'll soon see," said Robin. "But if you would rather follow your friends, or wait me here, I'll think no worse of you—for joking apart, I have no idea at all what might be on the hilltop."

"Whatever it is, I'm coming with you," said Osmund. "Why, Robin, surely you don't think I would run away if you are going into danger?"

"Come you from courage or curiosity?" inquired Robin, who did not believe in taking anything over seriously.

"Curiosity, of course!"

Before the words were out of Osmund's mouth, Robin had leaped the stream, landing with unerring balance on a slippery stone, and was gliding through the tangle of young wood on the farther side as quickly and noiselessly as a questing hound. He paused from time to time to peer up at the horizon, and at one of these pauses pointed out the gulls circling lazily round and round in the warm summer air.

"There is carrion or offal of some kind there—mark the gulls! But a few moments ago plover flew steadily over, so there can scarce be men about."

"It might be just a dead sheep," hazarded the boy.

"Would there be sheep up there exposed to wolves and foxes without a shepherd? But of course shepherds may have left a dead beast unburied."

They went on; presently the stream bent to the left, and Robin crossed back. Osmund pointed out the hazel grove, and when they came to the traces of horses Robin whistled under his breath. He did not stop to examine either track but hastened on till they reached the edge of the beechwood and faced the wide sweep of heathery hill.

"Oh, look, Robin!" cried Osmund. "There's a road! A secret road—I mean a Roman road, like the one at home."

He pointed to the grassy causeway raised above the level of the moor.

Robin made no answer. He was sniffing the breeze. Above them the queer circle of stones crowned the little hill and jutted out against the sky.

"What said the maid?" he whispered.

"Why—she said she rode round the camp—as she called it— and something glittered in the sun, and she got off the pony to look, and through a crack between two rocks she saw a company of armed men and——"

"That's all I want to know," interrupted Robin. "See, here went the pony's feet, crushing the turf. And here we must follow; stay to my right and don't speak a word."

Robin strode on, keeping his own body between Osmund and the point whence danger threatened—the largest jutting stone which might well hide a man.

CHAPTER ELEVEN

WONDERFUL TALES were current of the strange persons and creatures that might be met with in Wales. Robin Hood was none too sure of his ground: even highly educated people believed in monsters and fairies, and he was quite prepared to believe that a poetical Welsh child might see a vision of her country's hero. On the other hand he was shrewd and had no intention of being slain in someone else's quarrel—hence he circled the mound at a good bowshot from the stones. Having satisfied himself that there was no movement about them, he dropped down behind the slight shelter of the raised track and crawled cautiously forward until he was able to creep between the tall heather bushes which covered the base of the hillock. Osmund copied him as faithfully as he could, but was soon gasping for breath and streaming with perspiration as he worked his way along.

From time to time Robin raised his head with infinite precaution and scanned the hill-side: some feeding curlew had risen and were flying about aloft in a way which would certainly have given them away had there been anyone watching—they would drop down as though to alight and then sweep upward again with frightened cries.

At last, after a long halt, Robin writhed his long form into a winding sheep-track and advanced boldly up the mount. The dewy path bore the impress of the pony's little feet and rose steeply to within a few yards of the standing stones. Sundry huge fragments of rock, which had once perhaps formed part of the circle, lay where they had fallen centuries before, and Robin examined each in turn. As he parted the rough grass and seedling whins, which sprouted about the third crag, he gave a smothered exclamation and recoiled violently on top of Osmund.

"Lord protect us!" muttered Robin. "Keep back, lad, I reckon it's no canny sight."

Osmund made the Sign of the Cross very carefully.

"Where you look, I look," he said, and creeping forward he craned his head over a dark fissure between two great slabs of stone. For a moment he could see nothing save a little fern bleached by the darkness, which fluttered in the draught from below. Then something glittered and the amazing scene became visible, like something painted on a dark background. He was looking into a cavern where men in armour were lying one on top of another—dead, as he thought at first. Then as he stared he became aware of red faces and open mouths from which came noisy breaths.

"Robin—they are drunken men!" he whispered. "They are real—no phantasy."

But though he spoke boldly his shaking limbs would scarcely hold him up. Creeping a little nearer, Osmund thrust his head into the cleft; at the same moment Robin approached and pressed down a large frond of bracken, letting a ray of light stream into the cave.

"Why," muttered Osmund, "we're dreaming! There lies Sir Elian, or his double."

Robin Hood pushed him aside and stared down for a tense minute. There was Sir Elian sure enough, gagged and bound like a criminal, and as Robin gazed he saw two small hands, tied together, stretch out from the darkness and shake the little man urgently by the arm.

Osmund was startled to hear Robin Hood whisper:

"We be friends. Lie still and make no sound."

Then he squatted back on his heels and laughed soundlessly.

"Blackbird, Blackbird! I wager we have all our quarry under our feet. But 'tis a ticklish pass, and drunken men—if they wake—are ill to reckon with. I'll wage a hart royal to a coney but we'll find Eadgar and the lass here as well."

He crept into the circle; it was a wide, grassy space with a large, flat stone in the centre; it would not budge under his hand and seemed firmly bedded in the earth. The grass was trampled and there were remains of food flung about as though a large body of men had bivouacked there.

"Ha," muttered Robin, "the gulls hinted as much."

There was no sign of horses. Looking back along the way they had come, Robin decided that the horses must be hidden somewhere in the beechwood. He scrambled down the farther side of the mound, taking care not to show himself on the skyline, and presently discovered a hole under a large rock—such a hole as a fox might make only that a strong draught blew from it. Robin tested the rock with his hand and it rolled slightly; then he put forth all his strength, but could not budge it further.

"It is wedged on the inner side," he declared.

"I could get under it," whispered Osmund. "If we scrape away these small stones and gravel, I could wriggle through."

"We'll try the other rock first," declared the forester, and he went back to the original place, while Osmund scraped and tore at the turf until his hands were bleeding. When Robin Hood returned after vainly seeking for another entrance, Osmund had disappeared all but his feet which he now drew after him with a last convulsive movement.

It was a horrible moment as he pushed himself forward under the rock, his hands grasping slimy clay, his chin scraping on the soil. At length he was able to kneel up, and he found himself in a rude passage, where there was only room to advance on all fours.

He felt for his knife and crept forward with it in his hand. His stealthy movements seemed to make a great deal of noise, his breathing alone filled his ears. But presently loud snores from the cavern drowned every other sound, and creeping through the low entrance Osmund found himself in a large circular chamber. There was a strong smell of mead, and as his eyes became accustomed to the dim light he could see a huge cauldron in the centre of the cave, and horns still clasped in the sleepers' hands. His heart beat hard as he cautiously picked his way through the men. There were two or three persons of high degree among the soldiers, for they wore gold collars, hooked round their throats by twisted gold wire, just like Llewelyn and his kinsfolk.

A sniffing sound made the boy start violently. It came again—sniff, sniff! There was a second smaller cave opening out of the big one, and as he gazed towards it, clutching his dagger, a ruffled, dark head was raised from the floor, and Eadgar's eyes met his.

Osmund flattened himself against the wall—it was made of beaten clay—and crept slowly and carefully towards his brother. Eadgar's arms were tied behind him: his feet too were fastened together and he was gagged. It was very difficult to release him in the darkness: Osmund was afraid of hurting him, and was slow and bungling over the work. Together they found Hild and released her too, and Osmund hugged her silently. But when he stooped over Sir Elian Hild pinched him.

"He has had a lot of mead," she whispered.

Elian's eyes rolled despairingly, and Osmund wavered.

"He tried to rescue us—we can't leave him," declared Eadgar.

"Leave his gag then," said Hild.

Osmund cut the thongs which bound the little man's hands and put his dagger into them.

"Free your feet and follow me," he said, and while Elian was rubbing his numb fingers and fumbling with the dagger,

Osmund led the way past the snoring drunkards and pushed Hild before him down the passage. She stooped down and wriggled under the stone like a flash. The boys paused an instant to see if they could discover the mechanism by which the great slab was poised, but a noise behind them made them abandon the attempt. Robin's hand could be seen wildly groping under the stone and closing and unclosing in his frenzied impatience, so first one boy and then the other crept out on the hillside. The noise they had heard proved to have been caused by Sir Elian, who tripped over a steel helmet and sent it rolling with a clatter. No one was more frightened than himself, and Robin laughed so much as Elian's pale, agitated face appeared—still tightly gagged—that he could hardly exert his strength to drag him out.

"No time to lose," he said then, and caught up Hild in his arms. "Lads, take the dwarf one on each side. Come, Elian, run for the honour of Wales and the safety of Llewelyn!"

He leaped down the hillside as he spoke, swerving towards the beechwood. The boys followed, dragging Elian with them.

Far away on the opposite hill they heard the silver music of a bugle, and at the gallant sound a horse neighed below them in the coppice.

Robin stopped suddenly and looked back.

"There should be just time to break up their horse-lines," he cried. "Oh, Elian, what a tale this will make when thou canst open thy lips to tell it!"

He dived into the wood and the others, panting in his wake, came presently to lines of picketed horses. There seemed to be no one on guard, and still clutching Hild against his shoulder, Robin rushed down the rows, kicking the pegs out of the ground and slashing at the ropes with his knife. Soon a score of excited animals were plunging about, and the boys, by Robin's command, bridled four stout cobs and they all mounted.

FIRST ONE BOY AND THEN THE OTHER CREPT OUT ON THE HILLSIDE
(See page 291)

"No time for saddles!" cried Robin, and picking a long sapling he drove the loose horses before him, and sent them galloping wildly down the lane towards the river.

"If the folk up yonder are truly coming to do homage to the Prince of Aberffraw, they will not be best pleased with us," remarked Robin with a grin. "Elian may be some private enemy of theirs for all we know——"

"Nay, Robin," interrupted Eadgar, "the little man came to our aid and they threatened to slay him and then decided to keep him as a hostage. He said they are traitors and intend to surround Llewelyn's camp and put him to death."

"Good, strong beer seems to have interfered with their plans," remarked the forester. "Now, children, cross the ford: I will wait till you are safe over for fear of accidents. Ride close, Blackbird, and I'll put this little maid behind you."

"It wasn't beer it was mead," announced a dismal, croaking voice.

Elian had at last managed to work off the gag, which still hung round his neck. He intended to take up his position opposite Robin Hood in order to share his post as guard of the ford, but his pony decided otherwise and trotted nimbly in the wake of the others, with its rider clinging to its mane.

"Are not you coming, Master Robin?" called the children from the opposite bank.

"Nay—bid the Prince send a few archers to hold the ford——"

Before the words were out of his mouth a group of horsemen came galloping down from the Hall. The foremost wore a mantle of scarlet silk and a helmet surmounted by a scarlet wolf's head. It was Llewelyn himself.

While the Prince paused to speak to Elian, Robin dismounted, tied up his pony and produced the bow and quiver which he had previously hidden in the rushes at the water's brink. He selected an arrow with his customary coolness and glanced keenly at the thicket from which the enemy might be expected to emerge.

"Two hundred paces," he muttered. "'Twere best to aim at the track where it turns above the bridge."

"Let us over-run the woods like the wolf," exclaimed Gwyllim, speaking English for Robin's benefit. "Let their blood crimson the tide of the stream."

"Gently," said Llewelyn. "Their swords are still in the scabbard. We have but one man's testimony against them."

"They enlisted the slavers to fight for them," cried Elian, his voice cracking with rage. And he began to pour forth poetic vituperations which left Gwyllim's remarks completely in the shade.

"Let no man strike till I give the word," ordered Llewelyn; he glanced sternly round to see if his warriors were prepared to obey him. "Will you ride with us, Master Archer? We will encircle the hill and take them in the rear, while my two kinsmen here and their men keep the ford."

"I have not my harp," cried Elian, "but nevertheless I will sing the song of the onset."

"But first," said Llewelyn kindly, "you must have your wounds dressed and take some refreshment. You, fair children, lead him to the Hall and stay you all within the enclosure until we return. Do you understand? It is my command."

"Do as he says," shouted Robin, above the rippling water.

"We will obey," said Eadgar, speaking for them all.

Osmund heaved a deep sigh. He greatly longed to ride beside Robin and to see the end of the adventure. Llewelyn turned to him.

"You shall be my representative," he said. "Take this as a token to the Lady Cristin, my kinswoman, and she will provide entertainment for you all."

He laid a beautiful rosary of chased gold in Osmund's hand and went forward across the river.

Chapter Twelve

THE LADIES of Llewelyn's family were standing at the entrance of the courtyard, gazing anxiously in the wake of the horsemen.

Osmund felt very awkward as he slipped down from his pony and came forward with Llewelyn's rosary in his hand. All the womenfolk, the serfs and the old Seneschal burst into Welsh speech, sounding for all the world like a flock of starlings settling for the night in the great holly tree beyond the moat at home.

Luckily Rhun was there and he translated Osmund's shy speeches, and all the ladies then clustered round Elian and Hild and Eadgar, with even shriller outcry.

It must be owned that Hild immensely enjoyed the sensation she had created and longed to be able to relate her experiences. The two brothers stole away to a quiet corner, where Gwen presently followed them with a foaming mug of new milk in one hand and a large dish of oaten flummery in the other. There were two spoons, one of gold and the other of horn, and the boys fell to with a will, sharing the bowl between them. They talked hard between mouthfuls.

Presently Rhun joined them, carrying a big platter of bilberries and cream and a pile of buttered oat-cake.

"The ladies are all ministering to the bard," he said. "They hope he will put their names in his next ode and say that they are all divinely beautiful."

"There seem to be a great many bards in Wales," said Eadgar.

"I wish I could understand Welsh—I know they have wonderful rules for their verse—it must be very interesting."

"My father was a poet," said Rhun. "But he died before I can remember. His name was Howel, and after his death we were sent as hostages to Randulf Blundeville at Chester."

"So that is where you learnt English," said Osmund.

"Yes, and French too. He is married to the Lady Constance, you know, the heiress of Brittany, and the Bretons are kin to the Cymri. Only for her and her son Arthur, Randulf would have killed us both. Why do the English kill hostages? I think it is most unjust."

"I suppose it is when a treaty is broken or something," said Eadgar. "When barons begin warring with each other, they don't seem to mind a bit whom they kill. Except knights like my father, of course—true and faithful knights."

"Like Llewelyn too," agreed Rhun.

"I think Prince Llewelyn is splendid," cried Osmund warmly. "I should think his knights would follow him everywhere like Arthur's. I say, isn't it rather a joke that Gwen's Knights of the Round Table prove to be a crew of drunken enemies?"

They all burst into shouts of laughter.

"All the same, who could tell what was there?" cried Eadgar, interrupting himself. "My father will be proud of Osmund when I tell him the tale."

"That was nothing—Robin Hood was with me!" exclaimed Osmund, flushing at his brother's praise.

"Not when you crept under that rock," declared Eadgar. "I shall put it all in my chronicle. Hild was very brave too."

"Let's see if there is any sign of the men," cried Osmund, to change the subject, and they all went to the door.

The gate of the enclosure was barred, but by climbing an ash tree they were able to look over it. There was nothing to be seen except peasants peacefully cutting hay, and swans sailing on the river, and great shining white clouds rising slowly behind Llantisilio Mountain. But far away Osmund detected the gay lilt of a horn.

Tantivy-tantivy-tan-tallo!

"That's Robin Hood!" he cried. "It's the home call and means that all goes well."

An hour later the warriors returned. They had vanquished the rebels after a sharp skirmish and had taken their leader. Meredith ap Conan, prisoner. Two of the slavers had been killed in the fight, the others had fled. Robin Hood had done gallant service and was unhurt. As soon as he could push his way through the throng he called the boys and asked if they had done anything about Elian's harp. Osmund was obliged to confess that he had never once remembered it, but Gwen, who was standing by, declared that her sister had put it safely aside. Robin sent Osmund to the river for silver sand, and Eadgar to whisper in Elian's ear that his harp was found and would be restored to him by supper-time.

"We cannot, in courtesy, depart today," said Robin. "Though maybe Elian will find us a messenger by whom we can get word to Little-John that he may send back the Castle men with the tidings that you are safe."

"Make him find the messenger before you give him the harp," suggested Osmund, laughing.

Robin thought this a good suggestion, and while he was talking the matter over with the little bard, Gwyllim Sassenach came up and very civilly proposed to take the message himself.

"For that kindness, we must offer him the least good of our two Spanish horses," said Robin, as he and the boys sat on the grass scrubbing most unmercifully at the frame of the harp.

"And how shall we get gold to repay the beggar?" inquired Osmund. "Had we not better send a letter to our mother, asking her to provide it as soon as she can?"

"Nay, there is no haste. The beggar can stay in my band and

I will settle the matter with him in due time. When you go adventuring with me, Blackbird, Heaven provides the cost."

"But, Robin, you came for our sake," cried Eadgar. "And never can we repay you for saving us from worse than death. I do not know how to thank you, Master Robin, but if ever you have a service a boy can do, I'll be proud to render it."

"And I too!" exclaimed Osmund.

Hilda had been carried off by the Welsh girls to their own inner room. She appeared at the feast that evening, beautifully dressed in one of Gwen's garments, with a gold collar round her neck, and a green fillet in her hair.

Llewelyn noticed her and said she looked more like a dryad than a maid, and no one there, except his chaplain, a learned monk from the new Abbey of Valle Crucis, had the least idea what he meant. Rhun and his sisters were allowed to sit with the visitors, and they pointed out the notables who had come to the feast. All day the neighbouring lords had been riding in to do homage, and now, towards evening, folk from further away came hurrying up, for the news of the skirmish had spread like wild-fire. The fierce tribesmen of Meirionydd were eager to protest their loyalty, and the more sophisticated chieftains from Maelor and the border were not to be outdone.

Rhun pointed out Ednyved Vychan, a chief of Gwynedd, who was Llewelyn's great friend; his wife, Gwenllian was godmother to Rhun's sister.

"And the lady in white velvet is Eva, the daughter of Madoc-ap-Meredith—she's supposed to be wonderfully beautiful—white as the spray on the wave and all that."

The boys glanced critically at the young woman in question.

"She is very fair but I like Maid Marian's looks better," remarked Osmund. "Maid Marian would look beautiful whatever she wore—she has such laughing eyes."

"Her voice makes you glad," chimed in Eadgar.

"I could not praise her better myself," said Robin, "and I would she were here."

The Welsh drank from horns, and Robin Hood had been supplied with a large one, mounted in gold, and filled to the brim with wine. He rose to his feet and trolled forth:

> "I drink to the maid
> Of the forest glade
> And fair she is to see,
> Her eyes are bright
> As the stars o' night,
> And her shape like the sapling tree.
>
> "In weal or woe
> She will with me go,
> For truer than gold is she,
> By my arrow and bow
> I can prove it so,
> O, the archer's target is she."

With the last words he emptied his horn in one prolonged draught.

"Well sung, Master Archer," exclaimed Llewelyn. "There is a pretty play upon words in the last line, for I warrant the lady is the target of your thoughts and her prayers your shield in danger."

Robin bowed civilly: plays upon words were more than he could manage, though he could throw off a rhyme easily enough.

"If you had consulted me, my good friend, I would have polished the rude verse for you," said Elian patronizingly. "Why, even for the English mode you should have alliteration, if not assonance."

"Heavens!" muttered Robin. "I'd rather have eel-pie," and he helped himself generously to the said dainty. "Here, Eadgar, change places with me—alliterance and assonation are more in your line than mine."

Eadgar obeyed, and soon he and the bard were deep in discussion, passing from the rules of poetry to the quotation of syllogisms. It was observed that Eadgar forgot his food in his absorption, but that Elian never missed a dish, though he talked without ceasing.

He was called upon presently for a song, and came forward with great dignity, bearing his recovered harp—somewhat scratched as to frame, but none the worse otherwise. He had an ode all ready and introduced a special verse to praise Robin Hood. Otherwise the ode, though ostensibly in honour of Llewelyn, was all about the prowess of Elian, who seemed to think that he had waylaid the rebel Meredith and captured him single-handed.

The children were sitting round the hearth by this time, and Rhun whispered this comment. Mischievous Hild pulled a charred stick from the fire and drew on the clean flagstone a lively caricature of the little man, crawling from under the rock. Eadgar rubbed it out with his foot, but not before Rhun and Gwenllian had hailed it with appreciative giggles.

When Elian had finished his ode he struck up a livelier air and began to sing 'englynion'—a particular kind of extempore verse, with sly jokes against some person or persons in the audience. Soon the lords and ladies at the upper end of the hall began to stand up in turns and sing each an englyn in reply—then the folk at the lower end had their chance.

The English children could not understand the words, but they laughed when the other people laughed, and enjoyed watching the people jump up and take part. Eluned said the fun would be kept up till one or two in the morning. It was a regular 'Merry Night' she said, such as they often had in Wales. People would gather from all the houses and farms about and each one would bring something to eat or drink, so as to make things easy for the host and hostess.

When it grew late the Lady Cristin sent the girls to bed in one of the inner rooms. The boys rolled themselves up in the coarse, home-made blankets which were spread over heaps of sweet-smelling rushes on the sleeping-bench. The noise of laughter, singing and playing went on as merrily as ever, and whenever they opened their eyes the great fire was flaming vigorously and no one seemed to dream of breaking up the party.

.   .   .   .   .

The 'merry night' fun was indeed kept up until light began to dawn. At last the harps were wheeled aside, blankets were spread and the ladies withdrew. Llewelyn invited Robin Hood to walk out with him into the fresh air. Such guests as could not be accommodated in the hall were making their way to tents and huts set up within the enclosure. Llewelyn bade the porter open the outer doors and strode up the pasture to the hill-top, where he paused and looked around him.

"See, friend," he said. "Those little white buildings scattered like stars on the green are churches. Mass will be said anon all over this land of ours, and we are Christian men."

"Yet your cousin could plot treachery against you and find a following too," remarked Robin. His keen eyes wandered from one simple little barn-like building to another: from the eminence on which they stood four or five were to be seen. They were whitewashed all over, including the reed-thatched roofs.

"The Prince of Peace dwells in our midst," said the Welshman. "And for His sake, and for my policy of peace, I will not slay Meredith. Nevertheless, I must keep him prisoned until my power is supreme."

"And then you will attack England, I suppose?" said Robin cheerfully.

"Not unless your King attacks me. I would even do homage to Richard, if he would keep his barons in order. 'Tis my mind that the two countries should be as sisters, the older protecting the younger. Yes, England should guard the Eastern confines of the land and repel invaders. We can keep our coasts ourselves."

"You will pardon me, Sir Prince, but are you not very young to direct a princedom single-handed? But no doubt you have councillors?" said Robin, stifling a yawn.

"My father, Davydd, was my counsellor," said Llewelyn. "He impressed his views on my mind when I was a child. 'Strike with the sword only as a last extremity,' he taught me, 'and then strike hard.'"

"Good counsel," agreed Robin. "Would it be deemed a discourtesy if I slept awhile beneath that group of rowan trees? For I am not used to lying under a roof."

"It were safer within the garth. But, good fellow, I brought you here to ask you—will you not throw in your lot with ours for a while? My cousins would like marvellous well to have your young friends for playmates."

"Aye, but the Lady Etheldreda expects me to bring them back without delay," cried Robin.

"Then when my affairs are more settled, you, good Sir Forester, must visit us at my own castle at Aber," said Llewelyn kindly.

"With all my heart!" Robin rejoined.

The young Prince held out his hand with that gracious friendliness which won all hearts to him. After the hand-clasp, he took a silk purse from under his mantle; the long ends hung down, heavily weighted, and the gleam of gold showed through the strands.

"I would not have you the poorer for your sojourn in Wales," he said, and laid his gift on Robin's palm.

"Great thanks," cried the forester, carelessly sticking the purse in his belt. "A good gift, nobly bestowed! And may I, in my turn, crave your acceptance of my Spanish horse? The other I would fain give to Gwyllim in gratitude for his kindness."

Llewelyn could not forbear a smile at the way in which Robin Hood linked prince and vassal in his bestowal of 'vails' or parting gifts. He was accustomed to be treated with almost exaggerated consideration in his own court, and his ancient lineage and exalted position were always being brought forward.

But it was evident that Robin spoke in all simplicity, and with no intention of giving offence.

"It is a noble gift, and Gwyllim and I thank you most heartily," cried Llewelyn. "When I ride in the jousts, or to meet your King—in conference—I will bestride your horse."

"Good day, then," said the forester.

He did not wait to be dismissed by the Prince, but turned aside to the cluster of mountain ash trees and rolling himself in his cloak, threw himself down to rest.

Presently a little bell, hung over the roof of a white-washed chapel in the valley, began to ring the Angelus.

Robin Hood got up and said the prayer, for he was ever most devout to Our Blessed Lady.

He noted that Llewelyn too was praying, still standing at his vantage-point on the hilltop, with his tall figure silhouetted against the sunrise.

Robin Hood only slept for a couple of hours and then strolled down to the hall to break his fast. Sentries had been posted overnight, and he was not allowed to pass until Gwyllim came out, yawning, and brought him in. The children were up and had gone to see the cows milked. The Welsh attached great importance to their herds and milk, and its products formed a large portion of their diet.

"Some day you must come to visit us," said Gwen. "And you shall ride my pony, and we'll share everything with you. What fun it will be to show you our mountains."

"I'll take you fishing in the lakes," said Rhun.

"And I'll show you where the little yellow water-lilies grow," said Eluned. "We have a Roman road, too, which comes right down the mountain to our Castle—Llewelyn says there are Roman milestones on it, and we could go and look for them."

"Who told you about *our* Roman road?" asked Hild. "It's a secret and nobody is to know!"

"How can it be a secret?" exclaimed Rhun. "Everyone is aware that the Saxons did not know how to make roads—as we Cymri do—and all the highways you have in England are Roman ones."

Osmund glanced at his brother: it was surely the scholar of the family who ought to be able to refute a remark like that. But Eadgar was following out his own train of thought.

"I never told any secret," he said slowly. "I said we were tracing out an old Roman road when we walked into the slavers' camp unawares. I didn't say where we started from."

"English folk are as good road-builders as anyone else—better!" declared Osmund, as it seemed as though Eadgar would not take up the challenge. "But we have the sense to use the good Roman roads when they are there—some of them. And we make new roads too."

"But we are free as birds, or the wild deer that wander over the hill," said Rhun. "We scorn roads—our good little mountain horses carry us wherever we will."

"One Roman road always leads to another Roman road," remarked Eadgar, still tenacious of his idea. "And so at last they all lead to Rome, like the spokes of a wheel going to the same centre."

"I have an idea!" cried Osmund. "Perhaps *our* road leads to Rhun's road, and some day we'll all come riding down it to visit the Prince. You had better give us a password, so that your folk will know us when we come."

"It must be something about Arthur," chimed in Gwen eagerly. "Arthur's cave—Ogof Arthur—how would that do?"

Eadgar had been listening to the children without speaking, and now seeing Llewelyn's chaplain, Friar Gwryd, emerge from the house, he waylaid him.

"Is it not true, good Friar, that one Roman road leads to another?" he asked eagerly. "I know you are a learned man, and can give me a safe answer."

"Why, as to that, I am better read in spiritual matters than in worldly ones," returned the priest, smiling. "They say 'all roads lead to Rome,' so it was true once; but since the time of the Roman occupation of England many hundred years have flown. So, doubtless, rivers have changed their courses and roads have been ploughed up, interrupted or built upon."

"We still use Watling Street and Rycknield Street, and the Fosse Way as main highways," declared Eadgar.

"We have Sarn Helen connecting North and South Wales, and merchants occasionally use it," said Gwryd. "But this is deep talk for such an early hour, and I must leave you to say Mass in the church below there."

"Give us ten minutes to make our farewells, and we will hear your Mass," cried Robin Hood. "Quick, children, get your cloaks—give your thanks—we must be gone!"

Elian, roused by one of the serfs, came hurrying out to bid them farewell.

"You will find me when you visit the Prince," he declared. "For I am duly appointed Household Bard as a reward for my share in yesterday's noble slaughter."

"H'm, three men killed and a few wounded," commented Rhun in Osmund's ear.

Robin waved his cap and rode on down the slope, followed

helter-skelter by the children. Eluned walked behind with great sedateness until a turn in the path took her out of sight of the Hall, and then she ran faster than any of them.

The little church was very poor—there were no chairs or benches and everyone knelt on the floor. A circle of peasants were gathered round the altar, with their dogs crouching at their feet. The men joined in the responses to the Mass, and at the moment of the Elevation a great sigh went up from all: "Welcome to the Son of Mary!"

As soon as Mass was over Robin Hood went out and jumped on to his cob. He did not love prolonged farewells, and was anxious to rejoin his band. But before he could move off Rhun came hastening up.

"The Prince sends you this ring," he said, holding up a jewel set in delicate Celtic craftsmanship. "He says 'twill be your passport when you come to visit him. You have only to show it and say his name, and his vassals will bring you to him wherever he may be."

Robin thanked him, and pulling up a chain which hung about his neck, slung the ring on to it in company with a medal of Our Lady and one of St. Hubert, patron of hunters.

The journey to Southwell was uneventful. The Lady Etheldreda had received Robin's message some days previously, and was therefore out of acute anxiety. Stephen thought the time would never pass; he could not settle either to work or play, but was continually running from window to window to see if his brothers and sister were yet in sight.

Stephen and Sibell were saying their night prayers in the chapel when at last the lilt of Robin's bugle came to their ears. The Manor House was so near the Minster that the lady only had a small oratory in the battlements, with a slit in the wall through which a sentry could hear Mass without leaving his post. No sentries were posted during times of peace, so Sibell and her brother sprang up from their prayers and hurried out to the windy platform. Sibell was not tall enough to look over the parapet, and Stephen could not see anything in the gathering dusk. So they rushed down to tell their mother that Robin was coming, and then to carry her orders to the lieutenant to lift the portcullis and drop the drawbridge. After that, they had to wait for what seemed ages until the bugle sang again and the sound of trotting horses sounded first far away, then clattering on the village cobblestones, and at last, soft and dull, mounting up the grassy slope.

Stephen and Sibell rushed out and were the first to greet the wanderers. Robin Hood, Hild, and the boys rode at the head, followed by Scarlet, Friar Tuck, Little-John, Much, and many another old friend. The lady came running into the courtyard with her veil flying out behind her and seized her children in her arms.

All was bustle in the house. The cook sent the scullions to the poultry-yard to slay half-a-dozen fowl. He had the pie-crusts for huge pasties all ready in the buttery, and soon savoury smells streamed forth from the kitchen. Sam butler broached a new barrel of ale, Dame Alice insisted on embracing Eadgar, and all was a joyous hubbub.

Robin Hood and his followers departed at dawn next day, and the children of the Castle settled down to their usual work and play as though the exciting adventures of the past week had never happened.

The End

Also by Agnes Blundell

View a sample chapter from each title at www.staidanpress.com.

The Net

"Roger felt a freezing dew break out upon his forehead. The net was over him it seemed; in vain he told himself that he could establish his identity. His head was worth forty pounds to the vile creatures at the stair foot, and once in their clutches who knew if he could ever communicate with his friends?"

$16.00 — 264 pages. Available at amazon.com.

Other Titles Available From St. Aidan Press

The Queen's Tragedy, by Msgr. Robert Hugh Benson

"Upon the publication of former books of mine several kindly critics remarked that the reign of Mary Tudor told a very different story with regard to the Catholic character. It is that story which I am now attempting to set forth as honestly as I can."

$19.00 — 364 pages. Available at amazon.com.

Mangled Hands, by Fr. Neil Boyton, S.J.

Tarcisius Tandihetsi, the chief's son, has seen wonderful things in the Great Villages of the French and is going home. But the canoes are ambushed by the Iroquois, and he will soon learn what it is to be a captive alone among pagans. If only he could escape and find his Blackrobe, Father Isaac Jogues!

$14.00 — 186 pages. Available at amazon.com.

Redrobes, by Fr. Neil Boyton, S.J.

Thirteen-year-old orphan Jacques gets into trouble in Quebec, and decides to run away to Huronia and become an interpreter for his Jesuit guardian, Father John Brebeuf. But his journey along the Iroquois-infested river may not be so easy as he hopes!

$17.00 — 300 pages. Available at amazon.com.

The Anchorhold, by Enid Dinnis

A chaplain's sermon drove Editha de Beauville to give up the world and enter the religious life. But could a strong-willed noblewoman accept and embrace full seclusion in an anchorhold? Read on to learn how she fared, and how her life affected those around her: Sir Aleric, her erstwhile suitor, now a crusader knight; Fr. Nicholas, a young priest who was quite bright, and thought so too; and Fiddlemee, the witty yet wise court jester whose past held a surprising secret.

$14.00 — 196 pages. Available at amazon.com.

THE ROAD TO SOMEWHERE, by Enid Dinnis

Richard and Ann discover a real Tudor house in London being sold cheap, complete with leather latch-strings, a tale of hidden treasure, and a wonderful piper. But the treasure turns out to be an old altar-stone. Will it lose them the house and each other, or set them on the real road to Somewhere?

$10.00 — 106 pages. Available at amazon.com.

THE SHEPHERD OF WEEPINGWOLD, by Enid Dinnis

Sir Robert Luffkyn, rich grandson of a peasant, has purchased the manor of Weepingwold from the noble but impoverished de Lessels, intending to make the renamed Luffkynwold a busy center of his tanning trade. He sends Petronilla, last de Lessels, to Gracerood, intending her for its future Abbess, and plucks little Brother Kit from the cloister to become the new parson of the long-abandoned church. How will Father Kit fare with the parish and his own soul? Will Petronilla find her true vocation? And is there really a witch in the parish?

$14.00 — 202 pages. Available at amazon.com.

SCOUTING FOR SECRET SERVICE, by Fr. Bernard F. J. Dooley

Frank and George are going to spend their summer vacation in the Adirondacks, thanks to Frank's uncle Ed. But once they get there, they realize something fishy is going on. Can they trust Pete, their Indian guide, or is he mixed up in it too? And is Frank's mysterious uncle really behind it all?

$14.00 — 188 pages. Available at amazon.com.

THE COMING OF THE MONSTER, by Fr. Owen Francis Dudley

The Masterful Monk returns to England to fight against the Bolshevik cause, to find beautiful, idealistic Verna Wray torn between her family's wealth and her French Catholic suitor. But how much suffering is Red hate still to cause them all?

$15.00 — 218 pages. Available at amazon.com.

THE MASTERFUL MONK, by Fr. Owen Francis Dudley

Brother Anselm comes back to England to counter the Atheist's efforts to destroy the influence of Catholic morals. Between his lectures he is drawn into a struggle for the soul of Beauty Dethier, who is Catholic but fascinated by the "freedom" of the world and the Atheist.

$18.00 — 342 pages. Available at amazon.com.

WILL MEN BE LIKE GODS? & THE SHADOW ON THE EARTH, by Fr. Owen Francis Dudley

Father Dudley's first two books on human happiness are published together here—his rare collection of essays together with the novel which introduces his most famous character, the Masterful Monk.

$15.00 — 216 pages. Available at amazon.com.

CANDLELIGHT ATTIC & ODD JOB'S, by Cecily Hallack

Here are seven true stories in honour of the Seven Joys of Our Blessed Lady, and ten more invented ones about the delightful Barnabas Job, to make a comfortable book for those who are afraid of the dark.

$14.00 — 192 pages. Available at amazon.com.

THE HAPPINESS OF FATHER HAPPÉ, by Cecily Hallack

Shingle Bay did not know what to make of Fr. Savinius Happé. He was a cheerful, rotund Franciscan, a famous author of books on everything from Etruscan civilization to Alpine meadows to beetles, and someone who had never quite mastered the English language. His jovial demeanor concealed a wisdom that alternately bewildered, astonished, but ultimately won over the people of Shingle Bay.

$10.00 — 112 pages. Available at amazon.com.

THREE RELIGIOUS REBELS, by M. Raymond, O.C.S.O.

The stories of the three Saints who founded the Cistercian order— St. Robert of Molesme, St. Alberic, and St. Stephen Harding.

$17.00 — 294 pages. Available at amazon.com.

THE RED INN OF SAINT LYPHAR, by Anna T. Sadlier

Richard Duplessis is leaving his sweetheart to fight under Jambe d'Argent, when his envious rival denounces him to the Revolution. Can even his wily commander save him and his friends from the guillotine?

$13.00 — 168 pages. Available at amazon.com.

CON OF MISTY MOUNTAIN, by Mary T. Waggaman

"It had been a long night for Con. Just what had happened to him he was at first too dazed to know. Dennis had flung him into the smoking-room with no very gentle hand, turned the key and left him to himself. And, sinking down dully upon a rug that felt very soft and warm after the hard flight over the mountain, Con was glad to rest his bruised, aching limbs, his dizzy head, without any thought of what was to come upon him next."

$14.00 — 190 pages. Available at amazon.com.

NON-FICTION

THE STORY OF THE WAR IN LA VENDÉE AND THE LITTLE CHOUAN-NERIE, by George J. Hill, M.A.

The story of the brave French Catholics who rose up in arms against the revolutionary government.

$18.00 — 342 pages. Available at amazon.com.

THE AMERICAN HERESY, by Christopher Hollis

The history of Jeffersonian America and of its downfall is told here in the lives of four famous statesmen: Thomas Jefferson, John C. Calhoun, Abraham Lincoln, and Woodrow Wilson.

$18.00 — 358 pages. Available at amazon.com.

CATHOLICISM AND SCOTLAND, by Compton Mackenzie

The little known history of the Scots who sought to defend their country and their Faith from the onslaught of Protestantism.

$12.00 — 138 pages. Available at amazon.com.

DOMINICAN SAINTS, by the Novices of the Dominican House of Studies

The astonishing lives of fourteen saints of the Dominican Order, with an encyclical on the Dominican Order by Pope Benedict XV and a list of all the Dominican Saints and Blesseds (as of 1921).

$19.00 — 392 pages. Available at amazon.com.